TIMELINE

THE MINUTEMAN PROJECT

BY: STEVEN FOSTER

TOUCH PUBLISHING

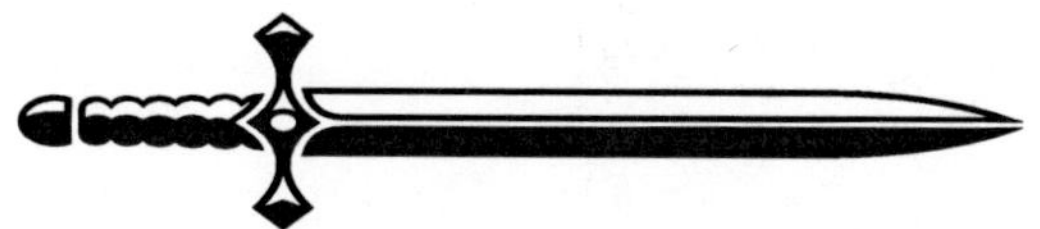

Author photo by Josh Stelting

ISBN: 978-0-9919839-2-6

Published by Touch Publishing
Requests should be directed to:
P.O. Box 180303
Arlington, Texas 76096
www.TouchPublishingServices.com

Printed in the United States of America

Library of Congress Control Number: 2014934727

Foster, Steven N.
The Minuteman Project / Steven Foster.
356 p. 21 cm. – (Timeline ; # 1)
Summary: Three teenagers who have been held captive by a pharmaceutical company escape, only to find that the experimental testing that they were subjected to has given them extraordinary powers.
ISBN: 978-0-9919839-2-6
[1. Time travel– Juvenile fiction. 2. Orphans–Juvenile fiction.
3. Science fiction.]

PZ7 .F815167 Ti 2014

This book is dedicated to my mother and father.

Thank you for being so amazing.

A special thanks to David and Kim and Touch Publishing.

Without you, this would not be possible.

For Shannon Lake Elemetary,

Fiction is an escape from the world. Use it to let your imagination run wild!

CHAPTERS

1 ESCAPE! OR NOT.

The bright moon was surrounded by a mass of dark clouds. Droplets of water quietly poured from them in an endless torrent, soaking the dirt and forming mud puddles that glistened where the moonlight touched them. Despite the rain, it would have been a peaceful scene, had I not been running for my life.

I sprinted through the woods, branches jabbing harshly at me with every turn I made. It was an endless maze of trees, bushes, and mud. With every group of branches I launched myself through, I was greeted with more cuts, staining my short blonde hair and cheeks scarlet with blood. I continued to run; stopping was not an option.

The rain intensified, as if it were getting angrier with me. I jumped over a small ledge, not realizing how slippery the surface would be. I fell onto the slick mud, and began to roll down a rough, jagged hill. Each tumble brought more pain, as rocks joined with the branches to tear at me from every angle.

I stopped my slide and waited before moving. I could hear voices. They were getting closer.

I pulled myself up, refusing to accept defeat. I kept running; my legs burned as if on fire. Out of the corner of my eye, I caught a glimpse of light shining past me.

A flashlight!

They're too close now, there's no way I can outrun them, I thought to myself. I stopped, looking for somewhere to take cover, and ducked out of sight behind a tree. This is where I would take my stand. I would not let them take me back without a fight.

A figure emerged from the bushes. He wore a dark uniform and I could see he held a gun. He was walking straight toward the tree I hid behind. Leaves crunched and mud spattered beneath his feet as he stepped closer and closer. As he approached the tree, I jumped out from behind it and hurled my entire body towards my assailant. The element of surprise was on my side and he didn't know what hit him. Our bodies collided, my momentum pushing the man backward into the mud, causing him to lose grip on his gun.

I unleashed a hailstorm of punches on him. Most were blocked, but a few connected. He swung an arm that hit me squarely in the face, and sent me sprawling backwards. By the time I had recovered from the blow, he was on his feet, sending a kick to my midsection that knocked the wind out of me. I hit the ground hard, but I managed to push myself back up.

Then a searing pain shot through my body. I looked down and saw a metal rod sticking out on both sides of my right shoulder. The tip of each end of the rod had claw-like metal prongs which shot inwards, and dug into my shoulder. Sparks flickered from where the claw dug in. My right side was quickly becoming numb. I was losing strength fast. Three other men had joined the first. One had his gun pointed at me.

I turned away, trying to run, but the man pulled the trigger. Another rod pierced me, this time through my leg. The claws separated and dug in, finding their mark. I collapsed. My face crashed into mud and the rain poured down, soaking my crumpled body. I tried crawling away with no luck. Something struck the back of my head.

My eyes fluttered open, but they were met with darkness. As I came to, I became aware of the bitter pain shooting through my body, especially in my shoulder and leg. I winced as I pulled myself up against the cold stone wall of my cell.

Yeah, that's right. You heard me; a *cell.*

My cell was surrounded on three sides by a stone wall. Floor-to-ceiling metal bars and the door to the cell lined the fourth. It was just big enough for me to stand in, and just long enough for me to lie down. No bed. No pillow. Only a bucket that sat in the corner. I'm sure you can guess what that was used for.

I looked around, and my eyes slowly started to adjust to the dark room that once again held me prisoner. The room was all too familiar to me. As I became more conscious I could see that it wasn't completely dark. A dim light flickered through the moldy bulb which hung sadly from the concrete ceiling. My cell was one of many identical cells that held other kids. The cells lined the perimeter of a large room, with the metal bars facing the room's center. Most of the others were younger than me, but some looked like they could have been my age. We didn't really know how old we were.

"So how far did you make it this time?" asked a voice from across the way.

I turned my head, trying to limit the movement of my shoulder. I could tell that Jessica was standing. Her clothes were tattered and much too big for her small frame, but we didn't exactly have a wardrobe to choose from. Her dirty blonde hair reached down a little past her shoulders and her blue eyes were bright, even in the darkness. She leaned against the front of her cell, hands gripping the bars.

"Just past the creek," I replied.

"Oh. A new record," she smiled. "How many times have you tried escaping?"

"I've lost count," I said weakly, smiling back at her in spite of the pain. If anything could shine a light in this place, it was her smile.

Another voice pierced through the dark room. "Francis, when will you figure out that you can't escape The Island?"

I turned toward Will, whose cell was beside Jessica's. Will was around 18 years old, just a little older than me, if we are keeping track of time correctly. He was lying down in his cell, hands running through a mess of dark brown hair. His eyes were an even darker brown, staring at the ceiling.

"Well it's better than sitting in a cell all day," I snapped back with a hint of anger that came more from the pain searing my shoulder and leg than it did because of Will's comment. I gently touched the scar where the rod had hit, and traced the circle of cuts from the claw attachment with my finger.

Will was like a brother to me, but sometimes his outlook on life was pretty bleak. I guess if you've spent your entire life living in a cell, you could get depressed from time to time. One thing I was thankful for was that we could see and talk to one another through the metal bars.

"Whatever," came his casual reply.

A door opened on the opposite end of the room. A tall figure stepped through, dressed in a black uniform. He was a guard at The Island. They all wore the same uniform, and had the same style of gun. It was a cross between a pistol and a machine gun, but instead of bullets, it launched those excruciating metal rods. As if the the claw at each end digging into the skin wasn't bad enough, they also sent an electric shock through your body, numbing the place where you got hit. The bottom-line: you don't want to mess with the guards here. They don't exactly hire the people who greet you at Walmart.

The guard continued into the room, banging his weapon against each cell's bars. "That's enough chit-chat, freaks," he said in a cold voice. He did a lap around the room and left. We were all dead quiet.

"You should get some rest. You'll need it," Jessica whispered.

"Yeah, I guess so," I murmured, sliding down on my back, trying to get as comfortable as possible on the hard rock floor.

I guess now would be a good time for me to fill you in on what is going on. You may be wondering why I am in a cell. I've been asking myself that question for years. I was born in New York City, where I lived with my mom, dad, and sister.

They were really kind and caring, and my memories of them are happy ones. I knew they loved me. I was top of my class and dominated the playground in soccer, freeze tag, and pretty much anything I did. Freeze tag is like regular tag, but when the person who is "it" touches you, you have to stay perfectly still, as if frozen, until another player touches you. Sometimes, in the middle of a long and lonely night (at least, what I assume is night), I long to play freeze tag.

When I was eight years old, my family and I were in a bad car accident. I was the only survivor. My parents had no other living relatives, so I was sent to an orphanage. I am not sure who was in charge of this orphanage, but I am pretty sure they were crooked. Instead of finding me a good home, within the first year of my being there, they sold me to a big corporation called "The Island."

The Island.

Sounds nice, right? Yeah, well on the surface I'm sure they appear to be a nice company. They develop and manufacture medical drugs and products that can do anything from stopping headaches to instantly repairing damaged skin. What people don't know about The Island Corporation is that they test their drugs on orphaned kids who are kept prisoners and used for whatever purposes they want. Yep. That's where we come in.

When The Island develops a new product, they test it out on us first, to see if there are any side effects. Basically, we're all guinea pigs. The results are not always pleasant. Once, a kid named Ryan was given a new drug to treat acne, and the next day he began to grow mold on his hands and feet. Then, 48 hours later, permanent burn scars appeared all over his face. Needless to say, he's not going to get a date any time soon. (Not that there is much dating going on here.)

There you have it. I had eight years of childhood, then BOOM! No more family, no more sports, no T.V. Just me. And my weekly poking and prodding with needles. They keep us in cells to prevent us from escaping, and feed us twice a day. No, they're not nice meals. I'm actually not sure what it is, but it is brown and chunky, and as dry as dirt.

For as long as I've been here I've been in the cell across from Jessica and Will. Will got here when he was about three. He doesn't know or remember his family, let alone the world outside. I feel bad for him. Jessica was thrown in here about three weeks before me, so she can relate to me when I quote *Star Wars* or something.

It is nice to have Jessica. I don't mean it's nice that we're here, but it is nice to have someone who understands me nearby. Jessica's parents died in a plane crash when she was six, and she was tossed from orphanage to orphanage until The Island Corporation acquired her. We stick together and look out for one another as best we can. We are the closest thing we have to family.

Most children who are brought to The Island aren't even old enough to be in school. They spend the first few years of captivity getting a basic education from the scientists. They learn to read, write, and think like regular people. They even show us popular movies and make us read current books. That being said, nobody learns French or anything exciting like that. Just the basics–history, English, and math.

Once a child is old enough and hearty enough to survive the experiments, he or she becomes a test subject. We are all branded with a barcode and The Island's logo so we can be identified by our test groups. Will and I were assigned to be test subjects for neurological enhancement drugs designed to increase brainpower. Do they work? Some do, most don't. Usually we just have massive headaches.

Like I said, we are grouped according to the drugs tested on us. Jessica is the guinea pig for skin-related products. Others are tested for improved mobility, fast-healing injuries, or pretty much anything else that has potential to improve the livelihood of the general public.

Island life is not worth living.

We have no future to look forward to, or *anything* to look forward to, for that matter. The few of us who are strong enough try to escape. As you can tell, it hasn't gone well for us yet.

I rolled over in my cell and tried to ignore the lingering pain in my shoulder. I closed my eyes, hoping to escape from reality. In my dreams, I am free. In my dreams I recall a different life, one without needles or cells. As I drifted into a deep sleep, I did so with the knowledge that my life was pathetic. *I have to get out of here!* The thought crosses my mind too many times to count. *This place is slowly driving me insane.* My last thought of the evening was that I hoped tomorrow would never come.

Guess what? It came. There are no windows for the sunlight to peek through, letting us know morning has arrived. Our wake-up call comes when the guards burst through the doors, drag a kid out of his or her cell, and then slam the doors again. Would you like being woken up in that way? I'm sure you wouldn't.

"Morning, Buttercup," Will said, as I pulled myself up. The pain in my shoulder and leg was gone. Not even a scar remained to prove that it had happened. You see, the only perk to this whole situation is the fact that every now and then a drug actually works. Thanks to a few needles in my brain from a prior experiment, I have the ability to heal faster than most people.

"Morning," I said, rubbing my eyes. "How long have you been up?"

"I dunno. A few hours."

"Couldn't sleep?" I asked.

Will shook his head.

Will suffered terribly from nightmares. A while ago he was tested on a new drug that did something to his brain. We aren't sure what, but it affected his sleep patterns. Now he can't get so much as a few hours of sleep each night. And if he does manage to get some rest, the drug induces horrific nightmares. One time I woke up in the middle of the night to hear him yelling, "The badgers have my pants!" over and over. I didn't ask him about it the next morning, mainly because I didn't want to know why badgers were stealing his pants.

"Yeah, they seriously messed up my head," he replied, rubbing his temples.

"Don't worry, we'll get out of here eventually. You'll see," Jessica entered our conversation.

I have to hand it to her, she always looks on the bright side. Will is more of a glass-half-empty kind of guy.

"Oh yeah, 'cause all of our other attempts worked out so well," came Will's sarcastic reply.

"You'll see," she promised.

The metal door to the large room opened, creaking as it slid inward, like nails on a chalkboard. Two guards emerged, dragging a boy back to his cell. One pointed towards me and Will. "You two are next," he grunted.

I glanced at Will. His eyes were scared, but his face told another story. He did his best to look fearless as the guards opened our cells and dragged us out, literally throwing us to the ground. My face hit the cement floor, giving me another headache, but I managed to quickly get up to my feet. The guards pushed us into the hallway, closing the door behind them.

The hallways were similar to our holding room. They seemed to go on forever, lit by dim lights which flickered on and off like a scene from a bad horror movie. The walls were rusted metal. Several pipes ran along the walls and dripped water onto the ground at various intervals. The floor was part concrete and part dirt, and if you looked hard enough, you'd see small bugs crawling around. Every ten feet there was a numbered black door. I noticed the numbers began at 112 and decreased down this particular hallway. We reached the end of the hallway and a much taller door, deep red in color, loomed before us.

"Open it," said the cold, dark voice of the guard beside me.

I hesitated. Wrong move. The guard's fist collided with my face. I fell to my knees. Will, of course, made no attempt to help me. I can't blame him though; he would have been hit, too. The guards were not fond of us.

"Open it!" the guard shouted again.

I reached up, turned the knob, and pushed open the door, using the handle to pull myself to my feet. I was not prepared for what greeted us on the other side. I shut my eyes to avoid the bright lights. The room was completely white; walls, ceilings, floor, you name it. It was like they let a maniac loose in there with a bucket of bleach. In the middle of the room were two operating beds, and standing beside them was one of the scientists. He, too, was dressed in white, with an operating mask covering his face.

"Sit," he said, gesturing towards the two tables.

We walked forward. Will and I exchanged looks, neither of us knowing what was about to happen. Normally we were separated during experiments and operated on in isolated rooms packed with scientists and guards, but never with other kids. This? This definitely had a different feel to it. I was suddenly quite nervous and I'd bet my lunch that Will was too.

We each went to a table and sat. We knew any hesitation would result in a beating. The guards laid us back and strapped us down. I tried to flex my arms, but the restraints were too tight.

"There is no use struggling," came the calm voice of the scientist, "and it would be in your best interest to stay still."

This didn't make me feel any better.

"What's going on?" I asked.

He chuckled. "Today we are going to try a new type of compound. One that, if properly executed in this operation, could change the entire look of civilization."

"Oh, and I suppose we get this compound for free?" Will said sarcastically.

A guard stepped forward and smacked him square in the face with his gun. "No wise-cracks."

Will cringed in pain, his nose dripping blood down his neck. I couldn't resist joining in. "You know, for all the drugs they've created, you'd think they could fix that ugly face of yours."

Wouldn't you know it, that made him angry. He started moving towards me. I braced for the impact of his punch, but it never came.

"Don't even think about it, Frank. I need these subjects in decent condition for this operation," the scientist said sternly, grabbing the guard's arm just inches from my head.

Big, tall, ugly Frank backed off. I couldn't help letting a cocky smirk slide across my face. It was a small victory for me. I take them where I can.

"Island Corporation has developed a new chemical procedure. We're calling it *The Minuteman Project*," the scientist began.

"How cute, you and all your little friends come up with code names and everything," I interrupted, still reveling in my success.

"Yes, well, if successful this new brain enhancement will allow the body to control its aging process. Do you understand what that means?" he asked, with a tone suggesting we were three-year-olds.

"I got this one, Francis," Will said.

"Go right ahead," I replied.

"OK, so what Mr. White here is trying to say is that they're going to test another drug on us, which in all likelihood will be painful, so that old people in the real world can pretend to be young."

"Oh, is that it? Well I can't see anything wrong with that, can you?" I replied.

"Nope. By all means, Mr. White, do continue," said Will, nodding at the scientist.

Our sarcasm put Mr. White momentarily at a loss for words, but he quickly regained his composure. "In a manner of speaking, yes. It will allow older people to control their skin's aging process."

"Uh-huh. And people can't just get old and die, because …?" I paused, waiting for an answer.

"Because, normal people don't want to die. They want to live forever, living life to its fullest. And you're going to help them achieve that," he said, pointing a gloved finger at us.

"Yay for us," I said dryly.

Mr. White pushed his tray of operating tools towards us. "Don't worry, it will all be over soon, with little or no pain to you."

"How convenient," I snarled.

I looked over at Will. He seemed calm and peaceful. Mr. White swung a scanner over Will's wrist, and after several beeps a robotic voice spoke, "Patient 178442, a.k.a. 'William Tapper.' Procedure: Minuteman Project. Dosage: 8 milligrams of anesthetic."

He grabbed a needle off of the tray, took hold of Will's arm, and slid the needle into a vein. I hate needles. Will's eyes shut and his body went limp. I hadn't seen anyone else go under before and I couldn't help but notice how completely vulnerable Will looked.

"Your turn," Mr. White said, moving towards me.

I became panicked. I tried to break free of the restraints, but there was no use. I was trapped. He scanned my wrist and again the robotic voice spoke, "Patient 195682, a.k.a. 'Francis Parker.' Procedure: Minuteman Project. Dosage: 8 milligrams of anesthetic."

He grabbed another needle and placed an icy hand on my arm. I felt the needle hit my skin, and a rush of cold liquid pumped into my veins. Did I mention that I hate needles? I could feel myself beginning to lose consciousness. This was going to hurt in the morning. I became lost in complete darkness.

"Francis, what is the most important thing to remember?" My father was crouching in front of me. He was tall with brown hair, and hazel eyes that stared right through you (in a good way, not a creepy weird way).

"Always keep your promises," a young, eight year old me answered.

I was so happy my dad was home. He traveled a lot for business, and this was the first time in weeks that we were planning to do something as a family. One of the theaters downtown was playing the old *Batman* movie. It was one of my favorites and I couldn't wait to get going.

"That's right. Always keep your promises, and don't make one unless you plan on seeing it through," he smiled and ran his hand through my hair.

"Can we go see *Batman* now?" I asked, anxiously.

My dad gave a deep chuckle. "You know, Mom says you've seen that movie about six times in the last three weeks."

"And it's still awesome," I smiled.

"Alright then. I obviously can't talk you out of it. Get in the car."

I ran outside, climbed into the backseat, and buckled up. My sister Amy strolled casually from the house with earbuds in and iPod blaring. She got in the other side. Amy was six years older than me and didn't like *Batman*. I never understood how it's possible to not like *Batman*, but that's beside the point. She was only going because her boyfriend worked at the theater. I unbuckled momentarily to lean over the front seat and honk the horn. Amy shook her head at me. My mom and dad finally joined us and off we went.

"Francis, honey, can we maybe see a different movie next time?" my mom asked.

I frowned, but saw my dad grinning at me through the rear-view mirror. "I promise, Mom."

"Thanks, Francis," she turned her head and smiled back at me. "I could use the change."

The last thing I remember of my mom was that smile. That was when everything went wrong. As I gazed at my mom, I noticed a large truck coming fast toward her side of the car. I opened my mouth to scream, but have no idea if I did or not. The sound of the truck hitting our car is one that wakes me from my sleep in the dead of night.

I woke up with a catch of my breath. I saw nothing. After a few blinks, the knowledge that I wasn't in the car with my family, but lying in my cell, came clear in my head. *Oh, my head!* The headache was one of the worst yet. Go figure. I slowly sat up, resting my head against the concrete wall.

"You're awake!" came a familiar voice.

I looked over to see Jessica lying down in her cell.

"What? Did you actually think they could hurt me?" I said with a lame smile.

"You've been out for days," she said with a worried look in her eyes.

Usually after an operation I was awake within a few hours. But days? That was unusual.

"That's weird," I said, rubbing my forehead with my hand.

"What did they do to you?" asked Jessica.

"I'm not sure," I paused, thinking to myself. "They're testing a chemical that allows control over the body's aging process."

"What?" she exclaimed.

I chuckled. "Yeah, that's what I thought, too. Apparently people don't want to be old in the outside world. Supposedly they want to be young forever."

"Well that's just stupid," she agreed.

I looked towards Will's cell. He was still asleep. "Has he woken up at all?" I asked.

"Nope. He's been passed out just like you. By the way, you drool in your sleep," she said with a wink.

"It could be worse—" I started, but before I could get another word out I crumpled into a heap. My head burst with pain. It felt like my brain was slowly being crushed. I screamed in agony. Then, as suddenly as it began, it stopped, leaving me lying in silence with the other children staring at me.

"Are you OK? What happened?" I heard Jessica ask, her voice desperate with concern.

I rolled onto my back and took several deep breaths before answering.

"I'm not sure. It felt like an explosion detonated inside my skull."

"Yeah, mine too," Will's voice was soft, almost as if it hurt him to speak.

I could feel Will and I processing this information together, then I realized, we felt that pain at the same time. When I collapsed in pain, he woke up in the same pain.

Weird.

"You both started screaming at the same time! Oh, that was creepy," Jessica said, shaking her head.

Will glanced my way. "Any ideas?" he wondered.

I thought about it for a second. "The only logical explanation is that we had the same reaction to the operation."

"Logical explanation?" Will gave a slightly deranged laugh.

"There is nothing logical about kids being locked in a cell and treated like lab rats!" He let out a long, calming breath. "We need to get out of here, before this place kills us."

The reality of that statement hit all of us. We had been stuck in cells for most of our lives. How lame is that? Would we die here?

"So, are you up for one more escape attempt?" I asked.

"Always," smiled Jessica.

"We start planning tomorrow," Will said, determination in his voice.

The room fell silent. Will and I needed to rest from the operation and recover from whatever had happened to us. The three of us were the most talkative of the group, probably as we were the oldest, and we usually kept the others awake late into the night with our shenanigans. Tonight, however, we were quiet. As the hours passed I began thinking of another escape plan, and I eventually fell asleep.

The car was spinning. My body bounced back and forth like a pinball. Then something hit me hard. Everything went black. Flashes of reality pierced the darkness. I saw red lights. Then I saw nothing. I heard murmurs. Then I heard nothing. I was coherent enough to be afraid. The moments of silence were eerie.

When my eyes finally opened with some semblance of clarity, I realized I was in a hospital bed. There were tubes entering and exiting my body from various places and an oxygen mask covered most of my face. I tried moving, but nothing happened. I glanced my eyes downward to look at my body. It was covered in bandages and casts.

Why am I so mangled? I wondered.

Then I remembered the crash. As I lay in that bed I started to remember all the details. The truck coming toward us. The initial hit, which sent us into a spastic spin. The realization that we were headed for oncoming traffic. We were upside down. I saw a flash of my sister, she was looking back at me. She seemed to be OK. I heard my mom's voice, and I remember thinking we would be alright. But then another car hit us. Our car spun around and around before coming to a shuddering stop.

My head felt fuzzy, but I looked around the car to see my family. I wish I hadn't looked. If they were alive before, they certainly weren't anymore. I knew that final image of them would be permanently imprinted on my mind. I blacked out.

A doctor came into my hospital room. I opened my eyes. His face was grim. I knew before he even said a word that he was about to tell me that the others didn't survive the accident.

I was eight years old.

I jolted awake to the sound of a boy being dragged out of the cell area. This kid had wings. I'm not talking about tiny pigeon wings, or small growths on his shoulder blades. I mean, this kid had big freaking eagle wings. I felt sorry for him. How many kids wish they could fly? This kid actually could, but would never try it in the open sky. The only place he was tested was in a big warehouse-type room from which he could not escape.

I sat up, trying to stretch out my back. The dreams didn't bother me like they used to, because they've been a part of my life since that day. At first I'd drive myself crazy when I woke up, wondering if I could have done something to stop it. If only I'd picked a different movie. Then we'd have been travelling down a different street. If only. If only. Eventually I had to stop that line of thinking. It was slowly crushing me. I couldn't do anything to change the past, and I had to accept that.

I looked around the room at the other children, still lying in their cages, unawakened by the commotion. Some had normal bodies, while others had been subject to harsher treatments that left permanent damage. One kid was blind and had burns on his skin. Another actually had scales, like a fish, in patches all over his body. Most had given up hope of ever leaving these confines. You could see it in their faces.

I have to get them out of here, I thought to myself.

"They don't stand a chance in here," I declared.

"Then we'd better start thinking of a plan," Jessica said, interrupting my thoughts.

"You've got that right," I replied.

"Do you have any ideas?" she asked.

"Nothing new. What about you?"

She shook her head, looking at the floor, defeated.

"We'll find a way," Will, awake, joined our conversation.

Will's dark brown eyes stared at the door with a burning intensity.

"You know, no matter how hard you look at that door, it's not going to open," I said.

"Ha, ha, very funny, Francis."

The door opened suddenly, causing us all to jump. Two guards emerged from the lit hallway and walked towards us.

"You two," the first guard said, pointing his two index fingers at me and Will, "time for your checkup."

They opened our cells. The last time I escaped, I slid a small rock between the bolt and lock, which jammed it just enough to keep it from locking. *I can probably pull that off again*, I thought.

We crawled out, slowly standing to our feet (when you spend all day in a cell your legs get kind of sore). I took note of the guards. One was … how do I put this delicately? He looked like he had spent too many days in a donut shop, while the other seemed relatively fit. *We could definitely take them*, I thought. I looked over at Will, who nodded, thinking the same thing.

I swung a punch at the fat one. My fist collided with his

stomach. It didn't hurt, his blubber cushioned the blow for my hand, and he went down, gasping for air. Almost immediately the other guard bashed the back of my head with his gun. I collapsed to the ground, the room spinning around me. Will just watched how the guards reacted. There was no point in both of us getting a beating.

"You had better think twice about doing that again, punk," said Chubby. His fist connected with my face, which sent me sprawling over. Will ran over to help me up.

"Nice one," he whispered.

I grinned through bloody teeth. Hopefully he had paid close attention to how the guards reacted. If we were going to have any chance of escape, we needed to know how adequate the guards were. It appeared to me that we could take them if we had the right timing, not to mention an actual plan.

"C'mon you two. No more outbursts," threatened the fit guard, pushing both of us forward.

We walked down the dim hallway, and this time took a left turn through a grungy green door. We entered a room that was full of lab equipment. Scientists hurried across the room, doing various evil lab activities. I despised them. We walked past rows of desks, which had computers and other machines sitting on top of them. At the end of the room was another door. This one was gray. The guards opened it and pushed us through into a white room that looked depressingly like the one in which Will and I had our previous operation. This room not only had the same fancy lab equipment, but also was full of exercise machines.

Now that might not sound unusual to you, but it gave me concern. I'd never had any experiments that required physical testing. Will and I were guinea pigs for neurological products. It made no sense that they would send us here, unless they expected the latest test to screw us up completely.

Will seemed just as confused as I was. *What were they testing us for?* I wondered, as a scientist approached us.

"Both of you have recently been implanted with our latest chemical compound. We need to see if there have been any side effects on your body," he said calmly.

"Hear that, Will?" I interrupted, "They might actually care about our health."

"Imagine that," he whistled.

"Don't flatter yourselves. We don't really care much about you at all. We don't want the public being hit with any side effects. If they were, we'd be looking at a serious law suit."

"Ah yes. God forbid the outside world gets a headache. Let the kids die from testing the drug," I snorted.

"Precisely," he said, unfazed by my comment. "We'll need you two to spend some time on these exercise machines. We need to get an accurate reading of your stamina."

"Uh-huh," Will paused, looking around at the machines, "so you want us to run around, so you can see if we were affected by one of your experimental drugs, which we were forced to take?"

"Yes."

"Oh. Well if that's all," Will said, rolling his eyes. He sat down on a nearby chair, not budging. You can always count on Will to refuse to participate in whatever they wanted from us.

"This would go so much easier if you cooperated," the scientist said, staring at Will.

"I'm sure it would," was all he could get out before a guard punched him in the face.

If you haven't noticed, Will can be childish from time to time. Most of the time he just cracked bad jokes, but every now and then he'd do something like this, which usually resulted in a butt-kicking. He didn't know how to pick his battles.

Will rolled over, wiped the blood from his mouth, and growled, "Well, since you asked nicely."

He got to his feet and we made our way to the first machine. The scientist attached several wires to us, which were attached to other machines. He scanned both of our wrists, and I saw our pictures pop up on his clipboard. We spent the next few hours running, lifting weights, and doing other vigorous exercises. It wasn't very exciting, so I won't bore you with details, but all I can say is, my body felt like Jell-O, which, sadly, it had been years since I had. Will had never had Jell-O, as I learned one day while reminiscing about things we missed from the outside.

The scientist watched us the entire time we worked out and jotted notes on his clipboard. After what seemed forever he spoke up, "That's enough."

I was so relieved. I sat down on the floor, catching my breath. Sweat rained off my body. I know, I know, that's gross. Get over it.

Will gasped for breath not too far away from me. As you can probably tell, we don't work out much.

"That wasn't so bad, was it?" the scientist asked.

"Sure," I gasped. "You try running for a couple of hours straight."

The scientist just laughed. "I'm done with these two. Guards, remove them from my sight."

"Oh, how kind of you," said an oxygen-starved Will.

The guards escorted us back to our room, locked the cells, and removed the boy with fish scales. He didn't even put up a fight. He never did. He was only six, and fighting off the guards would probably never cross his mind. I was finally able to relax as I sat down in my cell. My muscles were sore beyond reason, and I had a headache that did not want to quit.

I looked around the room. Jessica wasn't there. *They must've taken her for tests,* I assumed. Hopefully she had better luck than we did.

"Is your head killing you right now?" I asked Will.

He nodded. "It feels like I was hit by a bus."

"Maybe several," I groaned.

"Jessica's not here?"

"Nope. Probably testing some skin product."

We sat in silence, trying to recover from the strenuous workout. I thought about the guards. If Will and I could escape our cells, we could take those two down without too much commotion. Then we could get Jessica out, and the rest of this unfortunate bunch.

I thought through what we'd do next. We could go out the door and make our way down the hallway. The last time I made it to the exit without sounding the alarm, but with a bigger group I worried we wouldn't make it that far before someone saw us. There was a door about a hundred feet down the hallway to the left of our room. Through it was the boiler room. That was where I slipped through an air conditioning vent, and made my way through the facility undetected. I crawled around the vent for a bit, until I found an opening to the outside. However, the opening I found was in plain sight of the guard towers, which was where I was spotted. You know how the rest went.

We would need to be quick and precise if we were going to have any hope of succeeding.

Will broke my concentration, "I've seen that look before. You've got a plan don't you?"

"I think so."

"The vents?" He asked.

"Yup. We can't be detected in there as far as I know."

"It's worth a try. You almost made it last time."

I nodded, preoccupied with counting the number of kids in the room. There were 36 of us. Will and I were the oldest. If I could fit, the rest of them, who were smaller, should have no trouble getting through the vents.

"We need to get these kids out too," I said firmly.

"What?" he exclaimed. "No way! There is no freaking way we'd be able to escape if we have to drag a bunch of crybabies with us. You couldn't even escape alone! What do you think will happen with a large group?"

That went well, I thought. I knew Will would be against it, but I was determined to save the others. "We can't just leave them here!"

"And why not?" he paused. "It's not like they're going to be able to survive out there if we do escape."

I hesitated. He had a point. Even if we did manage to escape, the kids would be helpless in the real world. "That doesn't matter. They don't deserve to be stuck here."

He lowered his voice, "Look, if we have any hope of escape, we need to go just the three of us. Forget about these kids. They're a lost cause. We'll tell someone on the outside about them and send help back for them."

The doors opened, halting our conversation. I looked over to see a guard dragging Jessica back. He threw her in her cell and left without saying a word. Jessica was distraught. She held her head in her arms.

"What did they do?" I asked.

She looked up slowly. "I'm not really sure how to put this, but I can become invisible."

"What?" I asked, puzzled.

"I mean I can literally become see-through!" she snapped.

"As in, your whole body?" Will asked.

She nodded. "Yup."

"Cool," was all I could think of to say. After everything I've seen happen here, turning invisible wasn't so bad.

"Cool? Cool?!" she shouted. "I can turn invisible. That's not normal! That's just another addition to my life as a freak!"

"Hey, look on the bright side. It *is* kinda cool," said Will.

"Yeah, you are, like, a ninja or something! Can you show me?" I couldn't resist asking.

She nodded. She remained still and fixed her eyes on the ground in front of her. At first, nothing happened. Then, my jaw dropped as I watched her transform. She went from being in my plain sight to slowly becoming see-through. Eventually I couldn't see her at all. She reappeared seconds later. It was a little bit creepy, but at the same time, incredibly wicked-awesome.

"Wow. That's intense," I whistled.

"Really?" asked Jessica, on the verge of tears.

"Yeah," I continued, "I mean that's like some type of superpower right there."

"Thanks," she smiled, wiping her eyes. "I guess it is kind of neat. It's just hard to deal with the fact that I can do it. I mean, all I want to be is normal, and this isn't helping."

"No doubt," I said. "How did they do it?"

"They injected something into my blood. They told me it was a research project for soldiers in the army. It allows me, and sometimes whatever is touching me, to become invisible. I spent three hours getting the hang of it."

"Wow."

"So how is the escape plan going?" she whispered, changing the subject.

"Mr. High and Mighty here wants to save everyone else too," said Will.

"We can't just leave them here!" I shot back.

"Francis is right. We can't abandon these kids," she agreed.

"Exactly," I said.

"So it's two against one, eh?" replied Will. "Fine. But I hope you realize how impossible it will be to escape undetected with all these kids."

"We have to try," Jessica reassured him. "So what's the plan?"

"I think we should try escaping through the vents like I did last time," I explained. "The next time the guards come to get us, Will and I can jump them, hopefully before they sound the alarm. Then we'll release you and the others and make a run for it."

"It's a long shot, but it's the best chance we have," said Will. "This has been the first time they're taking Francis and I out at the same time. Who knows how many more times they'll come for both of us together?"

Jessica nodded in agreement. "Sounds like a plan. When do we give it a go?"

"Tomorrow," I surmised. "If not, we might not live long enough to get another chance."

"We will need to make sure these kids are good to go when we are," Will said looking around the room.

"Right," I affirmed. I raised my voice so everyone could hear. "OK, listen up guys. Look over here," I waited until all eyes were looking at me. "We're not gonna sit here and take this anymore. Tomorrow, we make our escape. All of you will need to be prepared to go. When the guards come for me and Will, we're going to jump them and open the cells. Be ready! If you're too weak to run, we will carry you. Any questions?"

The room remained silent, but I could see several of the kids nodding, a glimmer of hope in their eyes. Many were too young to understand what was going on, or where they were.

This might just work, I thought. *We can make it.*

"Then we better get some rest," I concluded, lying down on the cold concrete of my cell, wishing it were a nice soft bed.

Everyone went to sleep, dreaming of freedom and escape. *We're going to need all the luck we can get*, I thought to myself, allowing my eyes to close.

Maybe it was just the uncomfortable coldness of the ground, but after a few minutes something inside me suddenly thought, *there's no way this is going to work.* I rolled over, refusing to accept that fact. Rest is what I needed, not negative thoughts. I fell asleep before another one could enter my mind.

TIMELINE: THE MINUTEMAN PROJECT

2 WE DID WHAT?

I woke up the next morning with a new-found strength, or maybe it was just gas from my lumpy brown breakfast, but my body felt like it was ready for anything. I looked around. Jessica was still asleep, but Will was awake, crouched against the side of his cell in deep thought. I saw that everyone else was sleeping.

"Are you sure you want to take all the kids?" Will asked in a hushed tone. "They'll only slow us down."

He never was much of a team player.

"I know. But it's not right to leave them here to die during some experiment," I replied.

"I just can't reason with you, can I?"

I chuckled. "No, I guess not."

"Even if we took only a few of them, there's no chance we'll actually be able to escape. You know that."

"Maybe," I paused, "but we have to try."

Will let out a deep sigh.

He was right, I thought. *We won't make it out of here with this big of a group.* I felt, though, that if I could get at least one kid free, that would be enough. Will is a great guy, but The Island was slowly killing him inside.

There was movement in the room now. Some of the kids were waking up. Jessica's blonde hair was in a bundle as she sat up against the back of her cell. Her blue eyes looked over at us.

"Today's the big day," she said, taking a deep breath.

"Yep," Will replied.

"Are you guys ready for this?" she asked.

We didn't have a chance to answer. The door suddenly opened, and two guards came through. Perfect. They were not extremely big and intimidating. We would be able to overpower them easily. They walked toward us, but instead of opening Will's cell, they opened Jessica's and mine.

This could screw things up, I thought. I gave a quick look to Will. I could tell he wanted us to go through with the escape.

Jessica gave me a determined nod, fire burning in her eyes. I mouthed the countdown as we approached the door, with one guard in front and one behind.

Three.

Two.

One.

I wasted no time, swinging my hardest punch right at the guard behind us. I then threw a series of hits at his face. He managed to grab his gun, bashing the side of my cheek with it. I rolled off of him, dazed, but regained focus quickly as I hurled my body at him. We collided, my impact sending us both to the ground. I saw his gun slide away from his hand, and I dove for it. I stretched my arm as far as I could, trying to grab the handle. I used my fingertips to pull the gun into my palm and my index finger found the trigger. In one fluent motion I spun, faced the guard, and squeezed with all my might.

A metal rod launched from the weapon, colliding with the guard's chest. Bull's eye! I got to my feet, looking to see how Jessica was doing. She was struggling. The guard was triple her size (and could probably eat her if he wanted to). She flickered in and out of view as she tried to become invisible. She was struggling to control it. The guard had his radio in his hand and was about to sound the alarm. I ran over to help her, shooting the guard in the back as I reached them, but I was too late. A loud buzzer sounded and red lights began flashing.

"Not good!" I shouted over the alarm.

"Don't just stand there! Get me outta here!" screamed Will.

I grabbed the keys from the unconscious guard and ran to Will's cell, unlocking the bolt as fast as I could. His cell opened. Will immediately jumped out, wasting no time.

"Let's move!" he shouted, running to the downed guard, grabbing the other gun.

"What about the others? We can't just leave them!" I retorted.

"There's no time! If we want to get out of here, we need to go now!" Will yelled, his face burning red.

"He's right," Jessica said, somewhat defeated. "I'm sorry."

I looked at all the kids, who stared helplessly back at me.

"I'll come back to get you," I declared. "I promise."

We took off down the hallway, sprinting towards the boiler room. I chanced a look behind us. Two new guards were in pursuit.

"Don't stop running!" I shouted at Jessica and Will.

We reached the door and Will jerked it open. I turned, pointing my gun at the guards and pulled the trigger twice, sending two rods in their direction. I couldn't believe it–I hit my targets, and the two guards hit the floor like sacks of potatoes.

"Nice shot," said Will from the inside of the boiler room.

"No biggie," I smirked, as I grabbed a gun from the crumpled body of the guard closest to me.

We slammed the door shut, locked it, and ran towards the vent that Jessica was trying to open.

"It's bolted shut!" she shouted.

Will shot at the bolted covering with the gun I'd given him, but it was no use.

"What do we do now?" panicked Will.

"There's nothing we can do!" cried Jessica.

"We make our last stand here. We can take down most of the guards, and try to find another escape route," I said over the commotion, handing the other gun I had picked up to Jessica.

The boiler room door started to rattle. The guards were outside! The door groaned as the guards slammed into it again and again. We had no escape route. We had no option but to stand and fight.

This was it.

We huddled together. It was odd to touch each other, but the contact made us feel stronger. The pounding grew louder as the door began to crack under the pressure.

"Jessica, you can save yourself. Turn invisible and hide. Wait for things to calm down then try and get out of here," I said, looking into her blue eyes.

"I'm not going to leave you guys here," she replied firmly.

"This is it!" Will shouted.

The door burst open. Guards poured in and surrounded us. We didn't even have time to react or fire off a shot. I looked around. No hope of escape anywhere. It was over. We huddled closer, backs together, still not wanting to accept defeat.

"Put down the guns!" shouted one of the guards.

We didn't move. It was like we were honoring an unspoken pact to stand our ground. We stayed in contact with each other, shoulder to shoulder.

"If you do not cooperate, we will be forced to shoot you," the guard warned.

We didn't move.

"Very well."

In a matter of seconds we would be showered with electrified metal rods. I shut my eyes, bracing for the impact. My entire body tensed up. Pressure was building in my head. It felt like it was going to explode. I waited for the pain to sink in, but it never came. Instead, my body was launched forward and I felt my face smash against something soft, and then … nothing.

I opened my eyes and saw a clear blue sky. A breeze floated gently over my body. *What?* This made no sense. We were underground. There shouldn't be a breeze or blue sky here.

I rolled onto my side and realized that my hand still grasped the gun. What I saw shocked me beyond all reason. There, right in front of me was an open field. I was lying in grass? I saw trees, bushes, above me was a blue sky, and … and … could it be?

Sunshine!

I couldn't remember the last time I saw the sun. Will and Jessica were lying a few feet away from me, unconscious.

I stood up slowly, my body crying out in pain. I limped over to Jessica and Will.

I gently shook both of them, trying to wake them. After a few seconds, they started to stir. Their eyes fluttered open and blinked at the bright sky.

"Is this a dream?" Jessica asked in disbelief.

Will sat up, staring in awe at the sight before us.

"It can't be," I replied. "It's too real, and we're all here."

"How is this possible?" Jessica asked, running fingers through the tall grass around her knees.

"I have no idea. But we're free!" shouted Will, standing up. He threw his arms to the sky as if he had not a care in the world.

"But the guards? The boiler room?" said Jessica, confused with furrowed eyebrows. "How could we have gotten here?"

"I don't know. But Will's right. We're free. I mean, look around, there are no guards or anything. This isn't even what the outside of The Island looks like," I said with a smile.

I took another look around us. Perhaps we were dead. I mean, if there was a heaven, this could be it. In front of us were rolling hills. A forest stretched to our left. A small stream cut through the grass to our right. I jogged towards it and knelt beside the slow, trickling water. I dipped my hands in, receiving a rush of refreshment. I dunked my head under and gulped a mouthful. It had been so long since I drank pure, fresh water.

I felt a shove to my back and fell face-first into the stream. I rose to the surface and caught a glimpse of Will laughing, right before he jumped in himself. Jessica was right behind him. The water felt so nice, I didn't mind the bath. I relaxed.

I couldn't comprehend how it was possible, but in that moment I didn't care. Everything was perfect. We were free.

We must've stayed in that stream for a good hour before we felt like getting out. I climbed onto the bank, and the grass formed a soft blanket against my back as I looked up at the sky. The clouds were like puffy white marshmallows immersed in endless blue sky.

"It's beautiful here, isn't it?" said Jessica, sitting down beside me.

"You've got that right," said Will, emerging from the stream.

"Mhmm," I agreed.

"But where exactly is 'here'?" she said, staring into the forest.

"I don't know, but hopefully somewhere far away from The Island," said Will.

Francis, what's the most important thing to remember?

My dad's question suddenly echoed in my head. I thought of the promise I made the kids as we ran from the cell room. "I'll come back for you," I had said. I needed to keep that promise. I couldn't let them down. *They won't survive without my help,* I thought.

"I have to go back," I said quietly, staring into the distance.

"I'm sorry, I must be crazy, because for a minute there, I thought you said you needed to go back," said Will, laughing.

"I did."

"After all the years we've dreamed of freedom, we finally

have it, and you want to go back?" Will sounded angry.

"Before we escaped, I promised those kids I'd come back for them. I'm not about to renege on that," I replied.

"They must've hit your head harder than mine, because you're insane," he shot back. He was stunned at my suggestion.

"You're serious about this?" Jessica asked.

"Yep," I said, slowly standing to my feet. "I can't sit here knowing what they're going through. So, yes, I'm going back to help them, and no, you don't have to come along."

"Fine. Have fun taking on The Island," huffed Will.

"I'm not going to let you go alone," Jessica asserted.

"Thanks," I smiled, and then looked back at Will.

It was a long moment before he budged. Then he rolled his eyes and grunted as he stood. "Well, I'm not gonna enjoy my freedom, knowing you two are getting yourselves killed, am I?"

"Alright. But first things first, we have to figure out where we are," I stated, as I surveyed our surroundings.

"Right," agreed Will. "Let's head over those hills. Maybe there'll be something on the other side."

"Good idea," said Jessica, jogging towards the green hillside.

"Hey, wait up!" I shouted, as Will and I tried to catch up.

She was fast, and was almost halfway up the hill before we reached her. That's when I heard the noise. It sounded like metal banging on metal. Not in a melodic way. It was industrial.

That's weird, I thought to myself. I stopped.

Jessica and Will stopped running.

"What's wrong?" Jessica asked.

"Shhh," I paused, "do you hear that?"

We stood still, listening. There it was again! This time, louder. Metal against metal. Over and over again. There was a lot of noise coming from beyond the hilltop.

"What is that sound?" asked Will.

"It doesn't sound inviting," replied Jessica.

"It could be The Island. We'd better stay out of sight until we know what it is. Have your guns ready," I said, moving cautiously up the hill, holding my weapon in my right hand.

We laid flat on our stomachs and crawled the rest of the way up the hillside. The noise grew louder as we reached the top. I peeked over the edge and was completely stunned.

"Hey guys," I said in a low voice, "I may not know much about the outside world, but I know it doesn't look like this."

There, in front of us, was a castle. I don't mean a tiny fort or a model of a castle. It was a big, huge, ginormous, freakin' castle! It was surrounded by large stone walls, and was flanked on five sides by tall towers that reached high into the sky. There was even a moat, complete with wooden drawbridge, which currently was upright, and for good reason.

The strange metal sound came from the scene in front of the castle. A battle in progress. It wasn't a battle with guns, like we had seen at The Island, they were fighting with swords.

Yeah.

Swords.

Straight, sharp, pointy, metal swords.

We could tell by the warriors' gear that there were two armies fighting. One was obviously defending the castle, while the other attacked. Yellow and red flags that bore a strange creature on them adorned the tops of the guard towers and rose from the spindles on the castle. The creature appeared to be a horse with wings. Flag bearers on the opposing side displayed their banner: a blue and black checkered flag.

The yellow-red side seemed to be dominating the fight. All over the battlefield, men were dressed in metal armor, wielded swords, and attacked each other. The defenders outnumbered the blue-black side, who seemed on the verge of retreat. The metal sound was the clashing of the swords against armor, as men came together in the heated battle.

Even from a distance, we could feel the intensity of the fight. The brutality of it overwhelmed me. I could see the swords plunge into men, who collapsed and either writhed in pain or died immediately. It wasn't pretty. Both sides fought with fearless energy. I had never witnessed anything so violent (and this is coming from a guy who was raised in a cell as a test subject).

The blue-black side was in a full retreat now. However, they weren't in the clear yet. A cloud of arrows rained down on them from skilled archers, who lined the top of the castle wall.

We watched in horror as the torrent of arrows fell upon the retreating soldiers, causing most to hit the ground, dead.

"Oh, snap!" Will said, staring at the remains of the battlefield.

"What the heck is going on?" asked Jessica, traumatized by the scene before us.

"I have no idea," I said in complete honesty.

"This is intense," said Will, mesmerized by the fight.

"Dude, that was insane," I agreed. I was shocked, but awed at what we saw.

OK, side-note here: It's not that Will and I are violent people, we're just guys. And guys think violence is cool. Girls on the other hand (not mentioning names here, *cough* *Jessica*) think violence is revolting. Believe me, any guy who witnessed what we just saw would think it was cool. It was a battle of epic proportions. Girls, on the other hand, would be disgusted. It's a fact, so just accept it.

Will and I looked at each other with a shared appreciation for it all. Jessica rolled her eyes at us, trying to force the gruesome images out of her head. We scooted back down the hill a little ways to remain out of sight.

"Aren't you guys bothered by what just happened?" she

exclaimed.

"Umm, nope. We're guys, Jessica. It was extremely cool," said Will.

"Ditto," was all I could say.

"Typical," Jessica said. "Well what about where we are? I mean this isn't exactly what the outside world looks like. Is it?"

Will piped up dramatically, "I know. Although it's extremely cool, it's also extremely weird. Like, swords? Really?"

"No, stupid. I mean people dressed in armor and living in a castle. This is a step backward from The Island," she explained.

"You're right, Jess," I replied, thinking of what New York looked like. "This is all wrong."

"Maybe it's just the area we landed in," said Will hopefully. He had no real memory of the outside world. He only knew what he'd seen in movies and in books.

I began to walk back down the hillside, away from the battle. "I doubt it."

I started racking my brain for a reasonable excuse for what we just saw. I started thinking of all the things we learned at The Island. You see, although we didn't have a high-class education, we got the basics, so we could achieve relatively "normal" brain function. I searched my memory to try and put some pieces together. I also tried to remember anything from the schooling I got before I was sent to The Island.

"Wait a minute," I said. "Do you guys remember the lessons we got back at The Island?"

"How could I forget?" came Will's sarcastic reply. "Biggest waste of my time."

"Maybe not," I paused. "Remember the history part? Where we learned about things in the past like the wars and stuff?"

Jessica nodded emphatically. "Yeah! Wasn't there something about medieval times? They rode horses and fought battles."

"Figures. You'd remember the stuff about pretty horsies," teased Will.

Jessica was about to argue, but I interrupted.

"Anyway," I continued, "we learned about knights and castles, things like that. Well, any of that look familiar here?"

"What are you saying?" asked Jessica. "That we went back to medieval times?"

"Well it would explain the castle and the battle," I replied.

Will burst out laughing. "So let me get this straight: we escaped from The Island by traveling back in time to the Medieval Ages? Be serious."

"I am," I said bluntly. "Remember what the scientist called that project?"

"*The Minuteman Project* or something like that," he replied.

"Exactly! Well, what if instead of allowing us to control our age, it actually allowed us to control time itself?"

Jessica and Will stared at me blankly. I couldn't blame them, what I was suggesting sounded crazy, even to me.

"Think about it. How else can you explain the fact that we vanished from the boiler room, moments from being captured, and arrived at a place that I know for a fact isn't anything like the forest surrounding The Island. Not only that, but we also land right near a battle, where we witness a massacre?" I persisted.

"That's crazy," said Will slowly.

"Actually, it kind of makes sense, in a really messed up way," Jessica pitched in.

I nodded, still thinking about what I had just said. *It is messed up,* I thought to myself, but it's the only reasoning I could think of. I was freaking out in my head.

Did we travel back in time?

Was it really possible?

How would we get back?

I took a deep breath, and put on a strong face. I couldn't show my friends how worried I was. Someone had to stay calm, and I guessed it would have to be me.

"OK, if we did travel back in time, how did we do it? You can't exactly just magically whoosh off into the past," Will asked waving his hands in the air.

"Just before the guards shot at us, I closed my eyes, mainly to brace for the impact," I paused, "but then my head got that massive pain, and I was launched forward, and when I woke up, we were here. Maybe that had something to do with it."

"Right. You wished us all here, just like that," Will snapped his fingers together.

"What I mean is, maybe *The Minuteman Project* made me able to control time or changed something in my brain, which allowed me to do it. It's a long shot, but it's the only thing we have right now. Besides, it's just as crazy as Jess being able to turn invisible," I reasoned.

"Well, it's a theory," said Jessica, ignoring my comment about her power being crazy. "At least for now."

"It's a stupid theory," Will stated.

"Well, when you come up with something better, be sure to let us know," I said.

"Yeah, like he's ever gotten an idea before," teased Jessica.

"Very funny," retorted Will. "Here's an idea, if we are in the past, let's get Francis to send us back to the future."

"I'd try, but I have no idea how I did it in the first place, or if it even was me who did it."

"That's great," sneered Will. "We're stuck with a bunch of guys, dressed in metal, armed with pointy sticks."

"It could be worse," said Jessica. "We could still be stuck inside The Island."

"True enough," I replied.

"Sitting here talking is useless," Will said after a long pause. "We should try and figure out where we are. Or maybe I should say, *when* we are."

"Yeah, real good plan there, bud," said Jessica. "Perhaps we should go ask those nice people in the castle, who just finished kicking the crap out of an army."

I laughed. Will glared at me and said, "All I'm saying is that we can't do nothing."

"He's right, you know," I said to Jessica.

She nodded. "I know. But we can't simply walk right up to the castle."

"We need a plan," I agreed.

"Actually, why *can't* we just walk in?" suggested Will.

"Why do you even bother talking?" asked Jessica.

"I'm serious," he explained. "It's not like we look like an army or anything. Why would they be hostile to us?"

"What if they are?" I retorted.

He paused, actually thinking about what he had said. He responded seriously, "Then we will most likely be stabbed to death."

"That sounds like a fantastic plan," said Jessica, rolling her eyes.

"It's a risk we might have to take," I said.

"Surely you can't be serious," Jessica snorted.

"I'm dead serious. And don't call me Shurly," I winked. (It was something my dad used to say.)

"Thanks Francis, at least someone agrees with me," Will said.

"We don't have many options," I said to Jessica.

"Alright. You have a point," conceded Jessica, "but we'll at least have to think it through."

We ascended the hill again, crouching to stay hidden from the view of the tower guards. We weren't going to be able to get close without being spotted. The drawbridge was lowered to allow the yellow and red troops back inside the castle walls. Even if we got close, we were going to have trouble crossing the moat.

"So you want to talk me through this plan of yours?" asked Jessica.

I frowned. "I never said it was going to be a piece of cake."

"Why don't we just make it obvious that we're going to the castle?" Will asked.

"What do you mean?" I questioned.

"I mean, why don't we make sure they can see us coming, so they don't think we're attacking them?" he replied.

"That could work," said Jessica. "What will we do if we get in there?"

I considered the question. "We should try and find a place to stay, get some rest, and then figure out where and when we are."

"Sounds reasonable," approved Will.

Jessica nodded in agreement, but she didn't seem too pleased with the fact that we could end up dead from this plan. I couldn't blame her.

"Then it's settled. We'll head towards the castle from the front," I said, "And if all goes well we'll be fine. Besides, look at us. It's not like we look threatening."

"Hey!" argued Will. "I can be quite threatening when I want to be."

Jessica burst out laughing. "Yeah, you look quite ferocious there, what with your rags for clothes."

Will opened his mouth to protest, but I interrupted him before he could start, "Cut it out, you two. What I meant was, those guards are not going to be threatened by three teenagers."

"Good point," said Will.

"Well, what are we waiting for?" asked Jessica, who was now standing. "We've got a castle to break into."

3 A KING'S WELCOME

We followed Jessica down the hill, and steered toward the dirt road leading to the castle. We cut through the forest, dodging the bushes and branches that poked out at us.

"At least you picked the easiest route to get us there," complained Will, nearly knee deep in a puddle of mud.

"Having fun, are you?" I teased.

Will frowned at me as he stepped to drier ground and did his best to wipe off the mud that covered him. "Oh just tons of fun. I love being covered in mud."

Up ahead Jessica laughed. She turned to face Will. "What's the matter?" she said. "My trail too hard for you?"

"Trail?" he protested. "This isn't a trail! This is just ridiculous."

"If you don't like it, you can lead the way," she said, extending an arm out.

"Maybe I will," retorted Will as he passed her, stepping over a fallen tree. He tripped, landing face-first in another puddle of mud.

The forest erupted with laughter as Jessica and I watched him slowly get up.

"I hate this place," muttered Will, letting Jessica lead the way again.

Our hike through the forest was so peaceful. The sun shone through the trees, which seemed to touch the sky. Flowers and moss were abundant. The further we went, the more the forest began to open up. Soon, there were no more fallen trees or obstacles. Before us spanned an open field of grass.

Jessica stopped. "We're here," she declared.

In the distance, across the field, I saw the stone walls. The drawbridge was no longer down.

"This is it," I sighed, as we walked out of the woods, exposing ourselves, and began to cross the field.

We moved slowly towards the castle. As we got nearer, we met up with the dirt path. The dirt crunched beneath our feet. Blood still lingered on the grass from the battle. Hard as I tried, I couldn't help but look at the dead bodies. As we got closer to the drawbridge, I heard shouts from inside the walls. I couldn't make out what they were saying, but it didn't sound good.

"This was a bad idea," whispered Jessica.

"We aren't dead yet," said Will as we approached the moat.

I looked up to see several guards staring down at us. They were armed with bows, pointed at our chests.

"What is your business here?" shouted one of the archers.

"We are … travelers," I shouted back. "We're looking for a place to stay the night."

Laughs echoed from atop the castle walls. I'm not sure why that was amusing.

The archer stopped laughing. "And what makes you think we'll let you inside the kingdom of Camelot, eh? There's a war going on right now, if you haven't noticed."

I mouthed the word *Camelot* to Will. He shrugged.

I persisted, "We are from a distant land, and have nothing to do with this war. Please let us in."

Another eruption of laughter. "The war is spread throughout all the land. How is it you haven't heard of it? You could be enemy assassins for all we know."

"Please, you must help us," I begged. "We aren't any danger to you."

No reply. The archer who spoke disappeared from the ledge above, but the others remained, arrows steadied in our direction.

This is not good, I thought. I reached behind me, putting a hand on the gun in my waistband. I looked to Will to see that he was doing the same. If things went south, we had to be ready to fight back. Jessica made no move for her gun.

Suddenly the drawbridge began to lower. We watched as it descended across the moat, revealing the inside of this place, Camelot. The first thing we noticed were ten guards running towards us with swords drawn. The archer was among them.

Before I could say anything, Will pulled out his gun and aimed it toward the guards.

"No!" I shouted at him.

He kept his eyes on the guards and said, "They're going to kill us!"

"You don't know that," I responded, but drew my gun as well. Just in case.

The guards formed a circle, pointing their swords at us. We were surrounded. They wore silver armor, with chain mail underneath. They all wore the same tunic, yellow and red with the horse-bird thing on it.

"Stay back!" warned Will, but the guards did not move or even flinch when he pointed the gun towards them.

"Will, I don't think they know what that is," I whispered.

Before he could reply, the archer who talked with us moments before approached us.

"It would be in your best interest to follow us without any retaliation. If you resist, you will find yourself hanging by a noose before dawn," he said in a cold voice.

"Guys," Jessica urged, "I think we should do as he says."

Will looked at me.

I lowered my gun, and said quietly, "Turn the safety on."

The guards grabbed the guns and stared at them, confused.

"What sort of weapon is this? It wouldn't last a second against my broadsword," one said, waving his sword around. Several of the guards chuckled.

"If you think so, why don't you give it back to me so we can find out?" asked Will, cockily.

The guard just grunted at him.

The archer stepped forward. He was younger than the guards, but still older than us. He had black curly hair, and dark stubble dotting his jawline.

"Follow us. And for your sake, don't try anything," he warned.

We crossed the drawbridge, flanked by the guards. When we stepped inside the castle walls, we were stunned. There was an entire village inside! The actual castle, that we saw from beyond the forest, sat on a hill beyond this town. Rows of houses, made out of wood, mud, and straw, stood side by side along cobbled streets. Villagers walked out onto the road to see us as we walked by, whispering to one another. Clearly they didn't get many visitors here. The way some people looked at us, you'd think we were aliens.

They aren't that far off, I thought.

The houses grew in size as we got closer to the castle. We walked through a marketplace where people paused in the middle of trading their wares to watch us pass. A larger wooden building stood just after the marketplace. I guessed it was an armory. There was a large, barn-like door that was open. Just inside it, a fat man with a fluffy beard banged a hammer against a red-hot sword. Everyone had one thing in common in this place: they were all dirty. We actually blended in perfectly in our dirty, mud covered, tattered clothes.

Further up loomed the castle. It was monstrous; towering over us as we approached. I was surprised that they could build something like this with their technology.

A smaller version of the stone wall that surrounded the village surrounded the castle. The wall was sealed with large gates that opened as we approached. As we entered them, I noticed something odd.

In front of the castle, just off of the road, sat a large rock. I did a double take. There was the hilt of a sword sticking out of the rock. Did someone actually stab a rock with a sword?

What a stupid thing to have in front of your castle, I thought.

I didn't think about it long, though, because the next thing I knew, we were entering the actual castle. Large stone pillars, which held up the roof, lined the path we were walking. It was an enormous hallway that stretched farther than I could see. We passed staircase after staircase both to the left and right. We walked in silence; the only noise was the chink of the metal armor on the guards. I couldn't help but wonder where we were going.

"So," I broke the silence, "where are we going?"

"You are to be brought before the king," replied the archer, who didn't even turn to face me. "You will speak only when spoken to, and it would be wise not to play games."

"What kind of games? Like Monopoly?" joked Will.

The archer did not respond. Apparently they did not have a sense of humor in the past (and they probably didn't have Monopoly either). Jessica glared at Will.

She was the mature one, in case you hadn't noticed.

The guards made us turn into one of the staircases. The stone walls had torches nailed to them. The dim flames flickered as we walked by, like a bunch of dying flashlights. After walking up dozens of steps, we reached a door. It was wooden, painted red, and had weird metal notches all over it. The archer knocked twice on the door, but said nothing.

"Enter," came a deep voice from inside the room.

The archer grasped the doorknob and pushed open the door. We stepped inside. We were in the king's room. It was enormous. Gone was the old stone and rotting wood. It was tiled with a slick, shiny stone material, speckled with white and black flecks that at once reminded me of the flooring from my parents' bathroom. Marble. The sudden recollection of something from my old life brought a pang to my chest.

There was a large bed in the corner, with four bedposts that reached a good ten feet high. Heavy curtains matched the bed covering. Paintings of men wearing crowns covered every wall. The eyes on the paintings were bizarre. They followed you around, staring right through you. I shuddered.

Opposite the bed was a fireplace. A dark figure stood against the fireplace, leaning with an arm on the stone. I couldn't make out his features. The heat of the crackling flames felt great against my face.

"What is it you want, Lancelot?" asked the figure, who I assumed was the king.

The archer stepped forward and kneeled. "Forgive me, sire, but we caught these three trying to enter the castle."

"Caught us!" blurted Will. "We walked right up to the gates!"

"Silence!" shouted Lancelot, his face whipping toward Will and turning red with anger.

Will held his tongue, unsure of the consequences of another interruption.

Lancelot continued, "They say they are looking for a place to spend the night, but I don't trust them."

The king sighed, and turned to face us. He did not wear a crown, but his clothes were neat and clean. He wore a red long-sleeved shirt with gold buttons, and dark pants tucked into jet-black boots. His face was tired, the wrinkles revealing his advanced age, although I had no idea what that might be. His scruffy beard was short and gray. He peered at the three of us with cold, dark hazel eyes as if he were trying to peer into our souls.

"Where do you hail from?" he asked.

I looked at Will. *How did we not anticipate that question?*

"Umm … we're from …" I paused. Then I figured, *Wait, if we were really in the past, then it didn't really matter where we say we're from, because they won't recognize it.* I smiled. "We're from California," I said calmly.

Jessica and Will both turned to me. Their mouths fell open like I was the dumbest person in the world.

Whatever, I thought, smiling. I always wanted to live in California. I shrugged at them.

"California?" the king thought for a moment. "I have never heard of such a land."

"Yes, well no surprise," I replied. "It's quite far away."

"Yeah, a few hundred years away, give or take a few," Jessica whispered to Will.

"I see," nodded the king. "And what are your names?"

This froze me. I wasn't sure if we should use our real names or not. I decided not. "Arthur. My name is Arthur," I told him.

Again, I got surprised looks from both Will and Jessica, but not from the king. He stood there nodding. "Arthur. A good, strong name. And what of you two?"

After seeing the king's reaction, Jessica got it.

"My name is Gwen," Jessica lied.

The king turned to Will, who was still confused. "And you?" he asked.

"My name is …" Will took a deep breath, paused, and then said the most ridiculous name in the world, "Merlin."

I couldn't even think of a response to that. He would've been better off saying, "Chuck Norris." I mean, *Merlin*? C'mon! That's embarrassing. For the record, if we die here, I'm blaming it on Will and his stupidity.

The king nodded again, and turned to Lancelot. “They don’t seem to be of any threat,” he determined.

Unbelievable! He bought the fake name Merlin? *How dumb is this king?* I thought. Nevermind that. How dumb are these people who made him king?

Lancelot, the archer, stepped forward holding one of our guns. “They were armed with these,” he cautioned.

The king grabbed it out of Lancelot’s hands, and his eyes widened with a cat’s curiosity. He flipped it around like a sword, trying to figure it out. We flinched when the king’s finger found the trigger and he toggled it.

“It’s a good thing we put the safety on, eh?” I whispered to Will. He nodded in reply, watching the king closely.

“What kind of weapon is this? I’ve never seen anything like it,” he asked.

“It’s a bit like a bow,” I lied.

“You will have to show me how to operate it. Its design intrigues me,” he said.

“Yeah. That’s not going to happen,” said Will cockily.

“If you refuse, I will take it as an act of aggression towards Camelot. I will have no other choice but to throw you in the dungeons,” the king said coldly. I don’t think he liked Will’s tone.

There was no way we could teach him how to use a gun. I wasn’t stupid. It would mess up the entire past. They’ve never even heard of a gun. The sheer power behind it could ruin history, and even worse, change the future.

“Sorry, but we can’t teach you,” I said.

“Yeah, family secret,” Will tried to make a joke.

The king shook his head. “Then I am sorry. Take them to the dungeons, maybe a night in there will bring them to their senses.”

“Oh joy. Out of one prison, and into another,” said Will, rolling his eyes.

Lancelot bowed to the king, then led us outside to descend the never-ending staircase. After an eternity of walking down the stairs we reached the hallway again. He turned right, leading us down another, smaller, hallway. I looked behind us. The guards were still following, leaving no chance for escape. We went down a small spiraled staircase, which was, like every other place in the castle, lit by torches. Lancelot stopped at an old wooden door with a rusted knob. He stepped inside and held out an arm, indicating us to enter. We stepped into the room, and were overwhelmed by a blast of cold, damp air. I felt my skin shudder with goosebumps.

There were four iron-barred cells in the room. Lancelot pulled a ring of keys out of his pocket and opened one of the cells. He gestured inside. One by one we walked into the cell, and once we were clear of the door, Lancelot slammed it shut.

"You should be grateful that the king is so curious about these weapons," he said nodding to our guns, which he piled in the corner beside the door.

He lowered his voice so we could barely hear him. "If I were in the king's position, you three would've been dead before you set one foot inside Camelot."

Lancelot turned and walked out of the room, closing and locking the wooden door behind him.

"He seems rather chipper," I quipped.

"At least this is a step up from our last cell," said Jessica cheerfully. "Look, we even get a bed."

Will chuckled. "Yeah Francis, next time you decide to time-warp us, find a place that doesn't have cells or prisons."

"Well excuse me, Merlin. By the way, who in their right mind picks *Merlin* as a fake name?" I asked.

Jessica giggled.

"Merlin's probably the most common name in this age dude,

they all have stupid names. Lancelot, like that's just dumb," he reasoned, and then looked at Jessica. "And what about you? Gwen? Really?"

I shook my head at him, but couldn't help laughing.

"Hey! I think it sounds like a medieval name," she argued.

"Yeah, really smooth," I teased.

Before she could say another word, Will collapsed to the stone floor holding his head and screaming in pain. Jessica and I rushed over. I knelt beside him and put my hands on his shoulders to keep him from thrashing around.

"What's going on?" asked Jessica, staring at Will in shock.

I was about to ask the same thing when something caught my eye. Objects in the room were floating in the air, like a Harry-freaking-Potter levitation. (Yeah, I've read *Harry Potter*). I shut my eyes for a full three seconds, then opened them for a second look. Our guns, which were piled in the corner, were hovering about three feet off the ground. They weren't the only objects defying gravity. A table in the opposite corner was now close to the ceiling.

Jessica was yelling at Will, trying to shake him out of it.

"Jessica …" I said, still staring at the floating objects.

She looked up. "What?" she screamed.

I didn't answer her. I couldn't. I was mesmerized.

Jessica followed my gaze. She rested her eyes on the guns and table floating in the air. Her jaw dropped.

After a few moments, the table and guns fell to the floor with a clatter, snapping us out of our trance. We looked at each other, then to Will. He was sitting up slowly, no longer in pain. We stared at him, then at the objects on the floor, then back at Will.

"Why are you guys looking at me like that? You're seriously creeping me out. It was just another headache," he said, holding his head in his hands.

"Umm, I don't think so," I said.

"What do you mean?" he asked.

"He means, when you had your little temper-tantrum, things in the room started to float … in the air," Jessica blurted out.

He looked at us, smiled as if we were joking, but his face turned serious after a few seconds. "Come again?"

"When you had your headache, or whatever, the guns and table started to float in the air, and when it stopped, they crashed to the floor," I said.

"Uh-huh," he replied in disbelief. "So let me get this straight. She can turn herself invisible, you can control time, and I can move objects with my mind?"

"It would appear so," Jessica said.

"Wow," he said, breathing deeply. "Are you guys drunk?"

I smiled. Will could always make a joke when times were rough. The silence was thick, as each of us considered what we've been through, and pondered our unique abilities. I mean, *time travel? Invisibility? Telekinesis? C'mon, this has to be a dream.*

Wait. Telekinesis. If Will has that ability, then technically speaking, he could move the guns closer to our cell.

"Will!" I shouted in excitement. "Can you try that again?"

He looked at me, surprised by my sudden yell. "What? Get another migraine? No thanks."

"C'mon," I persisted, "think about it. If you can use your floaty power thing and focus on moving our guns towards us, then we could break out of here."

Jessica sat up, realizing the potential. "He's right! Will, give it another try."

He stared at us with a cocked eyebrow. "Alright, alright. I'll try. But don't laugh at me, it's not like I move objects with my mind on a daily basis."

I smiled. Will stood up and walked to the bars of our cell. He stared at our guns, which were scattered in the corner of the room.

He concentrated extremely hard, and his face was priceless. I couldn't resist letting out a small laugh.

Will glared at me with anger in his voice, "What did I say about laughing?"

The smile faded from my face quickly, but that's not all that happened. Simultaneous with his outburst, the guns moved toward him. He stared at them in shock.

"Did … did I just do that?" he stuttered, staring at the guns.

I knelt down and tried touching the weapons. "I can't reach them. Try again."

He nodded and kept his focus on the guns.

Nothing happened.

Will frowned in confusion. "Why isn't it working?"

"Maybe it's your anger," Jessica quietly remarked.

"What?" he asked.

"Your anger," she replied. "Both times when you moved those things you were either angry, or in pain."

"She's right," I said, looking from Jessica to Will. "Maybe your anger gives you an extra push or something. Try getting angry at me, you might move the guns closer."

"How can I get angry at such a cute face?" he teased.

I grinned and stood slowly. I took a step towards him, and before I knew what I was doing, my fist collided with his face. He spun in the air, then hit the ground.

He looked at me, eyes burning with rage. He stood up with his own fist clenched, and headed for me.

"What did you do that for?" he yelled.

Just as he was about to hit me, the sound of our guns scraping the floor echoed in the room. He stopped mid-swing and gaped at the guns, which were now sliding toward us.

I smiled and patted him on the back, "That's why I hit you, buddy."

"Oh, well if that's all …" he said lowering his fist, only to bring the other one to meet my cheekbone.

I took a step back. He caught me off-guard.

"Hey look!" Will smiled, pointing a thumb to the floor. "It worked."

Sure enough, our guns were at the edge of our cell, and within reach. I rushed over, picked them up and tossed one over to Will and another to Jessica.

"Right, let's break out of another prison shall we?" I said, pointing my gun at the lock on our cell.

I squeezed the trigger, which sent a metal rod flying at the lock, shattering it. I smiled, but then realized the loud noise the collision had just made.

"Someone probably heard that," I observed.

"Gee, you think?" said Will sarcastically.

"Shut up," I snapped. "We need to move. Now."

We exited the cell and made for the door. The only problem was, the door was opening. As it swung open I whispered to Will, "Wait till I fire …"

I looked around and realized, Jessica was gone! It was like she just vanished into thin air. Will saw my shock, then recognized what was wrong. He turned his focus on the door. Two guards entered with swords drawn.

CLANG!

The loud sound of metal hitting metal rang out. The two guards swayed in place, then collapsed to the ground, out cold.

I looked at Will, who was just as confused as I. Before our eyes, a third figure appeared. Will yelped in shock.

It was Jessica.

"I can turn invisible, remember?" she said in a matter-of-fact tone. "There's no need to scream like a little girl, Will."

"Hey!" retorted Will, but Jessica was heading up the stairs.

"Let's go!" I said, jogging towards the staircase.

Will followed, explaining himself, "I wasn't scared, it was just … the sudden appearance that got me."

I mirrored Jessica's footsteps and took the stairs two at a time. "I know, buddy," I said with empathy. I had seen Jessica turn invisible in the cell, so I at least had a notion of what to expect.

We reached the top of the staircase. I stuck my head out, checking to see if the coast was clear. Four guards were trotting down the hallway in our direction. I ducked back into the stairwell before they saw me.

"OK, I've got good news and bad news," I whispered. "Good news is that the guards haven't spotted us … bad news … they're headed right for us."

"We'll have to run for it then," Will stated.

I quickly bolted out of the stairwell, running towards the front of the castle. Will and Jess were right behind me. Shouts came from the guards.

"The prisoners have escaped!"

"Sound the alarm!"

I sighed. *Why couldn't our escapes ever go smoothly?* We continued running, still twenty yards ahead of the guards pursuing us. A bell began ringing in the distance. An alarm. We reached the front gate of the castle, only to see at least twenty more guards surrounding us.

I looked back. The guards were closing the gap quickly. My eyes darted back and forth, looking for an escape route. Ahead was the rock with the sword sticking out of it. I sprinted for it, with Will and Jessica following closely. We were going to need all the weaponry we could get. The guards had us surrounded.

"They're not going to take us down without a fight!" I tossed my gun to Will, who caught it and pointed it at the guards.

I grasped the sword's hilt and pulled with all my strength. I didn't expect it to budge, so I was surprised when it slid out without any resistance. I turned and pointed the sword at the guards. They stopped moving. They began to whisper to each other, and some were pointing at me.

"What?" I yelled. "Are you guys scared of us?"

But the guards remained silent and still. Then, all at once, they dropped to one knee, and lowered their heads so their eyes were looking at the ground.

I was taken aback by their movement. "Uhh … guys … I may not be the smartest person when it comes to fighting, but this can't be very tactical can it?"

"Maybe they're giving up?" suggested Jessica.

"Yeah. Like an army of guards is gonna surrender to three teenagers," sneered Will, still pointing the guns at them.

"Why are you all kneeling?" I shouted. "Are none of you brave enough to take us on?"

No one moved. The guards' heads remained down. Not a single one looked up.

"Uhh, Franc—I mean Arthur … I wouldn't encourage them to fight us. They kind of have us outnumbered," Jessica cautioned.

My mind was spinning as I tried to figure out why the guards were bowed before us. Was it a trick?

"What are you fools doing?" shouted a deep voice. "Why are you kneeling before the prisoners?"

Lancelot, with his sword drawn, came up from behind the guards. He stopped dead in his tracks once he reached me. His snarl turned into a frown, then to shock, as his eyes went from me, to the sword, to the rock, then back to me.

"What?" I asked him.

"Did you pull that sword from the stone?" he asked quietly.

"Uhh … if you mean that rock there," I said pointing the sword at the rock. "Then yes … yes I did."

He frowned at me in disbelief.

"You lie!" he spat.

Before I realized what was going on, he swung his sword at my head. I dropped to my knee and whipped my sword up at the speed of light, blocking his attack. I had never been in a sword fight before.

Hold on, did I actually just say that? Of course I've never been in a sword fight before, that's just stupid. What I meant to say was that I had no idea what I was doing. The only experience I had with fighting was with the guards back at The Island.

I had no idea what to expect, but I wasn't afraid at all. It was quite the opposite. I felt … fearless. The sword had power, and I could feel it flow through my arms as Lancelot lunged, swung, and stabbed at me. Each time, I moved quickly, easily blocking his attacks. Don't ask me how I did it, because I have no idea. The sword was a part of me. The movement felt natural, like I had done it all my life.

I swung the sword at Lancelot, who just barely managed to block the blow, which sent him a few steps backwards. The guards formed a circle around the two of us, and were holding Will and Jessica captive. It appeared to be a one-on-one match for our freedom.

This just got interesting.

Lancelot lunged towards me, swinging his sword at my head. I ducked, turned, and swung my blade, nicking the side of his arm. He growled in pain, but didn't back down. He came at me again. This time I sidestepped, and punched his wrist with the hilt of my sword. He hissed at the impact, dropping his sword to the ground, rendering him defenseless.

I touched the tip of my blade to his throat. "Does anyone else want to try?" I said, sounding pretty tough, if I do say so myself.

Silence.

Lancelot's eyes were full of anger, and his nostrils flared.

"You will let my friends go," I said, edging the blade closer. It drew a tiny drop of blood.

He nodded to the guards. The two guards who were holding Will and Jess let them go, and gave them back their weapons.

"Thank you," I said, pulling my sword away from him. "Now, can somebody please tell me exactly what's going on?"

I waited for someone to step forward. Lancelot rose to his feet and brushed the dirt off of his clothes. His eyes glared at me with a burning intensity that made me wonder if he was going to attack me again. I tightened my grip on the sword.

"I'll take you to the scribe. He'll explain everything," he said, his words laced with hate.

Lancelot turned and walked through the group of guards, who stepped aside to form a path. I followed him with Jessica and Will right behind me.

"Dude, how did you do that?" whispered Will, eyes wide from the intensity of the duel.

"I … I don't know," I said, keeping my distance from Lancelot. "But it felt natural, like the sword was a part of me."

"Who's this scribe he's taking us to?" asked Jessica.

I looked at her as if to say, *Do you not care that I almost just died in that duel?*

She must've understood my look because she said, "Not that I'm not glad to see that you're OK, and I'm very impressed with your dueling skills, I just was wondering what's going on?"

"It must have something to do with the sword," Will said, nodding towards the metal blade still grasped in my hand.

I looked down and wondered, "Maybe?"

"Here we are," grunted Lancelot, indicating a small house.

The house was constructed of large stones. Piles of straw, bundled together, covered the roof. A window next to the door gave us a peek inside. A candle on a table flickered, casting dancing shadows on the wall. Lancelot banged on the wooden door with a closed fist.

"Blaine!" he shouted. "Open the door."

I heard a rustle of papers, followed by the frantic scuttle of feet. The door swung open to reveal a tall, skinny man wearing glasses and holding several scrolls of paper. He had dark hair, a short beard, and bright green eyes.

"Excalibur has been pulled from the stone," Lancelot said, nodding towards me. "By this one. His name is Arthur."

He emphasized my name with a tone of disgust.

The tall man looked at me, then at the sword. "Oh my. In all my years I never expected …" he paused, considering me. "Come in, come in. Don't just stand there like a bunch of buffoons. This is important!"

He scurried back into his house. I walked past Lancelot, who refused to look me in the eyes. I shook my head and stepped inside. It was larger than it looked on the outside. The room before us was littered with paper and scrolls. They leaned against walls, were spread open on tables, and lay stacked in piles on the floor.

The man was running around the room, trying to clear a space free of parchment, talking under his breath, "Such a mess … last thing I expected to see …"

He rushed out of the room with his arms full of scrolls. He returned holding chairs. Lancelot whispered something to Blaine then left, slamming the door behind him.

"Please, please, sit down," he said, placing the chairs on the floor next to a table.

We sat. I welcomed the offer of rest.

"My name's Arthur and this is Merlin and Gwen," I said, indicating my friends.

"I assume Gwen is short for Guinevere?" he asked.

"Umm, yeah … I guess," Jessica responded with uncertainty.

"I see. Forgive me for not introducing myself earlier," he stammered. "My name is Blaine, and I am Camelot's scribe. I record, write, and sort all of its history down on parchment."

"That's nice, but what does that have to do with us?" asked Will.

Will's question drew a confused look from Blaine. "You mean to tell me that you pulled the sword from the stone, and you know nothing of the prophecy?" Blaine responded.

"Umm … yeah," I replied, not sure what to say.

Blaine shook his head, incredulous. "For generations that sword has been lodged in the stone. The sword has tremendous powers. Ancient prophecy says that whoever can pull the sword from the stone is destined to become king of Camelot. Men from all over the realm have come to test their worth, but none prevailed.

"The other kings of the realm have allied themselves together, hoping to overthrow Camelot, seeking the power of the sword for themselves. That sword has been inseparable from the stone. That is, until now. You pulled Excalibur from the stone. Arthur, you are destined to become king."

An eerie silence hung heavy in the room. My mouth was wide open, but I had no idea what to say. My mind struggled to comprehend what I just heard. *I was destined to become king?* No way. I had pulled that sword, Excalibur, like it was nothing. Why couldn't anyone else do that?

Jessica's and Will's faces were twisted in stunned confusion.

"That's not possible," I said. "I'm not even from here."

"Oh, but it is, Arthur. Destiny has a funny way of showing itself, making a foreigner our new king," replied Blaine.

If he only knew where I was from.

"But I'm just a kid!" I tried reasoning with him. "How can I be king of some random place that I've never been to?"

"It is the prophecy: 'He who pulls the sword, will become king, regardless of his age.' You must accept your destiny."

"This is insane," I responded, shaking my head.

"That's stupid. Just because he pulled a sword out of a piece of rock, that shouldn't make him king," Will said.

"You may question the ancient prophecy, but everyone in this land believes in it, including me. You are the new king, Arthur, whether you like it or not," Blaine said with authority.

This has to be a dream, I thought. *I've spent my entire life in a prison. I'm the very definition of a nobody, and now ... now I was king?* I couldn't say another word. How could I? This was crazy.

Jessica spoke up, "This is impossible."

"I heard that you beat Lancelot in a duel," Blaine said, looking at me and ignoring Jessica's remark. "How is it, I wonder, that a foreigner who has, by the looks of it, never wielded a sword, bested our top swordsman? Hm?"

No one replied. It was true. I had never touched a sword in my life, yet I dominated Lancelot in the fight.

Blaine smiled, making his point, "You see, Excalibur chose you to rule this land. If you still doubt the prophecy, stab the sword back into the stone and let your friends try to pull it, for they will fail where you have succeeded."

I found my voice, "Yes, let's do that."

I picked up Excalibur from the table, and headed for the door. Jessica, Will, and Blaine followed. The moon was full, illuminating the highest turret on the castle like a candle in the sky. As we approached the empty stone, I started to have doubts.

What if they pull it out? After all, they're from the future, too.

I stopped in front of the stone. A small slit showed where the sword used to be. I looked over to Blaine. He nodded. I raised the sword up high and slammed it down into the rock. It could've been a trick of the moonlight, but I could've sworn I saw a light glow from inside the rock as I put the sword back in.

"Go ahead, give it a try," Blaine beckoned Will.

"Alright then, it can't be too hard if Fra—Arthur can do it," Will said confidently.

He placed his two hands on the hilt. He braced himself and then pulled up with all his strength. The sword didn't budge. He stared at it with a frown, "That's not possible."

"Here, let me try," Jessica said, pushing him aside.

She placed her hands around the hilt, just like Will did. She took a deep breath and pulled on the sword.

Nothing happened.

She, too, frowned.

Now it was Blaine's turn to try pulling the sword from the stone. He pulled as hard as he could, grunting to prove his effort. Again the sword did not budge.

He looked at me. "Now you try," he instructed.

I stepped forward. "Here goes nothing."

I grabbed Excalibur. The grip on the hilt felt soft and smooth against my palms. I took a breath and pulled up on the sword with all my strength. Just like before, it slid up with no resistance. Again, I held Excalibur in my hands. I could feel its power flow through me, as if something took hold of my body. I felt like I could do anything.

I studied the sword closely. The hilt was golden, with black leather straps running around the stem. Its blade was pure silver, and shone like a star burning in the darkest night sky. There were strange markings on the blade. They were in an entirely different language, and a small ruby was implanted in the bottom of the hilt.

Blaine's voice broke through my focus, "Now do you believe in the prophecy?"

I looked at him. He smiled as if it were the happiest day of his life. My friends' reactions were quite the opposite. Will looked at me with disbelief, unable to figure out how I could pull it and not him.

I've known him long enough to be able to tell he was angry. Jessica just stared at me, puzzled.

"But why me?" I asked Blaine.

He shrugged. "Excalibur chooses its owner. For some reason, it chose you above all others. You must possess a unique personality."

"Wait. For a moment there it sounded like you were saying Excalibur is alive," I said.

"In a way … yes," he paused. "Excalibur possesses unimaginable power, some have even guessed that it holds an entire spirit inside it. I believe that it has a will of its own."

"So what now?" Jessica asked.

"Now Arthur will become king of Camelot. There will be a great festival tomorrow to celebrate, and inevitably … a war," replied Blaine. "But for now let's just worry about the festival."

"Did you just say that there will be a war?" demanded Will.

Blaine hesitated before answering, "Do not worry about it just yet. For now let's focus on the celebration."

Before any of us could protest, he turned and started walking for the castle.

He looked back. "Come, you all must rest for tomorrow."

Will looked at me. I shrugged.

"We'll figure it out tomorrow. It's too much to take in right now," I said.

We jogged to catch up with Blaine. The moon was untouched by the clouds in the night sky. Now all of Camelot was engulfed in its bright light; the entire castle glowed like a firefly.

We caught up to Blaine as he reached the castle.

"Follow me. I'll show you to your rooms, and you can sleep the rest of the night."

We walked down the hallway, our shadows cast by the flicker of numerous torches. It was quiet, except for footsteps of the few guards who patrolled the corridors. Blaine led us down a small hallway, opposite of the dungeons. We passed several rooms; each had the same wooden frame. Blaine stopped in front of one.

He pointed to the door. “Gwen, this room is yours. The one across belongs to Arthur and Merlin.”

“Thank you,” she replied.

He bowed. “Now if you’ll excuse me I must get back to recording these past few events.”

With that, he turned and walked back down the empty corridor.

“We’ll see you in the morning,” I said to Jessica.

She nodded, closing the door behind her.

“Looks like it’s just you and me for tonight, your highness,” Will smiled, opening the door and giving me a mocked curtsy.

“Shut up,” I said, shoving him into the room.

The room was much smaller than the king’s room that Lancelot had brought us to. One window looked out into the courtyard. Of course the walls were stone, and there were two beds. A small fireplace gave the room light and heat.

Will laughed. “C’mon, admit it. You must be pretty happy.”

“Sure it’s cool, but they can’t honestly expect me to become king, can they?”

“Well they’re dumb enough to let a sword figure out who’s king so … yeah, I’d say they expect you to lead them.”

I chuckled. “It does sound pretty stupid, letting a sword choose your leader.”

“Ya think?” he agreed.

“We’d best be getting some sleep.”

“Yeah, we wouldn’t want the new *king* to be tired for his big day,” Will winked.

We crawled into our beds, which had soft warm cushions and blankets on them. The fire crackled throughout the night. The sound soothed me to sleep. It was the first time in I don't know how many years that I slept on an actual soft bed. Needless to say, I slept like a rock.

4 ROUND TABLES

Tap Tap Tap.

The noise woke me. I blinked at the dim light which streamed in from the window. I looked around. Will was asleep in his bed, and the fire and wall torch had gone out at some point during the night.

Tap Tap Tap.

It was the door. I got out of bed, rubbing the sleep from my eyes. My bare feet scraped across the stone floor.

"Don't worry, I got the door. No, seriously, don't get up, I wouldn't want you to strain yourself," I said to Will as I walked past him.

I opened the door. In the hallway stood Blaine, holding a bundle of clothes in his arms.

"Ah. Good to see you're up and about, my lord," he said.

"What?" I asked groggily.

"It's morning, and your kingdom awaits you," he bowed.

I stared at him. For a moment, I completely forgot about what happened last night.

The sword. The prophecy. Me. King.

"Oh. Right. My kingdom," I said slowly.

"What's all the commotion?" Will's voice carried across the room.

I glanced back. He rolled over and pulled the covers over his head.

"These are for you to wear," said Blaine, handing me the

clothes.

"We'll be out in a few," I replied to Blaine, who smiled, bowed, and then left. I shut the door.

Will moaned.

I grabbed a pillow from my bed. "Hey, Will. It's time to get up."

He moaned again.

"Always the hard way," I said, shaking my head.

I swung the pillow and smacked him squarely in the face.

"Alright! Alright! I'm up, jeez," yelled Will, throwing his own pillow at me, banking it off my shoulder. "You could've asked nicely."

"Now where's the fun in that?"

"Who was at the door?"

"Blaine."

"Ughh. That weird old man needs to do something better with his life," Will said.

"Yeah, I guess writing on paper all day is kind of lame. He gave us these clothes to wear," I tossed him one of the outfits.

"You've got to be joking," Will said, staring at the clothes. "He can't expect me to wear a dress."

"I believe it's a robe."

"Well it looks like a dress to me."

"Oh just shut up and put it on," I said, as I put on the other robe. "It's probably what they wear here, and we have to blend in with their time."

Will's face was doubtful. "Fine," he said resentfully.

There was no mirror in the room, but I couldn't help but think I looked like a fool. Yet, it was the nicest thing we'd worn in years.

"Yeah, I think it's a dress," I said with a chuckle.

Will stepped out from behind his bed. He wore a dark blue robe covered in white patches.

"How do I look?" he asked.

"Well, I'm sure your boyfriend will be very happy to see you," I snickered.

He glared at me. He tried to hit me, but tripped over the robe. I laughed and handed him a pair of the boots that Blaine brought in.

"This is stupid," he pouted, as he put on his new shoes. "Why doesn't mine look like yours?"

I looked down at my own attire. My robes were deep red, with a white collar and gold lines at the seams. Needless to say, I looked good … even if it was a dress.

"Probably because you're not the king," I teased. "Stop whining. You look terrific. Let's go."

"Yeah. Let's see what your kingdom has in store for us," mocked Will.

I didn't bother to reply. I grabbed Excalibur and opened the door. Jessica stood in the hallway. "What took you guys so long?"

She looked beautiful. Her gown was a pure red, with white swirls that surrounded the red in a dance. I could tell Blaine had brought her new sandals, too. I was speechless.

"We're not morning people, OK?" Will frowned.

"Whatever," she shrugged and looked at me. "Did Blaine wake you up?"

"Yeah."

"Then we'd better get going," she said briskly.

Jessica turned and started walking down the hallway, leaving us standing in the hallway.

"You know, if I didn't know her better, I'd say she's way too comfortable with being stuck in the past," Will observed as we followed her.

"Well, it *is* a step up from The Island."

"I don't know, being king … being prisoner …" Will smiled, weighing the two with his hands.

"It's a toss-up, really," I joked.

Blaine greeted us at the end of the hallway, "Did you get a nice rest?"

We nodded, and I'm sure all of us had the same thought. It was the first time in many years that we awoke in a bed and free from a concrete cell. Blaine held what looked like a case for Excalibur.

"Good," he smiled. "This is a sheath for Excalibur. It's leather bound and handcrafted by the best blacksmith in Camelot."

I grabbed the sheath, and tied it around my waist. I slid Excalibur inside. "Thanks."

"Now, we have much to discuss," he said urgently.

"Where do we begin?" I asked.

He started walking, and gestured for us to follow. "For starters, the old king isn't too happy to hear Excalibur was pulled free."

"I'm sorry to hear that," I replied. I couldn't keep the sarcasm from my voice.

Blaine chuckled. "Oh do not be sorry. He never was much of a king. And he knew it was always a possibility that the true king would be revealed. He'll go quietly."

Blaine led us up a staircase, and into another hallway. This hallway was large, but not as large as the main entrance. The walls were lined with stained glass windows, each with a different, beautifully crafted picture. I wanted to stop and stare, but Blaine led us past them.

"Here we are," he said, stopping in front of a door. "All the nobles and highest-ranked knights are gathered in this room. The old king is here, too. The purpose is to talk about you and the prophecy."

"Uh-huh," was all I could think of.

He opened the door. "May I introduce, King Arthur."

I was greeted with applause. It was a weird feeling. I walked down the steps. The room held close to twenty men; all standing around a rectangular wooden table. There were three empty seats, which I assumed were for us. As we walked toward our seats, some gave us a cheerful nod as we passed, while others glared.

"They are not used to being in a meeting with a woman," Blaine whispered to me.

"Why not?" I asked softly.

"I don't know where you're from, but here, women are not highly valued. They are never involved in the business of men. They care for children and take care of the household. Some consider it to be an insult that Guinevere is here."

I frowned. Will snickered. Jessica gave him a punch on the shoulder, silencing him. This was definitely not like the future.

"Why are they still standing?" I asked Blaine quietly.

"The king sits first in a meeting, you must sit before they can be seated themselves," he replied.

I was grateful Blaine was there to help us along; otherwise we surely would have ended up doing something stupid. We approached our seats, one at the head of the table, the other two on either side of the head seat.

"I'm guessing I sit at the head of the table?" I whispered.

Blaine smiled. "You catch on quickly, Arthur."

I took a seat. Almost immediately, all the other men sat down, as did Jessica and Will. Blaine remained standing next to me.

"Are you not going to sit down?" I asked him.

He shook his head. "Only nobles are allowed at the table. I am a mere scribe."

I looked at the faces around the table. I could only clearly see some the men, the rest were blocked from my angle, although I could see the bottom of a large beard sticking out at the other end of the table.

Blaine spoke first, "As you are well aware, Excalibur was pulled from the stone, revealing our new king: Arthur."

Blaine paused and pointed at me. I did one of those awkward

hand waves. You know, the kind where you twist your hand slightly, not quite sure if a wave is needed. Jessica put a hand over her face, and Will shook his head in embarrassment.

Blaine rattled off the facts of what happened like a laundry list, "He and his companions, Guinevere and Merlin, arrived at the castle yesterday. They were brought before the former king. He was intrigued with weapons they carried, but when he could not ascertain how the weapons worked, he instructed they be put into the dungeon for one night, while he considered what to do with them. They mysteriously escaped their cells and were pursued to the stone. Arthur pulled Excalibur from the stone, and defeated Lancelot in a one-on-one duel."

This statement brought several murmurs among the men, one of whom glared at me. Lancelot. Apparently he didn't like the fact that I kicked his butt.

One of the men spoke out, "Are you sure that this runt pulled Excalibur?"

Did he just call me runt?

"He did indeed pull it from the stone, I saw it myself," interjected Blaine.

He just called me runt.

"So he is truly our new king?" asked another man.

Lancelot nodded. "Yes Galahad, he is."

The man named Galahad sat back in approval. His dark brown hair was curled behind his ears. "The prophecy tells of a traveler who comes to our land and pulls the sword from the stone. It also says whoever can pull the sword was chosen for a reason, therefore I have faith in Arthur."

Several other men gave verbal agreement.

"Then we have an understanding. Arthur is the new King of Camelot," Lancelot said, the bitterness of his words left a stinging feeling in the air.

The entire table looked at me.

"Uh, hi. I'm Arthur," I said blankly. "And these are my friends, Gwen and Merlin."

Several men smiled, but most just stared at me with empty expressions.

"You are a foreigner, are you not?" asked Galahad. "Where do you hail from?"

"California. It is a distant and warm—erm—realm," I replied, pleased to see that at least one knight seemed to like me.

"I have never heard of such a place. It has quite the unusual name too," Galahad said.

"Yes. I guess it does," I wasn't sure how to respond.

Will spoke up, "Uh, can I ask something?"

I nodded.

"Cool," he paused. "So why is the table rectangular? Because I can hardly see anyone except the guys beside me … and that dude's beard at the end."

A husky grunt came from the bearded man at the end of the table.

Blaine responded, "The table is shaped to give the king the respect and power of the head of the table."

"I see," said Will.

"But shouldn't everyone be considered equal?" I blurted out. "I mean if we all know who's who, does it really matter where we sit? Like, if we had a round table we could all see each other."

I heard several gasps echo the room.

"A round table? That's absurd! Demonic, even," shouted a noble.

"I will not be considered equal status as a knight. I am a noble," shouted another.

I raised my hand and they all fell silent. I smiled. I could get used to being king. "Look, I'm the new king, right? And I want us all to be considered equals here, so I say we need a round table. How can we talk to each other and make decisions if we can't even see each other's faces? I'm the only one who can see everyone. That's not right."

The knights liked my suggestion that we be seated as equals, but the nobles glared. Obviously they didn't want to be considered equal to the knights.

Galahad stood up. "Enough of this bickering. Arthur is our king now, and we should all learn to trust his judgment," he stated. "And, we must repect his wishes."

I was thankful for Galahad. The knight seemed to be very trustworthy and honest.

"Thank you, Galahad," I said.

"I shall get our men working on it immediately," said Blaine, jotting down a note on his parchment.

"Now about this prophecy …" I said.

Several men nodded. I guess they had their doubts about it also.

Blaine stepped up to the table and spread out several pieces of paper. They were tattered and stained with a yellow tint.

"We all know of the sword in the stone," he paused. "But there is much more to the legend than most of you are aware of."

Confused murmurs came from the men.

Blaine continued, "You have all heard of the prophecy which states that Excalibur holds unimaginable power, and the one who can pull it from the stone is destined to become king, but there is another part to that prophecy."

He delicately picked up a torn piece of paper, handling it with great care. He read :

"Excalibur's power can be controlled by only one,
One who is pure of heart, and of soul.
Trials lie ahead, leaving a wake of

Destruction in their path.
War shall arise, that cannot be won alone.
A journey is key for victory,
Allies called upon from great lengths,
Enemies must be vanquished,
If the one fails, darkness shall overcome the land,
The world will be overwhelmed with chaos,
And all hope will cease to exist."

No one knew what to make of this doom and gloom part of the prophecy. It didn't exactly sound like the new king would bring with him a century of happiness. I started the apocalypse and I'm the only one who stands between it and peace.

Yay, me.

Blaine placed the paper back on the table. "As you can see, dark times are ahead of Camelot," he said. "We suspected a war was coming, we've had glimpses into it, and this proves it."

"Once they find out that Excalibur is out of the stone, they'll come in full force to get it," Lancelot warned.

"So it is my fault?" I asked, vocalizing what they were all thinking.

"We were at war long before Arthur pulled the sword. Our enemies were attacking us to gain possession of Excalibur. That didn't have anything to do with Arthur's arrival," stated a noble.

There was an awkward silence in which everyone averted their eyes from me. I couldn't blame them. Telling the new king that he brought a war upon everyone might not go over too well.

"In a way, it *is* your fault, sire," Blaine said, but not unkindly. "But understand that we were already at war with the other realms before all this happened. A war like this was inevitable."

Well, that made me feel better. I started a war by pulling a sword out of a rock. Great. The past is officially warped.

Will gave me a thumbs up and whispered, "Way to go, buddy. You're king for one day and you already started a war."

"You always know what to say, don't you?" I asked.

He just smiled.

"So how many of you actually believe in this prophecy?" Jessica asked.

A few men humphed at the prospect of answering a girl's question. The others, Lancelot and Galahad included, nodded their heads in response. The men who initially scoffed followed the knights' example and nodded their heads too. Everyone in the room believed in the prophecy. Everyone believed that a war was coming.

"So we're pretty much screwed here?" asked Will.

All eyes stared at him. "I'm not sure what you mean," Blaine said, puzzled.

"What I meant was that we don't really stand a chance, do we?"

Blaine was quick to respond, "Not necessarily. The prophecy told of a quest for he who wields Excalibur. It said that he must go out and confront our allies, asking for help. And if he fails, Camelot will fall, and chaos will consume the land," he paused. "Arthur, you pulled Excalibur out, you must fulfill the prophecy. You must call our allies to help us."

I froze. What did he expect me to say to that? You don't just tell a teenager that it's up to him to save the world. I mean, who does that?

"I'm sorry but I think you have the wrong guy for the job," I said firmly.

"I beg to differ," persisted Blaine. "Excalibur wouldn't release itself to just anybody. You have a destiny. Accept it."

I looked down the table. The knights seemed eager to go on this quest, but the rest of the nobles looked like they'd rather see me leave. I looked to my friends for help. Will didn't look too enthusiastic about this quest thing.

He leaned over and whispered, "This isn't our fight, man. Let them deal with it. We need to figure out how to get back to the future."

"No!" hissed Jessica. "We brought this fight on them, we have to finish it. Or at least help them until it's obvious that there's no chance that we will win. Then we can bail."

I chuckled sarcastically.

"What?" she asked.

"Great plan–help everyone but then ditch them when they're going to die," my voice couldn't hide my frustration.

"Well, there's no way I'm going to die for something that I had nothing to do with," she huffed.

"You're so kind," teased Will.

Jessica just shrugged.

"Well it *is* my fault that they're going to war," I said. "I don't think I really have a choice in this matter."

"It's your funeral. Well, *our* funeral, technically," surmised Will, leaning back in his chair.

"Alright. We'll go on this quest to get allies," I declared.

Blaine smiled.

"Excellent. The knights will accompany you on this journey," exclaimed Galahad. He truly seemed pleased.

I liked him. "Thanks," I said to Galahad.

Lancelot clearly wasn't thrilled at the idea of being stuck with me on a quest.

"But if there's a war coming shouldn't we have the knights protecting Camelot?" he asked.

I answered, "Good point. What if the three of us went out, and have Blaine as our guide?"

"I would be honored," replied Blaine.

Galahad argued, "But you'll need protection on your quest,

which our knights can provide."

"Yes, but if Camelot were to be attacked while we're on our quest, there would be no one to protect the castle. My friends and I will go on this journey alone, with Blaine to guide us. That way you can protect Camelot if we take longer than expected," I countered.

The knights seemed to nod their heads in approval.

"It's your choice, but I would recommend at least one knight accompany you," replied Galahad.

I thought about it for a minute. Who knew what we'd come across out there?

"Very well," I allowed. "One of the knights can join us, but I'm not going to force anyone to go, it'll be your choice to come along."

"I will accompany you on this quest," came the bold voice of Galahad, without a second's hesitation.

I definitely liked this guy. "Thank you. It seems we have our group managed, but who are our allies as of this moment?"

Blaine stepped forward again. He explained, "We have several allegiances with the realms of Carleton, Montego, and Guilderbane. Men from those realms will come and fight by our side."

"Good, if we send messengers to them right now, they could send their men over here immediately," I said.

Lancelot spoke up, "I'll send my best men right away."

"Anyone else?" I asked Blaine.

He hesitated before answering, "A war of this magnitude will need more than the men of three realms."

"So what do you suggest?" asked Galahad.

"Long ago Camelot had alliances with all kinds of other beings. Non-human ones, I mean. Mainly the dwarves and elves," Blaine continued.

"You can't possibly be suggesting we ally ourselves with them again?" protested a noble.

"Without their help, we won't win. The enemy is massed throughout all of the country," replied Lancelot.

Silence filled the room as everyone processed this. For the most part, I was stunned that elves and dwarves existed.

"Would they be willing to help us?" I asked Blaine tentatively.

"Under the circumstances I believe they will come to our aid, but you will need to be the one who asks them, not some messenger. I believe that is the quest the prophecy speaks of."

"I understand. Do we know where they are?" I asked.

"The last known locations of the dwarves were the mountains of Elsador. The elves are believed to live beyond Brentwood Forest."

Several hushed whispers filled the room. They didn't sound good.

"What's so bad about those places?" asked Will.

"Well, the mountains of Elsador are said to be guarded by a ferocious dragon, and the forests of Brentwood are cursed by a witch," replied Galahad.

"Oh. Is that all?" said Will sarcastically.

"That doesn't sound promising," I agreed.

"I never said it would be easy," replied Blaine.

"And how far away are these places?" asked Jessica.

Lancelot answered, "The mountains are several days away, and the forests are several days beyond the mountains. It will be a long journey."

"Then we'd better get started," I remarked.

"Galahad and I will help you train in combat before you leave. You may run into trouble on this journey," Lancelot stated.

"Thank you," I said sincerely. Then I turned to Blaine. "Are we done here?"

He nodded. "I believe so."

"Great, because I'm starving," mumbled Will.

5 HORSE PEOPLE

The meeting ended with a discussion to plan a feast. I was glad because I didn't feel like talking about the coming war anymore. We were the first to leave the room, accompanied by Blaine. We stepped out into the hallway and closed the door behind us.

"Well, that was fun," smirked Will. "Who knew a bunch of old guys could be so boring?"

"Now just who are you calling boring?" questioned Blaine.

Will stiffened, "Umm ..."

Blaine chuckled. "No need to make up an excuse, my boy, we have lost our youth, some of us."

Will let out a sigh of relief. Blaine led us back down the hallway.

"Where are we going now?" I asked.

"If you are to be our king," he related, "it would be good for you to know your kingdom and its people."

"I suppose so," I said, following him.

As we neared the gigantic doorway to leave the castle, the intensity of the sunlight made me shield my eyes. I paused a moment in the courtyard to adjust. I could see that the castle and outer courtyard were surrounded by a tremendous wall. Guards patrolled along the top of the wall, which was much like the wall that surrounded the entire kingdom, but even bigger. Mud and patches of grass covered the ground. Several stone statues of lions were strategically placed around the walkways. We passed the empty boulder that once held Excalibur.

We walked through the gateway and out of the castle's courtyard. There were dozens and dozens of huts and stone buildings on both sides of the walkway; most had straw roofs with bricks lining the walls. People walked busily to and from the buildings and along the path. I felt extremely awkward, considering they were wearing "normal" clothes, that may have been a bit on the dirty side, while we were wearing bright and vibrant robes. To be honest, we stuck out like sore thumbs.

"Do we have to wear these ridiculous outfits?" I whispered to Blaine, avoiding eye contact with the people staring at us. As we passed, each person bowed in respect to us, which made us stick out even more.

Blaine laughed. "I suppose you aren't accustomed to such prestige in California?"

"No, not really," replied Will.

"Well the robes show your status of nobility. It's what sets you apart from all the commoners," Blaine stated. "But if you'd like to change, I can hardly deny the king."

I looked at Will and Jessica. "Do you guys feel like getting out of these?"

"I don't know, I think Merlin looks rather stunning in that dress," teased Jessica.

"Alright that's it, I'm getting out of this stupid thing," said Will, his voice muffled as he pulled the robe over his head.

"Is there any place where we can find more casual clothes?" I asked Blaine.

He nodded. "There is a tailor just around the corner."

We turned right after passing a butcher shop, which I won't describe in great detail because it was kind of gross. Even for me. The side street we turned onto wasn't as busy as the main street, and it wasn't as clean either. Piles of mud and hay lay on the path, which was also littered with several pigs and chickens.

Blaine stopped in front of a rundown shack on the left of the road. The shack was a wreck. Worn pieces of wood hung from the walls, there were holes in the roof. It was definitely sketchy.

"Blaine … not that I don't trust you, but this looks like the home of some psycho killer," I said, staring at the shack.

I'm not sure Blaine understood what I meant, but it didn't stop him from knocking on the door. "Appearances aren't everything," he warned.

"They are when we're getting clothes from the guy," I countered.

I heard footsteps heading toward the door, followed by a husky voice, "Who's making all the ruckus out there?"

"It's Blaine, Charles. I've brought you some business," Blaine yelled to the voice behind the door.

"Is that right?" the voice called back. "Last time you brought me business I ended up with that weird green fungus, and it took me weeks to get it off!"

I raised an eyebrow at Blaine.

"It's a long story," he brushed me off, and turned back to the door. "That wasn't my fault. Besides, all I need are some clothes."

There was no reply for a few seconds. Then Charles called, "Who's with you? Because if it's those French stable boys, don't even think about it."

"Just open the door, Charles."

Another pause.

"Very well," came the reply, followed by the sound of several locks being opened.

The door opened slightly, revealing the face of a scrawny man with glasses. He had dark hair and a scruffy beard.

"Who's the royalty?" he quizzed staring at us, his eyes darting back and forth. "Never mind, you'd better get inside quickly."

"You don't get out much anymore, do you Charles?" asked Blaine.

"Well, no. It's far too dangerous out there. All kinds of danger," he said in a low voice, eyes staring down the street.

He opened the door and I couldn't help but notice he was wearing dirty gray pants and an equally filthy shirt.

"Get inside," he ordered.

One at a time we stepped into the small shack. The smell was terrible, like a mix of rotten eggs and mud.

I wrinkled my nose. "What's that smell?"

Charles turned and stared at me for a quick second before replying, "It's either yesterday's stew, or the rats in the walls. I haven't quite figured out which."

"Oh, that's nice," Will grumbled under his breath.

Charles didn't seem to care. He walked around the room, piling clothes and fabric into a corner. He pulled out four small stools for us to sit on. A small orange cat leapt onto the pile of fabric in the corner of the room.

"Josephine, get down from there!" fussed Charles, scuttling over to the clothes, picking up the cat, and disappearing around a corner.

"Oh come now, he isn't as bad as he appears to be. He's just a little out there," Blaine responded to our judgmental stares.

"Blaine, he lives alone with a cat named Josephine," I stated.

"Oh all right, he's crazy. But he's the best tailor in Camelot, so try to be nice," said Blaine.

Charles reappeared moments later without the cat. He grabbed another stool and sat around a small table with us.

"So what exactly have you gotten me into this time Blaine?" he asked, staring at Blaine with dark beady eyes.

"May I introduce Merlin, Guinevere, and Arthur," Blaine said with a gesture in our direction.

“That’s very nice, but as you can see I’m quite busy, and don’t have time for your friends,” he replied.

Blaine looked around the cluttered room. “Yes, I can see you have a lot of other guests to entertain,” he quipped.

Charles narrowed his eyes. “Fine. You said you needed some clothes?”

“Yes, the king and his friends need some regular clothes to wear,” he nodded to me.

“The king?” he said, eyeing me down. “Blaine, I may not get out much, but I know the king is older than him.”

Blaine smiled. “And this is why you should get out more my friend. Arthur pulled Excalibur from the stone.”

A wide smile broke over Charles’ face. “Your pranks never get old, Blaine,” he grinned.

He obviously needed some proof. Blaine gave me a nod, so I pulled Excalibur out of my robe, holding it in front of him.

“My word, it’s true,” he said with shock. “When did this happen?”

“Just last night,” replied Blaine.

“Fantastic!” shouted Charles. “I never did like that rusty old man.”

“Indeed,” agreed Blaine. “Arthur and his friends would like more normal clothes so they don’t stand out in the marketplace.”

“Well I can’t really say no then, can I?” he said. “Very well, what type of clothes would you like? I can make you a light padded armor, regular cloth, cloaks, you name it.”

His sudden enthusiasm took me off guard. I said slowly, “Umm, I honestly don’t know, maybe the padded armor might be best since we’re leaving soon?”

He gave Blaine a quizzical look.

“The other realms will want Excalibur, so we’re leaving to get more troops,” Blaine elaborated.

"I see. Yes, the padded armor will suit you nicely. It's light, maneuverable, and will protect you from most enemy blows."

I nodded in appreciation as he grabbed a piece of string and started measuring my size. After a few measurements he turned to Will, "And what shall I make for you?"

"Oh, regular clothes will do for me. As long as I don't stick out, and it doesn't look like a dress, I'll be fine with it," Will smiled.

Blaine chuckled, and Charles took his measurements as well. "And what can I get the lady?" he asked Jessica.

Jessica smiled, "Normal clothes work for me too, but something comfortable please."

He nodded, measuring her sizes. After recording all our measurements, he looked at us, "This should take me an hour or two. If you return after midday I shall have them ready for you."

"Thank you," Blaine said. "We'll return then."

We left his house quickly. He didn't leave us much choice, as he shoved us out the door.

"Only an hour?" Jessica asked.

"I told you, he's the best tailor in Camelot. He may be crazy, but he works like a dog."

"So how are we going to kill time?" asked Will.

"I can finish giving you the tour of Camelot," Blaine replied.

"Sounds exciting," said Will dryly.

"Oh come on, that'll be fun," Jessica encouraged.

Blaine led us back to the main street. We walked past several houses, a blacksmith, and a pottery shed before reaching the front gates of Camelot. Blaine signalled for the drawbridge to be lowered. A couple of guards opened the gates, and we stepped inside. We skirted the outside of the castle. Because the castle sat on a hill, when we got behind it I could see a large forest behind the back wall.

It was quiet and peaceful. You'd hardly know that in front of the castle was a busy town. Blaine read my mind.

"The forest stretches behind the castle for quite a long way, with only one road in and out," he said, pointing to a dirt road that snaked into the trees. "The forest gives us plenty of food, and there is a river back there that supplies our water. The closest town is about four hours away by horse on that road."

We took in the view.

"It's so peaceful," said Jessica.

"Yes, it's quite the place," agreed Blaine.

"Oh it's so beautiful, I wish I could stay here instead of doing something fun," said Will sarcastically.

Blaine caught the hint, "Very well, we shall continue."

He led us around to the front gates. "As you can see, the added moat gives us more protection in battle. Although you can't quite tell, there are alligators in the water, so I'd keep my distance."

"Why alligators?" I asked.

He shrugged. "You'd have to ask the old king, but they do help keep unwanted visitors away."

"It's a good thing we didn't try sneaking in," Jessica remarked quietly.

We reached the gates, which were guarded by six men; four on the walkway above, and two outside the gates. We crossed the bridge again, and Blaine led us down a path to the right. We passed a few houses and then came to a clearing. The clearing was in the shape of a large ring surrounded by bleachers. It reminded me of the football stadiums I recalled seeing in books, except older and dustier.

"This is our arena. We host tournaments where knights from all over the country come to battle for prizes. They joust and also do other contests."

"This is so wicked," admired Will, jumping the wooden fence and stepping into the center of the arena.

"This is where you three will train with Lancelot and Galahad to prepare yourselves for the journey ahead."

I stepped into the ring with Will. I could picture the people in the stands around me, cheering while a one-on-one match raged. It was pretty awesome.

Suddenly we heard a loud ringing. I looked around and spotted a large bell, swinging at the top of one of the towers.

"That's the warning alert. Someone's attacking Camelot!" shouted Blaine.

He ran back up the hill towards the gates. We hurried after him. As we approached the gates I could see guards running in different directions, getting ready. The drawbridge began to raise the second we reached the other side. Blaine turned sharply and led us up a set of stone steps. We were on the walkway above the drawbridge. I looked out into the large field in front of us to see a large group of men on horses charging towards us.

"False alarm!" shouted one of the guards.

"What do you mean? They're headed straight for us!" I exclaimed.

"It's only the centaurs, my lord," replied the guard.

I looked at Blaine.

He explained, "The centaurs are wild animals. They are allied to no one, and are only looking for a good time. Every now and then they find it amusing to make it look like they're attacking us and shoot designs into our wall using their bows and arrows. I believe they think that it annoys us. They mean us no harm. Last week it was a flower, I wonder what they'll do this time?"

Jessica pointed at the centaurs. "You've got to be kidding me! Those things can't be centaurs. Centaurs aren't real," she doubted.

"See for yourself," replied Blaine.

We stared with uneasiness at the creatures charging toward the castle. As they got closer I realized that they weren't men *riding* horses, they were men *attached* to horses. Where the horse's head should be was the waist up body of a man, literally attached to the body of a horse.

"Wow," was all I could say.

"They look so cool," Will said in wonderment.

There were about forty centaurs in the group, all loading arrows into their bow and shouting loudly. Some of what they yelled was quite offensive, so I won't tell you what they said, but they were having a good time. All at once they released their arrows. The three of us ducked, but Blaine just stood there watching.

"There's nothing to fear," he said. "Look."

We straightened up and looked out into the field again. The centaurs were now running away from the castle, still yelling obsenities and high-fiving one another.

"Let's see what they did, shall we?" asked Blaine.

"Sure," I said, still trying to figure out what just happened.

We walked down the steps and out the gates. After walking a good distance away from the castle, we turned around to look at the walls of Camelot. In front of us, where the arrows had hit the wall, was the off-centered picture of a sword in a stone. It was really neat … even though it was a little crooked.

I whistled, "That's pretty awesome."

Will and Jessica nodded in agreement.

"It wouldn't be so crooked if they weren't drunk all the time. It looks like they heard you pulled Excalibur out of the stone, Arthur," Blaine shook his head studying the picture.

"So it seems. And they just do this for fun?" I asked.

"They tend to keep to themselves, but they'll do anything that is amusing to them. Mostly that means they get drunk and race around the forest," Blaine said.

"I see."

"Well, after all this excitement I'm sure Charles will have your clothes ready," said Blaine. "He works faster when he hears the warning bell."

"Let's not waste any more time. I can't wait to get out of this stupid thing," Will replied, already heading toward the gates.

He came to a stop under the gates, his head turning in every direction. "Right, so which way was the crazy guy's house again?"

Blaine chuckled. "Follow me."

We walked back up the dirt path and turned left down the familiar street where Charles lived. We reached his shack and Blaine once again knocked on the wooden door.

"Who is it?" demanded Charles from inside the house.

"Charles, we really need to talk about getting you outside more," replied Blaine.

After several locks were undone, the door opened slightly. "Oh, it's you," he said.

He opened the door completely. He held a pointed stick in one hand and a broken bottle in another.

Will stared at him, "Who were you expecting?"

Charles glanced down at the weapons in his hands and nervously cast them aside, "Oh … no one, I heard the warning bell and, well, I don't get many visitors."

"Gee, I wonder why?" Jessica whispered to me.

I let out a quiet laugh as we stepped back into the ragged house. Charles led us over to the table. We took our seats expecting Charles to bring us our clothes, but he sat down, too and just stared at us.

After a few seconds he stood up. "What do you want?" he asked with frustration.

We couldn't hide our confusion.

Blaine spoke slowly, "We came by earlier … asking for clothes … that you said you would have ready by now …"

"Right!" he shouted in excitement after taking a few moments to process what Blaine said. "Of course! You want the clothes. I have them all finished in the other room, I'll just be a second."

He walked out of the room and disappeared around the corner.

"So what exactly is wrong with him?" I asked.

"I don't quite know," Blaine said honestly.

"That's always good," I replied with an eye roll.

A loud crash came from the other room.

"I'm okay!" reassured Charles. His voice was muffled.

Will shook his head, "The man's a lunatic."

Charles returned, holding a bundle of clothing. "Here we are. Sorry about the wait, I couldn't remember where I put them."

"Of course," I gibed under my breath. The guy was a wreck.

He dumped the pile of clothes onto the table, which shifted under the weight. He handed a set of clothes to each of us.

"Well, go on. Try them out."

"Buddy, I am not going to change in front of you," I stated.

Charles blinked. "Oh, right. I understand. You can change in that room," he instructed, pointing to a wooden door behind us.

"Thank you," Jessica said.

We stood up, and walked into the other room. Every free space was heaped with fabric, except for one small shelf which held a few dishes of what I thought was chicken, but could have been vegetables. Or something else. I'll never know.

Will put a hand over his nose, "I think I'd almost prefer changing in front of him."

"Me too," I said, holding my breath.

"You guys are such babies. Yeah it's bad, but I've smelled worse, so if you'll excuse me I'd like to change," said Jessica.

We crashed back through the door, breathing in fresh air.

"Oh my god! I thought I'd never breathe clean air again," Will said, and he took in a deep breath.

"That smelled like a pile of crap … mixed with … a dead animal … covered in more crap," I said between breaths. I pointed to the door and demanded, "What exactly died in there? And how long ago did it die?"

Charles pondered for a moment before he replied, "I wondered where my pet badger went."

I asked with disbelief, "How could you lose a pet badger? Nevermind. Why do you have a pet badger?"

"Correction: did. I did have a badger, because I had this theory about talking to animals."

"I can't even think of a response to that," I said.

Charles just smiled. Face it, the man was insane.

And we were getting clothes from him.

Great.

"If you don't mind, we'll use the other room where there's no decaying animal bodies. I hope," said Will, heading for the other room where Charles had retrieved our clothes.

Charles continued to smile at us (it was kind of creepy, really). I gave Blaine a look as I passed him; he shrugged.

"The man has a cat named Josephine and a pet badger that is currently rotting away in that room. I really don't see why we should wear his clothes," Will said, eyeing his clothes suspiciously.

"Well they can't be any worse than what we've got on already," I said, taking my robe off.

"Alright but if they don't fit, I'm out of here."

I inspected the clothes Charles had made for me. There was a dark green long-sleeved shirt with a hood, and brown leather padded armor that reminded me of football pads I had seen when I was younger. The pants were a dark color that I couldn't really make out in the light of the room. I took off the heavy red robe and put the new things on. The hoodie was surprisingly comfortable, and fit me perfectly. I threw the brown padding over my shoulders, tying the strings in the center, keeping it tight to my body. I picked up more of the same padding and slid it up my arms, tying them to the shoulder pads. The sleeves protected my arms and wrists, but I was still able to move them freely. I rolled my shoulders to find the armor padding was maneuverable and light. I looked over at Will. He wore a blue shirt with a red tunic and a brown long-sleeved jacket over top. He seemed pleased.

"You know, he may be crazy, but he sure knows what he's doing with clothing," he said with appreciation.

I agreed, "It's definitely better than the robes. Hey, punch me in the chest, I wanna see if this armor actually works."

Will didn't even hesitate. He swung a hard punch, which collided with my chest. I didn't feel a thing, but Will did. He cringed in pain, holding his hand. "Ow!" he yelped.

I smiled. "Yup, it works."

We went back into the other room. Charles stood and inspected his handiwork.

"A perfect fit, if I do say so," he said smiling.

The door in the corner opened and out stepped Jessica, wearing a light blue dress. It wasn't fancy, but it looked quite comfortable.

"Well, what do you think?" she asked, twirling around.

"It suits you," I replied.

"I'm glad you are all pleased with my clothes, now if that is all, I have much to do," Charles said, the smile vanishing.

"We have much to do as well," Blaine said as he stood. "Thank you for your help, old friend, I'll stop by soon."

Charles nodded, shooing us out of his house with his arms, "Just don't bring any company next time."

Blaine smiled, and Charles shut the door behind us. We heard several locks click. Blaine stepped back into the street. "Now that we've gotten you some normal clothing, we can finish the tour."

"You mean there's more?" groaned Will.

"There are still the fields to see, and the rest of the village," Blaine continued.

He brought us past the arena where we had been when the commotion started with the centaurs. We walked up a path that led to another part of town. Thanks to the clothes, people stopped giving us a second look, and it was much more relaxing. We passed more houses until we reached a circular courtyard. A wooden stockade in the middle held an old man. His arms and head poked through the boards and he looked like he would collapse at any minute.

"Why's that man there?" Jessica asked.

Blaine sighed, "He was caught hunting deer in the king's forest—the old king that is—in order to feed his family and the punishment is three days in the stockade."

"That's ridiculous," I said. "He was only trying to feed his family."

"I agree, but that is the law. However, we are currently under new management, so you can change it if you want to."

I affirmed, "I guess I can, can't I?"

I walked up to the old man, and pulled out Excalibur. I swung at the bolts that held him in place. They shattered upon contact with my sword. I lifted the board off of the man and helped him stand up.

"Who are you, young man?" he managed to say.

"I'm Arthur. The new king," I replied boldly, moving him to a stoop so he could sit down.

"God bless you, Arthur."

The man had kind eyes. "Blaine can you make sure this man gets food for himself and his family?" I ordered.

"Of course, sire," Blaine replied.

"Thank you," the man said taking a few deep breaths.

"Take it easy for a bit and someone will come with some food for you," I said to him.

"Shall we continue?" asked Blaine.

"Sorry for interrupting," I said.

"Not at all, that was very noble of you. You'll be a great king," he smiled.

"Yeah, I don't know about that."

"Don't be so modest, that was a really nice thing you did back there," Jessica chipped in.

"Really?" I asked.

"Oh, totally. I mean, let's release all the convicts everywhere, it'll work great," teased Will.

"OK, he's like ninety years old and he killed a deer, not some person," I stated.

He laughed. "I know, I'm just messing with you."

"Thanks."

"Don't mention it."

"I won't."

"Good."

"Great."

"Are you two done?" interrupted Jessica.

We looked at Jessica who shook her head, "You guys are so immature."

"You're immature," I mimicked.

"You know you just proved my point right?" she pointed out.

I stopped and searched for a comeback. "Well … you're…you have a big nose," I blurted.

"I do not!" she argued. She let out a sigh and walked ahead with Blaine.

"That went well," Will said.

"I thought so," I said. I'll never say this out loud, but I couldn't think of a comeback. She doesn't actually have a big nose.

"You know, now that you mention it, she kind of does have a big nose," Will chuckled.

I changed the subject, "Blaine, where are we going now?"

He looked back, "As I was telling Gwen, I've shown you the courtyard, marketplace, town, the training arena, and some of the outside grounds of the castle. Oh, except for the stables and fields."

"Stables?" Will asked.

"Yes, it's where we keep all the horses," Blaine replied.

"Right. Horses. Awesome," Will said, unenthused.

"Yes, quite incredible creatures they are," continued Blaine, not noticing the sarcasm in Will's voice.

"Are we going to take some with us when we leave?" Jessica asked.

"Yes, they will speed up the trip significantly, but there will be some parts where we shall have to walk."

Up ahead I could see several long barns, which I assumed housed the horses. They were brown, with mud and straw covering the roof, and to the side of them were mounds of hay.

"How many horses does Camelot have?" Jessica asked with great interest.

"Camelot has hundreds of horses, but only about thirty are kept here. The rest are stabled in nearby towns."

We reached the door of the stables and I couldn't help but notice the stench coming from inside. I coughed out, "What's that smell?"

Blaine was unfazed. "Well, you don't think we're the only creatures who go to the bathroom, do you?"

The place reeked, which dampened my excitement for the impending horse ride.

Blaine opened the door, and the smell smacked us in the face with force. Rremember, we haven't been near animals in years.

We stepped inside. The floor was hay and mud. Thick wooden beams held up the roof. Each horse was in its own stock, and every color was represented in the horses' sleek coats.

"They're so calm," said Jessica, approaching a brown one. She reached out her hand, petting its head.

"That's Insontis. She's the oldest horse here, but she's also very strong. Her name means 'innocent,'" Blaine said.

"I like her," smiled Jessica, trailing her fingers down Insontis' nose.

I walked along, looking at each horse. I stopped when I reached a white one. Its eyes were jet black, and it was circling its stock.

"He's called Animi. That's Latin for 'courage.' I think he will suit you very nicely," Blaine said.

"Suit me?" I asked raising an eyebrow.

"Yes, you can each choose your own horse for the journey."

"I see."

"I want this one," Will said pointing at a black horse, which stared back at him blankly. "What's his name?"

Blaine walked up to the horse, "This one is Arbor."

"That sounds intimidating," Will said.

"It means 'tree.'"

Jessica and I burst out laughing, and even Blaine let a grin slip across his face.

"That's not funny. How come you guys get cool names and I get stuck with *tree*?" he asked.

"Hey, don't beat yourself up. Tree is a very intimidating name," I teased.

Will frowned, staring at his horse. "Well, I think Arbor is a wicked name," he justified.

"Despite the fact that it means tree?" laughed Jessica.

"Shut up," he retorted.

Blaine spoke up, "Have any of you ridden a horse before?"

We looked at each other. Considering that we've been stuck in cells for years, no, we didn't get to ride horses much. But we couldn't exactly tell that to Blaine.

"No, not really," I said.

Blaine looked puzzled, "You must truly come from a far away

place not to have ridden a horse before."

"It's not something we've had the chance to do," said Jessica.

Blaine shrugged, "Alright then, we'll just have to train you before we leave."

"Can we start now?" asked Jessica eagerly.

Blaine seemed to like that plan. "The feast isn't until sundown, so why not?"

"This is going to be so much fun," groused Will, rolling his eyes.

Blaine walked into Insontis' stall and pulled a saddle from the wall. He flipped it onto Jessica's horse and fastened the straps firmly.

"I've never taught anyone how to ride a horse, so bear with me," he said. "You mount your horse by putting your left foot on the stirrup and holding onto the pommel. Then swing your right leg up and over the horse …"

He attempted to demonstrate. He grunted, obviously struggling. I stepped forward and gave him a boost.

"Thank you. My body isn't what it used to be. Now where were we? Oh yes; now grab the reins and make sure you have a firm grip. We'll start off with a slow walk, nothing too fancy. You can do this by squeezing your legs together, and if the horse does not respond, give it a firm kick." He squeezed his legs and the horse moved out of the stock slowly.

"Make sure you keep your heels down, back straight, and chin up to keep your balance. Guide your horse by putting pressure with the opposite leg of the direction you'd like to go, and come to a stop by pulling the reins toward you and leaning back."

The horse stopped walking, and he slid off gingerly, petting the side of its head.

"Now you try it," he said, handing the reins to Jessica.

Jessica pressed her lips together with determination. She put her left foot on the stirrup and swung her other leg over its back effortlessly. She beamed with joy as she peered down from atop her horse. We applauded.

"Well done! That was excellent. Now, keep hold of the reins and gently squeeze your legs together," Blaine said, encouraging her.

Jessica was focused. She held the reins, squeezed her legs, and Insontis moved forward slowly. She giggled with delight. It was good to see her laughing. She reached the end of the stables, and continued outside.

"Umm, how do I stop again?" she panicked.

Blainc callcd out, "Pull back gently and lean back."

She did just as he said, and her horse came to a stop. She patted it on the head, and eased off of it, still holding onto the reins.

Her face was brighter than the sun. "That was so cool," she raved.

Blaine looked around, confused, "The sun is out and it is quite warm, how is it cool for you?"

She laughed. "Oh, it's an expression where I come from. Cool means great."

"Then I suppose riding a horse is quite … cool," he said.

"So who's next?" asked Jessica.

I took a step backwards and nudged Will ahead.

He frowned. "If you can do it, then I'll have no problem."

Blaine grabbed a saddle off the wall and fixed up Arbor for Will.

Will put his left foot on the stirrup, and grabbed the side of the saddle to pull himself onto the horse. The saddle shifted and slid towards him, causing him to fall backward into a pile of dirt. The three of us laughed as he tried to brush the mud off of him.

"A word of advice my friend, don't grab onto the saddle, because it will slide with you," Blaine grinned.

"Yeah, I kind of figured that out," Will replied, wiping the dirt off of his pants. He looked at Jessica and I, who were still laughing at him. “Shut up.”

I made the motion of zipping my lips with my hand. He glared, then turned to face the horse. He took a deep breath and tried again. After much grunting and wiggling he managed to pull himself upright onto the horse. He squeezed his legs and Arbor began to walk forward and out of the stables. Once outside, he pulled sharply on the reins. Arbor reeled back with a grunt, his front legs coming up off the ground. The sudden motion threw Will backward, off the horse and onto the grass.

Blaine was about to give him some advice, but Will shushed him with a look and a raised hand. “Not a word,” he said.

Blaine smiled and turned to me.

“My turn?” I asked.

“Your turn.”

“Right,” I nodded, and went into the stable.

I stopped in front of Animi’s stock, waiting for Blaine to set up the saddle. He tightened the straps and then backed off.

I walked up to Animi and whispered in his ear, “Take it easy on me, OK?”

I walked to his side and put my foot in the stirrup, climbing up onto the saddle with little trouble. I took another deep breath and squeezed with my legs, urging him forward. He obeyed without any resistance and trotted forward slowly. When I reached the other horses I pulled back on the reins and came to a stop.

Blaine approached me after I had climbed down, “Well done. Animi seems to like you.”

I patted him on the head (Animi, not Blaine. Patting Blaine on the head would just be silly).

“Yeah, that was … interesting,” I replied, feeling apprehensive, but excited at the same time.

“Why don’t we go on a little ride?” Blaine asked.

I looked at my friends. Jessica was eager for the opportunity, while Will shook his head, more interested in the feast.

"It would be good to get some riding practice before we leave," I suggested.

Blaine took that as affirmation. "Then we shall have a quick gander through the forest."

We remounted our horses and Blaine led us through the town and out the main gates. We followed at a trot. He took us along the path we'd used when we arrived at the castle on that first day. Soon, tall trees obscured our view of anything else. They reached towards the sky like arms outstretched to the heavens. Mud and grass surrounded us on both sides of the path, and flowers were in full bloom and in every color.

"It's so beautiful," said Jessica quietly.

We continued deeper into the woods. Our trot slowed to a walk. Blaine and I were side by side, with Jess and Will behind us. Squirrels scampered from tree to tree, and it seemed to me that they were following us.

"Ancient scrolls say that at one point animals could communicate with people. Over the ages, however, they lost the ability to do so," Blaine said, reading the expression on my face as I watched the squirrels. "Some believe that they still can communicate, but choose not to."

"Wait, you're saying that animals could talk?" I asked with a puzzled look on my face.

"Indeed. That is what the scrolls say, but most believe it to be a myth. However, there are those who still believe that some animals can communicate."

"Yeah, maybe those squirrels are chatting it up about the new King Arthur," teased Will.

"Ha ha, very funny," I replied. "But Blaine, you can't be serious. Animals can't talk."

Blaine smiled, obviously amused. He trotted forward a bit and started to whistle a tune.

"He's joking right?" asked Will.

"I don't know, he seemed pretty serious," said Jessica, also staring at the squirrels scampering about.

Will studied Blaine. "I think being cooped up with all those scrolls messed him up," he decided.

"Maybe …" I said, not fully convinced.

But animals couldn't talk. I mean, if they could talk, surely people in the future would've found out. The squirrels had stopped following us, and were now just staring in our direction with their beady black eyes.

"Where are we going?" I called out to Blaine.

He stopped whistling. "A little further up the path, and then we'll stop."

I had the feeling he wasn't telling us something. We continued our jaunt through the woods with the sun shining through the trees. After several minutes the woods began to clear. A large lake expanded before us.

Blaine dismounted his horse. "Here we are," he announced.

It was a perfectly nice day, but for some reason, a layer of fog hovered over the water. It was eerie, and I instantly felt nervous.

"What is this place?" I asked, frowning as I, too, dismounted. Jess and Will did likewise.

"It's the Dozmary Pool," he replied, staring at the lake.

"Why is it so foggy here?" asked Jessica.

Blaine hesitated before answering, "It's a long story. I think we should give Arthur a minute alone."

I was confused, "Why?"

"You'll find out," he said aloud. He then whispered in my ear,

"Don't get too close to the water."

He took Jessica and Will, who reluctantly agreed to accompany him, away from the lake. I was left alone in front of the foggy water, confused and a little bit scared, though I didn't know why.

As I stood there, I heard music rise up from the lake. It was a woman's voice, and she was singing a song. For some reason I was reminded of my mother. I was drawn to the sound and I took several steps closer to the lake. I stopped, remembering what Blaine said. As I gazed at the middle of the lake, I was startled to see that a woman was walking towards me. Now when I say she was walking towards me, I mean literally walking on the water towards me. Her eyes were closed, arms down at her sides. Step-by-step she continued closer, until she was at the water's edge, merely several feet away from me. Her eyes opened, and the music stopped. A chill went down my spine as her black eyes stared at me. Her eyes didn't *appear* black. They were completely black. She had no pupil and no white around the color.

"Hello," she said. Her voice was warm and kind, and it comforted me in a weird way that made no sense given how all this was shaking out.

"Umm, hi," I said awkwardly.

"My name is Nimue, and I am the lady of the lake," she said with a thin smile.

"Nice to meet you, I'm ..."

"Francis. Yes, I know," she interrupted.

I was shocked. She knew my real name. "How do you know my real name?" I wondered.

"I know everything about you, Francis. Everything. You're very far from your home."

"I don't have a home."

Her eyes twitched. "You know what I mean, little one. I'm

talking about The Island. The future," she drawled.

I stared at her. How could she know these things?

"So we are in the past?" I confirmed.

"Yes. Thanks to you," she laughed.

I hesitated, something in her eyes, something in her laugh, something in her voice made my skin crawl.

"How do you know about me?"

Her smile was crooked as she said, "I know everything, and I see everything. The things that have happened, the things that are happening, and the things that are going to happen."

I stared at her, "How?"

"That is a very long story, Francis, perhaps if you come closer I'll tell you."

Don't get too close to the water, Blaine's warning flashed in my mind.

"No thanks, I'd rather stay on dry land," I stated.

She chuckled. "I'm not going to bite you."

I smiled, but didn't budge.

"Very well," she said focusing her black eyes on my face. "You're not as stupid as you look."

"And you're much creepier than you look."

She laughed. "I wouldn't be too sure about that."

I looked around, hoping to see Blaine and my friends coming back, but there was nothing.

"Don't be scared, I'm not going to hurt you. You're much too important for that. Besides, your friends won't return until I want them to. And you won't leave until I'm done with you."

That statement freaked me out of my mind. It was like something out of a horror movie and I was at the part where someone goes to check out a weird noise and they end up dead. I tried to turn and run, but I couldn't move. I looked down at my legs, and they were in the water. I had no idea how I got there, or how I didn't notice my feet soaking wet, but there I was.

"Don't bother trying to run," she smiled. "You're in my kingdom now, young one."

OK don't panic, I thought, trying to reassure myself. *She's just a crazy, black-eyed woman. She looks like she wants to eat my soul, she has magically trapped me in a lake, but it'll be OK. Blaine won't let me die.*

"What do you want from me?" I asked nervously.

Suddenly I was moving across the lake. Nimue must have controlled the water, because I couldn't move my feet.

"What's going on?" I panicked, and felt like I was going to have a full-on anxiety attack. (Hey, don't judge me! I was hovering above the water.)

"Relax, Francis. Just breathe."

My body moved deeper into the lake. I tried to steady my voice, "I'm being dragged down. This isn't cool, Lake Lady."

Her cold, dark smile didn't help me feel any better.

"Uh, now's the time to let me go, here. If you're really all-knowing you should know I can't breathe under water," I said, struggling against the force dragging me down.

I held my breath as my head went under the water. I struggled, but no matter how hard I tried, I couldn't move. I opened my eyes when I felt Nimue grab my hand. She pulled me down even deeper.

I was running out of air and I couldn't hold it in any longer. *I am going to die at the bottom of a lake*, I thought to myself.

I opened my mouth. I expected to breathe in a mouthful of water, but instead, I got air. I gasped, taking a deep breath of air.

Wasn't I underwater?

What's going on?

"It's always amusing to read people's expressions when they realize they can breathe here," Nimue said cheerfully.

"What?" I asked instinctively.

Did I just ask her a question underwater?

"I control this lake," she paused. "You can breathe if I want you to, and since a one-way conversation is quite pointless, I'd like you to breathe and talk underwater. I prefer to have my conversations down here where I am more comfortable."

A fish passed by. I stared at it, so shocked about breathing and talking underwater, I didn't catch what Nimue had said.

"Are you even paying attention?" she asked sharply.

I looked at her. It was bizarre. "Sorry," I said. "It's just weird. I don't usually breathe and have conversations underwater."

"Is it weirder than time-traveling back to the medieval ages?" she asked pointedly.

"Good point," I said.

"Don't worry child, I will explain everything when we reach the bottom."

"The b-b-bottom?" I stammered.

I looked to my left. An enormous dark figure swam towards me.

"OK, that's a shark," I panicked.

Nimue was amused, "It's a salt water lake, so there are all kinds of creatures living here. But don't worry, it won't attack you unless I ask it to."

"Is that supposed to make me feel better?"

She stared forward, silent as we continued to sink. There were so many fish swimming nearby through the dark, cloudy water. I could feel their presence, and it was unsettling. I lost sense of time and have no idea how long we were underwater, but eventually it started to clear up. I could see the bottom. Seaweed reached up like long fingers trying to grab me. I gulped.

"Welcome to my humble home," Nimue said, stretching an arm out in front of her.

A row of old, broken columns made of stone stretched before

us. Two large thrones stood at the top of a small staircase, and one small cement chair faced them at the bottom.

"Sit down," she smiled at me as she took her seat at one of the thrones. Although, she didn't really give me a choice, seeing as I was pushed into the chair by a sudden current of water.

"Sure …"

She leaned toward me, "Now that we're comfortable, let's talk."

"Yeah, like what do you want from me, and how can we have a conversation at the bottom of a freaking lake?"

"I told you, it's a long story, but let's just say I control everything here."

"That doesn't help me at all," I muttered to myself. A fish swam in little circles near my head. I shooed it away.

"I brought you here because I want to help you."

"Right, 'cause nothing says 'friendship' like dragging someone to the bottom of a lake."

"I said I wanted to help you, I didn't say I wanted to be your friend," she replied sharply.

"Good to know."

"You've gotten yourself into quite the difficult situation."

"Thanks, Tips," I shot back. I was looking for a fight.

She glared at me. The water around me suddenly got colder, and I could no longer breathe. "You should keep in mind who you're dealing with, young one," she glowered.

I shut my mouth at once, concerned for my well-being. The cold went away and I breathed fresh air into my lungs.

"That's better. As I was saying, I'm here to help you. Your life up to this point has been somewhat bleak and depressing. You've been given a gift that's turned your world upside-down, and the ride hasn't even begun yet. I've seen your future, and it's not a thing of beauty, nor is it pleasant. The trials that lie ahead will test you beyond your capabilities. I'm puzzled because the outcome still eludes me. You're quite the mystery. But one thing's for sure; you will be tested, you will be broken, but you will find the strength you need to succeed, although it may not all come from you."

She let her words sink into my mind. What was I supposed to say to that? How could she possibly know these things about me?

"Umm … thanks. That really helps."

"I do not expect you to understand the hardships ahead right now, but in time you will come to understand my warnings, Francis."

That confused me, "What warnings?"

"There are some things that cannot be changed, and you will go mad if you try, because destiny is unavoidable. Betrayal lies ahead from someone you trust, so tread carefully, little one. The corruption of The Island burns deeper than you could imagine. If you think you are safe in the past, think again …"

This was like something out of a bad fortune cookie. Destiny? Betrayal? By someone that I trust? These weren't answers. She was creating more questions.

"What's that supposed to mean?" I asked.

There was that crooked smile again. I blinked, and she disappeared! Her body turned into bubbles. For a second I felt that panic again, and I wondered what to do. Then, I felt the grip of the water loosen on me, so I started to swim back to the surface.

Remember what I have told you Francis. You can't save everyone. If you survive these trials, we will talk again soon. Oh, and beware of the mice.

The voice was no more than a whisper in my ear as I breached the surface of the lake.

Beware of the mice? Why couldn't these people just tell me something that made sense? First the prophecy, and now this?

This is getting ridiculous, I thought to myself.

I had surfaced in the middle of the lake, so I swam back to

where I had been dragged in. I reached the water's edge and stood on the grass with my clothes dripping wet. I took a few steps in the direction the others had went. My boots made a squishing noise with each step. Great.

How long was I under for? I wondered.

Voices broke through my thoughts. To my left, Blaine, Jessica, and Will were walking out of the trees and towards me. As they got closer, they noticed I was soaking wet.

"What happened to you?" asked Jessica, staring at my clothes.

I narrowed my eyes at Blaine. "Oh nothing, really. I just had a lovely conversation at the bottom of the lake with some psychic lady, talking about my future."

Will grinned at me, "You know pal, I was tempted to try those mushrooms too, but now I'm glad I didn't. I could've ended up going for a swim like you."

I glared. "It's not like I went for a swim with my clothes on for fun. I was dragged in."

"Dragged in?" Jessica asked.

"Yeah. Some crazy lady dragged me in there and started talking to me about my future. Blaine, what kind of demonic crazy-lady was that?" I couldn't keep the frustration from my voice. I suspected he knew what was going to happen.

He didn't seem concerned. "You didn't stay away from the water like I warned you."

I looked down at my drenched clothes. "Gee, you think?" I barked.

"So, you met with Nimue," he said, as a statement, moreso than a question.

"You know her?" I asked, incredulously. Now I was mad. It was kind of hard not to be. I was soaked and had nearly drowned. *And Blaine knew her?*

Blaine responded, "It's a long story. She would never have hurt you though, you're too important."

"So I've been told," I hadn't been this annoyed in a while.

Jessica and Will were trying to follow the conversation.

"What's going on? Who's Nimue?" Will asked.

Blaine sighed, "Nimue is the lady of the lake. She is a spirit bound to the water itself. She cannot leave or control anything outside the lake. She is very powerful, and her voice has a hypnotic effect on humans."

I took a deep breath to curb my anger. "That explains how I ended up in the water in the first place," I observed.

"Nimue doesn't really care about the world, unless it affects her lake. She would only choose to show herself to you if you had a great destiny," Blaine continued.

I stared at the lake. The fog was still bound to the top of the water.

"She said some interesting things," I commented.

Blaine urged me to tell them more. I started at the beginning and explained how I was dragged to her underwater fortress.

"She said I can't change what will happen, and if I try I will go crazy," I paused, wondering if I should tell them the part about the betrayal. I decided not to. I also didn't say anything about the fact that she knew about The Island or my real name. "And she told me to beware of the mice."

Will didn't take it seriously at all. "So let me get this straight. You were pulled down to the bottom of that lake, had a nice chat with a spirit, and she told you beware of the mice?" he chortled.

He sat on a nearby log to keep himself from falling over with laughter. Even Jessica giggled a little bit. Blaine, however, did not.

"Heed her warnings, Arthur," Blaine said sternly. "She told you those things for a reason, no matter how strange they may seem now, it will become clearer later on."

I nodded, angry about all the riddles and destiny garbage. It was like some Yoda crap from *Star Wars*. Yes, I've seen *Star Wars*, I was raised like a normal kid until I was nearly nine, remember?

"So you think that we should be scared of these mice? They could be out to get us," joked Will.

"Any warnings Nimue gave Arthur should be taken seriously!" Blaine came as close to yelling as we'd heard yet, and he gave Will a look that silenced his jesting immediately.

"What do we do now?" asked Jessica. "Got any more surprises for us?"

Blaine shook his head. "Not for today, no."

I began walking toward the horses. "Good, 'cause I could use a break from all of this."

"Yeah," Will followed quickly, "and some food."

"Well, there is going to be a feast later this evening to celebrate our new king. As for rest, you're going to need it for tomorrow," Blaine declared.

I frowned. "Why's that?"

"Tomorrow, you three start your training."

"Wonderful, I'll bet Lancelot is just ecstatic to be training you, buddy," chuckled Will, patting my shoulder.

"Aw, crap. Couldn't I just train with Galahad? I mean, what's Lancelot's deal anyway? All I did was beat him."

Blaine interjected, "And that's exactly why he despises you, Arthur."

"What do you mean?" I asked.

"Lancelot is a proud warrior. He's trained his entire life, and has never lost a fight or battle … until you showed up. You threaten his skills. Don't worry, he'll get over it eventually," Blaine explained.

"Oh, that's just great. I've officially ticked off Mr. Muscles," I said, as we reached the horses and untied them from the log where Blaine had hooked their reins.

"Hey, look on the bright side," said Jessica. "At least Galahad will be there to keep him under control."

I mounted my horse, as did the others. Blaine took the lead. "What do you say we try speeding things up?"

I smiled. "Might as well."

Blaine kicked the sides of his horse, which reacted instantly by breaking into a run. I did the same and Animi started to move faster and faster. Before I knew it, I was catching up to Blaine. I quickly glanced behind me to see Jessica following and Will right on her tail. I looked forward and smiled.

I had to admit, I was having fun. For the first time in many years I was enjoying myself. I wasn't worried about The Island or my destiny, I was just … free. It felt good. That feeling held as we traversed the trail. As we breached the forest and one again caught sight of Camelot, I was sucked back into reality. I was in medieval times. That is not normal.

That shouldn't even be possible.

And yet, here we are. I shrugged the thoughts away as we approached the front gates. The horses slowed and shouts echoed from within, as the drawbridge lowered. We crossed the moat.

"We'll drop the horses off at the stables then head back to the castle and prepare for the feast," Blaine said as he directed us towards the stables.

"Yes!" agreed Will, eager to get food.

As we made our way to the stables, I noticed more people were out in the streets. They bowed their heads in respect as we passed. I felt powerful, and yet, fearful at the same time. These people had little or no free will. Their future was guided by the actions of one man, in this case, me. How can that much power be entrusted to one man? We exited the maze of houses and arrived back at the stables. Attendants took the horses. Blaine instructed them to give the horses a good rub down, watering, and feeding.

"What do you say we head back to the castle?" asked Blaine.

Our stomachs growled in agreement. Before long we were at the main entrance to the hall.

"On your left is the banquet room. That is where all our feasts are held, and where the celebrations will take place tonight," Blaine announced, gesturing to a great big door.

I couldn't see much of the room, but I could see servants hustling back and forth. We continued down the maze of hallways until we reached our rooms.

"The feast will not begin for a while. You may spend the time however you choose," Blaine said as we reached our rooms.

"Great," I said. I had been hoping that I could explore the castle.

"Well, what do you want to do?" asked Jessica as we watched Blaine walk away.

Will shrugged, "I don't know about you guys, but I'm going to catch up on some much-needed sleep."

That didn't surprise me. "Good for you," I said to Will. "I actually wouldn't mind checking out the rest of the castle."

"Sounds like fun," Jessica replied.

"I know, eh?" Will said, smirking.

She frowned at him, "I was talking about exploring the castle, stupid."

He chuckled as he walked away. "Fine, be that way. Wake me up when the food's ready."

I looked at Jessica, "So where should we start?"

"Up to you. You're the king after all," she shrugged.

"Really? You're going to play that card?"

She smiled nonchalantly. I looked up then down the corridor.

"Left it is," I said.

Jess followed without hesitation. We walked silently down the empty corridor, passing several tapestries, portraits and archways. We wandered aimlessly for a long time, climbing staircases and opening doors. Eventually we ended up in the old king's room. The bizarre paintings still hung on the wall. I found it curious that the fire still crackled in the hearth.

"You know, if I were you, I'd take down these paintings," Jessica said, staring at a particularly ugly one.

I came alongside of her. "Aw, you mean you don't like Frankenstein over here, watching your every move?"

She wrinkled her nose. "It's creepy and weird."

She sat down by the fire, holding her hands up to absorb the warmth. I pulled a chair close to the fire and sat down. We stayed that way for some time.

"How're we going to get back, Francis?" she asked finally, still staring into the flickering flames.

I pointed at the door, "It's out there and to the left."

She smiled, but said quietly, "You know what I mean."

I knew what she meant. I felt helpless, though. I responded softly, "I honestly don't know. We only got here by fluke, and getting back, let alone saving those kids at The Island, is going to be next to impossible. I don't even know if we're going to make it through training tomorrow."

She stared into the flames. "What if we can't save them?"

You can't save everyone ... Nimue's words fluttered softly into my head.

"We will," I determined.

The door flung open and Blaine burst into the room. "There you are!" he seemed relieved. "I've been searching the entire castle for you. The feast is about to begin."

He thrust a change of clothes at each of us. I started to protest, but he shook his head and said, "Don't argue. As the king and guest of honor, you do have to follow some tradition. You need to look the part tonight. It will gain you respect."

They stepped into the hall while I quickly changed, and then

Jessica did the same. We left our clothes in the room and Blaine assured us they would be cleaned and returned to our own rooms by morning.

We walked down the spiral stairs and soon found ourselves in the main hallway.

"The feast is through those doors," Blaine gestured to the massive doors in front of us.

After years of eating the slop served on The Island (which I wouldn't even classify as food), a medieval feast was sounding pretty good, but I didn't really know what to expect.

Blaine led us through the tremendous doorway, and almost immediately I was overtaken with delicious smells. I could not keep the smile from my face. There were rows and rows of tables, where the lower class people had to eat, but at the very end of the room was a giant table, facing the rest. Will was already there, ready for the feast to begin.

"Just to warn you, Arthur, the people will expect you to say something before the meal," Blaine advised quietly.

I rolled my eyes. "Great."

As we approached our seats, the room became deathly quiet. I stood in front of my chair and faced the crowd. Every eye was directed my way.

Fantastic. What did these people expect me to say?

"Umm, as you all know by now, I'm the new king. My name is Arthur," I paused, searching my brain for something intelligent to say. "Thank you for your warm welcome and this feast."

I sat down. The rest of the people sat in unison after I had done so. Servants and entertainers appeared from who-knows-where with food and well … entertainment. A huge roasted chicken was presented on my left, while a young boy poured some type of red liquid into my cup. I wasted no time and dug into the food (there were no forks or knives, by the way). Between gulps of food and licking my fingers I glanced around the room. Will was stuffing his face, while Jessica sipped her cup, watching the fire jugglers.

One more time for emphasis:

Fire jugglers!

They literally lit sticks of wood on fire and juggled them. It was intense! I looked around. There were musicians, dancers, and even fire jugglers. Did I already mention those guys?

"You seem to be enjoying yourself, my lord," a voice from behind me said.

I turned to see Galahad with a cup in his right hand and a drumstick in the other. "Hey. Yeah, this is great," I said.

Galahad nodded. "Indeed it is. They are currently the best performers in all the land."

I gazed at them in amazement. "Wow. Have you seen the fire jugglers?"

"Yes, quite talented, they are."

"I'll say."

"Well, I'd best let you get back to the food. I will see you tomorrow for training," he bowed and disappeared into the crowd.

I stared at my food. Suddenly I had lost my appetite. I had forgotten about training tomorrow, and had forgotten about the quest. Dang this good food and fire jugglers for distracting me.

"What do you think these are?" Will interrupted my thoughts, holding what looked like meatballs.

I stated the obvious, "Meatballs?"

He popped a couple into his mouth, and after a few bites, he smiled, "These actually aren't that bad."

A servant boy with a tray full of the meatball things walked up to Will. "More pig testicles, sir?" he said, holding them out.

"Pig what?" Will shouted, spitting what remained in his mouth onto his plate.

"Pig testicles. Very meaty and chewy eh?"

"Ughh! Get them away from me!"

The boy frowned and wandered to another table.

I looked to see if Jessica had caught any of this ordeal. She had. She was laughing uncontrollably.

"So you like those pig testicles?" she gasped.

I burst out laughing, as Will tried to eat and drink away the taste from his mouth.

"Shut up! Fra—Arthur said they were meatballs!" he said between mouthfuls of chicken.

"Hey, hey, hey. I said they looked like meatballs. I never said they were," I defended, amused at the disgusted look on Will's face. "And on that note, I think I'm done eating. I'm gonna head back to our room. See you guys later."

"Bye," Jessica said, still smiling at Will.

"Good riddance," put in Will, who was now inspecting all of his food.

I ducked out of the hall through a doorway I hadn't seen earlier. I wandered around the castle a bit before heading to my room. As I stepped inside, the warmth of the fire welcomed me back. I took my boots off and sat on a chair beside the window. The moon and stars were hidden behind clouds, which disappointed me. It had been a long time since I'd seen the night sky without running for my life underneath it.

I took off the fancy clothes and crawled into my bed. I hadn't realized how tired I was until I was in it. My eyes drooped shut, and an all-too familiar darkness engulfed me.

Snippets of scenery from the car crash haunted my dreams. Like a strobe light, they flashed in my mind. The faces of my family, the blood, the hospital.

It was a long night.

7 TRAINING DAY

I awoke before Will. I didn't even hear him come in, despite my restless sleep. I sat up and took a deep breath before sauntering over to my clothes, which were clean and neatly stacked on a chair. I pulled the light padding over my head and slid it onto my shoulders. Will was snoring, and I knew if I woke him up he'd be ticked. I opened the door quietly and slipped out of the room. I walked down the hallway and through the castle until I reached the courtyard. The sun was just rising.

I took the same path we'd gone the day before and I reached the gates. I climbed the steps that led to the walkway on the walls. A guard stood several feet away from me, leaning against the stone wall, focusing on the vast forest in front of the castle.

"Anything interesting out there?" I asked.

The guard jumped. "What? Erm, sorry, my lord. I didn't realize it was you. No, nothing's out there."

I leaned against the wall near him, staring just as he had been. The view was incredible. The pink sunrise was breathtaking and a slight fog rolled over top of the forest.

"So it's true? You're the one who pulled Excalibur from the stone?" the guard said, eyeing my sheath.

I glanced down at the sword, then back to the view. "Yup," I said casually.

"If you don't mind me asking, how'd you do it?"

I shrugged, "I don't know. It just happened."

He said wistfully, “I tried pulling it once. It didn’t budge.”

We stood in silence for a while until the guard worked up the courage to speak again, “You don’t seem like other kings.”

I laughed. “Trust me, I’m nothing like anyone here.”

“I’m not quite sure what you mean, my lord.”

“I just meant … people here seem to not care about the people around them. I saw an old man yesterday who was in chains just for trying to feed his family. That’s just wrong to me.”

The guard smiled. “You’re a good person, with a strong heart. Good qualities for a king. I think I like you as my king, Arthur.”

I chuckled. “Well thanks, but you might be the only one who thinks that. Others seem to disapprove. Myself included.”

The guard faced me, and stared into my eyes as he spoke, “You might not know why you were chosen as king, but what I’ve seen from you so far, you’re exactly what Camelot needs. You are a strong young man, who has a kind heart, and does not think only of himself. I’m sure you’ll be a great king. But for now I must return to my duties. It was nice to talk to you in person, my lord. The other king never conversed with the guards.”

I nodded goodbye, and the guard left without another word.

At least there’s someone who thinks I can do this, I thought.

The sun had risen and shone brightly down on the castle.

I decided to skip breakfast (I know, I know. It’s the most important meal of the day, but that’s the least of my worries). I headed straight down to the arena where our training was going to take place. I walked towards the empty ring and stepped inside. I pictured the fights, the crowd cheering, and the clash of swords.

“Decided to get a head start, have we?” came a familiar voice. It was Galahad, dressed in full armor, carrying several bags of equipment.

“I figured it wouldn’t hurt,” I answered.

“No, I suppose not.”

I hurried over to help him with the bags.

"Thanks, those things weigh as much as a horse," he said, dropping the bags on the ground.

"Yeah, what's in these things?" I opened one of the bags.

"Oh, the usual. Swords, shields, maces, bows, arrows, knives, and other pointy objects."

"Cool."

"Cool?"

"Yeah, cool. You know … never mind. It's great."

"I see," Galahad said, puzzled.

"Where do we start?" I asked, rummaging through the stuff.

"Well, if you're not going to wait for your friends, we can begin with a little warm-up," he said with intrigue.

"Yeah, let's get started. Merlin takes forever to wake up."

"Very well. We'll start with swords. In battle, it is rarely a one-on-one fight, but it does happen, and since there are only two of us, we shall begin with that."

"Alright," I said, pulling Excalibur from its sheath.

"Normally, we'd use blunted swords, but since Excalibur seems to have bonded with you, we shall train with the real deal."

I was not quite sure what he meant. We faced each other on opposite sides of the arena.

"The way duels are performed in Camelot is pretty basic. The first person to three strikes wins. A strike is not a lethal wound to the opponent; it is merely a bang or tap on their body. Like so …" He banged his sword against his armor so that it clanged but did not hurt him.

"Seems easy enough," I said taking a deep breath.

I gripped Excalibur with both hands, and began circling with Galahad. He faked a lunge at me, and I reacted with a jump backwards. He then swung at my side, and once again, before I realized what was happening, Excalibur had reacted for me and blocked the attack. Galahad backed away, which allowed me to start my own attack.

I swung high then low, and then to the side with quick, sharp thrusts. Galahad grunted in an attempt to block them, but I was too quick. At last, a swing connected with his side and clanged against his armor.

"That's one for me," I smiled, letting him regain his footing.

His hair was damp with sweat. "So it is," he said with a huff.

Galahad stepped it up a notch, because we battled for a long time before the second hit came. He had backed me into the edge of the arena and had me cornered. He swung his sword rapidly at my left side. I pulled mine up to block it just in time, rolled to my right and quickly swung, hitting his left shoulder.

"Quite the moves you have," he observed, smiling at me.

I took the moment to catch my breath, wishing I had some water or something. "Thanks, you too."

I hadn't realized earlier, but Jessica, Will, and Lancelot were watching our battle. Galahad took the opportunity of my distraction and quickly unleashed several jabs at me. My attention was flung back into the fight as I blocked each shot, moving with incredible speed. I swung a hard blow at him, which he blocked. Our swords clashed together and it became a battle of strength as we pushed our blades against each other, waiting for the other to yield. I pushed him backwards and then retreated, regaining my balance and footing.

We battled. Clang after clang of our swords beating against each other echoed in the arena. Galahad went for a high strike, which I blocked, then with a quick twist of my wrist, I turned and disarmed him. His sword clattered to the ground.

"Well done, Arthur," congratulated Galahad. "That was quite the battle."

I smiled, happy with my victory. But it didn't last long.

"Please, it was obvious Galahad was going easy on you. I, on the other hand, will not," snorted Lancelot.

"He seems rather chipper this morning," I snickered to Galahad.

Galahad tried hard not to show his amusement. "Lancelot, you've arrived," he declared. "Good. Now that we are all here, a proper set of training can begin."

"So how is this going to work?" asked Jessica.

Lancelot eagerly piped up, "Galahad and I will take turns teaching you separate skills and will test you in each."

"Great. I love tests," groaned Will.

"What do we start with?" I asked, ignoring Will.

Galahad picked up one of the bags, "I'll train with Guinevere and Merlin—"

"And I'll train you," interrupted Lancelot's cold voice.

Jessica and Will gave me the 'sorry we got the good knight and you got the jerk' look. I gave them a half-hearted smile in return.

"So what are we doing first?" I asked Lancelot. I watched sadly as Will, Jessica, and Galahad went to another part of the arena.

"Swords."

"Great," I said sarcastically. "Can I have a little rest first?"

"No."

"Awesome."

Lancelot reached into his own bag and pulled out his sword. He was dressed in the same type of armor that Galahad wore.

"First rule of battle: always be aware of your surroundings. You will often have to take on several opponents at once. You must be aware of their position at all times, as well as your own. The simplest mistake, like tripping on a rock, can get you killed."

"Good to know."

Anger flickered in his eyes, "With all due respect, my lord, I think you beat me by sheer dumb luck. I do not think you can fulfill this prophecy, and I do not want to be here right now."

Gee, who woke up on the wrong side of the bed this morning? I thought to myself.

But what I replied was, "For starters, I don't know how I beat you. Maybe it was luck. I honestly don't know how I'm going to fulfill this prophecy, but what I do know is that we're going to need to work together in order for this to work."

That seemed to wake him up.

He studied me for a few seconds. "Fine," he conceded.

We stood our ground, eyes locked in silence. It was a 'macho man' moment, where no one wanted to be the first to move. Eventually, he turned and walked into the arena.

"The second rule of battle is: don't hesitate. A split second could cost you your life. If you feel an impulse, use it."

I took that information in. "Makes sense."

"Of course it makes sense," he snapped. "Now, let's try this again. First point wins."

He positioned himself in a battle stance and made it known he was not joking around. I did the same. I gotta admit, I was nervous, but can you blame me? The one thing I did know about fighting was never make the first move (Thank you, *Karate Kid*). I waited for Lancelot to make the first move, which came like a flash of light.

His sword was slicing towards me with tremendous speed. I ducked, as my battle instinct kicked in again. As I came back up, I jabbed at his side, but he had already moved.

"Always keep moving," he said circling me. "It prevents you from getting caught flat-footed."

Before the last words had left his mouth, he lunged at me with swing after swing. I managed to block each attack, but I tripped as I was moving back. Lancelot took the opportunity and stabbed his sword at me. Before it hit, I rolled out of the way, and his sword pierced the dirt.

I got back on my feet, and attacked while he was still crouched on the ground. Somehow he saw it coming and pulled his sword out of the ground in time to block my attack. I retreated a few steps to catch my breath.

Make him angry.

The sudden voice inside my head distracted me, and before I knew what was happening, Lancelot was on his feet.

OK, voice. Let's see if you're any good, I thought.

I kept blocking his attacks, and eventually made it look like I wasn't even trying.

"C'mon. Is that all you got? I thought you were supposed to be good," I provoked.

He shouted in anger and charged at me. At the last moment, I crouched and let his momentum hit me. My back hit the ground, but my legs found Lancelot's stomach and I flung him over top of me.

I got up quickly. His sword was a few yards away from him, and he was on his back. I pointed Excalibur inches from his chest.

"Looks like it wasn't just luck," I said, putting Excalibur back in its sheath.

Lancelot's face turned beet-red. "I beg to differ," he growled. "Let's go again shall we? And this time, we'll use different swords."

"What do you mean?"

"I mean you'll use a different sword. Then we'll see."

From the pile of equipment, he grabbed a sword that was about the same size as Excalibur.

Lancelot tossed it at me. "Try this," he ordered.

I slid Excalibur into its sheath and set it to the side of the arena. "Bring it," I challenged.

The new sword felt heavier in my hand, but I didn't let it show. I did everything the same way I had done in the previous fight … the only problem was I got my butt whooped.

Lancelot came at me fast. His first attack was a jab at my side, which was fairly easy to block, followed by several more of the same shots. Before I knew what had happened, I was backed into another corner. This time I wasn't as lucky. When I tried to dodge Lancelot's attack, I was too slow and I felt the hard blow of steel against my side. I collapsed to the ground; the hit was hard, but thankfully my armor softened the blow.

"That's what I thought. You're nothing without Excalibur," he spat. "That was the only reason you beat me, and the only reason you're still alive."

That was it. I'd had it with this guy.

"What's your problem?" I shouted as I got to my feet. "Ever since I got here you've had it out for me."

He came at me, "*My* problem? I'll tell you what my problem is, Arthur. My problem is that the prophecy I've lived my life by has turned out to be a boy who can't hold his ground in a fight. A weak boy that I don't think can rule a kingdom."

"Look pal, I never wanted to be king. The only reason I pulled that sword in the first place was to protect my friends. Something I doubt you'd know anything about," I shot back at him. "I may not know anything about being a king, but I do know a thing or two about friends and how to treat people."

"What's all the commotion about?" shouted Jessica, running over with Will and Galahad.

Lancelot's face was blank, as he absorbed what I had just said. I grabbed Excalibur off the ground and walked over to my friends.

"Nothing, let's get on with training. I think it's time for us to switch teachers," I said, storming off to where they had been practicing.

Jessica was about to follow but Galahad grabbed her shoulder, "I'll deal with this if you don't mind. Lancelot, why don't you teach them archery, and play nice this time?"

I had almost reached the other bag of weapons when Galahad caught up to me.

"Arthur! Do you mind telling me what that was all about?"

I stopped and looked him in his eyes, "That guy's been after me ever since I showed up. He just took me down when I didn't have Excalibur, and because of that, he says I'm weak and not able to be king? It's crap."

Galahad eased my tension with a chuckle and wave of his hand, "Don't beat yourself up, Arthur. Lancelot is jealous. And, he was probably expecting an older man to pull Excalibur out of the stone. I don't know why Excalibur chose you, Arthur, but there must be a reason for it. You're a good kid; brave with a kind heart. Maybe that's what Camelot needs right now."

I sat on the wooden ledge surrounding the arena. "I don't know, Galahad," I sighed. "Maybe he's right. I have no idea how to be a king, let alone how to use a sword."

"Well then, let's change that. Besides, I'm sure you'll make a great king. Not everyone would accept the role and go on that quest."

I gave in, "I guess you're right. Let's get on with it."

Galahad clapped me on the back. "Now that's more like it," he said cheerfully. "Seeing as you clearly excel using Excalibur, why don't we try using different weapons? You never know when it might come in handy."

"Thanks, Galahad."

The day flew by after that. Galahad taught me how to use a sword a lot better than Lancelot did, and I was actually getting pretty good. We sparred again and again until I actually managed to beat him. If you haven't noticed, I'm a quick learner, compliments of The Island. After swords, we moved to archery. Galahad led me away from the arena where a target was set up. He showed me how to hold the bow, how to breathe while I shoot, and how to pull an arrow out of the quiver, which is way harder than it looks on *Robin Hood*. Shooting at the target calmed me down, seeing as I pictured Lancelot's head as the target.

Next, we moved to close-quarter combat. Galahad pulled some cool knife things from his bag. They looked like brass knuckles; only these had a curved blade attached to the knuckled side. If I punched someone with these on, they'd have a massive cut, at least a couple of inches deep.

"These are called fist knives," he said, putting his fingers in the grips. "They're effective during up close and personal fights, and are really just an extension of your fist."

"These are intense," I said in awe. They were sweet.

Galahad laughed. "Yes they are quite the fun little knives. Just be sure to know when to use them."

"What do you mean?"

"I mean, certain weapons should be used at certain times. These knives are a great weapon, but only if there isn't a massive army attacking you. They're small, quick, and fast … but they will wear you down quickly."

I punched the air a few times with them on. They were heavy. "I see what you mean," I understood.

He showed me how to use them, and the correct way to (and I quote) "cause the most damage."

He showed me weapons I'd never seen and tactics to help me in battle. We fought using each weapon and I almost beat him in every single one. He managed to beat me with the fist knives, but only because I have short arms that couldn't reach him. We kept going until my arms were numb.

I sat down to rest and catch my breath. We'd been going at it all day. My arms felt like lead, and my entire body ached.

"Are you ready for a break, my lord?" Galahad asked.

"Good idea," I said, massaging my shoulders.

I found a shady spot beneath a tree and sat down while Galahad went and got my friends. I let out a deep breath. This was getting to be too much for me to handle. All I wanted to do was save a few kids from The Island, and now I had become king of a nation that I had to save from war.

Jessica and Will walked towards me, and, by the looks of it, needed the rest too. Galahad was with them.

"I decided it was best to send Lancelot back to the castle," he said as he approached.

"Thanks," I appreciated his wisdom.

"It's no trouble. But if you don't mind I could use a rest as well," he bowed and waited for my approval.

"Galahad, you don't have to do that."

"Do what?"

"That thing … the waiting for my command thing. If you're tired, just say so and you can leave."

"You're too kind, Arthur," he bowed again and left us.

"How did you guys do?" I asked Jessica and Will.

Will groaned as he collapsed on the soft grass, "That was worse than when we had to run at The Island. Can we go eat now?"

Jessica laughed. "Oh c'mon, it wasn't that bad."

"That's because he made me do all the work while he let you take it easy," Will complained.

"Well it's not my fault he likes me better than you," taunted Jessica. "How about you, Francis?"

"It was rough at the start. There's something about Lancelot that I just can't get past. But after Galahad took over, it went pretty well. I'm almost as good with a regular sword now as I am with Excalibur," I said with a hint of pride in my voice.

"Nice!" congratulated Jessica. "I kind of suck at all the weapons, except for the bow and arrows."

"Kind of?" Will remarked from his supine position on the grass.

"Shut up. It's hard for me OK? Everything weighs like a hundred pounds," she protested.

I smirked. "What about you Will?"

"I need food," he moaned.

Jessica perked up, "He's a natural at all this fighting stuff. He did pretty good against Lancelot, for the most part."

"That's cool," I said, but Will made no sign that he heard me. "This day has flown by. It's starting to get dark."

"Mhmm," Jessica said thoughtfully. "So tomorrow we leave on that quest?"

"I think so," I said. "We should get back to the castle, get some food, then get some sleep. I think we're gonna need it."

Will sat up, "Food?"

"Food," I affirmed.

"Well what are we waiting for?" he asked, getting up.

I shook my head and gave Jessica a hand up. We walked through the town, and up to the castle. Blaine was waiting for us.

"Good. You're here, I was just about to come and get you."

"What's up?" I asked.

"Just a few last minute things to discuss before we leave tomorrow," he said calmly.

"Can we talk over dinner?" asked Will.

Blaine chuckled. "Of course."

Instead of going where we had the feast, Blaine led us up the stairs to the room where we'd first met the knights and nobles. He opened the door and motioned for us to enter. A fantastic round table stood where the long table had been. It was made of black and gray marble and was embedded throughout with fascinating symbols and markings, which made it look even more cool.

There were new chairs, too. They weren't your typical kitchen chairs. These were gigantic! They were made of dark wood and had similar symbols carved into them as were found throughout the table.

"Do you like it?" Blaine asked, as I took a closer look.

I stared at the table with awe. "It's incredible."

"Take a seat."

I would have never thought a chair made from wood could be so comfy.

"I thought we were going to have food," said Will, obviously disappointed.

Blaine put two fingers in his mouth and whistled. Servants promptly entered, carrying trays of food. They placed them in front of us on the table. It looked like some type of beef stew with chicken on the side. We dug in fiercely, and soon we were licking the plates and bowls clean.

"Now, what did you want to talk about?" I asked Blaine.

Blaine stood from his chair, walked over to me, and placed a giant map where my food had just been. "I'd just like to go over the journey," he spoke, sounding all-business.

"Please do," I agreed.

"Alright, we're here," he said pointing to the X marked Camelot (duh), and then pointed to a thick line that led to some jagged upside-down Vs. "We need to travel along this path until we reach the mountains of Elsador. The entrance will be halfway up a mountain, deep within Elsador, so it will be cold and very dangerous to climb in the snow. As for the dragon, I have no idea what to expect."

"Well, that's just awesome," said Will, sarcastically. "We hike up a snowy mountain only to get eaten by a mysterious dragon."

Blaine nodded, not catching Will's tone, "It's not ideal, but we should be relatively safe from the dragon if it's snowing. From there we'll find the dwarves and convince them to come to our aid."

"And how exactly do we do that?" asked Jessica.

"An excellent point, Guinevere, but I'm afraid I don't have an answer. We'll just have to find out when we get there."

"So far this doesn't sound promising," I stated the obvious.

"I know, but we don't have much of a choice."

I frowned, unsure of the quest I had accepted. "OK, where do we go from there?"

He pointed to another thick line that curved around many places until it reached a place labeled Brentwood Forest. "We travel east to Brentwood Forest."

"Isn't that where you said the witch lives?" asked Jessica.

Blaine hesitated before answering, "Yes. The forest is cursed. Anyone who's entered it has never come back, but stories of a witch have surfaced to provide an explanation."

"If no one survives, where do the stories come from?" Will questioned.

"Good point," Blaine considered. "Whatever the case, something dark resides in that forest that we will have to face before reaching the elves."

"Elves?" asked Jessica.

Blaine nodded again, "Elves. They're a proud race that is very wise and old. Elves are immortal—"

"Immortal? Like, they can't die?" Will guessed.

"They do not age, but they can die in a battle just like a man. They are a peaceful race, so it may be difficult to persuade them to help us."

"I'm most concerned about the dragon," I contributed.

"So to sum this quest up, we have to climb a mountain guarded by a dragon, to convince a bunch of short, dirty men to help us in a battle. Then, we have to navigate through a forest, apparently haunted by a witch, or something, to find a peaceful, immortal group of people, and convince them to also come and fight with us. That sound about right?" asked Jessica. She sounded much calmer than I felt.

Blaine paused, as if for the first time sensing our cold feet. "I know this seems like a death wish, but it's Camelot's only chance. Our messengers have already reached Carleton, Montego, and

Guilderbane, and they are sending troops to our aid, but those men will not be enough to keep even half of the enemies at bay. Our spies in other regions have already reported a massive army preparing for battle. Weapons, troops, catapults, everything needed for a complete siege. We won't stand a chance if we don't get the help of the dwarves and elves. We're Camelot's only hope of victory."

"Gee, when you put it that way, it's a piece of cake," said Will.

I rolled my eyes, "Yeah, no pressure or anything."

Blaine sighed.

Jessica stepped up, "It's not so bad …"

We looked at her skeptically. A mountain? OK, not so bad. A haunted forest? Alright. But a freaking dragon? What in this forsaken world am I supposed to do with that? It's not like I can fight a dragon with a sword (even if it is a magical sword). But then I took a breath and remembered, *it doesn't really matter anyway; dragons are not real. Period. Regardless of what Blaine says.*

"OK, so even if we convince everybody to join us, how are we supposed to fight a dragon and a witch slash haunted forest?" I asked.

Blaine pointed a finger at me and repeated, "Again I say, I have absolutely no idea."

"Outstanding," I replied.

"We'll just have to cross that bridge when we come to it, Arthur."

"So now there's a bridge, too?" groaned Will.

"No stupid, it's a saying. It means we'll figure it out when we get there," Jessica said.

"It's a saying," Will mimicked.

I sighed, "So are there anymore training sessions or practice before we go? This whole thing has come up pretty quick."

"Sadly, there isn't. You'll just have to learn by trial, I guess. I'm sorry that there wasn't more time for you to practice, but we have no time to waste. By the time we reach the dwarves and elves, our enemies will be at our gates. There is no time to spare for extra practice," explained Blaine.

I nodded. "It's a good thing we're quick learners."

"Indeed," Blaine continued. "This is going to be a very dangerous journey; don't take it lightly. Galahad has agreed to join us, and will meet us in the morning at the stables. I've had some extra clothes, and some warmer things, made for you. You'll find them packed in your room. The majority of our supplies are already packed. Be sure to get a good rest tonight, because it will be the last in safety for a while."

"Sounds like a plan," Jessica said.

Will and I agreed. We were happy to be done with this planning stuff.

Blaine stood up. "Glad to hear it. I'll send someone to wake you in the morning."

We said our goodnights and he left. The door slid shut and we were left alone.

"I guess this is it," I said.

"You got that right," Will said as he sat up. "Ain't no way we're gonna survive this thing."

Jessica punched him in the shoulder. "That's no way to talk, Will. I mean, sure, there's a haunted forest … and a dragon—which I don't think is possible by the way—but we can do it. And if not, we'll get Francis to teleport us back to the future."

"Once again I'd like to point out that I have no idea how I did it in the first place," I interjected.

Will hopped onto the table and started to pace around it, "In my opinion, we should just leave now."

"Will we can't leave them, seeing as I caused this whole thing ... and get off the table!" I said as he walked in front of my seat.

He frowned as he hopped down off the table, "Not my fault the table's cool."

"Let's just play this whole thing by ear, and if things start going bad, I'll do my best to get us back to modern time," I reasoned.

"Fine," agreed Will. "But only because I want to see how short the dwarves are."

"You're such an idiot," Jessica said.

Will shot her a look.

"OK guys, enough talking. Let's get some rest. I've got a feeling we're going to need it," I stepped in.

"Good idea. I was getting bored anyway," said Jessica with a huff.

She left without saying anything else, leaving Will and I alone in the room.

"I figured something out about you," he said, once again climbing onto the table and standing over me.

"Oh? And what's that?"

"You have a hero complex. You have to help everyone don't you? Like those kids back at The Island, and now these people. Why? It doesn't matter what happens to them; the only thing that matters is that we're free."

I paused, taking in the things he said. "You really don't care about anyone other than yourself, do you?" I accused.

He shrugged, "Well, you and Jessica matter to me, but these people, and those kids … I have no reason to care for them. It's not like I know any of them or anything."

"They're still people, Will. And if there's something I can do to help them, I'll do it."

"Even if it means facing a dragon, a witch, and a massive army, which will most likely result in death?"

"Yep. It's my fault these people are faced with a war, so it's my job to help them. And as for those kids? They're just like us, and I can't sit by knowing what they're going through. Besides, I made a promise."

"Pfft," scoffed Will, jumping off the table. He came alongside me and placed his hand on my shoulder. "Look, I've always been there with you buddy, but we should be enjoying our freedom, not running around fighting dragons. And if I die because of your need to keep your promises …"

He let the words hang in the air as he left the room. I let my head collapse into my hands. Why did Will have to be so selfish? Don't get me wrong, he's a great guy, but he just doesn't care about anything but himself. What was I supposed to do? Abandon these people and those kids, leaving them to die?

I don't think so.

My father gave me one guiding principle to live by before he died, and that was to always keep my promises. So that's what I intended on doing. And if that meant fighting a dragon and an army, then I'll die trying. At least I won't have gone back on my word.

I got to my feet and headed to my room. Moping around wasn't going to help us survive the coming days. I walked down several corridors and staircases before realizing I was going in circles.

Eventually I found it, but not before I walked in on several people, leaving them angry at my intrusion. I opened my door slowly, trying to avoid making the door creak. Will was already passed out on his bed. I gratefully jumped into the cool sheets on my mattress. I let out a deep breath and closed my eyes.

Tomorrow was going to be a long day.

8 FREEZE FRAME

Morning arrived quicker than I wanted it to. A sharp knock on the door woke us. I sat up in my bed and saw Will was doing the same.

"Surely not," he said, lying back down in his bed.

Shaking my head, I wandered to the door like a zombie. I twisted the knob, pulled the door open, and saw a young, very short boy nervously looking at his feet.

"T-t-t-they're waiting for you at the stables, sire," he stuttered. His eyes remained low.

"Thanks, we'll be out soon," I said, closing the door. I could hear the patter of his boots as he sprinted off.

Will sat up in his bed. "Last chance. We could back out and run away," he offered.

"I told you Will, I'm going to do this, and you can stay here if you want, but I'm not going to run from my problems."

He sighed, "I just don't see why you're risking your own life for these people. You don't even know them."

"Shut up, Will. Now are you coming or not?"

"Well, I can't let you see the dwarves and elves without me, now can I?" he smirked. He got out of his bed and dressed.

I pulled my own fresh clothes over my head and then slid the padding onto my shoulders. I tightened all the straps and laces around my arms and wrists. After I was satisfied with the placement of my armor, I wandered over to the window for one last enjoyment of the view. I was greeted by a small breeze that seemed to whisper goodbye. The sun was barely visible through the light pink sky.

The castle was quiet; the only movement was from the guards. The fresh air was soothing, despite the anticipation in my bones.

"You ready for this?" asked Will, coming up next to me.

The land stretched before us was vast. "Nope. But I'll be fine. You?"

"I'm always ready," he bragged.

I walked back to my bed, picked up Excalibur and tied it around my waist. "You're such a tool."

"You're a tool," he retorted.

"Nice comeback. Did you think of that all by yourself?"

"Yup."

Arguing was pointless. I gathered the rest of my things and walked out the door.

"Hey, wait up!" he called.

I knocked on Jessica's door. "Hey, you awake in there?"

"Yeah, be out in a sec," she called.

We waited for what seemed like an hour, and she still hadn't come out. Why does it take girls so long to get ready for things? It's not like she needs to look good for a bunch of dwarves. Finally, she opened the door and stepped out into the hallway. She was wearing the clothes that Charles made for her and carried a small pack.

"OK, I'm good to go," she said.

"What took you so long?" Will nagged.

"I had to get ready. Is that alright with you?" she snapped.

"Looks like someone got up on the wrong side of the bed this morning," Will whispered to me, out of Jessica's earshot.

I nodded, smiling at Jessica.

"Are you guys ready to go, or are we going to stand around here all day?" she growled and stormed down the hallway.

"I think she heard you," I advised Will as we followed at a safe distance. This was going to be a long day.

The three of us walked out of the castle, and slowly made our way through the town. It was early, so there really wasn't anyone up and about yet, except for the blacksmith whose hammer we heard banging as we passed his shop. I could also hear several birds chirping away. I looked up in the sky to see them circling us, and chasing each other in swoops and dives. We passed the training grounds and continued on to the stables.

Blaine and Galahad were pulling the horses outside. Each horse had several bags attached to its saddle, which I assumed were full of supplies.

"Hey, you three, we were beginning to think you weren't coming," joked Blaine, as Galahad returned inside the stable.

Galahad exited, hauling some more equipment. "We're all set to go. Oh, and the blacksmith made these for you."

He tossed the bags in our direction. They were large and clattered to the ground. We huddled around them, curious to see what was inside. I untied the knots that kept the first bag closed. Inside was an assortment of brand new weapons.

"Pick whatever appeals to you," Galahad winked.

"Awesome," said Will, pulling out a sword and a dagger. He tied the sheathed sword around his waist and put the dagger under his left pant leg, near his foot.

I searched the second bag, and retrieved a pair of fist knives, which were tucked into a vest. I reversed the vest and slid it on my back so that the two knives were on each of my shoulders. Seeing as I already had a sword, I didn't really need anything else. Jessica found a bow and a quiver full of arrows, that she affixed to her back. She also pulled out a thinner sword.

"The blacksmith made that sword specially for you. It's lighter than a normal sword, but just as strong," Galahad explained.

"Wow, thanks. I guess," Jessica replied. She wasn't

enthusiastic about having to carry weapons.

Blaine patted the horses. “I think that about does it. Are you ready to leave?”

I hesitated before answering, “I guess so. There’s really nothing else we can do to get ready.”

“Then let’s get going,” Galahad said, hopping gracefully onto his horse.

I walked up to Animi and patted him on his head. “You ready for this?” I asked him.

Animi snorted in reply.

I laughed. “Yeah, me neither.”

I jumped up easily and settled into a comfortable position. I was sore from training, but I grabbed hold of the reins and trotted over to Galahad and his horse. The others did the same, and soon the five of us were on our way to the gates.

“Hey Galahad, what’s in all of these bags?” asked Jessica.

“Food, blankets, and some other supplies.”

He whistled to the guards on the tower, who responded by opening the gates and lowering the drawbridge. The gates creaked as they opened, reminding me of the cages on The Island. I shivered. Our group passed through the gateway and over the bridge, which was raised immediately after we crossed. Soon we were moving in a quick trot down a different path than the one that led to the lake.

Our quest had begun.

The forest welcomed us. The trees were spaced widely apart and the grass waved in the cool breeze, as if to say hello. A bright sun had fully risen and was just visible through the treetops. The smooth dirt path was occasionally disturbed by small rock clusters. I felt uneasy when the trail got steep and rocky, but the horses seemed to manage the unevenness just fine. As the day dragged on, I became increasingly bored and sore. Apparently, so did Will.

“Are we there yet?” complained Will. “My butt is sore.”

Blaine chuckled. "This trip will take a few days. So no, we are not there yet. But we have been travelling a long time, so I suppose we could stop for a quick rest."

"Sounds good," I agreed.

We dismounted and tied the horses to nearby trees. I didn't feel like sitting, so I paced up and down and performed a few leg stretches that made Will smirk. I didn't care. When his muscles stiffen up, he won't be smirking.

Blaine and Galahad rummaged through their bags. They pulled out some bread and handed pieces to the three of us.

"Here, this should tide you over until our next stop," Blaine said.

"Where exactly is our next stop?" I asked between nibbles.

"Fernbrae. It's a small town that we can spend the night in. It's before we reach the mountains. Fernbrae's pretty isolated, but we should try to keep a low profile," Blaine replied.

"Why do we need to keep a low profile?" Will asked, his mouth full of bread.

"By now word has spread that Excalibur has been pulled. An army has been deployed to find Arthur and the sword, and destroy Camelot. If the wrong people find out who and where we are, we won't make it to the mountains alive. We need to stay inconspicuous," Galahad explained.

"Incon—what?" Will asked.

"Inconspicuous. It means not to draw attention to yourself, Merlin."

"Oh … I see," Will said with a swallow.

I frowned, "Do you think we'll run into trouble there?"

Blaine and Galahad exchanged a nervous look.

"What was that?" asked Jessica.

"What was what?" Blaine shrugged innocently.

"That look you and Galahad just gave each other."

Blaine sighed, “Fernbrae isn’t exactly a … friendly place.”

“What do you mean?” I asked Blaine.

Galahad stepped forward and replied, “He means Fernbrae has a reputation for violence. Bar fights, robberies, uprisings, and the like. They happen on a daily basis. It’s not an ideal place to spend a night, but we don’t have any other option. Fernbrae is the only town on the path to the mountains of Elsador.”

“Fantastic! Not only are we facing terrible odds with the dragon and haunted forest, but now we have to worry about avoiding bar fights?” shouted Will, waving his hands in the air.

“Why didn’t you say anything about this before?” asked Jessica with furrowed eyebrows.

“We didn’t want to concern you. You already had this whole prophecy business thrown at you. Besides, it’s nothing that we can’t handle,” Blaine reasoned.

An awkward silence followed as we each processed this new information. Even the chattery birds abandoned us.

“Are you sure there’s no other way to the mountains?” I asked, even though I figured I knew the answer.

Blaine and Galahad shook their heads.

“Then it doesn’t sound like we have much choice. We’ll spend the night in Fernbrae, and try not to draw attention to ourselves,” I said, feeling a twinge of authority.

“How much farther is Fernbrae? We’ve been riding all day,” Jessica asked, staring down the path.

Blaine rummaged through a bag on his horse. He pulled out a rolled piece of paper, tanned with age. The map. He unraveled and studied it before replying, “We’ve been riding pretty hard today. We’ve made good progress. We should reach Fernbrae around sundown.”

I looked up at the sky. The sun was still shining brightly, but was beginning to fall.

"Then we should probably get going," I suggested.

Soon we were back on the path to Fernbrae. The horses trod through the dirt, mud, and rocks until the forest began to open up. The dirt path turned into a field of tall grass, with no trees to be seen. In the vast and open space, Galahad took the initiative to urge his horse into a gallop. The rest followed suit. The ground wasn't flat. It rolled before us like an ocean's waves. The tall grass danced in the cool breeze that came and went. A few clouds dotted the sky, but they avoided the sun, so there was no shade to be had.

Galahad led, riding a few paces in front of us, followed by Jessica and Blaine. Will and I brought up the rear. It was a roller-coaster ride on horses! My stomach even lurched a couple of times as we would crest a hill. The air kissed my face as we flew by. This lasted for several glorious minutes, then, to my disappointment, the grassy plains turned back into a forest. We slowed. These trees seemed greener than the others and a strong pine smell wafted up my nostrils and filled my head. Dried leaves cracked under the horses' hooves.

We travelled a fair ways into these woods when the trail suddenly became steep. At the top of the path stood a cloaked figure, with a hood covering his face. In his left hand was a bow, and a quiver hung over his left shoulder. Galahad brought his horse to a halt about fifteen feet from the mysterious person. He remained so still, I wondered if it was a statue.

"Who are you?" questioned Galahad in a deep voice.

The figure did not move nor speak.

Blaine and Galahad exchanged concerned looks. I heard rustling of leaves around us, but I could not see what was making the noise. My hand went to the sheath of Excalibur.

"Why do you block our path?" Galahad asked, this time in a more threatening voice.

The figure did not move.

"Who are—" Blaine started to ask.

"My name is Robin," The hooded figure said in a deep and brisk voice.

"Robin? As in Robin Hood?" I asked Jessica in a quiet voice.

She whispered back, "I think so, but he wasn't evil in the cartoon."

I nodded. The Disney cartoon character Robin Hood was less threatening and violent than this guy. Not good.

"Why do you block our path?" repeated Galahad.

"There is a toll to go through this forest," he said, his voice bore the same deep tone, but it felt like he was toying with us.

"Rubbish," Galahad shouted at the man.

The figure raised his left hand, simultaneously pulling off his hood and drawing three arrows. His face was young, much like Lancelot's. He had brown hair and a clean-cut beard. He smiled as he notched each arrow onto the bow, quicker than I would've thought possible.

"I suggest you pay up. My friends and I aren't the patient type," he said with a wink.

I looked around us. There were six or seven men now surrounding us, each bearing some sort of weapon. The scruffiness of the men reminded me of homeless people from the streets of New York. Galahad surveyed the situation; there wasn't much we could do. We had two options:

Surrender.

Fight our way out.

"And if we don't?" Galahad asked.

Robin released his arrows. To my amazement, all three hit Galahad's saddle. One struck in front of his left quad, another by his right, and the third just in front of his … well let's just say it landed close to somewhere that would not be a good place for an arrow to hit. The horse jumped at the impact, but the arrows did not penetrate the heavy leather.

"Point taken," I heard Galahad mutter to himself.

"We can't let them take Excalibur," whispered Blaine harshly. "If we surrender, they'll steal everything from us."

Galahad nodded slowly and whispered, "Then we'll have to fight."

Option number two.

"Very well, you leave us no choice but to pay your toll," Galahad called to Robin, as he hopped off his horse. The four of us did the same.

Robin smiled as he walked down towards us, "I'm glad you've come to your senses."

My left hand was ready on Excalibur. Robin and his gang started to close in on us. As soon as Robin was five feet away from us, Galahad pulled out his sword faster than The Flash (a modern comic book superhero for those who don't know). The rest of us followed his example and pulled out our weapons, preparing for a fight.

"Tsk, tsk. I had rather hoped not to kill you," Robin said, pulling out a sword.

Galahad made the first swing at Robin, and with it, his gang attacked. Two men ran forward at me with swords drawn. One went for Jessica. Another two headed for Will. And one ran toward Blaine. The first man heading for me was much taller than his companion. The tall one swung at me first, aiming for my right shoulder. I shot Excalibur up and blocked it. Then, while moving forward, I swung my sword around and blocked the short man's lunge at my stomach.

I turned. They were between me and my friends. I moved quickly and gave the tall man two solid swings, which he blocked, then I pivoted just in time to repel another attack by the short man. This was intense.

I snuck a glance at the others. Will was handling the two men relatively well, and Jessica appeared to be doing fine. Blaine and Galahad were struggling with the fierce men opposing them.

My focus went back to the men before me. I had to beat them quickly in order to help the others.

OK, Excalibur, time to use those cool moves, I mentally spoke to my sword.

That seemed to work because as I advanced again on the short man, my instincts (or something) took over and I was able to use Excalibur to block the swing at my back from the tall man, while still facing the short man. I kicked the tall man behind me, sending him reeling back. I continued to duel the short man. Our swords collided again and again. I could sense that the tall man was coming up behind me. I blocked a swing and punched the short man in the face. Immediately, I turned and ducked as the tall man swung for my head. I instantly shot Excalibur upward and it plunged into the man's chest.

Excalibur had pierced the man effortlessly, the bones inside of him breaking through Excalibur's vibrations. I froze. He fell to his knees, then collapsed onto his back. Excalibur slid out in the process. This was way different than shooting those stupid Island guards had been. I killed him. With my hands. The shock of what just happened was short-lived. The short man was charging me, a battle cry escaping from his lips. I whipped around. His sword was high over his head. He swung at my head. I easily blocked it and knocked the weapon from his hands, but his body kept coming. I stepped back, forgetting there was a dead guy behind me. I tripped over him, as did the short man. I scrambled to my feet and thrust Excalibur to the short man's throat, stopping just before it penetrated skin.

"G-g-get out of here," I managed to choke out.

The man nodded, terrified. I let him get up and he immediately ran back into the woods from where he had come. I looked around to help the others. Will had killed one of his attackers and was battling with the other; Galahad had locked swords with Robin, and was holding his ground. Blaine was up against a tall husky man, who wasn't that skilled with a sword by the look of things.

Then I saw Jessica. She was on the ground, her sword far out of her reach. A man stood over her and was about to drive a sword through her chest.

"No!" I shouted, reaching out a hand to Jessica.

Then, everything stopped. It was like someone hit the pause button on life around me. My friends weren't moving, neither were the men who attacked us, and neither was the sword, inches away from Jessica's heart. I didn't have time to think of what was going on. The only thing running through my mind was that I had to save Jessica. I ran to her, my legs pumping, Excalibur gripped in my right hand. I leapt at the man, tackling him away from Jessica. As soon as my body touched his, everything was once again in motion. I was now rolling through the leaves with the man. He broke free of my grip and we were on our feet in seconds. But he had lost his sword while we were rolling.

"Leave now," I snarled, staring him straight in his eyes.

The man ran, just like the other had done. I ran back to Jessica and lent out a hand to help her up. "Are you okay?"

"Yeah. How did—"

"Not now," I replied.

I heard a whistle echo through the forest. The remaining bandits bolted into the forest, running from the fight.

"Consider yourselves lucky this time," shouted Robin as he followed his gang and disappeared into the forest.

"Is everyone alright?" Galahad asked, keeping an eye on the woods.

Blaine rubbed his back. "I think I might've strained my back, but other than that I'm fine."

"That was pretty intense," Will said inspecting the body he had killed. "I had to take on two of them, but I won, no big deal."

"What about you two?" Galahad asked Jessica and me.

"I—I'm fine. Just a little bit rattled," Jessica replied, with her eyes on me.

"Yeah, me too. I've never killed someone like that before," I said, almost apologetically. I glanced at the tall man's body.

"That's understandable Arthur. It's a normal reaction and a quality needed in a leader. Killing should not be for fun. Only kill when necessary, and in this situation it was most definitely necessary," Galahad said grimly.

Blaine chimed in, "Indeed. This was quite the unexpected event; rebels don't usually lurk in these parts."

Galahad jumped onto his horse. His armor was scratched in the places where Robin had hit him. "We had better get a move on. This unfortunate experience has set us back, and I would prefer to get to Fernbrae before nightfall," he said.

We were all in agreement. We didn't want a repeat of what just happened. We cleaned our weapons, then mounted our horses and took off up the trail quickly. Jessica was riding beside me. "So I've got two questions for you. One, why was Robin Hood attacking us? And two, how did you save me? You were too far to do anything, and then you appeared out of nowhere."

"I don't know. Wasn't Robin Hood supposed to be a good guy? At least that's what Disney said," I kept my voice low, so only she could hear me.

"That's what I thought too, but stop trying to avoid the main question, Francis."

"Honestly, I don't have a clue what happened. Time just froze. Everything was still and I was the only one who could move. It's just like how we got here in the first place; I have no idea how I did it."

She shook her head and said, "I'm not sure how you did it either, but if it wasn't for you, I'd be dead right now." Her voice cracked slightly.

Our eyes locked for a split second. I immediately looked away. “Don’t mention it,” I whispered.

I stared at the path ahead, but I could tell she was still looking at me. I also could sense she was smiling. I couldn’t help but smile too. I didn’t care what happened or how it happened, I was just glad she was OK. Galahad kept a fast and steady pace as we raced through the forest, hoping not to run into any more trouble. The sun was beginning to set, turning the sky crescent orange. We didn’t have much time before darkness would have a firm grip over us.

The path ahead faded as the sun vanished from our sight. Galahad slowed in order to follow the path without getting lost. I felt a sudden drop of coldness on my head. It was starting to rain.

“We need to hurry. If we get caught in the rain, we might lose the trail and I’d rather not get lost,” Galahad called back.

“Right, lead the way,” I yelled to him, the rain was now pouring on us.

Galahad nodded and we picked up speed. I pulled my hood over my head to keep the rain out of my eyes. The others did the same. The rain felt like ice as it pelted me from above. My hands shivered from the sudden cold. I tightened my grip on the reins. I urged Animi to go faster, following right behind Galahad. We were moving rather quickly. Eventually the path straightened and I sensed the presence of the town, even though I couldn’t see it. Galahad held up his arm, signalling us to stop.

He turned his head and talked in a low voice. “Remember, this is a place of little dignity,” he warned. “We should move quickly to find the closest inn and get to our rooms.”

“Hey guys,” Will whispered, “what does dignity mean?”

“It means we shouldn’t spend too much time here,” I strained my eyes and things came into a bit of focus.

It was dark and wet. Two lanterns lit the entrance to the town, flanking a large gate. We trotted up to the gate and were greeted by two guards.

"What's your business here?" the first questioned.

"We're travellers on our way to the mountains," Galahad replied.

The guard scoffed, "Right. No one goes to the mountains. And if they do, they don't come back. There happens to be a dragon guarding it, if you hadn't heard."

"That's for us to decide. Now please let us by. If you aren't aware, it is raining and we are cold."

He grunted, "Very well. Be warned, if you cause trouble, you will be hung."

"Thank you," Galahad said, nudging his horse onward.

We followed closely. He avoided the side streets. I chanced a glance down one of the alleyways. Several dark figures roughed each other up, fists a-swinging. Ahead of us were several houses, much like Camelot's, only dirtier. Three cloaked figures stumbled towards us. They were obviously drunk and shouted obscene comments at us as we passed. A few of the houses had a lit candle in the window, but most were pitch black. The horses splashed through the puddles on the road. I could hear a loud creaking noise. As I looked around, I saw a sign dangling from a pole, swinging back and forth in the rain. As we got closer, I noticed the lettering on the sign read: The Stable Inn. Galahad stopped in front of the inn and dismounted his horse.

"You four stay here while I get our rooms. Try not to get into any trouble while I'm gone," he said, as he disappeared through the door to the inn.

We sat on the horses and waited for Galahad to return. Water continued to drip down my face. My hood was useless. I looked around. There wasn't anyone walking around, though I could tell that a few motionless bodies leaned against some of the buildings. Light and noise flooded from the inn when Galahad opened the door and stepped out.

"I got us two rooms. They're inside and up the stairs on the right. It's quite rowdy in there, so let's not make any detours, OK?"

We nodded and got off our horses, tying them to the stocks on the side of the inn. We grabbed the bags that held the weapons and food supplies. Galahad held the door for us as we piled into the inn.

What a mess. Now when I say mess, I mean Mess. With a capital M. Tables were scattered around a large open area. Nearly every table had at least one drunken body slumped over it. We stepped over empty and broken bottles as we made our way through. We had to walk past the bar, where an obviously bagged bartender stood behind the counter, washing it with a cloth. Several men were fighting in the back corner. One threw a bottle at another and it shattered against his face. Ouch. I didn't get the chance to see any more because Galahad rushed us upstairs.

He opened the third door on our right. "This is your room. Blaine and I will be staying in that room if you run into any trouble," he said, pointing to the door right across from us.

"Thanks, we'll see you in the morning," I said, as we filed in and closed the door behind us.

The room was dim and quiet, which was surprising considering the zoo we had walked through to get there. There were two beds, one window, and a fireplace.

The fire crackled and flickered cheerfully, filling the room with enveloping warmth. The rain outside pelted the window with consistency, rattling the glass in its pane. Will went straight for the far bed and sat down on it.

"So is now a good time to talk about what happened?" Jessica asked me.

"What happened now?" Will asked, intrigued.

I shook my head. "I honestly don't know what happened, OK? Just like I don't know how we got here. One minute everything was normal, and then time froze."

"What are you talking about?" Will asked, confused.

Jessica turned to him with intensity. "During that fight in the woods, I was this close to dying," she said, pinching her thumb and forefinger together with only a hair's width of space in between, "and then Francis appeared out of nowhere and saved me. One moment he was too far away to help, and then the next instant he was on top of the man who was attacking me. How did he get to me in time?"

"I told you Jess, I have no idea what happened. Everything just suddenly ... stopped"

"Uh-huh. So you can now stop time too?" Will raised an eyebrow.

I shrugged, "I guess."

"OK there, Champ. Jessica, why didn't you just do your turning-invisible thing?"

"Shoot. I totally forgot about that," she said, slapping her head. "Well why didn't you use your force power thingy, huh, smart guy?"

"Hey don't go turning this on me. You're the one who almost died," Will retorted, as he laid down on one of the beds.

"Guys settle down. Look, something obviously happened to all of us at The Island. I don't think we can control what happens and when it happens. Maybe with practice we can, but for now we just have to deal with it as it comes and goes. Alright?" I reasoned.

"You're right Francis," Jessica said as she sat on the other bed. "And if we're going to survive this and save the other kids, we're going to need to learn how to control these things and use them against our enemies."

"That sounds like a lot of work," complained Will.

"Stop being such a baby," Jessica said. Will's mouth mimicked her words after she said them. He was so immature.

I sat on a chair in the corner of the room. "So tomorrow we climb the mountain?" I asked.

"More work," Will muttered to himself.

"I think so. Does that mean we have to face that dragon?" Jessica answered.

I held my hands closer to the fire. "I'm still not convinced there is a dragon."

"I guess we'll find out then, won't we?"

"Mhmm."

"Could you guys be quiet? Some of us are trying to sleep here," Will groaned.

Jessica and I rolled our eyes at the same time, which made us laugh. Will was quite the character sometimes.

"Alright Will, because you need your beauty rest so much, we'll go to bed, just for you," she teased.

"Thank you," Will ignored the criticism.

I didn't feel like going in the bed with Will (and if you're thinking I should sleep in the bed with Jessica, forget it. That would just be weird), so I sat down next to the fire and got comfy. I had gotten used to the rough and cold floor after spending the many years in The Island's cells. The fire kept me warm, and I rested my head on one of our packs. I closed my eyes and let the popping of the fire (and Will's snoring), lull me to sleep.

I should've stayed awake, because my dreams got weirder. First off, you know the type of dreams that feel real? Yeah, I had one of those. Secondly, this time it wasn't the car accident. I was in a war. Mangled bodies were scattered all around me with grotesque features. It was bloody and kind of gross. In front of me was a vast battlefield, lined with catapults. A castle stood in the distance off to my right. Twenty men, armed with swords, were charging the castle. Guarding the fortress was a single warrior, dressed in a unique armor. On his right shoulder was a round metal plate, that had a sharp point protruding out from its center. His shins were protected by similar plating, which curved around his legs beginning at his ankles and ending in sharp points extending from his knees that would do some damage if he kneed someone. Along his arms were long metal gloves with a jagged tip outreaching from his fists. His head bore a sleek helmet that curved back, as if a giant fan was blowing in front of him. A ragged cape drifted in the breeze behind him, and a hood from a dark tunic covered most of his face. His right hand gripped a thin, curved sword. He did not move. He did not back down. He only stared at the men charging him.

When they were about twenty feet from him, he charged forward to meet them head-on. He ducked and dodged their swords, while at the same time slicing them with precision. He twisted and bent his body to avoid oncoming attacks, and at one point he reminded me of Neo from *The Matrix*. (They actually made me watch *The Matrix* on The Island once.) The attackers couldn't touch him. He moved too fast and guarded himself too well.

I heard a yell from behind me. Another group of men were charging at me with swords drawn. I had no time to react; all I could do was cover my face and brace for death. When nothing happened, I peeked my eyes out from underneath my arms. The men ran right past me, as if I was invisible. One man was inches from me and again I braced for impact. He passed right through me, my body dissolving into gold dust, then reforming on the other side of him.

"What just happened?" I shuddered.

I looked back to the man fighting in front of the castle. He had quickly defeated the attackers and was left standing alone atop a pile of dead bodies. He hopped down and walked straight towards me. I tried to move, but I was paralyzed with fear. (Cut me some slack, the guy just kicked the crap out of at least thirty guys, and looked pretty badass.) He wiped the blade of his sword on his cloak and sheathed it over his left shoulder.

"You don't need to fear me, Francis," he said calmly. His voice was deep and hollow.

"Who are you? And how do you know my name?" I worked up the courage to ask.

"I am Excalibur."

"Dude. I'm pretty sure Excalibur is a sword."

The warrior chuckled, "Do you know how Excalibur was created?"

I shook my head.

"My name is Excalibur, and I was once the greatest warrior ever known. I was fast, strong, and smart. I won many battles that most ordinary men would've perished in. Until one fateful day," he paused, almost wistfully, "the enemy emperor had employed a witch to help him. When I was about to strike a fatal blow to him, the witch cursed me. She took my very soul–my essence–and transferred it into a sword. I've been trapped there for God knows how many years. She bound me to that stone, and I've been there ever since."

"That," I wasn't sure what to say, "… sucks."

"Yes," he agreed. "It certainly hasn't been pleasant. But now that's over. You freed me. Well, you've freed me from the stone."

"I'm so confused. You were a real guy who got transferred by witchcraft into a sword and sat in a rock until I pulled you out?"

"Precisely."

"Why me?"

"Whenever someone attempted to pull the sword, I was privy to all their thoughts and memories. That was how I knew you were the right person, Francis. You may be from the future, but you can help me, and I can help you."

"What do you mean?"

"The witch that cursed me resides in Brentwood Forest. If you kill her, I will be free. I will return to human form and I can live again. In return, I give you my battle instinct and power."

I nodded, following along. But then I realized what he said. "Wait … what?" I asked.

"No doubt you've felt the power within the sword. That's me. I was the reason you beat Lancelot. When you used a different weapon, I couldn't help you and you were left on your own, which is why you lost to him. If you help free me, I will leave that power with you. You'll need it in the trials ahead."

"I see," I said slowly. *But did I?*

He laughed. "I know you've had a lot thrown at you recently, but with my help, you'll make it through."

"Thanks," I thought about what he said. "Um, where exactly are we?"

Excalibur looked around the battlefield. "To put it simply, you're in my mind. I can share my thoughts and memories with you, and as you can see, a lot of them are battle-related. This was the easiest way to talk with you."

"Right. So are you like my guardian angel type of thing?"

"I guess you could call it that."

"You're going to help me fight this dragon and witch, and survive this whole war thing?"

"Indeed."

"Sounds good to me," I said clasping my hands together. "So how does this work?"

"Leave that to me. I'll take over like I have before. You just worry about getting the elves and dwarves on our side."

"Right, I like the sound of that. Any advice?"

He chuckled. "The elves are a proud race. They avoid violence, only using it when no other course is available, so try to play with that. As for the dwarves … they're greedy and stupid. Just offer them something shiny and they'll most likely agree to help us."

"Doesn't seem too difficult. I'll do my best and hopefully won't die, but I can't promise anything. I'm not exactly used to talking with mythological creatures, you know?"

"I understand. This situation can't be easy for you, but you must succeed. Camelot depends on it."

"I've been told," I affirmed. "So, do I like, go back to sleep now? Or do you snap your fingers and disappear?"

He smiled. "Not exactly ..."

He whipped out his sword and plunged it into my stomach. The pain was white hot and I cried out. The next moment, I was sitting up, clutching my stomach. I looked down; there was no scar or wound. There was no battlefield. Just a room, a fireplace, and my friends, still sound asleep.

I was in a cold sweat. The effect of that "dream" made me not want to fall back asleep. I got up and walked over to sit by the window. It was still raining. I watched it trickle down the windowsill, the drops racing each other to the bottom. I heard shouts coming from the streets and shifted my position to see. Four men chased a hooded figure down the middle of the street. The cloaked person tripped and plummeted face-first into a puddle. He tried to get up but the men had caught up to him. They kicked and punched him, as he lay helpless on the ground. As soon as I realized what was happening, I grabbed Excalibur and rushed out of the room. I didn't stop to wake Jess or Will, and Galahad said not to cause trouble, so I wasn't about to knock on his door. Besides, there wasn't any time to waste. I booked it down the stairs and flung open the door to the street. I stepped out into the storm and was greeted with hundreds of raindrops pelting me.

"Hey!" I shouted at the men. "Let him go."

The men stopped attacking the crumpled body. One of them stepped forward. "This doesn't concern you, boy. Just be on your way and I'll let that outburst go."

I shook my head, "No."

"Do you have a death wish kid?" another man asked.

I gripped Excalibur tightly in my hand and gave it a couple turns, showing them I was ready for a fight.

"Get him," the first man said to the others.

The three men rushed me. Each was holding a large dagger. The spirit, or whatever it was, must've been telling the truth because as the men came at me I was able to size up the situation. I backed quickly towards an empty barrel sitting by the inn. I kicked it over and rolled it at my attackers. It knocked the first man to the ground, but the other two dodged it. I jumped onto the barrel. I used it to pin the man on the ground, while at the same time this gave me higher ground against the other two. The two men still on their feet came at me swinging their daggers wildly. It was hard to parry their attacks while balancing on the barrel, but somehow I managed to do both. I didn't want to kill the men, but at the same time, I didn't want to die. So I compromised, deciding to clip them with my sword to draw blood. I hoped it would be enough to stop them. I jumped off the barrel and cut the first man on the arm, then the leg. The other charged at me. I quickly sidestepped and slashed him across the back, then followed through with a light slice on the chest of the man under the barrel. The two retreated behind their leader, holding their wounds and cringing in pain. The third remained on the ground.

"That's a nice sword boy," the leader said in a cold voice. His dark eyes bore right through me. "Looks awfully familiar."

I tried to hide my nervousness. "Yeah, well they're all long and pointy so I can see where you'd get confused."

The man didn't laugh. "Looks remarkably like Excalibur. And I've heard it's been pulled by a young man."

"Well, you've got the wrong guy, but thanks for thinking I could be that strong."

"Give me the sword, boy, and no one will get hurt," he snarled.

"Huh," I looked at his men. The third guy had gotten to his feet. "Seems to me like you're the one who's going to get hurt."

"You best be watching your back, kid," the man said as he turned and started to walk away. His men followed him. "I'll be seeing you around."

I shuddered. (I'm going to blame my shivers on the rain.) I stretched out a hand to the broken man on the ground and helped him up. I supported him into the inn and lowered him into a chair by the bar.

"Thank you," he managed to whisper.

I smiled and gave him a nod.

"Is it true? About …" he said in a low voice, eyeing my sword.

"Yes."

He nodded. "Then there is still hope for the land."

"Thanks. Are you going to be alright?"

"I should be fine, thanks again …?"

"Arthur."

"Arthur. You're a good man," he said softly.

I let out a deep breath. I walked back up the stairs to my room. I tried to be as quiet as possible, so I tiptoed to my spot by the fire and sat down. Excalibur had followed through with his part of the bargain. I was still alive. I closed my eyes, hoping for a chance to actually get some rest for once, and drifted into a deep sleep.

9 AMBUSH

We awoke to the ever-familiar sound of knocking at our door. Jessica was the first to get up. She twisted the knob and pulled the door open. Blaine and Galahad stood in the hallway, already packed and fully dressed.

"I see you're not ready yet," Blaine said eyeing the room.

Jessica gave an apologetic look over her shoulder.

"We'll get ready quickly," she promised.

"Please hurry," insisted Galahad, glancing nervously down the hallway.

She shut the door and began gathering her things. "Hey guys, you should probably step on it. Sounds like we have to split."

Will groaned (another ever-familiar morning sound). I got to my feet slowly; the previous night's events had worn me out. I put my clothes on (not that I was naked, I mean my armor and stuff) and went into the hallway. Blaine and Galahad were waiting. Galahad looked rather tense. I figured I'd better come clean.

"Something happened last night," I said.

"What do you mean?" he asked.

I looked down the hallway to make sure no one was listening. "Last night someone was getting attacked by four guys in the street. I saw them out my window. I don't know why I didn't get you, but I went out to help him on my own. The good news is the man is OK. The bad news is one of them recognized Excalibur and told me to watch my back."

Galahad cursed. “We have to get out of here now. If people know we’re here, they’ll be after us. That group sounds like a band of mercenaries; people who will do anything for the right price. If they know, they’ll want Excalibur for the money its worth, and will kill us for it.”

Blaine gave a low whistle. “This isn’t good. From this point on, we’re going to be hunted.”

“What was I supposed to do? Just let them kill him?”

Blaine held his hand out. “No, no. You did the right thing. It’s just … going to be more difficult now.”

“More difficult indeed. But Blaine is right, you did good,” Galahad agreed. “But we will have to be extra careful now, especially at night. We should leave immediately.”

Jessica and Will were standing in the doorway when I turned around. No doubt they heard what happened.

“We just can’t take you anywhere anymore, can we? I mean you keep getting into fights and making people mad,” teased Will.

“Shouldn’t we get moving?” insisted Jessica.

Galahad wasted no time bustling us out the door of the inn. We followed him to the horse posts and packed up our gear. Once everything was tucked safely away, we mounted and Galahad led us out of the town. It was early in the morning, so there wasn’t much activity in the streets, but several townsfolk were starting to move about. The road was damp and muddy from the night’s storm.

The gate at the back end of the town was much like the gate we had entered by. Thankfully, it was open. A wooden tower stood on either side of it, with a guard standing in each. Another guard was near the gate’s opening. He made no effort to stop us, but as we passed he gave us a look I can only describe as hateful. The other side of the town was much different from the lush forest that preceded it. There were mountains far off in the distance where we were headed. Some were jagged and looked like they were made of granite, while others were covered in snow. The path before us was a mix of rock and grass. Rolling hills stretched off to either side of the path.

We rode towards the mountains, thinking the path would be smooth, but soon found out it would be more difficult to cross these plains than it first appeared. The hills would stop suddenly, plummeting into a rocky abyss. There were steep ledges that we had to navigate around. All in all, it was a pain in the butt to travel. I mean that literally, by the way. My butt was getting sore from all the bumps.

"This path is terrible," Will complained as we slowly maneuvered down a sharp slope.

Galahad chuckled. "You're quite right, Merlin. It's probably because it's not a path at all. I'm trying to make sure no one follows us, and if they do, it will be rather difficult."

"Great," he groaned back.

"And now that you mention it, we might have to walk for the next while," Galahad stopped and dismounted his horse. He took one of the packs from the horse and slung it over his shoulder. "Put a bag or two over your shoulders to lighten the load for the horses as we go down the slope," he instructed.

"Awesome," I said, eagerly jumping off Animi and following his orders. "I was beginning to lose feeling in my legs."

"That's understandable," Galahad nodded. "Sorry for the inconvenience, I'm just taking precautions."

After we were all ready, Galahad led us one at a time down the steep, unstable path. It was a slow process and a few times one or another of us would slip and fall, or slide a few feet, but eventually we all made it safely down. I surveyed our surroundings. We were at the bottom of a valley. Sharp rocks blocked us from going back up. Before us, the path was narrow and although we could ride the horses again, we were forced to travel one behind another in a straight line. The pace was slow, but we had no other choice. Dark, black clouds began to encroach the once bright sky.

"Just our luck. It's going to rain now," Blaine observed.

"Oh come on," Will said. "Just because there are dark clouds, doesn't mean it's going to rain."

Not two seconds after Will finished talking, it started to rain. He frowned.

"I'm sorry Merlin, I couldn't hear you over the sudden rain," Blaine joked.

Will remained silent, not wanting to embarrass himself further. The rain trickled gently onto us, like drops of water falling one after another from a tap. This calm, slow rain didn't last long though. After a few minutes, the sky opened up.

"The weather turns a bit bleak when we get near the mountains," Galahad shouted over the downpour. "The valley should become a marsh soon."

"A marsh?" I asked.

"Yes," Blaine took over. "A wetland. Very grassy. Water everywhere. Foggy. Nothing exciting."

"Sounds lovely," I replied.

"You left out the part about snakes," called Galahad.

"Oh right!" Blaine snapped his fingers. "I forgot about those buggers. There are snakes, too.'"

"Snakes?" Jessica panicked.

Blaine nodded and replied, "Serpentas to be exact. Nasty creatures. They range in size from three to twenty-five feet long. The smaller ones cluster around the large ones. They're very territorial, and won't venture from their claimed area. If you go too deep in the water, the large ones will bite. Their venom will paralyze you, and then the small ones will attack, releasing their venom—which is deadly by the way—into your body, and you will die within seconds."

"You've got to be kidding me," Jessica said.

"I wish I was. But we shouldn't run into any. We'll only be in trouble if we run into the large ones. The little snakes are too afraid to attack if they are not accompanied by the large ones."

"This just keeps getting better and better," Will lamented.

"Don't worry," Galahad said effortlessly, "some believe the Serpentas are more of a legend anyways."

I rolled my eyes, "Yeah, like the dragon?"

We continued along the valley in the rain. The rocky slopes slowly disappeared, leaving us in an open field of tall grass. As we got closer to the marsh I could see that it was full of water, grass, mud, and fog. In the far distance were huge mountains overlooking the enormous wetland.

"We've reached the marsh," Galahad stated. "We'll need to stick close togeth—"

He never finished his sentence. An arrow pierced the back of his left shoulder, and two more hit his horse in the side. He hunched forward, grunting in pain, and immediately jumped off the wounded horse. He grabbed a shield that was attached to his saddle and faced the direction of the attack. We quickly followed his example and grouped together, each of us holding a shield for protection.

THWANG!

An arrow collided with my shield, and the momentum took me back a step. I could see our attackers now. They were at the top of the hill we had just descended. They had both the advantage of surprise and high ground. I couldn't make out how many there were, but I didn't feel like counting because another arrow whipped past my head. I backed up even closer against the others.

"They have us cornered," Galahad grunted as he snapped the arrow out of his shoulder. "Our only option is to head for the marsh. They're too well-guarded up there."

Another arrow hit my shield. An instant later Jessica's and

Will's shields has arrows protruding from them, too.

"We need to stay close together. Watch your step and keep an eye on the valley," Galahad cautioned. As a group we started to back up very slowly.

"Jessica," I said urgently, "give me your bow."

Her eyes radiated fear. She nodded and carefully took the bow and quiver off her back and handed it to me. More arrows collided with our shields as we backed towards the marsh. I looped my arm through the arm straps on my shield. I pulled an arrow from the quiver and stepped closed to Will to benefit from the extra cover of his shield. I took aim at one of our attackers and launched the arrow. It disappeared into the air and I had no clue if it hit anything. A moment later we saw him collapse and roll down the hill.

"Nice shot, Arthur," Galahad said. His arm was through his shield and he quickly fired off his own arrow.

Jessica glanced behind us, "We're at the edge of the marsh now."

"Alright, we need to go one by one," Galahad said. "Blaine, you take the front, Arthur and I will take care of as many of these men as we can before following. We'll meet you on the other end."

Blaine surveyed the marsh to identify a path. "Quickly, follow me," he said.

Blaine, Will, and Jessica moved into the marsh and soon disappeared into the fog. Galahad and I were on our own, crouched down in the mud. The attackers moved closer to get in range.

"Arthur, we need to work together to cover one another as we counterattack."

"Right, just tell me what to do," I said.

"Every time I say, 'cover,' you move and keep the shield in front of me while I fire arrows. Every time I say, 'attack,' I'll cover and you fire. Understand?"

I nodded.

"Good. Cover!"

I lunged in front of him, pulling my shield in front of both of us. I could hear his arrows screeching past me. Ten men were attacking us.

"Attack!" he instructed, and took position with his shield.

I pulled out an arrow and aimed at the closest man. I let go. The arrow slid out of the bow and into the chest of the man. He went down. I took aim at a farther target halfway down the valley. I let out my breath as I released the arrow. I ducked behind my shield just as the arrow connected with its target. Now there were eight men. Two archers left. The rest were on foot, charging us.

"Take out the archer to the left on my go!" shouted Galahad.

I nodded.

"Go!"

We both stood tall, each aiming for one of the two archers. I fired a clean shot, which hit the archer in the head. Galahad also succeeded in killing his target. He dropped his bow and drew his sword.

"Arthur, keep backing into the fog. We'll use it against them."

"Right," I said, my pulse racing.

With our swords drawn, we quickly moved deeper into the marsh. The fog provided cover and the snake-infested water limited their approach.

"Here they come," Galahad whispered.

Out of the fog emerged two men; one with a sword, and the other with an axe. The axed dude came at me, and the other headed for Galahad. This guy was pretty stupid. He didn't realize charging an opponent wasn't the smartest idea. I used his momentum against him by crouching down as he reached me. His axe was high above his head. Just as he was about to swing, I grabbed him by his chest and fell on my back, pulling him over my body and flinging him into the water with a loud splash. I turned my attention back to the fog from where he'd come, but out of the corner of my eye I saw a giant green snake twisting around the man's body.

Blaine wasn't kidding around, I thought.

Four more men appeared from the fog. Galahad sheathed his sword and pulled out two fist knives, anticipating close-quarters combat. One of them was the man from the alley.

"We meet again, my young friend," he said calmly, glancing at the scene behind me. "Nasty business those Serpentas. Why don't you save yourself the pain, and hand over Excalibur? We clearly have you outnumbered."

I laughed, trying to sound more confident than I felt, and winked at Galahad, "Something tells me we can take you."

"I think not."

The four men attacked. However, three of them went for Galahad, while the leader came for me. He came at me with quick, precise jabs. I swung high and low, trying with no luck to find the weak spot in the man's defense. He blocked my attacks and almost clipped me a few times. Then, suddenly, he unleashed a fury of attacks that I didn't expect. I realized he was driving me backward, nearer and nearer to the edge of the marsh water.

"Give it up, boy, and I might let you live," he growled.

I gave him a sly smile, "Funny, I was about to say the same thing to you."

He glared and raised his sword high above his head. He didn't realize my knees were in the water. I dove to my left onto solid ground, just as a massive snake lunged at me from behind. Because my body was no longer there, the snake soared through the air, straight into the man's chest. I felt sick inside as I watched the snake sink its fangs into his neck and drag him into the water. Flashes of black and blue repeatedly lunged at the motionless body. There must've been hundreds of the small poisonous snakes now munching on their manwich meal. I forced the sight out of my head and turned to help Galahad. He had killed one of the three, but was struggling to defeat the other two. I had the element of surprise and stabbed one of the men in the back. The other hesitated at the activity and Galahad took advantage of the confusion and swung fist after fist into the man's chest. His crumpled body fell to the ground with a dull thud.

We took a full minute to catch our breath, then Galahad spoke, "The blood will attract more of the Serpentas. We need to get away from here fast and catch up with the others."

I didn't argue. The two of us moved quickly through the rest of the marsh, avoiding the water. It took a long time to cross, but eventually we saw the others. Jessica was standing guard, while Blaine knelt down beside Will. My heart sank. Will wasn't moving.

"What happened?" I asked.

"We ran into one of those huge snakes," Jessica explained. "It bit him, but before it could drag him to the water, I killed it."

"He'll be fine. The large Serpentas only paralyze the body. He will be stuck like this for an hour, at the most," Blaine elaborated.

"He's going to be fine?" I asked, the concern in my voice was strong.

Blaine nodded.

"After these events, I think we should set up camp here," Galahad said, surveying the area. "From here on in, we need to keep watch during the nights. We'll take turns and rotate every few hours. We can't risk another ambush like that. Next time we may not be so lucky."

I agreed, "So we spend the night here, and in the morning continue to the mountains?"

Blaine stood as he replied, "Yes, we're close to the dwarves now. We need to travel through some of the mountains before we reach them, but it won't take more than a day, maybe two."

"Is there *anything* we can do for him?" Jessica asked, staring at Will.

Galahad shook his head, "The venom of the Serpentas has no cure. All we can do is keep him comfortable. And you're sure he was not bit by any of the little ones?"

Jessica affirmed, "Positive."

"Then we will just have to wait it out. I'm going to go look for any food or firewood, seeing as our horses are now gone," Galahad said, and he headed for the trees.

It hit me then: We didn't have the horses! We had left them on the other side in the ambush … along with many of our supplies. Crap!

"Should we go back and get them?" I asked, looking into the foggy marsh. We had a few things in our shoulder bags, but a lot was lost.

"No," Blaine warned. "It's too dangerous and we can't risk anyone getting hurt, besides there could've been other bandits who took them. It would be a fool's errand."

I moaned in frustration, "I guess that makes sense."

"What should we do right now?" Jessica asked.

"Galahad has gone to find food and firewood. He should be back in an hour or so. Merlin is immobile for a while. There's not much we can do, I'd take this time to catch up on some rest. Or maybe practice your combat skills."

I looked at Jessica with questioning eyes.

"Might as well. But you'll probably beat me," she shrugged.

"Don't worry, I'll go easy on you," I winked.

The next hour or so went by quickly. Blaine stayed beside Will, frequently checking on his condition, while Jessica and I practiced with swords and bows until we got too tired to continue. She was actually starting to get really good with a sword, and she was determined to get better.

The setting sun turned the sky a bright orange over the mountaintop that was in all honesty, beautiful. I stared at the mountains ahead of us. They were monstrous. The first few were just regular mountains, but the further I looked, the more snow I saw. It was going to take a long time to get over them. Especially with no horses.

Galahad still hadn't returned from whatever he was doing out there. Will had not moved either.

"Blaine," I said casually, "would you mind going out to look for Galahad?"

He nodded courteously. "Anything you ask."

I waited till Blaine was out of sight, then I turned to Jessica and asked, "Jessica, do you still have your gun?"

"Yes, why?" she replied.

"I just wanted to make sure we still had them. We got lucky this time, seeing as it only paralyzed him, but next time it could be worse. I should be fine because I have Excalibur, but you and Will should use the guns instead of swords."

"OK, I doubt I'd do that good in a sword fight anyway. Does Will still have his?"

I knelt down and checked him.

"Why are you feeling me up, dude?" he groaned.

I laughed with relief, and helped him sit up. "You seem to be back to normal."

"Thanks. What happened?"

Jessica passed him some water. "You were bit by one of those huge snakes. I saved you. You've been paralyzed since."

"You saved me?" he asked doubtfully.

She nodded and put her hands on her hips. "What? Are you embarrassed a girl saved you?"

"Pffft ... no," he lied.

"Do you still have your gun?" I asked before Jessica could tease him again.

He pulled out the gun from the waistband of his pants and held it up. “That answer your question?”

“Maybe you should stick to using that instead of swords,” I hinted.

He picked up on it. “Yeah, we’re not as good as you are with those things. I guess it will make things easier.”

I heard rustling in the bushes so I drew my sword and Jessica aimed her gun towards the noise. Galahad and Blaine emerged. Galahad was carrying several dead rabbits, and Blaine held a bundle of firewood.

“Not quite the welcome I was expecting, but it’s good to see you’re on your guard,” Galahad said.

I sheathed the sword. “Just taking precautions,” I said. “You were gone a long time, but I see you did pretty well.”

He plopped the rabbits on the ground beside a log. “Yes, it was quite hard to find them in these parts. I see Merlin has recovered.”

“Did you bring food?” Will asked eagerly.

I laughed. “Yeah, he’ll be fine.”

Blaine set the firewood down near the rabbits. He took several sticks and we watched him arrange them to make a fire. It only took him a few minutes to successfully ignite the wood and soon flames rose from the pile. The sun had just passed over the mountains, so the fire provided us with light and heat. We huddled around the fire while Galahad used a sharp stick to roast the rabbits.

“We’re seriously going to eat that?” Jessica stared with disgust at the charred meat.

“There’s nothing wrong with rabbit, Gwen,” Blaine said. “It tastes just like chicken.”

She didn’t buy it. “So where do we go from here?” she asked, changing the subject.

Galahad used his dagger to cut the rabbit into edible portions. “The entrance to the dwarves’ kingdom is deep within the mountains. We’ll have to travel through them until we reach Tristan’s

Peak, which will take a while, seeing as it's covered in snow. Once we reach it, we'll have to climb until we reach a cave, which will lead us to the dwarves."

"So it's going to be cold from here on?" I asked.

"Yes."

"Awesome."

Galahad handed cooked rabbit to everyone. I didn't really care where the food came from, just as long as it tasted good. I tore a small piece off and shoved it in my mouth. Blaine was right; it did taste like chicken. I ate until my hands were empty. Jessica hesitantly nibbled on hers. I'm sure she was trying not to think about what she was eating. Will demolished every piece of meat given to him within seconds, and then looked at Galahad for more. Galahad shook his head and Will looked down at the ground with sad eyes.

"We should get some rest now," Galahad stated. "Tomorrow will be a long day. I'll take the first watch."

We each found a comfy spot near the fire. I closed my eyes, letting my body relax. The crackling of the flames eased me to sleep.

Excalibur visited me again, wearing his heavy cloak. This time we were in a throne room covered with gold coins and gems.

"You did well today," he greeted me.

"Don't you mean we?" I asked.

He nodded graciously, "I suppose I do, thank you for noticing."

"So, I've gotta ask … what do you do all day? I mean, I'm out there doing everything, are you just stuck here doing nothing?" I asked, waving around the room.

He chuckled as he answered, "That is a good question. My essence is tied to the sword. So when it isn't with you, I do just sit around doing nothing. But when you are in trouble, like today, I can see through your eyes and react using my power."

"Uh-huh … that's not creepy at all."

"You worry too much about the little things, Francis. Just focus on the things that are important," he paused. "Like your gift."

"My gift?"

"Your control over time of course."

"How do you know? Oh, right. The whole 'reading my mind' thing. What exactly do you want me to do?"

"Like all gifts, you must learn to control it. So far, it's only happened in times of great emotion, or peril. But if you practice, you can learn to control it, and you will be able to do so much more."

I sighed, "I understand why, but how exactly would I practice using it? I don't even know what I do when it happens."

He thought for a moment. "Try focusing on stopping time. Like you did to save the girl."

"Jessica."

"Yes, that's who I meant."

I nodded. "I should think really hard about freezing everything, and hope it works?"

"You have to start somewhere," he shrugged.

"I guess so."

He began to pull out his sword.

"Hey! Whoa there, big guy," I backed away. (What do you expect? He stabbed me last time.)

He laughed. "Relax, Francis, I only did that to see the look on your face, besides, someone is coming for you anyway."

"What do you—" I started to ask what he meant, but I was whisked back to reality.

Blaine was standing over me, between me and the campfire. "Your turn to keep watch," he said sleepily.

I rubbed my eyes, "OK, thanks."

He curled himself up in a spot near Galahad and went to sleep. I walked around for a bit to wake myself up and then sat down on the log. If I was up anyway, and everyone else was sleeping, I decided to try and use my abilities. I stared at the fire with a deep concentration. I focused on freezing everything around me. I tried as hard as I could for what seemed hours, but nothing happened.

I frowned in anger, "Stupid powers."

Time rolled on, like the moon in the sky. The stars were abundant and shining brightly. Crickets chirped incessantly. By the way, I have officially decided I hate crickets more than anything. The sound was driving me crazy.

"Get out of my head!" Will shouted, grabbing his head in pain.

I ran over to him, "Are you OK?"

His eyes were unfocused, as if he wasn't sure where he was. "Oh. Yeah. It was just a dream."

I didn't have the courage to ask him what it was that put that frightened look on his face.

"I'm up, so I might as well take over for you," he said. I knew he didn't want to talk about it.

I let him be. I walked back to where I had slept before and tried to go back to sleep. I was worried about Will. His dreams seemed way worse than mine were, and after my experience with dreaming, I wondered if there might be something more to them. I shuddered at the thought. Thankfully, the crickets stopped chirping long enough for me to fall asleep.

Excalibur wasn't in my dreams this time, which I was kind of glad for (mainly because I didn't want to get stabbed again). However, a large turtle with a top hat was. His name was Gary. Don't ask.

10 SNOW WHITE'S FRIENDS

The sun rose in a beautifully vibrant orange sky. After sleeping and living in a dark room for what seemed eternity, I was glad to open my eyes to a bright world. Galahad was already up, packing the provisions we had left.

"Do we have enough stuff to make it to the dwarves?" I asked him quietly.

He sighed, "I don't know. We'll be cutting it close. If we had the horses and the rest of our gear it would be easier, but we can't risk crossing the marsh again."

I nodded. "Do you know exactly where the cave is?"

He shook his head. "No, but Blaine seems confident that he can find it."

"What's for breakfast?" Will asked groggily.

"Rabbit," smiled Galahad.

Will groaned, loud enough to wake the others.

"Good morning," Jessica said as she stood, shaking her legs awake.

"Morning," I replied.

Galahad made a fire and began roasting another rabbit. Birds chirped a happy tune in the trees at the bottom of the mountains. Clouds drifted slowly across the sky, and fog was cast ominously over the marsh. When the food was ready, Galahad divided it into equal amounts. We ate in silence because there really wasn't much to talk about, and we were all still pretty tired.

"We should get going," Galahad said once everyone had finished eating.

"Lead the way," I gestured.

Galahad and Blaine took the lead. The first bit of walking was through the woods, which wasn't bad, and before long we reached the bottom of the mountains.

"This path should lead us through the mountains right to Tristan's Peak," Blaine said, holding a map.

"It *should* lead us there?" I asked hesitantly.

Blaine replied, "This map is quite old, but we should be able to get there without too much trouble."

"Right."

"Just trust me," he looked over his shoulder and winked.

We followed the trail along the mountains. It led us up the rocky slope, and twisted up and down and over several obstacles. The ground beneath our feet wasn't exactly stable, so a few times my feet slipped out from under me and I slid with the small rocks a few feet. We moved in a straight line, one by one. The path led us through trees, over and around rocks, and, at one point, straight up. We had to climb using both our hands and feet.

We had only begun the journey, and my body already ached. My legs burned as we climbed higher and higher up the slope. I wasn't the only one struggling either. Will was constantly complaining, and Blaine lost his footing every few steps. We did not stop for a long time. Galahad kept us at a steady pace. Eventually we reached a slope that connected to the next mountain, which had a white-capped top. The cold kicked in and permeated my body.

"How much further do we have to go?" protested Will.

Blaine checked the map and said, "We're just getting started, Merlin. Do you see that tall peak off in the distance?"

I squinted, scanning the land for the peak. A fair ways into the mountains I finally spotted it. It was much bigger than the rest, and I would guess it compared in size to Mount Everest.

And we had to climb it.

Outstanding.

"You mean that giant mountain?" exclaimed Will. "We have to go that far? And then climb it?"

Galahad nodded. "Yes, it's going to be a cold and rough journey."

"Is it too late to go back?" Will asked quietly.

"C'mon, it's just a little cold, how bad can it be?" Jessica said in a chipper tone.

It was bad. And when I say bad, I mean, it totally sucked. Picture the coldest you've ever been, and multiply it by infinity. That's how cold it was. Looking back, I would've rather risked going back to the horses, if it meant a blanket or two. By the time we reached the snow-covered mountains, my feet were numb and I couldn't feel my hands. My teeth chattered so much I felt like a cartoon character. The shiver throughout my body made it difficult to focus. Each step took all of my concentration. I could actually see the redness of my nose through the corners of my eyes and I figured my ears must have frozen clean off my head and were buried in the snow somewhere, because I couldn't feel them anymore.

"H-h-how much f-f-further?" I managed to ask as my feet crunched through the snow.

Blaine was in the lead. "Just a bit more and we'll have reached the peak."

"It's f-f-freezing," Jessica said, rubbing her hands together.

"It's just a little cold. How b-b-b-bad can it be?" Will mocked her.

Jessica didn't reply. Talking was too much effort. As if things weren't bad enough, it started to snow as we went deeper into the mountain range. The flakes swirled in every direction because of the wind. I was pretty sure I would collapse at any moment and end up a popsicle on the side of the mountain. We kept our heads down to keep the wind from striking our faces. Our feet sank into the snow up to our knees, which didn't help at all.

I had no idea where we were, or if Blaine was leading us in the right direction. Fog had rolled in, so we couldn't even see more than a few feet in front of us.

"Hang on to the person in front of you, so that we don't get separated in this weather," Galahad commanded.

We were too weak to reply, so we grabbed hold of the person in front of us. I couldn't remember what being warm felt like. My mind was so disoriented I couldn't remember ever doing anything else but trudging through the snow. If we ever made it to the dwarves alive, someone was going to pay for making me go through this.

We had begun climbing another slope, when everything went wrong. A loud cracking noise beneath my feet made me pause. I figured I was hearing things, so I took another step. Bad idea. The ground beneath me gave away. I let go of Jessica, who was in front of me, as I was dragged down the mountain. Will, who was behind me, tumbled along with me and we grabbed onto each other. It was an avalanche. The last thing I saw was Jessica, shouting and reaching her hand for us. The snow pushed us down the slope at an alarming rate. Will clung to my arm for dear life as we were tossed through the snow. The terror of it all made me try and yell for help, but all I got was a mouthful of snow.

After a few moments of sliding, I was able to get my head out of the snow long enough to see where we were going. It was a cliff. Then I really panicked. My mind reeled as I tried to think of something to save us. All that came to mind was something I had seen in the movies once.

"Hang on to me!" I shouted to Will.

I pulled out Excalibur and shoved it as deep as I could in the snow. It dug itself into the hard-packed snow and we started to slow down. My arm burned from holding the sword, but miraculously I felt the sword catch on something and our momentum stopped completely. We were only a few feet away from the cliff's edge. The snow from the small avalanche continued to roll past us like a freight train. My right arm clung tightly to Excalibur, while my left held Will. His feet dangled over the edge. I screamed in pain from the weight my body was holding (I'm not exactly built like Arnold Schwarzenegger).

"Will, you need to use your sword, I can't hold you for much longer," I grunted.

He let go of me with his right hand and hastily pulled out his sword. He slammed it into the ground like I had done. He tested the stability cautiously. When he was convinced that the sword was firmly planted, he let go of my arm, releasing a tremendous burden of weight from me (and no, I'm not calling him fat). I rolled over and held onto Excalibur with both hands. I could see Will was doing the same with his sword. We could hear shouting further up the mountain, and I knew the others were trying to help us.

"There's no way they can reach us," I said to him.

He nodded. "What do we do?"

I had no idea. Then suddenly a light went on in my head. I let go of Excalibur with one hand, grabbed one of the fist knives from my shoulder, and handed it to Will.

"Thanks, but I don't think I can fight a mountain with this, buddy."

"Shut up. Use it and the sword together, and we might be able to climb up," I said, pulling the second one out for myself.

I dug into the snow with the fist knife, placing it a bit higher up the mountain than we were, and it held. I pulled Excalibur out of the snow and punched it back in above the knife. Sure enough, it held. It seemed I had found a way to climb back up to the others. Will mimicked what I had done. It was exhausting, but the glance over the cliff was all the incentive we needed to find the strength to keep going until we were high enough that the others could help us. As they pulled us up, I collapsed to the ground. My body was toast. My arms were strained beyond reason, and I was not only physically at my end, but mentally as well from the near-death experience. Will didn't look so good either. The cold stung with an unforgiving bitterness.

"Are you OK?" Jessica asked. She had tears in her eyes.

"The ground beneath us collapsed and we were thrown into an avalanche," I stated the obvious.

"We'll rest for a minute, but not too long, or else we'll freeze to death. It's not much further to Tristan's Peak," Galahad encouraged.

"I don't know if I can keep going," I said. "I can't feel my hands."

Jessica sat beside me and held my hands to warm them up. "We're almost there; you can make it. I've seen you get through worse."

I tried to smile. "Thanks."

Blaine held out the map. "One more pass and we'll reach it. We can't stop now. If we stop, Camelot will perish, as will we. We need to keep going."

"Will it be warm?" Will asked Blaine.

"What?"

"Will the dwarves' home be warm?"

"Yes, yes it will." (I don't think Blaine really knew.)

"Then I say, we suck it up and keep moving," Will said, surprising me with his attitude. He stood, and I found the strength to stand as well.

We all knew we needed to get someplace warm–and fast. Blaine led the way through the pass. Large peaks surrounded us as we moved closer to our goal. They towered over us ominously, like claws about to close in on us. Sharp icicles hung from the edges of the cliffs. We hiked until we reached a gap. Our mountain was connected to the next by an icy bridge. A small entrance to a cave awaited us on the other side. The five of us stood at the edge of the bridge, staring across the chasm. The bridge was just wide enough for one person to walk on, and it wasn't that thick.

"Is it safe?" I asked.

Galahad cautiously crouched down and placed his palm on the ice. "It should hold, but we'll need to go one at a time," he said. "And just in case it does collapse, I have a rope in my pack that we'll tie to one another for support."

"So who's going first?" Jessica asked.

We stared at her.

"No," she backed away. "No, no, no, no, no. There's no way I'm going first."

"Dearest Gwen, you're the lightest out of all of us, and we don't want it to collapse," Galahad explained.

"We'll be supporting you with the rope the entire way. If you fall, we'll pull you up," Blaine reassured.

"That doesn't inspire confidence," she said, staring across the bridge.

Blaine smiled as he tied the rope around her. "You'll be fine."

"For the record, I hate you guys."

Once Galahad (the heaviest of the group) had the rope secured around his waist, Jessica nervously stepped towards the Icy Bridge of Doom (that was the official name I gave the bridge). She hesitantly placed one foot on it. The ice creaked and moaned as she took a step forward. Step by step she inched her way across, with her arms out for balance. After what seemed like a lifetime, she reached the other side safely. She untied herself and Galahad pulled the rope back to the other side.

"You're next," Galahad motioned me to step forward.

The rope was fastened around my waist and I approached the bridge. I looked down. Bad idea. I couldn't even see the bottom of the cliff. I took a step onto the bridge. It was icy and hard to keep a solid footing on it without sliding. I moved slowly across, keeping my balance because there was no way I was going to fall to my death. The bridge groaned as I crossed it, but I made it through without slipping, so I was happy.

"Not as bad as I thought it would be," I said to Jessica when I reached the other side.

She frowned. "Well, I'm not doing it again."

Will was now making his way across. About halfway, he lost his footing, slipping on the icy surface. Jess and I gasped as Will went down. Will clung to the bridge on his stomach. His eyes were shut and he held tightly onto the sides.

"Am I alive?" he asked, freaked out of his mind.

"Just go slowly, you're almost there, buddy," I encouraged.

"Oh God, why did I let you talk me into this?" he asked, as he crawled the rest of the way.

When he was close enough for us to help him, we pulled him to safety. I untied Will and gave Blaine the thumbs up sign (I'm not sure he knew what I meant by it though). He nodded, tied himself to the rope, and began to move across the bridge. The bridge made its cracking noise, and he hurried the rest of the way. He remained tied to the rope and nodded to Galahad. From the second he set foot on the Icy Bridge of Doom, I knew it wouldn't hold him. He made it four steps, and then the bridge shattered.

It happened in slow motion. Cracking noises echoed across the chasm. Galahad looked up at us. His eyes locked on mine, and we both knew exactly what was happening. The bridge exploded into hundreds of pieces and Galahad disappeared into the endless pit. That was when things sped up. Instinctively, the three of us not tied to the rope grabbed Blaine to secure him in place. While we braced ourselves, there was a sudden yank that pulled us two feet forward. We dug our heels in hard to prevent ourselves from going over the edge. The rope held, and inch by inch we pulled Galahad up the side of the cliff. After several long pulls, we had him up.

Galahad exhaled as he said nervously, “See, that wasn’t so bad, now was it?”

I was still shaking. “It’s good to see you’re OK.”

He nodded. “I’ll be better once I’m out of this godforsaken cold.”

We all agreed and we hurried into the cave. The second we entered it I noticed two things. One, it felt so freaking good to get out of the snow. I felt instantly better as my body became less numb. Two, it was pitch black. I could not see anything or any of the others. Suddenly, something cold, metallic, and sharp pressed against my throat.

“Hey guys, anyone got a light?” I asked. Truth be told, I was scared to death.

“What’s going on?” Jessica’s panic-filled voice cut through the darkness.

“It seems we are not alone,” came Galahad’s shaky voice.

Someone lit a torch. The light illuminated probably one of the scariest sights I’d seen. Short, fat, bearded men, who I assumed were the dwarves, surrounded us. At about my waist level was a fearsome looking man with a wicked brown beard. I mean, the thing was monstrous (but that’s probably not the most important detail you need to know right now). He held an axe, which was the metal I felt against my throat. I didn’t dare move my body, but I surveyed the situation with my eyes. There were ten dwarves in the cave. Five of them were holding an axe to the five of us, and the others stood in front of a door at the back of the cave. They had axes too. I guess axes are standard issue for dwarves. One of them also had the torch. The flame on the torch flickered from the wind that entered the cave.

I'm sure there were other details, but that's the gist of it. I mean, give me a break–I had an axe against my throat.

None of us moved, none of us spoke, and none of us tried to do anything. We stood there, eyeing each other up. The dwarf in front of me glared with intense brown eyes. There was a loud thump and the back door opened. Out stepped another dwarf. He was wearing armor, similar Galahad's (only much, much smaller), and he had a long, gray beard. His axe was over his right shoulder.

"What are you doing here?" he asked in a deep, husky voice.

I knew I was the one to speak, so I chose my words carefully.

"My name is Arthur, and I am the King of Camelot. According to prophecy, a war is coming upon Camelot, and we came to ask for your help. We come in peace." (I always wanted to say that.)

The dwarf did not say anything for several long seconds. He stared me down, then eyed the rest of our group.

"Follow," he growled.

We didn't really have a choice. The dwarves lowered their weapons and shoved us in front of them. We traveled in a single file line, alternating one of us with one of them. Gray Beard led the way, after having grabbed the torch. There was a tunnel on the other side of the door that sloped down, deeper into the mountain. I looked around. There weren't any places for torches to hang, or any type of lighting at all. The tunnel was perfectly round and smooth, except for the ground, which was flat. If not for the axe nudging my back every few minutes, I might've found it extremely cool. We were in that tunnel forever! It kept going and going and going.

I could babble on about it, but what you need to know is that the tunnel seemed endless. Every now and then it split off in two directions, but there was never a light down either way. We walked in silence the entire time; the only sound was the crunch of dirt beneath our feet. I had no idea where we were going, but I didn't have a good feeling about it. Eventually it began to open up. The sides disappeared and we entered a long cavern. The torch only lit up a small area around us, but I could sense the width of the place. After walking a little bit further, the flicker of the flame brought a throne into view.

A husky dwarf wearing a golden crown sat on the giant, earthen throne. His silver beard glowed in the dim light. He wore dark boots, and a cloak covered his golden armor. A giant hammer leaned against the throne to his right. It was no doubt the biggest hammer I ever saw. I mean, it was almost as big as the dwarf himself. Its handle was made of some type of dark material, maybe wood, while the end itself was pure steel.

"What is this?" he hissed in anger. "You brought outsiders?"

The dwarf with the gray beard knelt before him. "Forgive me, King Backura, but they spoke of the prophecy."

"Why should we help these outsiders after they abandoned us last time?"

He seems like a nice guy, I thought.

Gray Beard shifted nervously as he replied, "It is not my place to make that decision, Great One, but perhaps we should hear what they have to say. They did manage to make it to the entrance at Tristan's Peak."

The dwarves' king thought long before answering, "Very well. Speak, outsiders. But do not waste my time."

Blaine gave me an encouraging nod. I stepped forward and the dwarf guarding me backed away to let me speak.

"My name is Arthur. I pulled Excalibur from the stone a few days ago, and have become the new King of Camelot," I paused, letting my words sink in. "Prophecy says that a war is coming. There are enemies who want Excalibur's power for themselves.

The prophecy instructed us to ask old allies for help. That's why we've come, to ask for your help. Without you, we won't stand a chance at winning."

The king dwarf, Backura, stared at me. Again, he did not speak for a long time. He stroked his beard as he thought. Finally he stood. He picked up his hammer and walked straight up to me. We would have been face to face, but he was really short. So it was more like face to chest.

"I have no desire to help you, Arthur. I do not care for humans. You brought this war upon yourself, so you should have to face the consequences. We won't be affected by who wins or loses. We will still be here in our peaceful mountains, where we hear nothing but the sound of hammer on dirt, and have no odor but the smell of aged ale. Besides, you haven't offered us anything in return."

I had no idea asking them for help was going to be this difficult. "Perhaps you will allow my friends and I to try and come up with something to convince you to help us?"

Backura pondered for a moment. "Very well," he replied.

He walked back up to his throne and sat down, while I brought our group in for a huddle. "OK, anyone have any ideas?"

"Dwarves are greedy creatures. They have an obsession with shiny objects, which is one of the reasons they stay in the mountains, to dig for jewels," Blaine explained.

"Great, do we have anything shiny?" Jessica asked.

"Not with us."

"Well, that was a good idea," Will rolled his eyes.

"Wait!" exclaimed Galahad. "We might be able to convince them if we offer to allow them to keep the gold from the enemies we defeat. Each kingdom has a stash of gold and wealth in their keep. We will give the dwarves that gold in exchange for their help."

"Awesome! Good thinking," I said, breaking out of the huddle.

"I think we have come up with a plan that will interest you."

"Go on," Backura said flatly.

"You must know that each kingdom has its own share of wealth. If you help us defeat our enemies in this war, we would give you all of the gold, jewels, and prized collections from the enemies' treasure stores."

Backura's eyes twinkled, "That is rather intriguing."

He motioned for Gray Beard to come to his side. They whispered back and forth for a few seconds, and then laughed heartedly. Gray Beard stepped back to his place.

"We will send our warriors, who would make Thor himself proud by the way, on one more condition."

I hesitated, "What condition?"

He smiled a sly, disgusting smile. "We have dug this mountain hollow, and have run out of places to mine. We would move to other mountains, but the rock is too solid to break from the underside. We would move outside and tunnel in if it weren't for one thing."

Uh-oh. I could see where this was going. "The dragon," I offered.

"The dragon," he affirmed. "It is quite the pest and will kill us. Frankly, I'm surprised you made it here without running into it. If you kill this dragon, we will fight by your side."

The room fell silent. I was mad.

Greedy, no-good jerk! I thought to myself. *You're not satisfied with a bunch of gold and jewels, so you want me to kill a dragon?* I won't lie. I wanted to punch him.

"And if I don't want to fight this dragon?" I asked sharply.

"Then we do not fight with you."

"I see."

I went back to my group huddle. "Is there any way we can avoid fighting a dragon?"

Blaine shook his head as he answered, "I warned you, the dwarves are greedy, smelly creatures. You won't be able to change his mind. And we need them."

"So we have to fight it?" Jessica asked.

Galahad nodded.

I separated from the group and faced the king. "Fine. If we kill this dragon, you'd better have one impressive army helping us."

"We?" he asked slyly.

"Yes. We. Me and my friends."

He smiled a cold, dark smile.

"No," I said, realizing what he meant. "No, you can't expect me to fight a dragon on my own."

Backura nodded to his guards, who immediately seized my friends. There was nothing they could do. "I want to see if this Excalibur is worth fighting for. If it has the power you say it does, you should be able to kill the dragon."

"Alone? Are you serious? The gold alone should be enough for you!" I was ticked.

He shook his head. "The gold is worth it for sure, but I hold my fellow dwarves before gold. I don't want to send them to fight, and possibly die, for something that will have no effect on the world."

My mind raced, trying to find a way out, but I came up with nothing. I tried sheer frustration, "So you expect me to abandon my friends and fight a freaking dragon on my own?"

"Yes, because if you don't, we will put all of you to work in the mines. And you don't want that, do you?"

"Just do it Arthur," Will encouraged. "How hard can it be? Besides, I don't want to work in the dark."

"We'd supply you with torches," Backura said.

"Speaking of which, why are there no torches anywhere? I can barely see where I'm going," Jessica asked.

"We can see perfectly in the dark. Our eyes have evolved to adjust to both darkness and light. It's one of the reasons we like it underground, because it's as clear as day to us."

"Aren't we getting a little off topic here?" I shouted.

I heard Will whisper under his breath, "That's so cool."

"King Arthur, do you accept my terms, or do you choose to spend your remaining life in the mines?" Backura asked harshly.

"I accept," I spat.

"Good, you may accompany your companions to their cells before you leave."

"How kind of you," I let my voice drip with sarcasm.

We were forced out of the hallway down a passage to our right. Gray Beard led us down the twisting tunnel until we reached a pit. It was round, about fifteen feet deep, and five feet wide.

"Down you go," he said, gesturing at the pit.

"This royally sucks," declared Will, climbing down.

One by one I watched my friends climb down until only Blaine was left. He approached me and whispered in my ear, "Tread carefully, Arthur. Our lives are in your hands. I'm sure you'll be fine, but keep in mind, a dragon's scales are impenetrable by any mortal weapon. And dragons are immortal."

"What?" I hissed "This sword might not even work on it?"

He shrugged. "Good luck," he said as he disappeared down into the pit.

Fantastic.

So let's sum up my position here. I have to kill a dragon (once again, so it can sink in, a DRAGON), which can't be hurt by any weapon, so that the dwarves will not only help us, but also release my friends. I officially hated my life at that moment. But I did have an idea.

"Will, toss me your … erm … crossbow."

"What?"

"You know," I winked, "the thing, from The Island?"

The light bulb clicked. "Ohhh! Right. The crossbow. Here you go, buddy, no pressure or anything, but if you don't kill that thing, we're stuck here," he said, tossing me the gun.

"Yeah I got that."

"Just making sure."

"Of course."

"Because we'd be working in a mine."

"I said I got it!" I shouted.

The light was terrible, but I could tell he was smiling. I tucked Will's gun, and mine, into my shoulder bag. I walked away from the pit, and my friends. I was going to take on a dragon.

Alone.

11 DRAGON? REALLY?

I was led back to the king's throne room through the dark, stinky tunnels. I didn't have time to notice before (seeing as there was an axe at my throat), but every single dwarf smelled terrible! The overwhelming stench wasn't coming from the dirt. It was coming from them. I couldn't believe a person could smell so bad. It was like they didn't shower, which, as soon as I had that thought, led me to believe that they didn't shower.

We reached the throne room and Backura was still lounging on his chair, doing absolutely nothing … except ticking me off. The guy was unbelievably greedy and manipulative. If I didn't kill this dragon, my friends would be condemned to an eternity of mining in a mountain. I could not bear that burden. A thousand thoughts raced through my mind as I was brought before Backura.

Why me? Why does it have to be a dragon? What if I can't do it? How can I kill something that can't be hurt by any weapon? Would my gun work? Would Excalibur? I won't go on, but there were a lot more questions in there.

My feet dragged lazily across the dirt. Even though we'd been inside for a while, my hands were still cold, as if a sharp wind was pounding them. My eyes burned with anger as I approached Backura.

"I've let you say goodbye to your friends, is there anything else you'll be needing for your … excursion?" he said it like he was doing me the biggest favor in the world.

I was mad, but I kept my cool, "As a matter of fact, there is."

His eyes narrowed. "Such as?"

I took a deep breath. "I'll need four strong daggers, some rope, some cloth, and some food," I requested.

Backura stared at me for several minutes before whispering in the ear of the dwarf next to him. He looked back at me and answered, "Very well. King Arthur, I wish you luck with the dragon, but if you do not return, I can make do parting with a few knives in exchange for your companions' work in the mines." His cold, dark laugh sent shivers down my spine.

He knew I had no choice but to fight the dragon. If I didn't, my friends would be forced into the mines, and if I died, they would still go to the mines. I was beginning to regret ever going on this quest.

"I know the consequences, but if I succeed, you will let me and my friends go, and you will help us in the war."

He waved his hand, "Yes, yes, I know."

I said with confidence, "You'd better."

Two dwarves escorted me to place where we had first entered the mountain. When we reached the room, I could see that the knives, rope, food, and cloth were waiting for me. Originally I was going to use the daggers to help my friends somehow, but that wouldn't work because I couldn't navigate in the dark through the tunnels.

A thought popped into my head. I asked, "Where does this dragon even live?"

It hadn't even occurred to me before now. I was more concerned with how I would kill it than where it was.

One of the dwarves answered, "The dragon dwells in a cave at the top of Tristan's Peak. You'll have to climb to get there."

"What?" I asked.

"The dragon resides at the top of the mountain. There is no path, so you shall have to climb."

"Great. So now I not only have to kill a dragon, but I have to climb a freezing cold mountain in order to do it," I muttered to myself.

I stared at the equipment I had been given, and then stepped outside the cave quickly to see what I was up against. The rest of the mountain was steep, icy, and looked impossible to climb. *If I make it through this, I'm going to kill Backura*, I thought.

I went back inside where it was warm. Even that short time outside chilled my body. The snow was blowing like crazy. I knelt down beside the cloth and began to cut it into different sizes. One piece I used to cover my face, except for my eyes, and the others I used for my hands and body. There was no way I was going to get halfway up there and freeze to death. I packed the food, which consisted of meat and bread, into pouches of my clothes. I cut the rope into 3 pieces, one long and two small. I used each of the small pieces of rope to tie the daggers to my boots, so that the blade was sticking out in front of the toes of the boots. I flung the rest of the rope over my shoulder and grabbed the remaining two knives, one in each hand, and went out into the cold.

I stabbed the daggers into the wall of ice in front of me. Next, I kicked one of my boots into the ice wall to see if the dagger would go in. It did. I kicked in the other and stood there for a full minute to test if the four knives would support my weight. I didn't slip or fall, so I kept going. My dad took me rock climbing when I was a kid, and it felt a bit like that, except there was no support rope if I fell. I moved slowly up the side of the mountain by stabbing each dagger in a little bit higher than the last. I would move as far as I could with the knives in my hands, and then use the ones tied to my feet to catch up. It was actually working better than I thought it would.

Progress was slow and painful. The wind and snow whipped at my back relentlessly. My eyes burned from the cold, and my arms and legs were getting tired. I constantly fought the urge to look down. I glanced up the slope for any sign of a flat edge I could sit and rest on. About twenty feet up, there appeared to be a platform.

Just a little bit further, I told myself, straining to find the energy to continue. I pushed onward, despite the numbness taking over my body. I reached the platform and felt my body relax as the weight came off my hands and toes and transferred to my butt. I sat for several minutes, resting and taking long, deep breaths.

It dawned on me that the higher I went, the harder it would be to breathe. The view was exhilarating. I would have enjoyed it, if not for the freezing cold…and the fact I was probably going to be eaten to death. But other than that, it was quite beautiful. Jagged peaks stretched up endlessly, twisting and turning their way through the sky. Clouds filled the stormy skies, blocking out any view of the sun. I rubbed my hands together for warmth, but I had gotten so cold that I was beginning to have a hard time feeling parts of my fingers. My body shivered worse than it ever had before, and I knew I was in trouble.

What was I thinking, trying to be king? Thinking I could make a difference? Now I was going to freeze to death in the middle of nowhere. Even if I managed to survive this weather, how on earth can I fight a dragon?

I jumped up and down to warm up as much as possible. I stared up at the remaining section I had to climb. It was huge. I let out a deep breath.

I hate this, I thought. I gripped the two daggers firmly and began again. With each stab into the icy mountain, chunks of snow tumbled to their doom. I tried not to think about how far I would fall if I slipped. The bitter cold slowed my progress, increasing my hate considerably. The air was thin and it felt like oxygen was abandoning me. I pushed forward, determined not to die out in the cold.

The wind picked up. Imagine the coldest you've ever been. I guarantee you it doesn't even compare to how I felt.

As I neared the summit, trouble struck. I dug the knife in my left hand into the mountainside, when the ice broke. I gripped tightly to the three remaining daggers. Fear and adrenaline coursed through my body. I swung the knife back into the mountain, this time making sure it stuck.

That was a close one, I thought as I looked down. That probably wasn't the greatest idea, because it was a long ways down. I'd have thrown up if I could have.

After that scare, I decided to move slower and more carefully. My system worked pretty well, until I reached a crack in the mountain's side. It was a small gap, but there wasn't a safer way to keep going up. I studied the crack before I made an attempt to climb it. It was a deep gash, about three or four feet wide, and continued into the mountain farther than I could see. It was a tight fit, but I managed to squeeze through. I walked through the crack for as long as I could. The icy crevice rocketed upward at a steep angle. I inched my way further through the gap until I reached a point where it narrowed. I could go on no longer. I peered up, wondering how to get up the icy cliff's side. I pushed my back against one side, and placed both my feet on the opposite wall. From there I was able to inch my way through the crack by moving my back up slowly, followed by my feet, using the two walls as leverage.

It was tough, and at times I found it difficult to continue because it was either too slippery or, I'll admit, it scared the crap out of me. The ice melted against my back because of my body heat, soaking through my clothes, which made the harsh cold sting even more. I moved up through the gash in the mountain, like a worm crawling through the dirt. There was no sound, save for the hiss of the wind as it blew past. Breathing became more and more difficult. If I didn't reach the top soon, I knew I would die.

I'm not going to let that happen.

I picked up my pace. My head spun, like when you stand up

too fast and you get dizzy. But this was worse, because I was climbing a mountain. As I braced myself against the frozen wall, my mind wandered through a barren wasteland of memories. The cold was winning. Images flashed through my head; the crash, The Island, my family, my friends … Jessica. I snapped back to reality. I couldn't let them down. Every part of my body felt like dying, but I couldn't do it. I kept climbing.

I didn't even notice that I had reached the top of the crack until I pushed back and found nothing but space behind me. I stood on the ledge, stretched my limbs, and inhaled deep breaths. I took in my surroundings. I was up so high that fog and clouds were well below me, and I gasped at the sight before me. A giant black hole was cut into the mountaintop. It was a cave. It had to be the entrance to the dragon's lair. I pulled Excalibur from its sheath and carefully walked towards the opening. As I neared, I could see the entrance was way bigger than I thought it was. It was at least twenty feet high and was even wider than it was tall (please don't ask for precise measurements, because I've never been good at math).

Anyways, the cave was huge. My jaw dropped as I thought with dismay, *if this was the entrance, how big was this dragon?* The unknown fear of what lurked in the dark gripped me. I cautiously stepped out of the unforgiving wind and cold and into the mouth of the cave. I warmed immediately. It was like opening an oven door.

The cave must have a built-in heater, I thought. Then I nearly fainted as I realized the heater was probably the dragon. I sat, letting the warmth engulf me like a blanket, and I took in my surroundings. Large spikes of rock jutted from the ground and ceiling. Despite their size, they looked delicate and unstable. The cave walls were rippled, like when you throw a stone in a pond. My eye caught the glint of metal, so I walked forward to investigate. I wished I hadn't. The shiny metal was armor, and it covered the charred remains of a person. As I looked around, sure enough, there were more bodies, bones, and armor.

Not exactly the encouragement I need right now, I shuddered.

My eyes darted back and forth, searching for any sign of the beast. There was none. Only an eerie silence that sent cold chills through me. Every step I took echoed through the cavern. I continued forward, really hoping I wouldn't die.

As I went deeper, it got warmer. Soon, I was practically sweating. Then, the ground suddenly stopped, and dropped sharply. The sight in front of me was exhilarating. The cave opened up completely, and it looked like the entire top of the mountain was hollowed out. In the middle of the roof, where the peak of the mountain should be, was a gaping hole, filling the empty cavern with light. The same rock spikes I saw when I entered the cavern were everywhere. Thousands. But these were much larger than the others. They were tight together on the ground, making a deadly obstacle course. To my left, a large winding staircase led downward.

What does a dragon need stairs for? I wondered.

I began my descent into the cavern. The stairs were carved into the stone. It was quiet, except for my steps which continued to echo through the cave. I sheathed Excalibur and took out my gun. If a dragon appeared anywhere in this cave, I wouldn't be able to get close enough to use a sword. As I neared the bottom of the stairs, my nose started to twitch. A foul stench drifted through the air. It was worse than the smell from Charles' hut.

To avoid filling my head with the smell, I breathed through my mouth. I kept the gun ready, using it as my eyes to scout the area for any sign of movement. Cautiously, I navigated the spiked maze. That's when I heard it. It was the slightest noise, but unmistakable. Somewhere in the cavern clumps and thuds of loose rock tumbled. It didn't last long, and wasn't that loud, but it happened. I wasn't alone. I dove behind a large spike and placed my back against it, listening. I peeked an eye to where I thought the noise came from, but the echoes made it impossible to tell. I remained crouched, and ready for anything.

A gust of wind hit me from the other side. I quickly moved behind another spike and pointed the gun where I had been. The sound of tumbling rocks again echoed through the cavern.

It's toying with me. It knows I'm here, and it's playing with me.

I kept my eyes open, searching for any sign of it. I saw something I hadn't noticed. Claw marks scarred the spike I was hiding behind. I looked around and noticed the others bore the same. This knowledge gave me an advantage.

It's hanging on to the spikes, I realized. *That's the cause of the noise. It is flying from spike to spike, trying to throw me off.*

Another cluster of falling rocks confirmed my theory.

How can I fight something that I can't see?

A chuckle bounced off the walls of the ginormous cavern. My body convulsed in shivers as I ran through the spikes, trying to find a safer spot. I slid under a rocky ledge, and my eyes wildly scanned the ceiling. That laugh hadn't come from me, but how could it have come from the dragon?

I felt the impact before I realized what was happening. The ledge was smashed from above, leaving me out in the open. Another sinister laugh drifted through the air. I ran like crazy to another spot, this time ducking behind several spikes. This time I was ready. When the gust of wind passed over me I dropped to my stomach. An instant later, three of the spikes near me were smashed in half. Pieces of rock bounced off my body. I needed to do something, and fast, or I would be dinner. I fired the gun once, launching a metal rod through the darkness to where I thought the dragon went. The electrical pulses lit the darkness, giving me a brief glimpse of the dragon.

It was big. It moved faster than I could keep track. I fired rods into the darkness, until the entire cavern was lit. Then I saw it. It clung to a large spike near the top of the cave. Its roar made me cover my ears. The ferocity of it sent vibrations that shook the cave violently, causing some of the spikes to fall. I jumped to the side, to avoid one that was heading right for me. I barely dodged it, but more were heading my way. I got to my feet quickly and ran like mad through the cave, twisting in and out to stay clear of falling spikes. In the commotion, I lost track of the dragon.

I whipped my head around, searching for it. I caught sight of it from the corner of my eye as it plummeted towards me, breathing fire out of its mouth. I side-stepped and the blaze landed right where I had been standing. The dragon flew past, leaving a wake of fire in its path. The flames didn't die down. They burned as if fueled by gasoline or something. I ran through the spikes, trying to hide from the great beast. It moved too fast for me to make out any of its details. I ducked behind another spike to catch my breath. I poked my head out, looking for the dragon. The fire had provided me with light and now I could view the entire cavern without squinting. The dragon was above, hanging, and stared straight into my eyes.

It was bigger than a fully-grown elephant. The wings were jet black and leathery. They stretched out much farther than I could've thought possible. Its body was also black, but was scaly, like a lizard, and golden orbs glowed from its eye sockets. Each wing bore three claws, and its legs and arms were bulky, with large points extending from its elbows and knees. Its tail was long, and had seven silver bony spikes protruding from it. Its head was long too, and was adorned with horns–two from the back and several from the sides. It roared again, and I could see three rows of razor sharp teeth glistening in the firelight.

I was terrified.

No. I was more than terrified.

I had no clue what to do, or how to fight it.

So I screamed. It wasn't a girly scream, but let's call it more of a war-cry. As I screamed, I fired off as many shots as I could with the gun, while charging towards it. As I got closer I realized that the rods were just bouncing off of the dragon.

Not good.

I could have sworn I saw the dragon smiling at me. It wasn't a casual, 'let's be best friends' smile, this was more of an, 'I'm going to eat you' smile.

Yup, I'm screwed, I thought. I felt glued to the floor. But then chaos broke loose. The dragon lunged at me, snapping its teeth wildly. I dove out of the way, but the dragon was faster. It clipped me in the side, mid-air, and I was flung into the side of a spike. I was disorientated and the cave was spinning around me. My left side burned with pain. I held my hand against it and when I looked down I could see it was covered in blood.

How did you think it was going to turn out? I thought to myself, collapsing to my knees.

The dragon landed in front of me with a thump that shook the mountain. Dust and dirt kicked up where its feet landed. I pulled out Excalibur, and forced myself to look into its eyes. It smiled again, and opened its mouth. I held the sword in front of me. I had planned to attack, but realized I was too weak. The sword just hung in front of me. I heard the dragon inhale, and the next moment fire ignited in its mouth, which it launched at my face.

"Oh sh—"

Shoot … I said shoot.

I shut my eyes, hoping death would be quick and painless. I could tell the fire surrounded me. It was a burning, intense heat. But I felt no pain.

I opened my eyes. The fire came steadily from the dragon, but Excalibur was blocking it from hitting me. Instead of allowing it to burn me to a crisp, Excalibur redirected it. The dragon ran out of breath, and the fire stopped.

I don't know what you did Excalibur, but thank you! I thought.

The dragon stared at me, and narrowed its eyes. "That's Excalibur isn't it?" it said.

Yeah, the dragon talked.

"What?" I asked, shocked. The pain from my side was excruciating.

"I said, that's Excalibur, isn't it?" it repeated with a voice so deep the ground trembled slightly. It spoke with a slight accent that I couldn't place.

"Umm, yeah," I said, my mind trying to grasp the fact that this thing was talking.

It sighed, "Well, this is awkward."

"What?" I asked again.

"You're not the smartest person, are you? You do know what awkward means, don't you?" it snapped, obvious anger in its voice.

"Yeah …"

"Then what's so confusing?"

"You can talk."

"Of course I can talk," he spat. "What? Did you think I was just some stupid beast? You humans are all the same, barging into my home, trying to kill me—which is impossible by the way—waking me up with your shouting and you don't even taste good."

"You can … talk."

It rolled its glowing golden eyes. "Of all the people to show up here with Excalibur, I get stuck with the incompetent one," it said.

"Hey!" I shouted, but I shut up quickly because my side burned with pain.

"Oh yeah, sorry about that," the dragon said, nodding at my side.

I stared at him. "Sorry?" I shrieked. "A second ago you were trying to turn me into a well-done steak."

He snorted, and smoke came from its nostrils. "I thought you were just another punk, trying to kill me."

"Well … I was. But that's not the point," I said, trying to make sense of everything. "What exactly just happened?"

The dragon groaned. It replied, "You mean to tell me that you pulled Excalibur, climbed my mountain, and you don't even know that Excalibur is the only weapon that can hurt me?"

"…Sure," I said. But I was still confused. "So why exactly are you not eating me right now?"

"I am a creature of ancient magic. The same magic that created Excalibur," he began. "No mortal weapon can harm a dragon, but since Excalibur was made from the old magic, it is the only thing that can hurt me … other than another dragon. Excalibur was too powerful for a common man, so it was cast in the stone. Only someone who is honest, pure, and has a great destiny could pull it out. You must be more than an ordinary human, and for that reason, certain creatures respect you.

"Excalibur has unimaginable power, such that it prevented you from being scorched by my flame. As soon as I realized you were the one, I became bound to the old magic to protect you. Do you understand?"

My side was pulsating in pain but I nodded. "Yeah, I guess. So are you like my … ally now?"

He nodded, advancing towards me and breathed warm air on my side. "Whether I like it or not."

At first I was creeped out, mainly because he was terrifying up close (but also because his breath was terrible). I had no idea what he was doing, until the pain in my side disappeared. I looked down and the cuts were gone. There wasn't even a scar.

"How did you do that?" I asked, standing to my feet.

"I told you, I am a creature of the ancient magic," he replied.

"Thank you," I said, still rubbing my hand over where the gash had been. "So what happens now?"

"Now, you can feel free to stop asking stupid questions."

I smiled. "I think we're going to get along just fine."

The dragon eyed me. "You're different than other men I've encountered."

"I'll take that as a complement."

"Hmm," the dragon pondered. "Perhaps I might be able to put up with you."

"That's good, because I could use your help ..." I paused, not knowing his name.

"Silas. My name is Silas, not that anyone cares to ask. And what exactly did you have in mind?"

"Well my name's Arthur, and when I pulled this stupid thing out of the stone," I gestured at Excalibur, "I started a war, and there's this prophecy that says I have to get the elves and dwarves to help us fight, or else the world will crumble into chaos. The dwarves agreed to help if I gave them a bunch of gold … and killed you."

Silas cocked his head to the side. "Typical dwarves," he said. "Greedy and stupid is how I would describe each and every one of them. So are you going to kill me now, Arthur?"

I shook my head. "That would just be stupid, seeing as you're actually on my side. I'm not the biggest fan of the dwarves either. They're holding my friends prisoner and if I don't return in one piece, they'll be forced to work in the mines."

Silas laughed. "I guess ol' Backura has it out for me."

"Why's that?" I asked.

"I was here long before the dwarves. When they came and started mining and digging through the mountains, I might've attacked them several times. It's just amusing to see their tiny bodies roll down the mountain; I don't actually eat them. Sheep are much tastier. We've been constantly fighting each other ever since."

"You just attack and throw them down the mountain for fun?"

"Yes."

"Interesting," I paused. An idea came to me, "What do you say we scare the crap out of some dwarves?"

Silas smiled. "Sounds great."

"Alright, but is there any way you could carry me down there? Because I really do not want to climb down that mountain."

"I suppose so. No human has ever ridden a dragon before, but I think I can make an exception for you."

I walked towards him and he crouched down so I could climb onto his back. "Thank you."

Silas' scales were razor sharp and I cut myself several times as I climbed up. They were harder than steel and glistened in the light like a firefly. I positioned myself so that I was in front of his wings and behind his long neck.

"Are you holding on?" he asked calmly.

"Yeah," I said. I grasped his neck tightly.

"Then here we go."

Silas launched himself with ease and flapped his wings, ascending to the top of the cave. He gave one last pump of his wings, folded them in, and shot through the opening. The wind and snow lashed at me, but Silas' body was so warm that I barely felt it. He was like a heater. He circled the peak of the mountain, and then plummeted toward the entrance to the dwarves' lair. That flight was one I will never forget. The air in my face and the freedom in the endless skies were simply amazing. My joy was cut short when I realized blood was rushing along my hands. I was holding onto Silas for dear life, and his scales were so sharp, they sliced up my hands.

Silas rocketed through the snow and wind, until we reached the platform where the ice bridge had been. He stretched out his wings and we slowly hovered above the entrance to the cave.

"Let me off here," I shouted. "I'll go in and get Backura to come out, and then you can roar and do your fire thing to scare him, but don't kill him okay?"

He smiled. "I can't make any promises."

I jumped from his back to avoid sliding on the sharp scales, and landed in the powdery snow. The snow turned red where my hands had been.

"Do you want me to fix that?" Silas asked me.

I smiled. "Not right now. Gotta make it look like you put up some kind of fight."

He chuckled, taking off and soaring through the sky again. I turned and walked into the cave. The darkness greeted me as I stepped inside. After several seconds the door opened and out came Gray Beard holding a torch. He seemed surprised to see me.

"By the beard of Zeus! You're back!"

I shook my head. "No, I'm actually a ghost coming back to haunt you."

He paused a moment, then glared, picking up on my sarcasm.

"If you don't mind, I'd like to see my friends and Backura now," I stated.

He didn't say a word to me as he led me through the tunnels. He muttered a few unpleasant sounding things, which I ignored. Blood trickled from my hands and fell in drops on the dirt, leaving a gruesome trail behind. We eventually reached the throne room. Backura was right where he was when I had left, sitting on the chair, chowing down on food.

"By the hammer of Thor!" he shouted.

"Great Odin's Raven!" another dwarf shouted.

"Poseidon's Trident!" came a voice from the corner.

Apparently they didn't think I'd make it. "I guess you didn't think you'd see me again, did you?" I challenged.

Backura stood from his throne and wandered over to me. "How did you survive? Is the beast truly dead?" he asked with a greedy gleam in his eyes. He glanced at my bloody hands.

"Where are my friends?" I asked sharply.

"Yes, of course, of course," he nodded. "Someone bring them here!"

I didn't speak to him at all as I waited to see if my friends were OK.

"You must be an extraordinary swordsman to have taken down such a creature. I suppose I will have to honor our agreement and fight alongside you for Camelot."

"Mhmm," I agreed.

I could hear voices approaching, "Where are you taking us? What happened to Arthur?"

I smiled. My friends were alright. Blaine, Galahad, Will, and Jessica entered through one of the tunnels, guarded by two dwarves.

"Arthur!" Jessica shouted as she ran towards me. She hugged me, squeezing tightly. "We thought we'd never see you again."

I laughed. "C'mon, you can't get rid of me that easily."

Will put his hand up to give me a high-five. "Nice man, how did you kill that dragon?" he asked.

I held out my hands to show him my injuries. "I'd high-five you, but as you can see that would kind of hurt."

Jessica's eyes widened. "Are you okay?"

I nodded. "I'll be fine."

Blaine and Galahad began to offer their congratulations, but Backura interrupted them, "Yes, yes, we're all happy he survived and killed the dragon. Now tell me how you did it."

Backura was seriously starting to tick me off, but I smiled. "How about I show you instead? Come outside."

Backura eagerly pushed past me with his hammer and tromped up the tunnel. I gestured for everyone to follow. I winked at them.

This was going to be amusing.

He hurried to the entrance. We followed. Two dwarves with torches came along for light. He flung open the door, and we walked out into the snow, just in front of the ledge.

"Well, where is it?" he asked impatiently.

I whistled. Silas was hanging onto the mountain above the cave's entrance. Silas let out a horrific roar that shook the entire mountain. Backura turned around, his eyes emanating fear and terror. Backura, and all my friends screamed. I wish I'd had a camera to capture their faces. Instead, I burst out laughing. I heard a deep chuckle come from Silas, who was also very amused.

"What is the meaning of this?" Backura shouted.

My friends stayed silent and studied the dragon with wide, uncertain eyes. I nodded for Silas to come down from the ledge. He swooped down and landed swiftly on the powdered snow. Everyone took a step backward.

"Relax, Backura," I said, calmly walking towards Silas. "Silas is on our side now."

Backura's face burned with anger. "Silas? What do you mean, Arthur?"

I smiled. "Silas is bound by some old magic to protect me because of Excalibur. He has agreed to help us in battle. So, whether you like it or not, he is our ally now."

A cocky grin slipped across the dragon's face. It was weird to see a dragon smile.

Backura grunted. "Our deal was for you to kill the dragon, not keep him as your pet."

I sighed, "Look, when this battle is done and over, Silas won't kill any more of your kind."

"What?" Silas asked.

"Hey," I pointed at him. "If we're going to make this work, you'll just have to stick to sheep, alright?"

He rolled his eyes. "Fine."

I turned back to Backura. "Do we have a deal?"

Backura eyed Silas. He was trying to look tough, but I could still see fear. He said quietly, "It doesn't look like you've left me any choice."

"Good. Gather your army and send them to Camelot right away, they'll be expecting you."

Backura grunted as he left us and ventured back into the mountain.

"Dude, that's a dragon," Will said, staring at Silas.

"Really?" I tossed some sarcasm his way.

Blaine cautiously stepped forward to examine him. "Remarkable. How did you manage this?"

I told them what happened, starting with climbing the mountain, and ending with almost getting scorched alive.

"Wow," was all Jessica could say.

"We've gained a dragon," Galahad stated.

Silas nodded. "And a pretty good one too."

I laughed. "You're so modest."

"I try," he said, studying his claws.

"Now that we've gotten the dwarves to fight, and a dragon, what do we do next?" Jessica asked.

"Now we make our way to Brentwood Forest to get the elves," Blaine said.

"And what do we do with Silas?" I asked.

Blaine thought for a moment. "I think he should go on ahead to the elves, and we'll meet up with him there. There's no way he'd be able to carry us all."

I looked at Silas. "You okay with that?"

He snuffed. "Very well. Who knows, I might even find a couple sheep on the way," he said, and he licked his lips.

"Wait!" I shouted as he was about to take off. I held out my hands. "Do you mind helping me out with this?"

He leaned in and breathed gently on my hands. The cuts sealed, leaving no evidence that the scratches had ever been there.

"Thanks."

He took off, flapping his wings elegantly. It was truly breathtaking. We all stared at the sky until he was out of sight.

"What just happened?" Jessica asked.

"Silas has some weird healing power. When we faced off in the mountain, he clawed my side and I would've died if he hadn't healed me."

"You're quite fortunate, Arthur," Blaine said studying my hands.

"Does this mean we have to go through the snow again to get there?" Will groaned, more concerned about himself.

"Actually, no," Blaine said. He walked back into the cave and we all followed. "I talked to one of the dwarves, and they apparently have tunnels that cut through the mountains. We can follow those until we come out at the other end of the mountain range."

"You mean we could've just gone through the tunnels before, instead of hiking through the snow?" Will whined.

"Yes, if we'd known where an entrance was, but the dwarves keep them a secret."

"Of course they do," he said, rolling his eyes.

"We have to ask Backura to show us the way?" Jessica asked.

Blaine nodded.

"Then we'd better go find him," I said.

One of the dwarves had left us a torch. I had gotten used to the smell of dirt and sweat, so it didn't really bother me anymore.

"Where do you think he'll be?" I asked.

"He's probably in the throne room, preparing for battle," Galahad said, glancing down a dark tunnel. He held the torch so that we could see where we were going.

We wandered past the side tunnels until we reached the throne room. Sure enough, Backura was there, putting on his armor.

"Hey Backura, you got a second?" I called.

He looked over his shoulder and continued fixing his armor.

"What is it now?" he grumbled.

I grinned. He didn't like me. "Do you mind showing us a tunnel that could lead us to the other side of the mountain, near Brentwood Forest?"

He huffed, "The locations of those tunnels are kept secret by the dwarves, we don't let anyone know about them."

"Well, we're not just anyone, are we?" I argued. "Besides, we're allies now."

He put his bulky helmet on his melon-shaped head and grabbed his hammer, using it to point at a tunnel off to the right. "I don't have time for this. I have to prepare for battle. Follow that tunnel, and it will lead you where you asked."

"Thanks," I said as he walked away.

He grunted in reply.

"Alright, should we get back on the road?" I asked the others.

"Indeed," Blaine said.

Galahad nodded, and led the way for us. We kept the torch and picked another from the wall as we exited.

12 MICE & OTTERS

The five of us made our way through the tunnel. It dipped, rose, and twisted, making it a slow and painful trek. Granted, we weren't frozen in the snow. But we had no idea where we were, or how much longer it would take. The tunnels all looked the same, and it felt like we were walking in circles. My legs felt the all-too familiar burn.

"Are we there yet?" Will spoke up, piercing the silent tunnel.

"I honestly don't know, Merlin. These mountains go on for miles; it could take a while. Just be glad we are not outside," Galahad said as he walked.

Will frowned and groaned, but we didn't slow our pace.

"Blaine, what do you know about this witch guarding the forest?" I asked.

"Nothing definite," he replied. "But there have been many rumors and stories. Some say she is old and revolting, while others say she is young and beautiful. There are many variations, but every single one agrees that whoever walks into the woods will not return. No one knows what she does, or how powerful she is. All I know for sure is she's a force to be reckoned with."

I whistled. "She almost sounds as bad as a dragon."

"It will not be easy," Blaine agreed.

"At least this time we'll all be able to work together, right?" Jessica asked.

"This is true," Galahad stated. "The more people we have, the better chance we have at beating whatever she throws at us."

"What do you think she'll do?" Will asked.

"Dark magic is the most unpredictable thing out there," Blaine said bluntly. "Depending on her experience, she might be able to manipulate the undead, perform transmutations, or even control the elements."

I frowned. "That could complicate things."

"Just a little bit," Jessica stated.

"So we don't really have a plan here, do we?" I asked.

An unnerving silence weighed heavy over us.

"No, not really," Galahad said. "Since no one has returned from the forest alive, we don't really know the layout of the forest. That being said, we have no idea what we're walking into. So no, we don't have a plan."

"Great."

"Does anyone have any food?" Will asked after a couple minutes of silence.

Blaine chuckled.

"Merlin, we ate before we left," Galahad said. "We need to make our supply of food last, otherwise we won't make it to the elves."

Will grumbled and complained, reluctantly agreeing to conserve the food.

I passed the time by kicking a pebble over and over in front of me, like one would dribble a soccer ball. Will kept mumbling about food, while Jessica just walked quietly.

Blaine and Galahad exchanged words with each other every now and then, most of which were wonderment about where we were and how much longer it'll take. Although I didn't really care for the dwarves, I had to give them credit for digging these tunnels. They were incredible and perfectly round.

And then, the tunnel stopped. When I say 'it stopped,' I mean, it flat out stopped. There was no door or opening or anything. We were at a dead end.

"You've got to be kidding me!" Will shouted.

"Umm, where's the exit?" I asked, staring at the dirt wall in front of us.

Galahad placed a hand on the wall. "There must be something else here," he said. He used the torch to begin examining different parts of the wall.

"I did *not* walk all that way for a dead end. You better be sure there's something else here," Jessica declared with anger.

Blaine stepped forward with the other torch. "Settle down everyone," he said. "These tunnels are one of the dwarves' best-kept secrets. They're not going to leave the opening out for the whole world to see. Just give us a minute, I'm sure we'll figure it out."

Tension filled the tunnel as we stood impatiently, waiting for Blaine and Galahad to find a way out. Blaine hummed a tune, and patted the wall with his right hand.

"Ah, here we are," he said confidently.

He slid his hand into a small hole near the bottom of the wall and fumbled around for a moment. Then, he removed his hand and the wall in front of us collapsed. A flood of light blinded us as the outside world welcomed us back. We had gotten used to the darkness of the tunnel, so the sudden burst of light actually hurt. I shielded my eyes with my arm as I stepped out into the sunlight.

The tunnel entrance, or exit (whichever way you look at it), had vines draped over the opening, which I swooped away with my hand. I walked out into the open and looked around. The tunnel dumped us at the bottom of the mountain range. In front of us was an open forest. A nearby dirt path cut into the trees.

"Looks like we made it through the mountains," I said, as we took in the sight of the forest.

"Good," Will muttered. "There are no more mountains that we

have to climb, are there?"

Galahad chuckled. He patted Will on the back as he said, "No, my young friend, only forest and trails."

"Thank God."

"So where do we go from here?" Jessica asked, as she stared at the trees.

"We'll follow that path until we reach Brentwood. We may have to stop somewhere for the night, though," Galahad instructed.

"Can we take a five-minute break or something first?" grumbled Will.

"Yeah, I'm down for that too," I said.

"Alright, I guess we can spare a moment or two for a little rest," Galahad said. He sat on a stump.

I took a seat in the soft grass and let my body relax and adjust to the outdoors. My feet were killing me. Relief drifted down my legs, and I allowed myself to sink into the smooth grass. Jessica found a spot next to me and did the same. Will collapsed face-down, with his arms sprawled out. Blaine remained standing, discussing the route with Galahad as they looked over a crinkled old map that Blaine had pulled from his pocket.

"We really should get moving now," Galahad urged after several long minutes. "We don't exactly have time to spare."

I sat up. "Yeah, it would probably be best if we get moving."

Will groaned. "Fine, but we should at least get food next time we stop."

"Yes, of course," Blaine sounded annoyed with Will's constant complaining. I couldn't blame him. Will had a one-track mind.

We began along the path. Blaine and Galahad led the way. The mountains disappeared from view behind us. The path was just like the one we took to get to the mountains, winding and twisting through trees. Soft dirt cushioned every step I took. It felt a hundred times better on my feet than the hard tunnel floor. A slight breeze rolled past, waving through my clothes and hair. The leaves crinkled and danced in the wind, while birds chirped elegantly as they soared past us. I let out a satisfied breath.

We kept a steady pace along the trail. It dawned on me that there were no other travelers. That struck me as bizarre.

"Hey Blaine?" I asked.

"Yes, Arthur?"

"Is it normal that we haven't run into any other people? I mean, besides the ones that have tried to kill us."

He chuckled. "Not entirely, no. Before the wars we might have run into folks, but ever since, very few people travel. Mainly because of the bandits."

"I see."

"Isn't there a way to stop the bandits?" Jessica asked innocently.

Galahad gave a hearty, deep laugh. "I wish there was, Gwen. Think about how far we've travelled and how much land we haven't even seen. How could we manage to patrol those areas? We don't have the resources for that. But, it is a good idea."

Will smirked. "Yeah, good thinking there, champ."

She punched him in the arm. "Shut up. I was just asking."

"Hey, old man," Will said, stepping over a fallen log.

"I assume you're talking to me, Merlin?" Blaine said, raising an eyebrow.

"Yup. How much farther until we can stop walking?"

He sighed, "We've been keeping a steady pace, but we have a fair ways to go still."

"Wow," Will said, rolling his eyes. "That just helped me so much."

"Relax, we'll get there when we get there," I chided Will.

The conversation died down as we all became lost in our thoughts. I contemplated if I would be able to live permanently in this time period. I didn't think I'd want to. Even though The Island had me prisoner for so long, I think I'd miss cars, technology, and other things I remembered from my youth. I'd have given anything for a car at that moment. Walking everywhere was exhausting and I just wanted to get the whole thing over with. I did, however, enjoy the outdoors. I liked the wind in my face, the scenery, and the smells of the forest. It was something I had never experienced before.

Time rolled on as slowly as the clouds in the sky. Eventually we reached an enclosed area. A steep rocky hill was in front of us, and thick forest surrounded us.

"This is where we will stop for the night," Galahad declared. "It is not far from Brentwood Forest, so we should be safe, but we'll still need to keep watch."

No one spoke against this, we were all in need of a break. Blaine set up a place for us to sleep, while Galahad and I went out to get firewood. Will and Jessica plopped down on the grass. Galahad and I each dumped an armload of wood in a pile next to Blaine, and he started a small fire.

"What do we have to eat?" Will asked.

"Do you really want to know?" Blaine asked, chopping things up and placing them in a small pot.

Will thought for a moment. "No, I guess not."

Blaine chuckled as he placed the pot over the fire to cook. The sun had just set behind the trees, and with it came a cold chill in the air. The five of us huddled closer to the flames, absorbing their heat.

"Do we have any blankets?" Jessica asked quietly.

Galahad responded, "Of course."

He had packed a bag of supplies before we had left the dwarves. From it, he pulled out a large dark blanket. He tossed it to Jessica.

"Thank you."

He nodded. None of us felt much like talking.

She wrapped it around herself. Blaine checked whatever was in the pot and smiled with satisfaction.

"Dinner's ready," he stated.

He poured it into several small bowls (which also came from the pack) and handed them out. I eyed the soupy mixture with suspicion, and slowly put the bowl to my lips. It was actually quite nice, at least, compared to The Island's food. We ate until there was nothing left. Our stomachs were full, and we were ready for some needed sleep.

"I'll take the first watch," Galahad stated.

"Alright. Wake me when it's my turn," I said, getting myself comfortable.

The crackle of the fire eased me to sleep. I thought about the prophecy, the war, then The Island, and then nothing. I drifted into a dream that I didn't remember and didn't last nearly long enough. Before I knew it, I was being shaken awake.

I opened my eyes to see Blaine standing over me. "It's your turn to keep watch," he said.

I nodded sleepily. "OK, thanks."

He found his sleeping spot, as I stood to stretch my muscles. The fire looked low, so I threw another chunk of wood onto it. I sat on a tree stump near the fire, and my body warmed as I gazed into the woods. The forest was silent for me.

Will, however, was not silent. He began to roll slightly as he slept, and his face started to twitch. Whether he was in fear or pain, I couldn't really tell. I was about to go over and wake him, when he sat up and shouted, "Stop it!"

His hands cradled his head for a moment, and then he realized that he was awake. He looked at me, but said nothing.

"Are you OK?" I asked quietly.

He continued to stare as if to say: *Do I look OK?*

I said gently, "You should get some rest."

He didn't reply. He just went back to sleep.

His nightmares are getting worse, I realized. I was worried for him, but there was nothing I could do. I continued my watch, and tried not to think about it. I edged closer to the fire, absorbing its warmth, and poking it with a stick every so often. Embers sparkled and kicked into the air. I kept busy by playing with the fire and swinging Excalibur around. I even tried talking to it (or him, whichever it is), but eventually my eyes began to droop.

They snapped open however when I heard a rustling in the bushes. I rose to my feet, faster than the speed of light, with Excalibur clutched tightly in my right hand. My eyes darted back and forth, searching the woods for the source of the sound. Another rustle drew my attention. I cautiously stepped toward the bush, keeping Excalibur ready. The bush continued to rustle until a small, furry creature jumped out into the open.

It was a mouse.

No, scratch that. It was a mouse on steroids.

This mouse wasn't your average household rodent. This mouse stood on its hind legs and was at least as tall as my knees. Its fur was honey-yellow and its eyes were bright green. White whiskers hung in the air at the side of its face, and two small teeth stuck out of its mouth. Now, understand that I am the last person that would say something like this, but this mouse was adorable.

Don't trust the mice.

That lake lady had told me not to trust the mice. Could this be what she was talking about? But then again, how could this cute little thing be dangerous? (Shut up, if you were there you would be thinking the same thing.)

I pointed Excalibur at it and hissed. "Shoo," I ordered.

It cocked its head to the side and stared at me. I shooed it again and the mouse turned, dropped to its four paws, and scurried away. I kept a sharper watch after that for a while, but inevitably my eyes began to droop again.

I woke Galahad. "Hey, Merlin's having a rough night, so could you take his shift? He hasn't had much sleep."

"I noticed," he said, standing to his feet. "It's no trouble at all, Arthur. I don't mind staying up."

"Thank you. Something weird just happened."

"What do you mean?"

"There was a rustling in the bushes, so I checked it out. It was a huge mouse. The thing was up to my knees, man. I shooed it away, but it might come back."

"I see," he pondered. "Do you think it has anything to do with Nimue's warning?"

"That's why I'm telling you," I said. "I'm not sure what she meant by it, but it didn't sound too good, so keep an eye out."

"Thanks for the heads-up."

"No problem."

He gave a courteous nod and took over the watch. I moved to where I had been sleeping earlier and after much tossing and turning, I forgot about the mice and went to sleep.

The night did not end there.

But I wish to God it did.

I awoke to chaos. I'm not sure if it was Galahad's screams that woke me, or the hissing of the mouse he was fighting. Whichever it was, I was suddenly wide awake, and so were the others. My brain tried to absorb what was happening. After a moment I understood. The mouse I had encountered earlier was sinking razor-sharp fangs into Galahad's neck. Galahad was writhing on the ground, screaming in pain. I saw him find a grip on his sword and slice clean through the savage mouse. Galahad's blood was everywhere, literally spewing from the gash in his neck.

"What's going on?" Jessica screamed.

More mice emerged from the bushes, all the same size as the

corpse lying on the ground. There must've been dozens of them, all scurrying towards us. I grabbed Excalibur, and looked at Galahad. He shook his head slightly. It was useless. There were too many.

"Run," he mouthed with a ghastly whisper, turning his back on us, and facing the horde of deadly mice. I nodded, understanding all too well that he was going to sacrifice himself to save us.

"We've gotta get out of here!" I shouted to the others.

Blaine quickly grabbed the bag and sprinted the opposite direction of the mice. "Follow me!" he called.

Will ran after him without a second's hesitation, but Jessica was frozen in shock. I grabbed her shoulders and looked her in the eyes. "Jess, we need to get out of here now. There's nothing we can do for Galahad, you have to run."

I began to push her in the direction the others had gone. With confused eyes, she began to run for her life. I was right behind her.

I looked back. Galahad was on his feet, slashing franticly at the army of mice. I watched in horror as three large mice brought him down. His body disappeared into a heap of fur and blood. The sight of those creatures tearing him apart is something I will never forget.

"Francis!" Jessica shouted in panic.

"I'm right behind you!" I yelled, turning my back to the gruesome scene, my feet pumping furiously to get away.

We ran for our lives as each of us followed the dark figure in front of us. Dawn was breaking, shedding light on the forest. I heard a noise behind me. Two of the mice were chasing after me. They were wicked fast, and gaining on me. Light reflected off their fangs. Blaine, Will, and Jessica were a good distance ahead.

One of the mice launched its body at me with surprising force, knocking me to the ground. In one swift move I unsheathed Excalibur, whipped around, and slashed the mouse in its side. It fell from my back. I stood and turned to face the other mouse. They both hissed at me with bitter hate. The mouse without the gash tried an attack, but I was ready for it. I swung Excalibur. I slashed the mouse mid-air, and pieces of its body flew in different directions. My arm was still extended, and the second mouse took advantage of that, digging its teeth into my arm.

I dropped Excalibur and shouted in pain. It was about to strike again, when a metal rod pierced it through the heart. Mercifully, it collapsed to the ground. I turned. Jessica was a few feet away, holding her gun at the ready.

"I thought you could use the help," she said. Her face was pale.

"Thanks," I said. I picked up Excalibur. I wiped it quickly on the grass and returned it to its sheath.

I grabbed her arm and we ran together to find Will and Blaine. We ducked and weaved through the trees until we wound up in an open field. I could see Will and Blaine in the distance, standing in the grass. The two of us hurried over to meet them.

"Is everyone alright?" Blaine asked.

Will and Jessica nodded.

Blaine turned to me with weary eyes. "… Galahad?"

I shook my head.

He understood. "He gave his life to buy us time to escape. He was a good man."

We stood in silence, as the truth of the situation sank in.

"What were those things?" Will asked after several minutes.

Blaine let a deep breath out. "They are called Raycuna. I thought they were extinct, or at least stayed in Brentwood, but it appears I was wrong."

"I saw one during my shift," I said. My face got hot, and I knew I wasn't far from crying. I stared at the ground. "It could've killed me. I warned Galahad …"

"It's not your fault, Arthur," Blaine assured me.

I didn't respond; somehow I felt responsible for his death.

"We didn't even try to help him," I said.

Blaine placed his hand on my shoulder, and I met his gaze. "There was nothing we could do to help him. He died for something he believed in, which was you, and the prophecy."

Another deathly silence followed. I realized that it wasn't just OK to help these people, and then leave when it was convenient for us. These were real people, like us, and Galahad's death made me keenly aware that we couldn't just leave them to die.

I found a new strength inside of me. "Then we'd better make sure he didn't die for nothing."

Blaine let a hint of a smile appear on his face. "We should get moving."

We followed as Blaine led us past the field and down a dirt path. No one spoke. We mourned the loss of Galahad. I kept running scenarios in my mind, wondering if there was anything I could've done differently. It was like dealing with the death of my parents all over again. Our quest had taken an ominous turn and we weren't even close to being finished.

The morning was dark and gloomy. Storm clouds hovered above, reflecting our dampened spirits. As if things weren't already bad enough, it started to rain after we crossed the field.

"That's just great," Will murmured.

"Keep moving," I said half-heartedly. My spirit was low.

Things were not going how I thought they would. I mean, I knew gaining allies, fighting enemies, and trekking on this journey wasn't going to be a piece of cake, but I sure didn't think it would turn out like this. Galahad was a good guy, and now he was gone.

Simple as that.

"Guys, I don't mean to be the girl who gives the cheesy motivational talk, but we need to keep it together," Jessica said. She had moved to the front of the group. She quit walking and turned to face us.

"I'm just saying, losing Galahad was terrible, but we need to focus on what we came here to do. Or else *we* might not make it."

"Gwen's right," Blaine stepped in. "Galahad knew the risks when he volunteered."

"What do we do now?" Will asked, almost in a way that made me question whether or not he was affected by what just happened.

Blaine stared at the path ahead. "We have to finish what we started. We need to recruit the elves and make it back to Camelot. Don't take this the wrong way, but to get through this, we must try and forget what happened to Galahad. Put it out of your mind and focus on what we came here to do."

It really was the only thing we could do.

"How far are we from Brentwood Forest?" Will asked.

Blaine began to walk again. "Not far," he said.

We trudged forward; through the rain, through the mud, and over yet another field. Internally we each did what we had to, to put the death of Galahad aside and focus on whatever lie ahead. Even though it was morning, the sky was as black as night, and the rain poured down, soaking me thoroughly.

This day is going to suck, I thought. I was drenched, tired, and one of my friends was just eaten alive by giant mice. Oh, did I mention we were about to enter a forest occupied by an evil witch?

Terrific.

"We should come up with a plan," I said.

Blaine did not look back. "And did you have any thoughts on that?"

"Well … no … but I'm thinking we should have one before going in there."

"You're right. We do need a plan. However, there isn't much we can do to prepare ourselves for the forest. There are creatures in there that no man has ever lived to talk about. All we can do is keep a sharp eye on our surroundings, and watch each other's back. If that witch decides to give us trouble, we'll send it right back at her."

"Uh-huh," Will added with uncertainty.

Rain continued to fall. Muddy puddles formed on the edges of the dirt path, and drops of water pelted us from the leaves on the trees. After several minutes we reached a sharp, steep drop that opened into a dark forest.

"My friends, I give you Brentwood Forest," Blaine said with a grand gesture.

The trees in the forest weren't green. They were black. It wasn't only the leaves though. The trunks, the space between the trees, the bushes; everything was black. Standing at the cliff's edge, all we could see was vast darkness. It was not what I imagined at all. Looking at it sent shivers down my spine. There was definitely something evil in that forest. (Not that I was afraid or anything.)

"That is one fierce forest," Will said with obvious appreciation in his voice.

The three of us stared at him.

"What?" Will said.

I shook my head. "You're not helping, buddy."

He shrugged.

"Are you sure we won't get lost in there?" Jessica asked, her eyes searching the blackness for any sign of light.

"I'm sure we'll be—"

Blaine was cut off by a sinister hissing noise. It was a haunting noise that could bring a grown man to tears. The mice had followed us. Behind us was a group of at least ten or so of the killer mice. They were about fifteen yards away from us, and they were staring, as if waiting for us to make the first move.

"What do we do?" I asked out of the corner of my mouth.

"Don't move," Will whispered. "They can't see us if we don't move."

"This isn't *Jurassic Park*, Merlin," Jessica chastened.

"What's *Jurassic Park*?" Blaine asked nervously.

"It's nothing," I said. "Just slowly pull out your weapons."

Each of us slid our weapons out of their cases and held them in front of us. The constant hissing coming from the mice was extremely unnerving. As my mind raced with possibilities, and my eyes scanned the horde of mice, two arrows came out of nowhere and pierced two of the mice's heads. The weird thing was (yeah, it's getting weirder) the arrows didn't come from anyone in our group.

"Chester's 'eading up the left field, a tricky shot, but 'e sticks it! The crowd is going wild!" a squeaky, British voice echoed through the woods.

"Brilliant shot, if I do say so me-self. Next up to bat is the infamous Malcom the Incredible," a new voice, with a similar accent said. Whoever they were, I could tell they were in the trees just off the path to our right.

Two more arrows connected with two more mice, killing them instantly.

"Blimey! What a shot by Malcom!"

The four of us were as dazed as the mice. Who did these voices belong to, and what was going on? The remaining mice scattered, darting away in every direction.

"Oi! Where do you think you're going, eh?" shouted one of the voices. Another two of the mice fell victim to the invisible attackers.

"I do love it when they run, don't you, Chester?"

"Right you are, Malcom."

Within a few seconds, all of the mice were dead.

"So that just happened," I said, confused out of my mind.

Two furry creatures jumped out of the trees and landed in front of us. We jumped, startled at the sight. Each had a quiver of arrows on his back and a bow in his hands. They were otters. One was as tall as my waist, and the other was a little bit shorter. Both had dark brown fur. Several whiskers stuck out of their faces and their tails were slick and thin. None of us knew what to say, or even how to react.

"Well, a thank you would be nice," the shorter one said.

Yeah, he spoke. Of course he did.

"Now, now, Malcom, don't be so forward," the other said. "My name's Chester, and this little dolt is Malcom."

"Who are you calling dolt?" the otter named Malcom said, and he tackled Chester to the ground.

They rolled around until Chester kicked Malcom off of him. "Would you grow up? You're embarrassin' me in front of the king," he said.

"You should try and act more professional," Malcom said. "Calling me dolt …"

Chester turned back to us. "Sorry about that," he said.

"We've been huntin' those fiends for a few days now. Nasty lil' buggers."

I was speechless. They were talking. Animals were talking to us. Talking! What was going on?

"Uhh …" was all I could get out.

"Some king," Malcom observed. "He can't even talk."

"Will you shut up?" Chester snapped. "Forgive me companion, 'e forgets 'is manners every now and then."

"You can talk," I said, stunned.

"Of course we can talk," Malcom scoffed. "Did you really think we were dumb animals?"

"Erm … no, but—"

"It's alrigh', Arthur. We don't usually communicate with humans," Chester said.

"Yeah, it's sort of an unwritten code," Malcom explained.

Will tugged my shirt like a child would. "Arthur … they're talking," he observed.

I was about to speak, but Jessica couldn't hold it in. "Aren't they just adorable?" she squealed.

"Not exactly the words I'd use, but OK," I replied.

"You're like, talking otters?" Will asked, stating the obvious.

"You're pretty sharp, aren't you?" Malcom rolled his eyes.

Will took a step forward. "Don't make me come over there, fur-brains."

I put my arm across his chest. "Relax dude, he's just teasing you."

"Look at their little whiskers," Jessica said. She was starry-eyed. (Must be a girl thing.)

"Thank you for helping us," I said. I spoke hesitantly, reconciling my mind to the fact that I was having a conversation with animals.

Chester and Malcom bowed.

"Nothin' to it," said Malcom.

"All in a day's work," Chester agreed.

"We 'eard that you were in need of some allies," Chester claimed, his eyes meeting mine. "We've come to join you on your quest. If you would take us, of course."

I let Blaine make the call. He nodded.

"We'd be happy to take all the help we can get. Besides, we owe you for helping us out back there," I replied.

The otters bowed with gratitude. "You won't regret it."

"So where are we going, exactly?" Malcom asked us.

"Through Brentwood Forest, to find the elves," Blaine responded.

He gasped. "Is it too late to take back our offer?"

We laughed.

Chester spoke up, "Just ignore him, that's what I do."

I looked at Will. "That sounds familiar."

"Shut up," Will said, shoving me.

“Well, are we going to just stand ’ere talking about finding the elves?” Chester asked. “Or are we going to do it?”

Blaine chuckled. “Follow me.”

“I’ll grab me arrows.”

13 THE WITCH

Our group had lost a great man, then gained two new furry companions. I was glad they offered to help, and, at the same time, thought it kind of cool that they could talk. Chester was kind and straight-forward, while Malcom reminded me of Will. They were quick and scurried on all fours as they gathered their arrows from the dead bodies. It was amazing to watch them leap from tree to tree and body to body, as if they were weightless. After collecting all of their arrows, they came back to us and waited patiently for Blaine to lead the way.

"We have to head down this trail," he said, pointing to a steep path leading downward. "And that will put us in front of the forest, and from there we will make our way to the elves. Hopefully without any trouble."

Blaine chose his steps carefully, as the path was slippery. My feet were extremely sore from all the walking, and navigating this rocky slope wasn't helping.

"Hey Blaine?" Will asked.

"Yes, Merlin?"

He paused for a moment as he took a large step down, past several loose rocks. "Sorry if this is a stupid question, but if this witch is as powerful as you say she is, is there a way to kill her if we actually run into her?"

"The only way to kill a witch is to burn her," he said between steps. "It's common knowledge in these parts."

"I see," Will said, with furrowed eyebrows. I could tell he was running it through in his head. "So if we run into her, how are we going to do that? We don't exactly have fire at the snap of our fingers."

Blaine did not speak for a few seconds. "I had not thought of that part. I suppose it would be a good thing to sort out before we enter the forest."

"Gee, you think?" I said incredulously. It was what I was trying to suggest all along.

We hiked until we reached the open flats in front of the mysterious Brentwood Forest. Blaine unpacked several pieces of cloth from his bag and began wrapping them onto several arrows.

"I got this material from Charles before we left. It is highly flammable and will ignite if struck against a rough surface, like a rock. We will each carry one, and if we run into her, with any luck one of us will be able to make the shot count."

"So you've been carrying extremely flammable fabric on your back this entire trip?" I asked.

"Yes."

"Not exactly safe, but good thing you brought it."

"Right, so we 'ave to go in there an' torch the witch?" Chester said, eyeing the black forest that stood in front of us.

"Not exactly," Blaine said. "We have to cut through the forest to find the elves. We only use these arrows if we run into her."

"Right-o."

Will stared into the vast darkness. "Blaine. Are you sure you're going to be able find your way through that?"

Blaine stopped wrapping arrows, took a look at the forest, then went back to the arrows. "Yeah, I should be fine."

"Should?"

"I'm going on instinct, seeing as no one has actually made it through alive. But I'm told I have an excellent sense of direction."

Will looked like he was having second thoughts. He shot me a concerned look. I shrugged. What did he expect me to do? It's not like I had a better plan.

Blaine finished wrapping the special arrows and handed one to each of us. I slid mine into the quiver on my back, but kept it separate from the others. Jessica did the same, and Will slid his into his pants. The six of us stood side by side, facing the ominous expanse before us.

"So who wants to go into the dark, creepy forest first?" I asked.

All of us looked to Blaine.

"If you insist," he said, walking forward.

I fell in behind Blaine, then came Jess and Will. The two otters brought up the rear. There were several things I noticed when I entered the forest. First, it was really dark. I knew it was still daytime, but the moment we set foot in the forest, it seemed as if were night. The thickness in the air was palpable. A thin layer of fog covered the ground, which made it even harder to see where we were going.

The second thing of note was the temperature. In an instant, it was almost as bad as the cold in the mountains.

My body tensed up with the sudden shock of cold, and I felt it throughout my bones.

My eyes began to adjust. The trees were either decaying or dying, and their trunks were clawed and scarred. As we ventured a little further, my foot suddenly began to sink sharply into the ground. Faster than a lightning strike, I jerked it back.

"Yeah, don't step there," I warned everyone, pointing to the spot that swallowed my foot.

Blaine furrowed his eyebrows, as he touched the ground I had pointed to. "That's not a good sign."

"What do you mean?"

He studied the material on his fingers. "It's quicksand."

"Quicksand," I repeated.

He nodded. "The forest must be hiding many secrets and dangers. We should tread carefully."

"It's not too late to turn back, you know?" Will whispered in my ear.

I rolled my eyes.

"How are we going to make it through this place alive, if every step we take could somehow kill us?" Jessica asked. She looked at the trees towering above us.

Blaine tore a long branch off of a tree and began to use it as a walking stick, tapping the ground in front of him. "We do it very carefully," he cautioned.

"Good plan."

In a single file line, we tracked in Blaine's footsteps, taking great care not to wander from the path. Except for our feet squishing through the mud, things were basically quiet. I continually scanned the forest for signs of danger. I couldn't see anything, which made me nervous. I thought about Excalibur, and wondered whether I could communicate with him when I was awake.

Yes.

"What?" I asked out loud.

Everyone looked at me. "Erm, sorry," I said.

You're the only one who can hear me. Just think it, and I'll hear you, Excalibur's voice echoed in my head.

So you can hear me right now? I asked.

Yes, he answered.

Cool.

Did you want something?

Oh, right, I thought. *It's really quiet here. Do you think something's wrong?*

Brentwood Forest is evil, he warned. *I sense it. It feels as if there are eyes watching our every move, which concerns me. We should keep our guard up.*

Sounds like a plan, I affirmed.

If I see anything out of the ordinary, I shall inform you, Francis, he assured.

Thanks, I thought. It was weird to hear him use my given name, instead of "Arthur," like Blaine and the others from the past used.

"Why is it so cold here?" Jessica's voice broke my thought conversation with Excalibur.

"Dark magic," Blaine replied. "It kills everything around it. That's why the trees are all dead. The witch's magic has cursed this forest beyond repair, and now, even the warmth is gone."

"That's comforting," she noted.

Blaine moved slowly through the mist, not taking a step without first poking the ground with the long stick. I realized I could hear a low moan. It seemed to come from the forest itself, as if it were warning the witch we were here. Blaine detoured several times around areas he designated unsafe and we even had to jump over a few trouble spots. I was almost feeling a sense of comfort, because we hadn't really run into any danger, but then again, I tend to speak too soon. The mist layering the ground began to dissipate, and the ground suddenly became clearer.

"Does this mean we're getting close to the elves?" Will asked.

Blaine frowned. "No. We're not even close to the edge of the forest yet. Something else is going on."

I gripped Excalibur with my right hand. The otters had arrows drawn, and loaded loosely on their bows. The strange sound echoed through the woods, bouncing off of the trees. All at once it reminded me of ... *uh-oh.*

"Blaine," I said, tensing up. "You don't think ..."

He nodded, pulling out his sword.

Out from the darkness appeared an army of the deadly mice. There must've been at least twenty of them, gnashing their teeth at us. Their eyes glowed in the blackness, their fur was ragged and messy.

"You take the five on the left, I'll take the fifteen on the right," Malcom commanded, loading another arrow onto his bow.

"Oi! What makes you think you can take more of em' on eh?" Chester retorted.

"Guys!" I hissed. "Not the time."

They hushed. Jessica and Will pulled out their guns. With Jessica's bow in my hand, I took aim for the mouse directly in front of me. He was only about twenty feet away.

"Fire!" I shouted.

Those of us with arrows released them, and we killed several mice. The remaining mice rushed us; claws ready to tear us apart. I dropped my bow and pulled out Excalibur. I sidestepped a mouse that lunged at me and slashed it mid-air. The otters began to jump from tree to tree, shooting arrows at any mouse that we couldn't see. Blaine swung his sword rapidly, fending off mouse after mouse. Will and Jessica used their guns to shoot as many as they could. Each time I thought we'd killed them all, more came at us.

"There's too many of them!" Blaine shouted.

I took a quick look around to see he was right. There were too many of them for us to handle. We were doomed.

"What is going on here?" a woman's voice cut through the air, louder than the noise of our battle.

The mice stopped in their tracks. We regrouped and I could tell the mice were afraid. I could see their whiskers quivering. We held our weapons, ready to fight against whatever belonged to the voice. There was a flash of red light in front of us, and a tall woman with dark brown hair appeared in front of us.

"Is that any way to treat our guests?" she said to the mice.

They answered by scurrying away as fast as their legs could carry them. Her voice was soft and innocent; it actually almost made me feel safe.

Don't be fooled, she's the witch, Excalibur whispered to me.

"What brings a group of travellers to my forest?" she asked with a warm smile.

I cleared my throat. "We're just passing through," I said.

She chuckled, although I wasn't trying to be amusing. "Just passing through? Who do you think you are? This is *my* forest."

I didn't know what to say. The last thing I wanted to do was tick her off. Lucky for me, Blaine stepped up.

"We meant no disrespect, ma'am."

Her body vaporized in shadowy smoke, and suddenly she reappeared right in front of me. "And who exactly are you?" she crooned.

"Umm …" I hesitated, "I'm Arthur, the new king of Camelot."

"The new king?" her eyes burned through me, staring me down until they rested upon Excalibur. "What do we have here? Is that Excalibur?"

Before I could nod, she turned into smoke again and reappeared several feet away from me. "So you're here to kill me, then?"

A cold, heartless laugh floated from her thin lips. "Well, that's not very nice, is it? Though I suppose we all have our flaws. Yours was coming here, Arthur. You and your friends will never leave here alive."

She vanished in another cloud of black smoke, leaving me wondering what she meant. Before I could say a word to Blaine, an invisible force threw me into a tree. As I got to my feet, I could see the same had happened to the others as well.

I could tell something was about to happen. "Guys!" I called. I was going to suggest we tighten our group and remain back to back.

Before I could get another word out, walls of dirt and vines shot up from the ground, separating us all. They launched up, higher than the treetops, within seconds.

They were too tall to climb and after trying to slash my way through with Excalibur, I realized they were too thick to cut through. I was cut off from my friends, and they were cut off from me.

"Jess! Will!" I shouted, not caring about using our fake names in my concern for their safety.

No reply.

The walls had not only separated me from my friends, but also removed me from the rest of the forest. They had sprouted up all around me, leaving only one path for me to go.

It was a labyrinth.

What am I supposed to do now? I wondered.

Stay calm. You have no choice but to go into the labyrinth. Make your way through it, and eventually you'll find the witch and your friends, Excalibur's voice echoed in my mind.

"Right. Stay calm," I said aloud. "I can do that."

I stared at the path, took a deep breath, and walked. The walls loomed over me, and the tight space between them made me nervous. I held Excalibur in front of me, and braced for any hidden dangers. I heard the witch giggling behind me, but when I turned around there was nothing there.

She's toying with you.

I nodded, and continued deeper into the maze. I went right, left, right, and right again, hoping that around each turn I would see my friends. But I never did. The wandering lasted so long, I drifted into a kind of trance. It felt aimless and pointless, as if she were simply leading me in circles. I wondered how my friends were doing, and if I was the only one separated. With Excalibur in front of me at all times, I was starting to believe this was my eternal fate. No sooner had I thought I would die in that place, then I turned one corner and became sure of it. Death was imminent.

There, standing several feet away from me was … well actually I don't know what it was, but it freaked the crap out of me. It looked like a wolf, but its skin was black and scaly, like the dragon's. It stared at me with blood-red eyes and crazy-huge fangs. Its tail was long and had several spikes poking out at the end of it. I had never seen anything like it, and was paralyzed with fear.

Stay calm. No sudden movements.

I didn't budge. I couldn't. Red eyes were locked on me and I could feel their fierce hatred. It started to growl. *Not good.* It bent its hind legs and lunged at me, jaw snapping. My instincts (or rather, Excalibur's instincts) kicked in, and I ducked and rolled underneath the wolf-thing. I turned just as it landed on the other side of me. Its tail almost whipped my face. It jumped forward and back, teasing me, as I swung Excalibur in defense. The creature got too close, and I slashed its neck. It roared in agony, and the pain made its eyes burn even brighter. It made one last attempt to kill me, lunging through the air towards me, but it wasn't good enough. I jumped to meet it head-on, and Excalibur found its underbelly, piercing it through. The creature's body went limp and collapsed onto me as dead weight. I was pinned to the ground for a few seconds, as I struggled to get it off of me. After much effort, I heaved it off, and got to my feet.

I caught my breath. Before me was a choice of two directions I could go. I started to walk one way, away from whatever it was I had just killed.

Other way, Excalibur's voice said.

I immediately turned around. I stepped over the corpse of the wolf-thing and forged ahead with determination. It kind of worried me how easy this whole killing thing had become for me, but I suppose if something's trying to kill you, you don't really have a choice. I didn't want to look too deeply into it. As I approached the next intersection of the maze, I poked my head out to check if there were any monsters waiting for me. There weren't. I let out a breath of relief and turned left.

I heard the playful giggle floating through the air again. The witch was enjoying this. I turned around, trying to follow the laughter. I jogged down the path until I reached a dead end. When I started to go back the way I had come, I heard something move behind me. I whipped around to see that the dead end was moving towards me, and it had sharp sticks protruding from it, aimed right at me. If I didn't move, the sticks would kill me. I sheathed my sword and took off in the other direction. The moving wall began to pick up speed. I turned a quick corner only to find another wall of spikes heading towards me. I twisted around, and sprinted the other way.

The walls were closing in on me. I saw an opening in the maze and ran for it. I pushed myself harder with the knowledge that I was running for my life. I was almost at the opening, but I didn't dare look behind me, knowing if I did, I would slow down and the spikes would hit me. I was inches away from being killed, so as I approached, I just dove through the opening, rolling to my side with the hopes that the spikes would not follow.

I was out of the maze. As I looked back, I saw the entire labyrinth itself collapse. I heard the sound of a person clapping their hands. The witch. In one quick motion, I got to my feet and pulled out Excalibur.

The witch stood about twenty feet from me, and continued to clap her hands together. "Well done, Arthur," she said. "After you killed my pet, I was getting tired of watching you circle the maze, so I decided to speed things up. Whether or not you survived, I didn't really care."

My friends were sitting on the ground behind her. All were unconscious and had their arms bound above their heads by thick vines.

She followed my gaze. "Don't worry about them. They're just

taking a nap. It's just you and me."

"Let them go."

She laughed. "Now why would I go and do a thing like that?"

"Because if you don't, I'll kill you."

"Strong words for such a young human."

My emotions had had enough. I felt nothing but raw hatred. I knew I wanted her dead.

She sighed. "I expected more from the new king. Thought he'd be … taller."

"I'm sorry to disappoint you," my voice sounded different to me. Older.

The witch studied me. "There's something different about you."

I shrugged. "Maybe it's my charm."

"No, that's not it," she said. She was smiling.

I remembered Blaine's insight that fire was the only way to kill a witch. I slowly sheathed Excalibur, and tried to think of a way to get the bow and fire arrow off my back and in position to strike.

"Let my friends go," I repeated.

"Not one for small talk, are you?" she asked. "I shall enjoy killing you."

She levitated and a silver, electrical ball began to form in her right hand. When it was as big as a bowling ball, she flung it towards me. I dove to the left and it missed. By the time I regained my footing, she'd launched another one. I dove again, but not quickly enough, and the blast caught my leg and drove me into the ground. My head was spinning, and somehow I managed to get to my feet again. The witch sent another ball of electricity at me. This one collided with my chest, sending me sprawling backwards and into something hard.

I tried to stand, but this time I was too weak. I couldn't focus, and all I heard was a loud ringing noise, mixed with her laughter. I sat up and noticed the clothing on my chest was charred.

Don't give up Francis! Excalibur's voice shouted at me.

There's nothing I can do.

Yes, there is.

"It's too bad that I have to kill you. I was enjoying this," the witch said with mock pity.

I got to one knee and hunched over it. I used all of my concentration to try and freeze time. The witch had another globe of electricity in her hand, and was in the midst of throwing it. With frustration and pain I yelled as loud as I could. It was an impressive roar, if I do say so myself. When I looked up, the globe was frozen, inches from my face.

I had done it. I had frozen time … again. I rose to my feet and limped across the battlefield, out of the way of the electric ball. I grabbed the bow off of my back, and scratched the arrow against a nearby rock. It ignited instantly, and I latched it onto the bow. I closed my eyes, and concentrated on unfreezing time. When I opened them I saw the lightning ball strike the ground where I had been moments earlier.

"Better luck next time," I said. And I released the arrow at the witch.

The confused look on her face was priceless. If she had a heart, my arrow pierced it. She burst into flames. I wondered whether the screams coming from her were from pain or frustration at her defeat. The flames grew brighter and brighter, and just when I thought I would go blind from the light, she exploded. The sound hung in the air for a moment, then died away. The forest became silent again. The vines which held my friends crumbled to the ground. That was the last thing I saw as my body collapsed and everything went black.

I woke up with the warmth of a campfire blanketing my body. My head rested on Blaine's bag. As I looked around, I could see several other fires formed a circle around me. There was a fire in the center and my friends were seated in front of it.

"He's awake!" Jessica said. She rushed to my side.

"Yeah, I suppose I am," I replied.

Blaine helped me sit up. "You gave us quite the scare, Arthur."

"I gave *you* a scare?" I snorted. "You guys practically left me on my own to face the witch."

Silence.

"So you did save us?" Chester asked.

I nodded, my head still hurt.

"Told you," he said. Malcom hung his head and handed him a fish. Chester smiled with delight and began to munch on his prize.

"What happened to you guys, anyway?" I asked.

Everyone except for Blaine averted their eyes.

"When you were separated from us," Blaine began, "we tried to cut our way through the wall, but the witch knocked us out."

"So you're telling me that all five of you were knocked out at the same time?" I realized how powerful the witch really had been.

Blaine nodded.

"Nice."

"How did you kill her?" Will asked.

"The fire arrow."

"It worked?" Blaine asked. He raised his eyebrows in shock.

I stared at him. "You mean to tell me you weren't sure if it would work?"

He shrugged. "I was pretty sure it would," he said.

I rolled my eyes. "Unbelievable."

"Are you alright?" Jessica asked.

I nodded. "My chest hurts, and I have a killer headache, but I'm fine."

"Your chest was severely burnt, Arthur. I had to put some herbal medicine on the wound," Blaine said.

"Thanks," I said. "Where are we?"

"We're still in the forest," Malcom replied.

"Great."

"You should get some rest, Arthur. The otters and I will keep watch tonight," Blaine said. "We'll get out of this place in the morning."

"Sounds good," I said. I laid back down and did my best to get comfortable. I closed my eyes and tried to fall asleep. Unfortunately, Excalibur had other plans. He met me on another battlefield.

"Francis, are you sure you're alright?"

"Yes. Just tired."

"I see."

I could tell something was wrong. "What do you want?"

Excalibur hesitated before answering, "Killing the witch was supposed to free me from this prison."

"Oh. Right. How's that working out for you?"

He stared at me.

I put my hands up in defense. "Hey, I'm sorry."

"I don't understand. Killing her was supposed to set me free."

I walked up to him and placed my hand on his shoulder. "I'm sorry man, but maybe this was supposed to happen."

"So I'm supposed to spend all eternity stuck in this godforsaken place? It makes no sense."

"How do you think I feel?" I asked him. "You know all of my memories; you know that I'm not even supposed to be here."

He nodded. "I suppose destiny has other plans for us," he said sadly.

"Mhmm."

He rose to his feet. "You did good today. You managed to harness your ability over time, and save your friends. However, I suggest you continue to practice, next time you might not be so lucky."

Before I could reply, he vanished, and I was left alone to dream.

I woke up to Blaine tapping my shoulder. "C'mon, we have to get moving," he said.

I sat up. The fires were all out, and the forest was still dark. Chester and Malcom were packing up their bows and arrows. Jessica was leaning against a tree with her arms folded across her chest. Will standing by me, stretching his arms. I grabbed my gear, threw it on my back, and got to my feet.

"Feeling better?" Jessica asked.

"Yeah. Actually, my head's fine."

"That's good."

I nodded. "So are we getting out of this place or what?"

Blaine hiked his pack over his shoulder. "Of course. Follow me. Just because the witch is dead, doesn't mean we're safe. There are still dark creatures lurking about."

He cautiously moved away from our campsite. We followed. We moved as a group, like we had done when we first entered the forest. Blaine led, tapping the ground with a stick, each of us behind the other, following in his footsteps. We moved quickly, less afraid of hidden dangers, seeing as the witch was dead. We travelled in and out of mud patches, through swampy grass, and around many fallen trees. The journey through the forest was painstakingly long and rough. My feet were soaked and cold. My body ached.

Time passed slowly in Brentwood. The lack of sunlight and the unchanging surroundings made it hard to tell how long we had been going. The eerie silence did not help. No one really spoke; there was no need. To be honest, my head still hurt, and the part of my chest where the lightning ball hit was tender. I was having a hard time keeping up with the group.

I hope the elves are close, I thought to myself.

The pain in my chest was getting worse. It throbbed with each breath. I tried to keep moving, but eventually the pain became unbearable. I lifted my shirt to check my chest. The burns were no longer red, but black. The veins on my chest were black as well. Before I could alert anyone, I collapsed. The last thing I heard was Will shouting.

I faded between reality and nothingness. Every now and then I got a flash of the ground. I was moving. Someone must have been carrying me. I had no idea what was happening, or if I was even alive. Eventually the flashes of reality stopped, and I blacked out.

14 CALYPSUS

My hearing was the first to come back, followed by vision, and then movement. I heard someone calling my name, but I didn't know who it was. I opened my eyes to a blinding light and immediately used my arm to shield it. As they adjusted, I could see that I was lying on my back on a beach. My fingers were pressed in the warm sand. I looked at my surroundings. There was open water in one direction, and Brentwood Forest in the other. My friends were standing around me with concerned looks and I saw Silas' head hanging over them.

"What's going on?" I asked groggily. "Where am I?"

"He's OK," Jessica said with a smile.

I tried to sit up, but Blaine held me down, "Not so fast. You need to take it easy. I'll explain everything, but you need to stay on your back for now."

I nodded, but didn't really understand.

"Drink this," he said. He poured water into my mouth. "Are you in any pain?"

"No," I replied. "Tell me what's going on."

"We were walking through the forest when you collapsed. We tried to wake you, but nothing worked. When I looked at your chest wound, it had gotten worse."

"Yeah man, your veins and blood were turning black," Will interrupted.

Blaine shut Will up with a look before continuing, "As I was saying, it had gotten worse. The dark magic that the witch used on you infected your body. It was turning your blood black. All the veins in your face and body were dark, as it spread rapidly through your system. There was nothing we could do but get you to Silas. His ancient magic could counter the witch's magic and save you. I carried you through the forest as quickly as possible, and when we finally made it out, Silas was waiting for us at the beach."

Silas interjected, "I met with the elves and they sent me here to wait for you. You can only pass through their barriers with help from someone with magical powers.

"I saw Blaine carry you out of the forest. He told me what had happened, and I immediately healed you."

"So I was poisoned?"

Blaine arched an eyebrow. "In a manner of speaking."

"Uh-huh," I breathed in. "Can I sit up now?"

He laughed. "Yes, I believe you can."

I sat up slowly, because my body still felt sore and weak. Blaine handed me some more water, which I gulped down. The ocean breeze helped clear my head.

Jessica gave me a concerned look.

"I'm fine," I told her. "So where are the elves?"

Silas nodded at the ocean. "They live on an island across the water. It would be easiest for me to carry two of you at a time. So we'll have to make several trips."

"Well, then let's get started," I said, and I stood.

"You should go first," Blaine said to me. "It would be best if you were the first person the elves saw."

"Alright, who else?"

"Yeah, I got this," Will indicated, raising his hand.

Silas grabbed the two of us with his giant claws. It was extremely uncomfortable, but I guess it was better than gripping his razor scales. We dangled from his claws as he soared into the air and made his way across the water. After several moments, I could see that we were approaching an island. As we got closer, I could see that it wasn't tropical. It looked very similar to the land we had travelled to get here. There were mountains, a thick forest, and lagoons.

Silas hovered over the beach, letting us go about ten feet from the ground. We hit the sand with a loud thump. "Oops, sorry about that."

Before we could reply, he took off, flying fast to pick up the next two.

"This is where the elves live?" I wondered aloud.

"Yeah, I'm disappointed, too," Will said.

I looked at him. "What do you mean?"

"When they said that they lived on an island, I expected something cooler. Like tropical trees and monkeys or something."

"So you're disappointed about seeing elves, who we didn't think even existed, because there are no monkeys?"

"Yup."

"Right."

I stared at the forest in front of us. It was full of bushy trees, much like the ones we had seen on our way to the mountains of Elsador. My eyes stopped when I saw a tall man, who I can only assume was an elf, standing at the forest line. As soon as I had spotted him, he walked towards us. He had bleach-white hair that went down to his shoulders. He wore fancy robes that were also pure white, and tight to the skin. A cape waved behind him in the breeze, and I could see a bow and quiver of arrows beneath it, on his back. His right hand held a long white staff that made him look very distinguished as he walked confidently toward us.

"Who's the magician?" Will asked.

"Dude, I'm pretty sure that's an elf."

"Then why does he have a staff?"

I rolled my eyes.

"I presume you are King Arthur?" the elf said. Now that he was closer, I could see that his ears were pointed back. His eyes were fascinating. They were narrow and really wide, with sky blue pupils. They reminded me of a cat's eyes.

I nodded. "Yes, I am."

He stood directly in front of me, staring. I kept waiting for him to say something. It was extremely unnerving. After what seemed like forever, he finally shifted his gaze out into the ocean. He spoke, "I know why you have come here. My name is Aiden. I am a member of the elves' high council. There is much to discuss, and much to learn."

"Uh-huh. So you're going to help us then?" I asked.

He continued to watch the water.

He did not respond.

I looked at Will, who shrugged and whispered, "Magicians never reveal their secrets."

"Shut up. He's not a magician."

I must've said that a little too loud, because the elf cocked his eyebrow at Will. "I am not a magician," he said.

"Told you," I said.

"However, magic is woven into the very being of an elf. You cannot have an elf unless you also have magic," Aiden said. It sounded like he was reading a fortune cookie.

"So you are a magician," Will confirmed.

"No, you missed the point. We are higher beings," Aiden let out a deep breath. "Magic is a part of us, but we are not sorcerers."

"Yeah, he's a magician," Will repeated confidently.

Aiden shook his head. Something caught his attention in the sky. "Silas has returned with the others," he said.

Silas was soaring towards us, with Blaine in one claw, Jessica in the other. The otters hung from his hind legs. He swooped down, and released them several feet from the ground. They hit the sand with a soft thump. He pumped his wings several times and disappeared to the other side of the island.

"Please tell me that I never have to do that again," Jessica said, holding her head. Her hair was in a wild mess.

Will snickered.

"Now that you are all here, I will show you the island of Calypsus, home of the elves," Aiden said, pointing to the island with his staff.

"Aiden?" I asked. "I don't mean to sound forward, but we don't have time to tour the island. Camelot is in danger right now, and we need to get back there as fast as possible."

Aiden smiled. "Do you know why Silas needed to be the one to bring you here?"

"Something about a magical barrier?" I replied.

He nodded. "Calypsus is an island protected by ancient magic. When you cross the barrier, everything changes. Including time. What seems like weeks here, is merely days on the outside. Do you understand?"

"So you're saying if we spent a week here, only a day would pass in Camelot?" I confirmed.

"Precisely."

"Cool," Will interjected.

"Therefore, we are in no rush. I shall show you the island, and then we shall discuss why you have come with the council elders."

"Seems reasonable enough," I said.

Jessica nodded. "Yeah, it would be nice to take a tour, and have a break from running for our lives."

"We've been through a lot these past few days," Blaine agreed.

"Very well," Aiden said, "I shall try to keep that in mind."

He led us into the forest. Everything was quiet and peaceful. The soothing, calm atmosphere was a complete change from the high-tension of Brentwood. Soft grass cushioned my feet. The sun shone through the treetops, illuminating the woods. The place vibrated with life and brilliance. Several birds chirped as they flew past us, singing a cheery tune. Thick batches of moss clung to the bottom of the taller trees.

"It's beautiful here," Jessica voiced, as we took it all in.

Aiden did not turn around or slow his pace when he responded, "Indeed. We elves respect nature and everything it offers. We have learned to become one with nature, unlike others who destroy it with fire or tools."

I couldn't help but feel that his last remark was most likely about humans. We hiked over ditches, under fallen trees, and down slopes until the forest opened up into a lagoon. It was breathtaking. In front of us was a calm and smooth, crescent-shaped lagoon, which fed into the ocean. We came out of the woods at the northern tip of the lagoon, on a rocky, slippery edge. Massive cliffs enclosed it, and a large waterfall rushed down the far side. The water was so crystal clear, we could count pebbles on the sandy bottom. Groups of vines and moss clung to the walls of the cliffs, and I could see several caves hidden behind them.

"Calypsus is divided into three different sections, according to the different races of elves. This is called the Sebian Lagoon. The Sebians live in caves along the cliffside," Aiden explained. "If you would like to stop, swim, and meet them, I can arrange it."

Everyone seemed eager to jump in the water, especially the otters, whose whiskers twitched at the sight of fish swimming in it.

"That would be fantastic," I replied.

He nodded. "This way."

He led us up the cliff, along the rocky path, until we neared the waterfall. The view from the top was incredible. The sun lit up the blue sky, making the water sparkle. Aiden approached the cliff's side, and grabbed a thick vine hanging over the edge.

"Wait here, I shall only be a moment," he said. And he jumped over the edge.

I gasped and ran to the edge. He had swung on the vine and disappeared into the cliff.

"Did he just commit suicide?" Will asked.

I shook my head. "No, I don't think so. I think he just swung into a cave."

"Like Tarzan?" Jessica asked.

I continued to look over the edge. "Yup."

"Is he coming back?" Jessica asked.

"He said he was."

Blaine sat on a nearby rock. "I'm sure he'll be back soon. Just relax, and enjoy the scenery."

We took Blaine's advice. The otters rolled in the soft grass, Will leaned against the cliff, and Jessica took a seat next to me. We dangled our feet over the cliff's edge. For the first time in days we had nothing to worry about. There was no conflict to solve and no troubles. It was nice. I mean, think about it. The recent chaos was enough to exhaust anyone. We escaped The Island after being chased by armed guards. We time-travelled. We were thrown into a dungeon. We escaped. I became king. We learned to fight. We hiked over ice-covered mountains. We were attacked. We met annoying dwarves. I battled the dragon. We lost our friend to giant mice. I killed a witch. Can you see why I may have needed a break?

The view was breathtaking. The sun seemed close enough to touch, and the water below was inviting. My break came to an end when several vines beside me started to shake. I peered over. Aiden and another elf were using them to climb up the steep cliff. Jessica scooted back and I got up on my knee and stretched out a hand. They didn't need my help, though. They climbed those vines with shocking ease.

"This is the Sebian leader, Capria," Aiden said, gesturing to the other elf.

Capria was exactly like Aiden, except he was blue. Blue robes. Blue hair. Yeah, blue.

"He's blue," Will whispered to me.

"I know."

"It's creeping me out."

"I know."

"He's, like, a blue magician."

"For the last time, they are not magicians!" I hissed.

"Aiden told me you are the new king of the human colony known as Camelot," he said, interrupting our private discussion.

I extended a hand. "I'm Arthur. It's nice to meet you."

"As the leader of the Sebians, I welcome you to Calypsus. Aiden has told me of the things you have been through. You are more than welcome to enjoy the beauty and prosperity of the lagoon. A word of caution," he paused, "most of the Sebians keep to themselves, and prefer to stay in the isolated caves. You are welcome to relax here, but do not overstep into their personal space."

His words were deep and hollow. I was left wondering if we should actually stay here. Capria bowed, then leapt over the edge and, I assume, swung back into a cave.

"So … we shouldn't go for a swim?" Will asked.

Aiden chuckled. "No. What Capria means is, do not stay here indefinitely."

Will still looked puzzled.

"We can go for a quick swim, then we better carry on with our purpose," I explained.

He nodded. "Got it."

Jessica wandered over to the edge. "How do we get down there?"

Aiden raised an eyebrow. "By jumping, of course."

"Of course."

I took another look over the edge; we must've been at least three stories high. "Umm, it's quite a ways down isn't it?"

"I forgot that you humans do not possess the same magic we do," he paused. "This lake has a surface charm on it."

"Of course! A surface charm, why didn't I think of that?" Will burst out sarcastically.

Aiden held his eyes to Will's for a minute, then he spoke, "The surface charm allows anything to hit the water, from any height, and it will not be harmed," he explained. "It will feel like you are just stepping into the lake, no matter how high you jump from."

"So you're saying if I jump off of this cliff, when I hit the water, I will be perfectly okay?" I asked.

"Precisely."

"Uh-huh."

"You do not trust me," Aiden challenged.

I hesitated. "Well … no, not really. No offense."

He smiled. "It's understandable. Perhaps the otters will show you."

Chester and Malcom perked up and scurried over.

"Right-o," Chester said.

"Not even a challenge, really," Malcom replied.

Without hesitation they scampered to the edge and hurled themselves off. They tucked into furry cannonballs. I cringed when they hit the water. Two small splashes were all I could see. I held my breath and began to think they were dead, until the small dark figures emerged from under the water's surface.

"Blimey! That was brilliant!" I heard Chester shouting.

"Oi!" Malcom yelled. "Are you coming or what?"

I looked at Will.

"Yeah right, buddy," he said, staring at the drop.

I shrugged at Will and took off my armor and the shirt underneath. "I dunno, they survived."

Jessica and Will hesitated.

"You guys gotta learn to live a little," I said with a little wave and then dove headfirst from the cliff. The air whipped my face as I plummeted toward the water. I'm not going to lie; it scared the crap out of me. It was like that uneasy feeling you get from the drop of a rollercoaster, but really it was incredible. I was flying … or falling to my death. Whatever. I picked up speed as the water got closer. I shut my eyes and braced for impact. Instead, when I broke the water surface it felt like my body was being slowly dipped into the water. I didn't have time to think about it all, I just enjoyed it.

The water was warm, like a hot spring. It was incredibly soothing on my still-aching body. I swam to the surface, and took in a glorious breath of fresh air.

"You guys have to come down here!" I shouted happily to my friends, who I could barely see at the top of the cliff.

The otters were happily splashing about, chasing the small fish swimming in the water. I swam on my back, away from where my friends would land when they jumped.

Suddenly, a high-pitched scream echoed throughout the lagoon. I could tell right away that it was Jessica. She screamed the entire way down, flailing her arms like a madman … or madwoman. Either way, it was funny. She hit the water just like I had; head first. As I watched it happen, nothing appeared to be out of the ordinary. She hit the water as the same speed she fell. The impact alone should kill a person, but sure enough, just like me, she came up smiling.

"That was amazing!" she squealed with delight. "It didn't even feel like I jumped into the water."

"I know, right?" I said, waiting for Will to come down. I knew he wouldn't want to be left behind.

Sure enough, moments later, Will tossed himself off the cliff. He yelped when he was about to hit it, and was engulfed in a splash of water.

He resurfaced shouting, "Ahhhh!"

"What's wrong? Are you alright?" I asked, concerned that the jump had hurt him.

"I got water up my nose!" Will complained.

Jessica splashed water in his face. "You idiot, we thought you were hurt."

"Hey! Don't splash me!" he shouted. "I hate getting water up my nose."

She shook her head, held her breath, and swam underneath the water away from him.

He looked to me and shrugged.

I ignored him and dove under the water as well. I swam to the sandy bottom and skimmed it with my stomach. I went up for air then dove back down. I loved how the water blocked the sound of the outside world. It was tranquil. I let my mind wander as I swam. I wasn't concerned about the prophecy, The Island, or even if I'd make it back to the future in one piece. I had no cares. I rose to the surface and swam to a shallow place where I could sit in the water.

We enjoyed the break. The otters spent their time chasing the fish. Will floated aimlessly across the lagoon. Jess swam near the waterfall and, at some point, Blaine and Aiden had come down too and sat talking at the water's edge. I looked down at my hands. Wrinkles were starting to form on my fingertips. My mom used to say my hands looked like prunes when I went swimming. The thought made me sad, and I shook the memory from my head. I decided it was time we move on.

"Hey, Aiden," I called out, "should we get going?"

He nodded. "Yes, I think that's a good idea."

He puckered his lips and a shrill whistle, almost like tinkling bells, filled the air. Four Sebians launched off the side of the cliff swinging on vines. They dropped our clothes in a pile on the grass, then continued to swing into a cave. It was extremely fascinating.

We dressed, and left the lagoon area.

"Aiden, where did Silas go?" I asked as we hiked through the forest. I realized that I hadn't seen Silas since he dropped off the second group on the beach.

"Don't worry Arthur, he is fine," he replied. "Silas is resting with the Pyras tribe, near the lava pits. He will find it most appealing."

"Lava pits?" Jessica perked up.

Aiden nodded. "Pyras is at the bottom of a volcano, making it the hottest place in Calypsus. Each time the volcano erupts, it fills the lava pits. Pyras is not the most pleasant place in Calypsus; most of us can't stand the heat. That is why we shall not be visiting it."

"Aw man, that sounds really cool," Will complained.

"I just said the heat there is unbearable, it is the opposite of cool, Merlin," Aiden replied.

Will forgot that they didn't understand many of our colloquialisms. "Erm, I meant something else. You know what? Nevermind."

"We will be going to Veritas, the forest tribe of Calypsus," Aiden said.

"Sounds pretty," Jessica said. "Who's the leader there?"

Aiden turned to meet her. "Why, me, of course."

"Of course," observed Will.

He led us deeper into the island. Sunlight twinkled from the treetops. Aiden expounded, "Since Veritas is in the center of Calypsus, the Tribunal is held there. The Tribunal is where the three leaders meet and collaborate in times like this. I shall show you my tribe, then we shall go to the Tribunal to discuss why you came here."

"Sounds like a plan," I replied.

"What do you guys do for fun around here?" Will asked. I could tell he was bored from all the walking.

"Fun?" Aiden questioned.

"Yeah, fun. You know, like entertainment, how do you pass the time cooped up on an island?"

"I suppose meditating for several hours is … fun."

"Meditating?"

"Indeed. It is an art of relaxation. We use it to connect to nature, calm our minds, and concentrate on aspects of life."

"Sounds like a riot," Will said, with one of his famous eye rolls.

Aiden didn't pick up on the sarcasm. Or maybe he ignored it. "It is quite liberating."

"Uh-huh."

I could have never imagined anything as bright and green as this forest. The green that reflected from the trees and moss was more vibrant and alive than any color I'd ever experienced. Aiden suddenly stopped in the middle of the forest.

"Is something wrong?" I asked him.

"Not at all," he replied. "We are here."

"I don't see anything," Jessica said. There was just mossy grass in front of us.

Aiden smiled and pointed upwards.

We looked up. The treetops held an entire village. Each tree was shaped and molded into a home with branches and leaves camouflaging it. Between each tree was either a long branch, a wooden bridge, or a vine which allowed the elves to transport from tree to tree.

"Incredible," I marveled.

"Welcome to Veritas," Aiden said.

"You mean your whole tribe lives up in the trees?" Jessica asked in awe.

Aiden nodded. "Indeed," he said with pride.

He showed us a large tree with a curved staircase carved into it. The stairs twisted upward along the trunk and were very smooth with weird symbols painted on them. Aiden began climbing and we followed. The top of the staircase led right into the hollowed-out tree. We found ourselves in a bedroom. There was a small hammock and several tables and chairs inside (keep in mind, it's a big tree), and out the opposite end of the bedroom was a doorway covered with a draping made of branches. Aiden pushed it aside and we stepped through to the outside. Before us was a large wooden bridge that led to several different trees.

"Each tree is a house, and is connected by these bridges. Everything here has been made from or out of the nature around us," Aiden said, as we walked across the bridge.

"You mean you didn't use any metal or anything?" Blaine asked.

"Nope," he replied. "The bridges are made from dead trees, held together by vines and sap. We do not waste what nature provides us, and we do not forsake it."

"Incredible," breathed Blaine, crouching to inspect the bridge.

"If you guys are one with nature, what do you eat?" Will asked.

"Whatever the forest provides. We have a variety of fruit, berries, plants, and herbs that grow naturally here."

"You don't eat meat?"

"No."

"That sucks."

Aiden raised his eyebrow at Will. I thought he was about to reply, but he must have decided it was better if he didn't. He was probably right. I got the distinct feeling that Will was a test to Aiden's patience. He led us through the village in the trees, showing us his tribe. The elves we came across were quiet and avoided talking to us. They all wore the same clothes as Aiden. I guess the different tribes were color-coded or something.

"We like to keep to ourselves, which is why we are on this

island in the first place. The world of man is far too destructive," Aiden explained, as if justifying his tribe's silence.

A long, piercing whistle rang out through the forest.

"What's that?" Jessica asked.

"It means the Tribunal is about to begin. We should get going."

We descended via a different tree. The Tribunal was a short walk away from the Veritas village. It didn't take long for us to reach a clearing. Large stones were pressed into the mossy grass to form a circle that was about 25 feet in diameter. Three stone chairs were positioned around the circle, facing its inside. The center of the circle was a couple of feet lower than the ground outside the circle. Capria sat on one of the stone chairs, while another elf, dressed in a black robe with black hair, sat in the other. Aiden took his place in the third chair and gestured for us to use the steps that would allow us to get to the middle of the circle. We did, and soon found ourselves in the flat center, looking up at Aiden.

"The Tribunal is now in session," he said in a deep voice. "Representing the Sebians is Capria, representing the Pyras is Marrek, and representing Veritas is myself, Aiden."

The elves raised their colored staffs when Aiden said their names.

This Tribunal seems very official, I thought to myself.

"The Tribunal has assembled upon the request of Arthur, King of Camelot," Aiden continued. The three elves stared down at us, or rather, at me, and I could tell they were waiting for me to respond.

"Don't screw up," whispered Will.

"I have come here to ask you for help," I entreated. "I pulled Excalibur from the stone, setting the ancient prophecy into motion. Apparently an unimaginably fierce army is gathering to attack Camelot and will attempt to steal Excalibur's power to use it for evil purposes. The prophecy reads that the only hope is for us to align with old allies; the dwarves and elves in particular. After much ...

trouble ... the dwarves agreed to help. We have come a long way, and even lost a great companion on our journey, in order to ask for your help in this battle. Please help us."

No one moved or spoke. After a few minutes, Marrek sat up in his chair and spoke a single word in his deep voice, "No."

"No?" Will asked, stepping forward angrily. "What do you mean, 'no'?"

Marrek's red eyes burned at Will, who shrunk back into the group. "The elves are no longer aligned with the human race. We are not concerned with the troubles of your kind."

"There must be something you can do to help us," I tried to reason. "The prophecy believed you can help."

"The elves are a peaceful race, and only fight when there is no other option," Capria said.

Aiden remained silent.

"You've got to be kidding me," I said. "We came all this way for nothing?!"

"Your anger only proves our point," Marrek said.

"My anger only proves my desire to help a kingdom that had nothing to do with me until a few days ago!" I shouted. "I don't even know them, but I'm not about to turn my back on them."

An uneasy silence followed my outburst. Jessica put her hand on my shoulder to calm me down, but I shrugged it off.

"If you won't fight because of some prophecy or … or allegiance, fine! Fight because it's the right thing to do. Fight because if you don't, good, innocent people will die, and their blood will be on your hands."

Aiden spoke up, "Our answer remains the same. We do not interfere with humans. We can offer you further training in your time here, but we will not send our army to help you. The Tribunal has reached its decision."

Capria and Marrek stood and walked away. Aiden walked

down to us. "I'm sorry," he said.

I didn't respond. My entire body was bursting with rage. I stormed off, away from my friends, away from Aiden, and away from the failed mission.

As I left I could hear Blaine saying, "No. Let him go."

I ran through the forest, trying to find my way back to the beach. I didn't look back. I was so full of anger and disappointment. I tore through the trees until the open sea air entered my lungs. The waves crashed onto the shore, and the sun beamed down on the sand. I collapsed against a piece of driftwood.

"Everything we've been through. Galahad. The dwarves. It was for nothing?" I put my head in my hands.

Calm down Francis, Excalibur's voice echoed into my head.

"Calm down?" I screamed out loud. "I don't understand why they won't help. I'm not even from this time period, and I'm helping."

I'm sure there's more to it than they are telling us. Maybe you should stay and take the training they offered.

"Pfft. The training. What a joke," I scoffed. "Maybe Will was right, maybe we should just go back to our own time."

And leave all these people to die? You and I both know that isn't who you are.

"I know. But without the elves we can't win, right?"

All the more reason for you to stay and train.

"You keep saying you."

Well, obviously I mean us. I'm trapped in a bloody sword. It's not like I can do anything.

"What about the others?"

I sense the elves' invitation was only for you. And besides, they won't listen to the others. You're royalty. They can return to Camelot, and we can use Silas to get there once the training is over.

"Uh-huh."

It wouldn't hurt. You would have more time to convince them to help. Their meditation might even help you harness your powers.

"They seem to have their minds made up already."

At the very least, we might annoy them then.

I laughed. "Yeah, I guess so."

Francis, believe me when I say that this will not be your hardest challenge. You must never lose sight of what's important.

"You're starting to sound like my father."

I'll take that as a compliment.

Before I could reply, Jessica's voice inturrupted, "Who are you talking to?"

"Oh. Nobody. Just myself," I answered.

She sat down beside me. "Mhmm. You alright? You kinda stormed off back there."

I let out a breath. "Yeah, I'm fine."

"Just because the elves said they wouldn't help, doesn't mean we're going to lose the battle. I think that prophecy is garbage anyway," she said. I could tell she was trying to cheer me up.

"I don't know what it means, but I've decided I'm going to stay and train with them."

"Great, we can all learn stuff from them."

"No, Jess, I mean *I'm* staying here. Aiden's invitation was only for me. You guys are going back to Camelot."

"What?" she asked. "There's no way we're leaving you here."

"They're not going to listen to you guys. I'm only staying to try and convince them to come fight with us. If I can do that, Camelot will be stronger, and we'd be less likely to die."

"What if something happens to us on the way back? It wasn't exactly easy getting here."

I thought for a moment. "I can ask Aiden to send an escort with you guys. Besides, you have the otters to protect you," I suggested.

She laughed. "Yeah, they're so reliable."

"I think those otters would die for us. This is the best way," I said. "You guys can go back and sort everything out in Camelot. Get our troops organized. Talk to Lancelot, I'm sure he'll know what to do. Meanwhile, I'll stay here and try to convince Aiden. If I can't, then I'll get Silas to fly me back to Camelot and meet up with you guys."

Jessica frowned. "I don't like the idea of us separating, but it sounds reasonable."

"Of course it's reasonable, I thought of it," I teased.

"Shut up," she laughed, hitting me on the shoulder. She stood up and stretched her legs. "C'mon, we should probably tell the others what's going on."

We made our way back to Veritas. I was completely lost, but Jessica knew exactly where she was going. When we reached Veritas, the gang was sitting on the ground, talking.

"Look who's back," Will observed.

Blaine and the others turned as we approached. "Ah, welcome back Arthur," Blaine said. "We were just discussing what we are going to do now."

"Good," I said, joining them on the ground. "As I was just telling Gwen, I'm staying here to train with the elves and try to convince them to join us. You guys are going to get back to Camelot and prepare for battle."

"What would you like us to do to prepare?" Blaine asked, unfazed at the thought of us splitting up.

"With the dwarves, and possibly the elves coming, I'm sure it will be chaos trying to organize everyone. I want you and Lancelot to sort everything out, and make sure Camelot is ready for anything."

"It shall be done. And how exactly are you getting back?" Blaine asked.

"Once I'm done here, I'll get Silas to take me back. It's faster that way. Remember, time moves differently here. It will probably be like I'm not far behind you at all."

Everyone nodded. I don't think any of them wanted to question the king's decision. Will didn't seem to care about leaving me here in the way that Jessica did. That kind of concern must be a chick thing.

"Right, then, when do we shove off?" Chester asked.

"I don't know, how about tomorrow morning?" I replied. "It would let us get a good rest in before everything happens."

The otters seemed pleased with the decision, and sprawled out on the grass. Blaine stood up. "I'll go talk to Aiden about finding us a place to stay."

"Thanks," I said as he left. I sat down beside Will.

"You seem to be getting comfortable as king," he said in a low voice. "Sure you don't want to stay here, instead of going back to The Island?"

I shook my head. "We don't belong here. Besides, I told you, we have to help the others."

He frowned and closed his eyes. "You and your hero complex are gonna get us killed."

I ignored him, which was starting to become a habit. I leaned back, resting my body on the smooth, cushy surface of the ground, and tried to relax.

15 TRUTH COMES OUT

The otters, Will, Jessica, and I were all enjoying ourselves, relaxing on the comfy grass when Blaine returned from talking with Aiden. "I've got good news. Aiden and his people will lodge us in Veritas," he announced.

"That's great!" Jessica replied cheerily.

"Yeah, it's always been one of my life goals to spend the night in a tree," grumbled Will.

"I have never spent the night in a tree either, Merlin. I also am quite looking forward to it," Blaine agreed. I couldn't help but think it was a good thing these people didn't pick up on Will's sarcasm.

"That's, um, nice," Will replied.

The otters, however, looked disappointed.

"You mean we can't stay by the lagoon?" Chester asked.

"No."

"Rubbish," Malcom muttered.

"So what are we going to do for the rest of the day?" Jessica asked Blaine.

"Well, it's going to get dark soon, so we should probably get something to eat, and then get some rest."

"Finally, some food," Will said. He stood up.

"Where do the elves eat, anyways?" I asked.

"Probably in a tree," guessed Will.

"Actually you're right," Blaine replied. "The elves usually eat separately in their homes, only coming together on special occasions.

We should find Aiden to see where we can eat."

The six of us wandered around Veritas until we came across Aiden, deep in discussion with a fellow elf. Once they were done talking, Aiden walked towards us. "What can I do for you?"

"We were wondering if you had any food?" I asked.

He thought for a moment. "I'll have someone bring a meal to your sleeping quarters."

"Alright, thank you."

He nodded and left us. Blaine led us to a large tree, which had openings at several levels of the trunk "The bottom floor is for the otters and myself, the middle is for Guinevere, and the top is for you and Merlin."

"Cool," Will said, staring at the tree. "Three levels in one tree!"

We said goodnight and went to our various sleeping quarters. As Will and I stepped inside the highest room, I noted it was surprisingly large, seeing as it was inside a tree. There were two beds carved out of the tree itself, with what appeared to be either grass or moss as the mattresses. The ceiling was dome-shaped, and, I kid you not, fireflies hovered at the top, lighting the room. In the corner of the room was a chair with a desk, also carved out of the tree. It was incredible to see how the elves didn't waste anything that the environment gave them.

"Wow," I said.

"Dude, I thought we learned in that stupid history class that tree huggers didn't come about until the 1960s," Will observed.

I laughed. "I don't think they're hippies, Will."

"Have you taken a look around? In case you haven't noticed, their entire village is in the trees."

"Yeah, well they're more like sophisticated hippies, then. I mean, they're incredibly smart; they have to be in order to build all of this."

"I guess so," he said, sitting down on a bed. "When do you think the food will get here?"

I shrugged, and sat down on my own bed. It was incredibly comfortable, and almost morphed to my body. I think I fell asleep for a bit. I was awakened by an elf who wore the same kind of robe and had the same white hair as Aiden. He was carrying two wooden plates of food. "Aiden told me you wanted something to eat," he said politely.

"Thanks," I said. He placed the trays on the table, and left the room.

"Oh man, I'm starving," Will said, jumping up and racing over to the table. He stopped abruptly and stared down at the food in disappointment.

"What's wrong?" I asked.

"It's ... salad," he said. He curled his lips in disgust.

I chuckled. "Oh come on, salad is good for you. Green food is healthy food."

"Green food also tastes like crap, buddy."

I grabbed my plate and began eating. It was actually pretty good. Will continued to stare at the salad, and started to poke it. Eventually he took a bite, but spat it right out.

"Man, this is worse than the food from The Island, and I didn't even know what that was."

I smiled and shook my head at him. "Well, I think I'm going to go to sleep."

"Whatever," he said poking at the green leafs on his plate.

I closed my eyes, and rested against the soft bed. I could hear Will complaining to himself about the food before I fell asleep. Excalibur was waiting for me in my dreams. He was sitting on a rock, cleaning his sword, which was dripping with blood. I stepped over several bodies in order to reach him.

"What's up?" I asked.

He looked solemn. “Not much. I’m still working out why I’m stuck here.”

“Uh-huh.”

“Tomorrow everyone’s heading back to Camelot and you’re staying to train?” he asked.

“Yup.”

“I see,” he said. He slid his sword back into its sheath. “I would recommend talking about honor and loyalty when speaking with Aiden one-on-one. But keep in mind that the elves value different things than we do. Their training might not be what you expect.”

“What do you mean?”

“You’ll see,” he smiled, and then vanished.

“Could you be more cryptic?” I yelled. No reply. I was alone. Eventually I faded back into my own dreams, and wasn’t bothered by Excalibur for the rest of the night.

Morning arrived with a beam of sunlight shining through the opening in the tree. I sat up in my bed, and looked around the room. Will was asleep, but he was tossing and turning. I could see the sweat on his brow. I wished there was something I could do to help him, but sadly, I had no idea what that would be. I walked outside, taking in the fresh air. I sat down on the ledge and let out a long exhale. I heard footsteps coming up the wooden staircase. It was Blaine.

He sat beside me. “Did you have a good night’s rest, my lord?”

“Yeah, how about you?”

“It was very relaxing,” he replied. “Are the others awake?”

I shook my head. “No. When are you all leaving?”

“Once everyone’s awake. I talked to Aiden, and he has agreed to send guards to escort us back to Camelot, in case we run into any trouble.”

“That’s good. With the way our luck has been, we’ll need it,” I said. "Will you be able to get Camelot ready for battle?"

He nodded. "I will inform Lancelot of the plan, and he shall organize the troops accordingly. The men from our allied villages shall be there. By now the dwarves will have reached Camelot, too. Lancelot probably has them already prepped for battle."

"Hopefully. Blaine, I'm not going to lie, I don't know if I can be this king that everyone expects me to be. If I can't get the elves' help, the prophecy says we can't win. What if all those people die, because I failed?"

Blaine sighed. "Arthur, you were chosen for a reason. It takes a good king to lead an army, but it takes an extraordinary king to put that army before himself. I have seen you put your life on the line for people you barely know. Trust me, you are a greater king than you realize."

I let his words sink in. "Thanks. I'll do my best."

"I'm sure you will," he said, as he got to his feet. "But for now, focus on the task at hand. Convince Aiden to help us, then meet us back at Camelot. I'm going to wake the otters, and then find Aiden."

I nodded. He descended the stairs and disappeared from my sight. I had to hand it to him, he was good at the whole motivational, pep-talk thing. I stood and returned to my room. Will had begun to twitch violently in his bed. I ran to his side and shook him awake. He was frightened and confused.

"It's all right, buddy, you're OK, " I said. I felt helpless to comfort him.

He was clearly shaken. We had a silent agreement that I would never ask him about his dreams; that if he wanted to talk about them, he'd let me know. So for now, I ignored his outbursts. I went to my bed and grabbed my pack. I put my armor and padding on, and slid the quiver of arrows onto my back. I placed the fist knives on the back of my shoulders.

"Is it morning?" he asked me.

"Yeah, you'd better get ready, you guys are leaving soon."

"Already?"

"Mhmm."

"What about breakfast?"

I laughed. "Do you want some more salad?"

"Nevermind. I can skip breakfast."

He dressed, then attached his sword to his belt. He walked out of the room, and I followed. We went down the stairs and stopped at Jessica's room.

"Hey Gwen, you in there?" I asked.

"Just a minute," she called. After a couple seconds she appeared in the entrance, ready to go. "Hey."

"Hey. You ready?"

She nodded. "Yeah, let's go."

We continued down the staircase. Blaine and the otters were waiting for us.

"Good to see you're all awake," Blaine said. "Are you ready to leave?"

I nodded, but then remembered I wasn't leaving.

"Aiden has a boat waiting for us at the beach."

Blaine led us through the forest, and towards the beach. I knew we were getting close when the salty breeze hit us. The trees opened up, and we were walking on sand. A large wooden boat was waiting. Three elves, one from each tribe, were on it.

Aiden stood beside the boat. "Are you ready to leave?"

"Yes," Blaine responded for the group.

"These three will escort you back to Camelot," Aiden said, as they climbed into the boat. "Arthur will remain here and train with me, as agreed."

"Be careful," I told them, as the boat began to pull away. I had a small lump in my throat. The three elves were paddling.

"Always," winked Will.

I waited until they were a fair ways out in the water before turning to Aiden. "So where do we start?" I asked.

He smiled and began walking back to Veritas, "Meditation. Battle is not just about strength and speed. It is about keeping a cool head, and always being aware of your surroundings."

"I see."

"Do you?"

"What do you mean?" I asked him.

"I know you have power, courage, and determination, but I believe you lack patience."

"Patience," I repeated.

"Indeed. Patience is necessary for victory. If you run into a situation without thinking, you will most likely die. But if you look and think and analyze the situation before attacking it …"

"I am less likely to die," I finished.

"Exactly. Humans are always in a rush, and are quite hot-headed. They do not take the time to appreciate the small things, like this flower," Aiden stopped and knelt down to smell it.

I was starting to see his point. "I've been pushing for us to start training, but we've already started, haven't we?"

He smiled. "You must learn to be more patient. Things have a way of working themselves out if we stop and take a moment."

"I've been too worried about the prophecy and everything to even think about anything else. Ever since I pulled Excalibur from the stone, I've been going nonstop."

"This training will help clear your mind, allowing you to focus, and observe everything around you. It is not about physical ability," he explained. We had reached an open patch of grass surrounded by trees. "Your first task is to sit here, and observe everything. Listen. Feel. Relax. Clear your mind and let go of everything you're holding onto."

"For how long?" I asked.

He smiled, but did not reply. He left me alone, disappearing into the woods.

"Great," I said to myself.

I sat cross-legged on a soft patch of grass. I stared at everything around me. I studied every tree, every flower, and every blade of grass. I closed my eyes and listened to the sounds, isolating each one, and figured out where it came from. I did this for hours. After a while it got kind of annoying. I grew impatient and began to fiddle with the grass around me. I figured the whole point of this was to see how long I could last before giving up or getting annoyed, so I went back to sitting still. Time rolled on and eventually it started to get dark. By then I was furious. Had Aiden forgotten about me? Did I do something wrong?

I had enough. I stood up and made my way back to Veritas to find Aiden. I didn't have time to sit still for a day, doing nothing, when I could be convincing the elves to help us. I reached Veritas just as the sun was going down. I found Aiden waiting for me at the entrance to my room.

"I was wondering when you'd show up," he said.

I walked past him and threw my gear on my bed. "Oh yeah? I was out there the entire day! What exactly was the purpose of that? Huh?"

He calmly stepped inside. "You lasted much longer than I expected. Meditation requires deep focus and concentration. If you could not last more than an hour doing nothing, you would not be able to carry on with the training. Seeing as you stayed the whole day, you have proved worthy of continuing training with me."

"So that was a test?"

"Yes. Elves can meditate for days. Humans do not have the same stamina. To last as long as you did without giving up required patience and self-control."

"Is the rest of the training going to be like this?" I questioned.

"Not exactly. From this point on you will be training with me, rather than alone, at least for the most part. We will begin tomorrow."

I was still angry with him, but if I wanted to get the elves on my side, I couldn't lash out. "Sounds good," I conceded.

He left, and I was alone. I noticed a plate of salad on the desk, which I ate with gusto. I then crawled into my bed, trying to relax and calm down. It took a while, but eventually I was able to fall asleep. Excalibur was in my dreams (again). I think he wanted to make sure I could keep my cool during the training.

"I told you it would be different," he said coolly.

"Yeah, thanks for the heads up there, champ," I replied. I wasn't in the mood for one of his talks.

"Francis, you've got to keep your emotions under control. If they control you, you will not survive the challenges that lie ahead."

"Uh-huh."

He let out a deep breath. "Just try to keep them in check, alright? Aiden knows what he's talking about. You need to listen. You need to focus."

"What do you think I did all day?"

"I know, but it was a test. Aiden will test your mental ability, your focus, and all of your emotions. If you want any chance of getting the elves to help, you need to pass all his tests."

"Super," I said. I turned and walked away from him.

"Where are you going?"

"I'm trying to get some sleep. Do you mind?"

"Just try to do what he asks you to," he called after me.

Aiden was standing over me, shaking me awake. "It's time to start training," he said. His white face was close to mine.

"What time is it?" I asked. I rubbed my eyes to wake them up.

"Early morning, just before dawn."

I looked out the door. The sun was just barely starting to rise.

"Why so early?" I asked, as I reached for my clothes.

"The mind works best in the morning. Plus, I like to watch the sun rise," Aiden replied, smiling. He ducked out of the room so I could dress.

I sighed, "Fair enough."

As soon as I was ready, Aiden led me down the stairs, and through the forest towards the beach. The sky was turning crimson red, with orange streaks. It was beautiful.

He sat on the sand, inches away from the waves. "Sit," he instructed.

I sat down next to him. The sand was cold against my hands. The waves reached towards us, but never actually touched us.

"I want you to clear your head and relax. Close your eyes, and take deep breaths."

I humored him and closed my eyes. I took a deep breath.

"Now, I want you to sense everything around you. Feel the environment. Know your surroundings."

I wasn't exactly sure what he meant, but I tried to do what he asked. After several seconds something hit my head. I opened my eyes. "Ouch! What was that for?"

Aiden had smacked my head with his hand. "You're not sensing your surroundings. You need to clear your mind, and focus on the sounds, the feelings, and the area around you. You need to be able to see everything around you, without using your eyes."

"How can I see without my eyes?"

He did not respond. I shook my head, and closed my eyes again. I strained my ears trying to hear him approach. I heard the waves hitting the shore, I heard the wind, but I couldn't hear Aiden moving around me. Another hard smack on my head signified my failure.

"Dig deep. Sense my footsteps, feel my movement, and anticipate my attack."

"OK."

I tried again and again. Each time I failed. There was no way I could tell when he would strike. I was getting angry.

"Again," Aiden said. He seemed to be enjoying himself.

Every time I tried to focus, the harder it was. My anger was building up to the point where I could no longer hear the waves.

"Can we try something else?" I asked.

Aiden smiled. "Now you see the power of this training. When we are finished, you will be able to sense my approach before I am anywhere near you. This will allow you to become aware of your surroundings at all times, but specifically, on the battlefield. It will let you see every attack coming from any angle."

"That would be quite useful. Are you sure you can teach me?" I asked him.

"Well, we'll find out, now won't we?"

I shrugged.

"This training will also help you learn to control your emotions. It is obvious you were getting frustrated during this exercise. If your emotions take over during a battle ... " Aiden didn't need to finish the sentence.

"Teach me."

He smiled. "Follow me."

Aiden led me off the beach and through the forest. His mysterious aura somewhat concerned me. We went around Veritas, journeying into a part of Calypsus I hadn't yet seen. After much walking, we ended up at the entrance to a dark cave. He looked at me, and then at the cave.

I shook my head. "Uh-uh. No way. I don't do dark, creepy caves."

He stared at me.

I let out a deep breath. "Aw, crap."

I followed him into the cave. Darkness consumed me. I was

worried for a few seconds, but then a bright light filled the cave. Aiden's staff was glowing.

"Whoa! How did you do that?"

"I told you, elves have access to ancient magic," he said. He ventured further into the cave. "But it's a different magic than you and your friends possess."

I stopped. "How did you know?"

"I can sense it. That, and Nimue told me about you."

"How did you talk to Nimue?"

"Magic has very little boundaries for communication, Arthur."

"I see." I thought about that for a moment, then continued, "You seem quite fine with the fact that I'm from the future."

"Magic can do unimaginable things. No, it doesn't come as a shock to me. Perhaps you should have another talk with Nimue, it might clear things up."

I nodded. Nimue might've told him of my powers and the future, but I could guess that she didn't tell him about The Island, and I knew there were things she didn't tell me.

"You do not belong here, and yet, here you are. I wanted to discuss this with you away from the others," he paused and looked back at me. "Like Nimue's lake, this cave is protected; no one can hear our conversation here."

"But there wasn't anyone on the way here, either. Why couldn't we talk out there, and not in some creepy cave?"

"As peaceful as Calypsus may appear, there are certain creatures, evil creatures, that can infiltrate our safe haven, and spy on us undetected. For that reason, we had to come here, so it would appear as though it was part of your training."

"I'm not sure I follow."

Aiden sat down on a rock. "There are dark forces attached to the prophecy. Things that aren't human. Demons, djinns, trolls, creatures that lurk in the darkest corners of the earth."

I looked around, suddenly extremely concerned.

"Not here of course," he said, sensing my thoughts. "I meant out there. The point is you will face more than just humans in this upcoming fight, and you will need all the help you can get. Everything up to this point has been a show—a front—to disguise our true plans. The elves will gladly help you in this battle. We lied in order to mislead any spies that were watching. We are already sending our troops out to Camelot, by a secret portal."

Relief flooded my body. "So you are helping us."

"Yes. Sorry for all the deceit."

I'm sure he could see me relax, even in the bad lighting. "I'm so glad you're on our side. But what about the forest, and everything I've done so far?"

He chuckled. "Oh that? That was more for my entertainment."

I smiled and shook my head. "Unbelievable."

"It was amusing to see how long you sat in that forest. But back to the main point. I need to help you control your powers in order to face your worst nightmares. We will do that here, out of sight from any and all spies. I knew I could trust you, because Excalibur did. I cannot be as sure with your friends. I could sense a great darkness in your friend, Merlin. I would not trust him."

I shook my head. "It's a long story, but he suffers from horrific nightmares, and gets very little sleep. He's my friend though, and I trust him."

"My warning still stands. Now, about your powers," he said.

"What about them?"

"I can help you control them."

"How?" I asked. Hope filled my chest.

"First, explain to me what you can do with them."

I told him about time-travelling, freezing time to save Jessica and then again to kill the witch, and pretty much everything else that I thought was important. I left out information on The Island and I didn't really talk about the future. Aiden nodded and took it all in.

"You have a tremendous gift, Arthur. And with great power, comes great—"

"Responsibility," I said, remembering the phrase from *Spiderman*.

"I was going to say 'obligation,' but responsibility works, too," Aiden said. "I'd like to see you try using your power."

"Alright, what do you want me to do?" I asked him.

He stood up and babbled something in a strange language. Several small spheres of fire came out of his staff, and danced in the air in front of us.

"I want you to focus your power, and try to freeze time," he said calmly, like it was easy for me to do.

"You do know that I have a hard time controlling it, right?"

"Relax and concentrate. Focus your thoughts on freezing this moment. Practice is the only way you'll ever control your powers."

"I'll try."

I took a few calming breaths, and stared at the globes of fire. I concentrated everything within me on freezing them, but they kept moving. I squinted and tensed my face, trying to make time stop, but still nothing happened.

"It's not working," I sighed. "I told you earlier, I don't know how I do it."

Aiden nodded. "I understand. Please keep trying, Arthur. You will need to be able to do this with the snap of your fingers in the future."

"I know. I just don't understand how it works."

"It's ok. That's what we're here to work on. This wasn't going to happen overnight, you know."

Nothing worked. I was disappointed with myself. If I couldn't learn to control my powers, we'd never get back to the future, and I'd never be able to help the others. I frowned in frustration, took another breath, and began to concentrate again. After much time passed with nothing happening, Aiden sucked the fire back into his staff.

"We'll try again tomorrow," he said.

I nodded, but didn't respond. I followed him out of the cave, and we arrived in Veritas just as it was getting dark. I said goodnight to Aiden when we reached my room. I sat down on the bed and sighed.

"Why can't I do it?" I asked myself. But, having no answers, I went to sleep.

My sleep was peaceful, and the next morning, Aiden greeted me at the bottom of the tree.

"Ready to continue your training?" he asked, handing me a fruit that looked a lot like an apple, but was better than any apple I ever had in my life.

I shrugged as I bit into it. "I guess so."

"Good, we will start with some battle simulations," he said. He led me back towards the cave. Once inside, we sat on the rocks again. "The creatures you face will have powers of their own. They will be difficult to kill," he warned.

"Like what?"

"Minotaurs," he said, waving his staff once we were inside. A 3D image of a creature that was half-man, half-bull appeared in the air before us. It startled me.

"Don't be scared. It's just a picture. Minotaurs are strong, ferocious creatures, and they fear nothing."

Another image flashed into view. It was a woman with wings and claws. Her face was twisted into a cruel grimace. "Harpies. Evil and ruthless creatures."

More scary portraits of monsters popped up, and Aiden described each one.

"So this fight isn't going to be as easy as I thought, is it?"

"No. The humans and dwarves should be able to handle the attacking humans, but it will be up to you and the rest of the elves to deal with these creatures."

"Why can't anyone else deal with them?"

"Most humans will be too petrified to attack creatures like the minotaurs, and most of the creatures can only die a certain way."

"What do you mean?"

Aiden pointed his staff, and a creature I recognized popped into view. "This is a—"

"Werewolf."

"Correct," he said. "Werewolves are extremely dangerous, and can only be killed by driving something silver through the heart."

"But werewolves are just myths."

Aiden raised his eyebrow. "Are they?"

I fell silent, suddenly terrified of what I had gotten myself into.

"The good news is that most dark creatures—like werewolves—can only come out at night."

"What if the battle goes into the night? Aren't sieges supposed to take a long time?" I asked.

"For our sake, I hope it doesn't come to that. Otherwise we will be dealing with a nightmare."

The shivers crawling up my spine caused an involuntary shudder. "Can we get back to training?"

Aiden nodded. "The point is, the elves know how to deal with these creatures, but people don't, and the dwarves are stupid. You'll be fine because the magic Excalibur contains allows it to kill anything."

"That makes me feel a little bit better."

"It should," Aiden said, taking my apple core and putting it in his pocket. (I figured he was going to plant it later.) "Come on."

We went deeper into the cave, until we reached a flat, open

space. He shot several globes of fire into the air. The cavern lit up. It was a huge space that reminded me of an arena.

"Today we will try a different approach to using your powers."

"And what's that?"

"Fear."

"Sounds good. Wait. What?"

Aiden vanished into a puff of smoke, leaving me alone in the large cavern. Several more fiery globes began to appear, and started to float towards me.

"Umm … Aiden?" I looked around nervously.

The globes launched towards me, but I was quick enough to dodge them. I got to my feet and began to run away. The balls of fire chased after me.

"Aiden, I don't like this plan!" I yelled.

There was no answer. *Great.* I continued to dodge the fire, but more balls began appearing. I started to panic, until I realized what Aiden was doing. He was creating a life-threatening situation, which would force me to use my powers like I had the other times. The only question was, would it work?

It dawned on me that the fire could actually kill me. Suddenly I feared for my life. I dove to my right, avoiding another ball of fire, but when I stood, the rest were screaming towards me. I narrowed my eyes and focused on freezing time in order to escape. The fiery globes were several feet from me when they all stopped.

I had done it! I jogged out of the way and unfroze time, letting the fire crash into the spot I had been moments ago.

"Well done!" Aiden said, appearing behind me.

Running for my life had winded me. "Never do that again," I said between breaths.

He smiled.

The next several days rolled on, much in the same way. Aiden and I would train my abilities inside the cave. Then, he would teach me about the creatures I might encounter, and afterward we would meditate outside. Anyone who was watching would think I was preparing for battle. It wasn't very exciting, but it did help me. Every day I became faster and better at stopping time. Aiden's encouragement was part of the reason, but I also started to understand where my powers were coming from, specifically, the area of my brain. I was pretty confident that I could get us back to the future, but I didn't dare practice time travel without Will and Jess, in case I couldn't return to the past to get them.

Enough days had passed that I began to wonder if I could get to Camelot in time for the battle. One day, during a lesson on djinns, I interrupted Aiden.

"Aiden, I should probably get to Camelot soon. I know that time moves differently here, but it's been such a long time that I feel like we've missed the battle already."

Aiden nodded. "I understand, Arthur. Besides, I believe we've covered everything I wanted to teach you, and we've made good progress with your abilities."

I thanked him for helping me. "So should I call Silas now?"

"You have enough time to spare to spend another night here, in which I would suggest getting as much sleep as possible. There is no telling how long this battle will go on."

"Alright," I said. I packed my gear. "Aiden?"

"Yes, Arthur?"

"Are the creatures we talked about really going to be there?"

He hesitated before answering, "I hope not. But there is evil out there that will stop at nothing to get Excalibur. It would not surprise me if we ran into any or all of those creatures."

I frowned in disappointment. "I have no idea what it's going to be like."

"What? Battle?"

I nodded. After the things I had been through in this time

period, I was beginning to think I wouldn't survive this fight.

"Arthur," he paused, "it will be like nothing you've experienced. Trust your instinct. It will keep you alive."

As we walked back to the village in the trees, I thought of my friends and wondered if they'd made it safely. Aiden led me to my room and simply left, without saying anything more. I laid on my bed and tried to fall asleep, but the excitement and fear of the coming battle kept me awake.

I left my room and wandered around Veritas in the dark. I saw a strange white light coming from the Tribunal area. I moved silently towards it. I peeked my head around a tree. The light was coming from Aiden. Actually, it came from Aiden's staff. He was practicing fighting moves, using his staff as a weapon. Occasionally white energy would fly from the staff at stone targets positioned around the clearing.

I watched him for a long time. His graceful and elegant strikes cut through the air smoothly. His staff moved at lethal speeds, and the stones shattered when they were hit by his magic. I had not seen Aiden do anything violent, or physical when we had been training. Now that I saw him practicing, I began to feel more confident with the fight. I was also happy he was on our side.

I must've stepped on a twig or something because Aiden snapped his head in my direction, his eyes staring into mine, and he pointed his staff at me.

"It's just me," I called out.

He lowered his staff and relaxed, "You should be resting."

"Funny, I was gonna say the same thing to you," I said, moving towards him. "You're pretty good with that thing."

He nodded. "Elves are deadly warriors, but only the tribe leaders have access to more intense magic."

"I see."

"You really should go back to sleep, Arthur," he said, resuming his training. "You will need all of your energy tomorrow."

I took his hint. He wanted to prepare for battle alone. I was just about back to my bed when Excalibur's voice echoed in my head.

Aiden's right, you need to get some rest. Battle is very strenuous on the body.

"I'll keep that in mind," I spoke out loud again to Excalibur.

Do not be scared of it.

"I'm not scared … you're scared."

I'm in your head, Francis. I know you're frightened. You can be honest with me.

"Alright, I'm freaked out. I didn't think there would be monsters and everything. I thought it would be …"

Easier?

"I dunno, just different. What if my friends get hurt?"

There will come a time where you must face your fears, and meet them head-on. Your friends know what they are getting into.

"No, they don't."

Maybe not about the dark creatures and whatnot, but they are loyal enough to fight beside you, and accompany you on your journey. Friends like that are rare, Francis. We will look out for them, but you must not let it distract you while you're in battle. That will get you killed.

I had reached my bed and climbed in. "Thanks for the advice, can I go to sleep now?" I asked with a yawn.

That would be best.

I rolled onto my side, and closed my eyes. I thought long and hard about if I'd survive whatever it was I had gotten myself into. I kept telling myself that helping people was worth putting my life in danger. It was something my father would be proud of.

16 NIGHT TERRORS

My dreams were haunted with images of my family on the day of the crash. I woke up in a cold sweat, my body weak from the ordeal. I took several deep breaths, trying to regain strength in my body. A dim beam of light shone through the doorway, signalling the dawn of a new day. I took my time getting up. I was in no rush to face the long day ahead of me. My armor and gear were piled in the corner of the room. I rubbed the sleep from my eyes, and carefully put all of my gear on, to make sure I didn't miss anything.

I gave my room one last look before I descended the stairs. Somehow, Aiden always knew when I was up, and greeted me at the bottom. "Did you sleep well?" he asked.

I was surprised how tired my voice sounded when I responded, "Well enough."

"Before you leave, I have several things to give you."

That intrigued me. "Like what?"

"Follow me," he said, leading me through Veritas one last time. He stopped in front of a large tree. There was a small doorway at the base of it. "Come in here."

I stepped through the doorway, ducking so I didn't hit my head. The room was hot and musky. It was much like the other tree-rooms, but in the center was a large table with armor on it.

"The armor you wore here will not do much against the claws of a harpy, or the horns of a minotaur, so I had my friends in Pyras forge this armor for you. It is laced with magic, and will protect you more than any other armor out there. It is also lighter than the armor humans make, which will allow you to be quick, but safe."

I walked to the table and studied the armor. It was a shiny silver metal, with gold lining the edges, and each joint was sharp and pointed. I picked up the helmet. It was lighter than a feather, which made me question whether it would protect me. The helmet left my eyes, nose, and mouth open, allowing me to see more of my surroundings. It had an unusual design in that it curved into three points on each side of my head. On the opposite side of the table was a bow with two curves in it, and a quiver full of black arrows with silver tips.

"That is an elven bow," Aiden explained. "It will give you a greater distance and finer accuracy than your current bow."

I stared at the gifts that Aiden had given me. "Aiden, I don't know what to say. This is great. Thank you."

He shook his head. "There is no need to thank me, Arthur. But there is more."

"What do you mean?"

"Exchange your armor, and then I will show you."

I did as he said, and switched my armor and bow for the new ones. The armor fit perfectly, and felt way better than what I'd had on. It was incredibly light and maneuverable. I placed the quiver on my back, and threw the bow over my head, so that it sat on my shoulder and I didn't have to carry it. There were two slits on the side of the armor, which were for my fist knives. I slid them in place. I saved Excalibur for last, tying its sheath around my waist. I met Aiden outside.

"A perfect fit," he said. "The last part of your gift is for you and Silas."

"For Silas?" I asked, wondering what a dragon needed.

Aiden nodded. A few moments later, I could see Silas circling above us, getting ready to land. He pumped his wings gracefully, kicking up dirt and loose earth. As he came closer to the ground, I could see that he, too, was wearing armor. His armor was black and matched his scales. It covered his head, tail, underbelly, and most of his body. The armor made him look even more intimidating, and I didn't think that was possible. There was also a saddle on his back in front of his wings, which I assumed was for me to ride on. I guess that's why I needed a better bow.

"I still do not believe I shall need this armor," he grumbled as his feet touched the ground. "My scales are stronger than any man-made weapon."

"It was made to protect you from the magic of dark creatures, to which I believe you are vulnerable," Aiden explained.

Silas' eyes narrowed. "Nobody said anything about dark magic."

"This battle will bring all sorts of darkness out from the crevices of the earth. It is a precaution, Silas."

He snorted.

"You should be on your way," Aiden said to me.

"You're not coming?" I asked.

"I have some things to attend to, but I shall meet you there," he replied.

I frowned. "Alright."

I was about to get on the saddle when Aiden grabbed my arm, a little tighter than I would've liked. "Arthur, a word of caution before you leave. I've heard rumors that a djinn is leading the army against Camelot."

"A djinn?" I asked.

Aiden hesitated, "Remember our training. A djinn is an evil creature that possesses unfathomable dark magic. It is one of the few creatures we elves fear. This djinn is particularly brutal. It has access to the dark magic, and will stop at nothing to get the power of Excalibur. It used a form of magic to gain control over the army of humans heading to Camelot. You must be extremely careful when you face it. Something this dark and this powerful can only be killed by something of equal power, like Excalibur."

"Why are you only just telling me about this djinn now?"

"I only just found out myself," he said. "But if this djinn is controlling the army against Camelot, it will be a much harder battle to win."

I let his words sink in. "Thanks for the warning."

He nodded. "Be careful. I shall meet you in Camelot."

I grabbed the saddle and climbed onto Silas' back. There were two coverings for my legs to slide into, and a leather strap for me to hold onto. It was definitely better than holding his scales. I held tight to the reigns.

"Ready to go?" I asked.

"It's what I live for," Silas said sarcastically. He pumped his wings, and we rose above the forest. Aiden became a small speck in the middle of all the trees. I took in the view of Calypsus. I could see the large mountain, and steam rising from Pyras. The lagoon looked incredible from the sky, and Veritas blended in completely with the forest.

"You should hold on," Silas said.

I took his advice and gripped the reigns even more tightly, bracing myself for the flight back to Camelot. Silas took off, soaring fast, cutting through the clouds with tremendous speed. He dipped and skimmed the surface of the water with his wings. Then he flew higher again as we approached Brentwood Forest. The trees passed as a dark blur as we headed for the mountains of Elsador. The journey, that had taken us so long, flashed by thanks to Silas. The air lapping my face became cold and harsh as we neared the mountains. Silas wove through the snow-covered mountaintops with ease. The blue sky had turned into a cloudy, gray storm. Snow whipped at my face as Silas soared quickly through the mountains. He raced around several more peaks, and I caught a glimpse of the forest on the other side. The air started to warm, and soon it stopped snowing.

I was amazed at how fast Silas could fly. We'd covered a lot of ground in such a short time. I spotted several clouds of smoke in the distance.

"Silas, what do you think that is?" I asked.

He veered towards the black clouds. "It appears to be what's left of Fernbrae."

"What do you mean?"

He cautiously flew towards the smoke. "See for yourself."

As we got closer I saw the town that we had spent the night in when we first started the quest. It was burned to a crisp. Every building was torched, and only ruins remained.

"What happened?"

Silas circled the town from a distance. "What do you think?"

I could see hundreds—maybe thousands—of soldiers camped by the ashes of Fernbrae. Terror shook my body. There were so many of them that I wasn't sure how we could possibly win this fight. The army covered such a large area, and the forest camouflaged even more of their troops. I suddenly realized what had happened.

"The army destroyed it on their way to Camelot. Everyone's dead," I said with a sick stomach.

Silas picked up the pace. "We should hurry."

We flew a safe enough distance away from Fernbrae, so that the army couldn't spot us. My mind was spinning from what I just saw. That army was massive! I was worried if my friends had even made it back alive. We rushed towards Camelot with a new sense of urgency. We needed to warn everyone about what we had seen.

Silas wasted no time soaring over the lush forest. After several minutes passed, I spotted the path we took when we had left Camelot. We were close. I squinted my eyes against the wind to scout ahead. The towering spires of Camelot were small specks in the distance. We moved through the sky like a comet.

Camelot had changed since we'd left. The town inside the castle walls was deserted. Soldiers patrolled the walkways. The marketplace was completely gone, and several large wooden objects stood in its place. I could hear shouts as we approached the castle. The walls were patrolled by triple the amount of guards as before, and they had absolutely no idea what to do when they saw us coming. That momentarily amused me, because I was wondering how I would feel if I saw a dragon coming at me. Oh wait, that already happened.

Silas ignored the guards and flew to the courtyard in front of the castle, and slowly descended. Guards surrounded us when we landed, not knowing what to do, or who we were. None of them looked too enthused to fight a dragon. I hopped off Silas and removed my helmet, revealing myself.

"Relax, guys," I ordered.

The guards realized who I was and backed off, returning to their duties. I could see the relief in their eyes as they ran away from Silas. I had to admit, Silas was pretty menacing. And it certainly helped that he let out a roar as we landed.

"Really? Was that necessary?" I asked Silas.

"I thought so."

"You're back!" Jessica's voice was music to my ears. She, Will, and Blaine were coming out of the castle. She threw her arms around me.

"Yeah, and we need to talk," I said, cutting to the chase as Will shook my hand.

"I'll say. What's going on? You're looking pretty sharp," he said, eyeing my armor.

"Can we talk inside?" I asked Blaine.

He nodded. "Right this way."

"Sure. Yeah. Let's all go in the castle and talk," Silas

grumbled. He was put out that he had to stay in the courtyard.

"I'm sorry Silas, if you want we can talk out here," I replied.

"No, I don't really care. I was there. I know what happened."

"Then why—" I started to say, but knew better. "Nevermind, let's go."

I shook my head at Silas' cocky smirk. We followed Blaine inside the castle. Jessica and Will looked curiously at me. I gave them the 'I'll explain everything soon' eyebrow raise in return. We went to the room where we had first met all the knights and nobles. (That seemed like years ago.) The room was the same as before. The large round table beckoned us to sit down.

"I totally forgot this thing was here," Will said, as he rubbed his hand over the smooth stone on the table. "Oh man, remind me to get one of these for my place. You know, when I get one."

Jessica tilted her head in annoyance at him.

"But you know, that's probably not relevant right now," he said.

"You think?" Jess jabbed.

"Guys!" I shouted, taking my seat.

Startled at my shout, my friends took their seats around the table, Will of course, sitting on the opposite side from me.

"So what's all the fuss about?" Will asked, kicking his feet up on the table.

"After you guys left, Aiden told me a few things," I paused. "First, the elves are actually on our side, and Aiden has sent their army here."

"Yeah dude, we know. They arrived after we got back, and so did the dwarves," Will said. "They look pretty serious."

"He's right. The elven army looks quite fierce. The dwarves looked … well you know, dirty," Blaine confirmed.

"That's good that they made it here safely," I said with relief.

"Why wouldn't they?" Jessica asked.

"I'll get to that soon, but there's more. Aiden told me some things about the enemy's army. For starters, it's led by something called a djinn."

"Please tell me you're not serious, Arthur," Blaine interjected.

I nodded.

"What's a dijon?" Will asked.

"It's a djinn, and it is a dark creature that possesses incredible black magic," Blaine explained.

"Exactly," I continued. "Aiden said that it used hypnosis to gain control of the army that is going to attack us."

"That can't be good," Jessica stated.

"It gets worse. That army doesn't just have people in it."

"What do you mean?" Blaine asked.

"Aiden says the djinn recruited some friends."

"You're not suggesting what I think you are. Are you?" Blaine's voice became low and concerned.

Jessica and Will were confused. "OK, what's going on?" Jessica said.

I took a breath. "Guys, remember stories we've heard about werewolves, trolls, and stuff?"

"Yeah, what about them?" Will asked.

"They're real. Apparently the djinn has a bunch of monsters fighting for him."

Will laughed. "Monsters aren't real, buddy."

After an awkward silence, Jessica said to Will, "You do know that there is a dragon in front of the castle, right?"

I cut in before Will could reply with a sarcastic remark. "The point is we're going to be facing more than just people in this fight. That's mainly why Aiden sent the elves," I explained.

"Where is he, by the way?" Blaine asked.

"I don't know, he said he had some things to attend to and then he would be here."

"So we're going to be fighting a bunch of terrifying monsters, on top of a bunch guys dressed in armor?" Will asked.

"Yup."

"Crap."

"Mhmm."

Blaine wasn't surprised. "I feared this would happen. Camelot has been fortunate, but the people outside have been attacked constantly by dark creatures. Especially near Brentwood."

"The elves are trained, and know how to kill most of the creatures, so we're pretty fortunate they're here. Our warriors wouldn't know what to do if they were faced with them. Aiden taught me how to fight them, too."

Blaine nodded. "So you and the elves will deal with the djinn and the creatures, and Camelot's knights and the dwarves will fight the rest of the army."

"Exactly," I replied. "Oh, and when we were on our way back, we saw their army. It's at Fernbrae. Or what used to be Fernbrae."

"What?" Jessica shouted.

"They burned Fernbrae?" Blaine asked.

"Yeah. The whole town is just ashes. Everyone's dead," I paused. "Their army was camped just outside of it. And it's massive."

"Wow, this is a nightmarish fairy tale if I've ever heard one," Will stated.

"Yeah. Hey, where is everyone? You said the elves and dwarves were here, but I didn't see anyone when I got here," I asked.

Blaine responded, "The dwarves are building tunnels that lead to the forest behind Camelot, so they're underground. The elves are everywhere from the forest to the stables. I can't really keep track of them, but they're here."

"What about the men from the other villages?" I asked.

"They have arrived safely, and are staying in the castle."

I ran everything through in my head. "Good. Do you know how many we have in our army?"

Blaine shook his head. "Not offhand, no. But if I were to guess, I'd say we have about 1,000 men, 400 elves, and about 300 dwarves."

"OK, that seems like we should have enough to face them, but I'm pretty sure they have more than us," I replied. "Should we get Backura and the leader of the elves in here?"

Blaine got out of his chair and went for the door. "I'll go get them now."

"Thanks."

Will piped up after Blaine had left the room, "So we're really gonna stay and fight this dark and evil army?"

"We have to. They only think they can win with Excalibur, and me doing my part to fulfill the prophecy."

"What if it gets too overwhelming?" he asked.

Jessica stepped in. "Wow. Big word, Will."

"Shut up," he snapped.

She smirked at him. "If things start going bad for our side, or if it looks like we're going to die, we can just get Francis to do his time-travel thing."

"Hopefully it won't come to that. After everything we've been through, I'd like to help these people," I paused. "Speaking of my powers … Aiden helped me control them."

"You mean you can get us back?" Jessica leaned forward in her seat.

"Not exactly. I still don't know how that part works, but he was able to help me control freezing time."

Will rolled his eyes. "Yeah, 'cause that'll come in handy."

My eyes narrowed as I concentrated hard. Time froze, and I stood from my chair and walked over to Will. I pulled Excalibur out and put it against his chest, then unfroze time as I said in his face,

"Yeah, it will come in handy."

He jumped in his seat at my sudden appearance. "What the ..."

Jessica laughed at my proven point. I sheathed my sword and returned to my seat. "As I was saying, he helped me harness my power, which should help out on the battlefield. Jess, you need to stay aware of yours, too. And Will, well, you'll get the hang of your powers eventually."

"What's that supposed to mean?" he protested. "I can control my power."

"Alright, move that chair," I said, pointing at a chair across the room.

"I will," he retorted. He stood and turned his focus onto the chair. His gaze was intense, but the chair didn't budge. "OK, so I can't use it on the spot, but I can use it when I need to."

Jessica giggled, "Suuuure."

He glared at her. Jessica's chair launched backwards several feet, but didn't tip over. She jumped from the sudden jolt, then narrowed her eyes at Will. Will kicked his feet back onto the table and let a cocky grin cross his face.

"That wasn't cool, Will," she said. She returned her chair back to the table.

"Alright, guys. So we all have powers. We're just learning to understand and control them. Except Jessica, but that's different," I said to calm the situation.

But Jessica wasn't calm. She seemed ticked. "What do you mean *but that's different*?" she challenged.

"I just meant you knew how to control your invisibility back at The Island. Will and I didn't," I replied. (Sheesh. Girls can be so emotional.) "Back to the point, which is, we must use our abilities if we get in trouble during the battle."

Our conversation came to a halt because Blaine burst through the doors. Behind him were Lancelot, Backura, and Marrek, from the

Pyras tribe of elves. They all took seats around the table.

"Now that we're all here, we should probably talk about our plan for battle," I started the discussion, hoping someone would know how to defend a castle.

Lancelot spoke first, "I have ordered most of our men to take up positions on the walls and towers of Camelot. From there we can fire arrows at the enemy once they are in range. Also, we have several small catapults, which will be set up by the stables. We will use those to disorganize their troops. Finally, the moat is full of alligators to guard the drawbridge from below. If they manage to get past them, we have cauldrons of burning oil to pour down, which should slow them."

"The dwarves have been tunnelling under Camelot. The citizens will remain there during the battle, and we have the tunnels in case we need an escape," Backura stated.

"Backura, where exactly are the tunnels?" I asked.

He shifted uncomfortably in the chair, which was not built for a dwarf. "The entrances are in the dungeons. They run underneath the castle, and lead out to the forest behind it. Why?"

I smiled as a thought occurred to me, "Do you think you can dig out under the field in front of Camelot before their army gets here?"

"Of course!" he exclaimed. "We're dwarves after all, but why would you want to do that?"

Several of the others smiled, as they realized what I was thinking. I explained, "They have to cross the field as they approach Camelot. If we dig under the field, we can do some crazy stuff, like make holes with sharp stakes at the bottom. Or we can have trap doors that lead to pits. Your dwarfs can be in the pits, waiting to attack. They won't see that coming."

"That's brilliant, Arthur!" Blaine said.

Backura agreed, "They certainly won't expect that. I'll get my people on it."

"And what of the elves?" Marrek's cold voice cut the room.

That was where I drew a blank. I shrugged, and looked at the others for help. Lancelot stepped in. "The elves can be in the courtyard and behind the drawbridge, using your long-range arrows to pick enemies off. If they breach Camelot, you can reroute them wherever needed," he suggested.

"Sounds like a good plan," I confirmed.

Marrek considered the plan. "That is adequate, but I would like some of my archers to be placed on Camelot's wall. We are more accurate than the archers of men."

Lancelot rose from his chair, offended by Marrek's words, "Better than our archers? You think your kind is so superior—"

"Lancelot!" I shouted.

He sat back down. Rage steamed from his face.

"Do you guys not realize what we're up against?" I asked. "I've seen their army. We will lose if we don't put our differences aside and work together. That's what this whole prophecy was about, right? Marrek, put some of your elves on the wall, and the rest behind the gates."

The room fell silent. No one expected my outburst. Marrek tipped his head in appreciation. The others thought about what I had said.

"Arthur's right," Blaine said. "I think it would be best if we all worked together and prepared Camelot for battle. If their army is at Fernbrae, they will be here by tomorrow night."

Backura and Marrek left to relay the plan to their troops. Lancelot bowed and left the room behind them, keeping his distance.

"That went well," Jessica stated.

Blaine stood up. "You know how Lancelot is. He's rather quick-tempered. Is there anything else I can do for you?"

"No, I think we covered everything." I thought for a moment.

"Oh wait! What exactly is the plan for now? Like, can we rest, or should we be keeping guard or something?"

He smiled. "One of the benefits of being king is that you can do whatever you want. If you want to rest, then rest. If you want to keep guard, then do so. It's up to you."

"Alright, thanks."

He bowed before he left. "If you need anything at all, let me know."

"So what are you guys gonna do?" Jessica asked. "I'm pretty tired, so I'm going to sleep."

"Yeah, me too. I'd like a good rest before dying a gruesome death," said Will dryly. "What about you, Francis?"

I shrugged. "I'm good. I think I'll wander around for a bit, and catch up later."

"OK, see you later," said Jessica, giving me a smile before she and Will left the room. I was alone.

I leaned my hands against the table and sighed. I wandered over to the window and stared out at Camelot. Knights filled the courtyard on patrol.

Is this really happening? Part of me still couldn't quite believe we had actually travelled back in time. I often wondered if it was all a bad dream and I would wake up and find myself in my little cell on The Island.

I left the room and headed towards the dungeons where the dwarves were tunnelling. I stopped along the way to take a torch off the wall, remembering how the dwarves lived in the dark. Two guards stood at the entrance to the tunnel, and they looked somewhat out to lunch. As I approached one bowed; the other hadn't noticed me.

"Christopher!" the one guard shouted at the other guard, nudging him. "It's the ruddy king. Hop to it!"

"Oh don't be daft, Bernard. Why would the king come down

'ere?" Christopher asked.

I smiled. "Just for fun."

"It is the king in't?" Christopher marveled, and stood up straight.

"I told you, din't I?" Bernard said.

"Guys, relax. I'm just looking for the dwarves," I told them.

Bernard sighed. "Oh well that's a relief. Thought we were going to get the stocks for a minute."

I shook my head. "No, don't worry. I'm not like that. Is this where the dwarves are digging?"

Christopher nodded. "Quite right, my lord. But it smells atrocious in there. 'Em dwarves got no sense of cleanliness whatsoever."

"Yeah, I know. Try going through their home."

Bernard chuckled as I passed into the cave. I could hear them talking even after I entered it.

"Well 'e was nice wasn't 'e?" Bernard said.

"Right you are," came Christopher's voice. "Much better than that grouchy old man."

With my torch to guide me, I ventured into the tunnel. Their voices became muffled, until I totally lost them. They reminded me of the otters. I think it was the accent. My nose twitched as the stench of the dwarves hit my nostrils. The tunnel widened, and I entered a large cavern. My torch wasn't as effective in the open space. I could see several dwarves walking around, glaring at me (or maybe they glared at the torch). I ignored them, and took a closer look at the elaborate tunnels. Eventually I found Backura, sitting on a large dirt throne in front of the escape tunnels for the townspeople. I don't think he ever did any work himself.

As I approached he shouted, "And what do you want now?"

"I'm just checking everything out. How're the tunnels leading into the field going?" I asked.

"They are well underway. We work best when not disturbed," he subtly hinted for me to leave. "The escape tunnels are back here."

It made me smile that he wanted me gone. "Thank you, I'll take a look."

I heard him grumble as I turned and continued down a tunnel. I hoped the townspeople wouldn't need to use them for escape, because that would mean that things went badly. It was quite large, which was good, considering people would need room to run for their lives. I continued until I began to see a light at the end.

I exited the tunnel and could tell that it was far away from the castle, and well-hidden in a thicket of bushes. The fact that we could make a quick getaway comforted me, and I immediately made my way back. I avoided Backura and moved quickly. I passed Christopher and Bernard, and continued up the staircase.

The day rolled on without incident. I wandered through the abandoned streets of Camelot; most people had boarded up their homes in anticipation of the move to the tunnels. I decided to leave the elves alone, seeing how they liked to keep to themselves. Camelot's men were moving the large wooden catapults into position, and gathering ammunition. The blacksmith was keeping busy, building swords and armor for the men.

Blaine was expecting the army to move quickly from Fernbrae, possibly reaching us by the following evening.

So much for not fighting at night, I thought to myself. I had been hoping I wouldn't have to deal with some of the night creatures that Aiden had described, but if their army was going to arrive at night, it looked like it was inevitable. Aiden still hadn't shown up, and the sun was beginning to set. I worried that he might not make it past the army to get here. I wondered if he was OK.

A cold breeze accompanied the setting sun. I decided it was a good time to return to my room. I could see lots of guards on the walkways, keeping a close eye in case the enemy showed up early. I could hear Lancelot yelling at someone in the distance. I didn't want to put up with him, so I kept walking. Besides, it wasn't like I had any advice to offer. Castle defense was new to me. By the time I made it back to my room the sun was gone, and darkness had taken over. Will lounged on his bed, with a drumstick of chicken in his hand.

"Do you know how good this thing tastes?" he asked with wide eyes. "I've never had so much chicken before."

"Yeah, chicken's a lot better than the stuff at The Island," I laughed. On my bed was a plate that was empty, except for a bare bone, which I can only assume was a chicken drumstick.

"Oh yeah, I ate yours too. Thought you wouldn't mind."

I rolled my eyes. "Mhmm, cause it's not like I wanted to eat or anything."

"Exactly," he smiled.

I opened the door and poked my head out. A guard was passing by. "Hey! You! You feel like bringing me some food?" I requested.

The guard looked shocked that I was talking to him. "Yes, of course, my lord. Right away."

"Thanks," I smiled at him, then shut the door.

"Tell him to get me one too!" Will shouted.

I opened the door again and called out, "And please bring a lot."

I don't know if he heard me or not, but I didn't really care. I removed my armor, and set it on a table near my bed. I admired the craftsmanship of it. I put on something comfortable to sleep in, then I went over to the window and stared out for a long time. A full moon lit the sky, and everything was quiet. A knock on the door forced me to turn away from the window. It was a servant, holding two large plates of chicken.

"Thank you," I said. The servant smiled, but then ran quickly down the hallway, almost as if he was afraid I'd do something to him if he stuck around.

Strange, I thought. I gave Will his plate and sat on my bed with my dinner. Will eagerly shovelled the food into his mouth. As I bit into the chicken, I was overtaken with a childhood memory. It was of my mom handing me a second helping of oven-roasted chicken with potatoes. My dad and sister were eating their dinner across the table. My mom sat next to me and picked up her fork.

My mom made good chicken, I remembered. I felt my eyes tear up at the thought. I'd forgotten that. It had been so long since I had chicken, or any decent meal for that matter. I was beginning to like the medieval times and their food. Except for the whole battle for the fate of the world thing, it wasn't so bad.

As I finished the meal, I felt my eyes droop. I crawled into my bed, hoping my mind would allow my body to rest. I drifted to sleep with the soothing sounds of Will chewing down on his third meal.

Unfortunately, my dreams were plagued by my family's death. Again. I was right in the middle of my own tossing and turning in bed when something woke me. It was Will screaming. I thought it was one of his nightmares, but as I sat up I could see it clearly wasn't.

A dark figure had Will by the throat, holding him in the air so he couldn't breathe. At the side of my bed was another dark figure, clothed in a black robe. It grabbed my shirt, and threw me across the room with one hand. I smashed into the table, knocking over all of my armor. The cloaked figure lunged at me with tremendous speed. I shut my eyes and stopped time. When I opened them, its face was right in front of mine. Fangs protruded from its frozen mouth, ready to take a chunk out of me. I screamed as complete fear overtook me. They were vampires! I backed away, my back hitting the wall, my legs pushing backward, as I tried to get as far away as possible. Golden eyes peered at me from its pale, wrinkled, white skin. One of its claws was stretched out to grab my face and likely tear it off.

If I hadn't stopped time, I would be dead right now, I thought with horror as I searched in panic for Excalibur. As soon as I gripped its hilt, the fear went away. My senses cleared, and I was able to focus calmly. I could not afford to freak out. Will was also about to be bitten by the vampire holding him. I decided to tackle Will's vampire first. Aiden had taught me about these things. They could only be killed by sunlight, or by cutting off their head. Seeing as it was the dead of night, I decided to go with the 'cutting off the head' thing.

Right beside Will was a large mirror. The vampire had no reflection. It distracted me momentarily as I looked from the mirror to the vampire then back to the mirror. I waved a hand behind it, which showed up, even though it was behind the vampire.

"Huh. That's interesting," I said.

I swung Excalibur, slicing the vampire's neck in one ferocious motion. Time resumed instantly. My head was filled with pain from the sudden pressure that time-freezing put on it. The vampire turned to dust, and Will collapsed to the ground.

"What is going on?" Will shouted, terrified.

I didn't have time to explain. I turned to deal with the other vampire that had crashed into the wall where I had been moments ago. It recovered quickly from my sudden disappearance. Outside, I could hear the warning bell clanging. The vampire hissed at me, and then vanished into a cloud of black smoke that wisped through the cracks of the window, out into the night.

I made sure it had left, and then ran over to Will. "Are you alright?"

"What kind of stupid question is that?" he shouted. "I was just about bitten by some ... what was that freaking thing?"

"Vampire," I offered.

He was shaking. "Is it gone now?"

I nodded. "I think so."

Jessica burst through the door. "What's going on? I heard noises, and now the warning bell's ringing."

I was pulling my elven armor on. "We were just attacked by two vampires. I killed one, the other went out the window."

"What?"

"You heard me," I said, running out the door. "Look after Will, he was clawed by one of them. I'll be back soon."

"Where are you going?" I heard her call, but I kept running. I had to find out what was happening.

Excalibur in hand, I ran through the hallways of the castle. I was almost to the main hallway when something large turned the corner in front of me, stopping me in my tracks. Ten feet away was a werewolf. It was about the size of a full-grown grizzly bear, and its teeth looked like blades. Its face was furry, just like a wolf's.

"Oh, you've got to be kidding me," I said to it.

It let out a deep and terrifying roar that sent shivers down my spine.

"Forget this," I declared, freezing time again. There was no way I was going to face that thing head-on. I ran up and sliced its head off with Excalibur. Werewolves are pretty much like vampires, but a silver blade in the heart can also kill them. I released time and the werewolf's body collapsed. It didn't even know what happened. I ran through the castle until I reached the courtyard.

There were more werewolves out here, tearing the guards apart, who had no idea how to attack the foul creatures. Elves were all over the place, firing silver arrows at the beasts, trying to save as many people as they could.

Behind you! Excalibur's voice shouted in my head.

I turned to see a werewolf charging towards me. Before I could react, I was pushed aside by Marrek. He fired a single arrow at the werewolf, who crashed to the ground and slid to Marrek's feet.

He extended a hand out to help me up.

"What's going on?" I asked him.

His face was smeared with blood. "It seems the djinn sent his dark creatures ahead of his army to take us by surprise for an easy victory."

"Yeah, two vampires almost killed me and Merlin."

His eyes narrowed. "Are you alright?"

I nodded.

Elves and guards were coming from all directions to aid in the sudden attack. Most of the werewolves were killed by the elves, but some fled, climbing over the outer walls with their claws. The elves ran up to the walkways and continued to fire arrows at them as they ran across the field. If Excalibur hadn't helped me through this whole ordeal, I would probably—nope, I would definitely—be dead.

Thanks, I said to my head.

It's what I do. You need to keep cool in situations like this, no matter how frightening they might be.

Blaine and Lancelot were now rushing towards me and Marrek. Blaine was clutching his arm with a bloody hand, while Lancelot's hair was matted to his head with sweat.

"Are you alright?" I asked Blaine, staring at his arm.

He nodded. "It's just a scratch. I'll be fine. What about you and the others?"

I told them about the vampires, and how one got away by turning into smoke. Lancelot spoke up, "The werewolves charged from the field. It must've been a diversion. None of my men saw any vampires."

"How many of our people died?" I asked solemnly.

"If I were to guess, I'd say about forty. That's including the elves that were killed."

"They knew the risks when we came here," Marrek said solemnly.

Lancelot was angry. "I'm going to attend to the wounded and dead after we post more guards around the castle. They will not catch us off-guard again!"

I nodded and let him go.

"I must discuss some things with my kin as well," Marrek said, leaving Blaine and I alone.

"You should get that looked at," I instructed, indicating his wounded arm.

"If you need anything, I shall be at the physician's hut." He bowed and left.

I let out a deep breath, trying to relax myself from the sudden wake-up call. I returned to Will and Jessica. Will was sitting against the bed, holding a cloth to his neck where the vampire had scratched him. Jessica was beside him, holding a glass of water.

"What was going on out there?" she asked me.

I explained to her about how two vampires tried to kill us, and then I told them about the werewolves. Jessica was pretty shaken up by the whole ordeal, and Will was still trying to recover his nerves.

"So is it over?" Jessica asked.

I shrugged. "For now it is, but you never know. Marrek thinks that the djinn sent them ahead of the army to try and steal Excalibur. To gain an easy victory."

"Dude, this was so not cool. I was actually sleeping for once, without nightmares, and then—boom—vampire pops up trying to bite my neck off. Thanks for saving me, by the way."

"Don't mention it," I said.

"So their army isn't here yet?" Jessica asked.

I shook my head. "No, this was just a preemptive strike. They'll be here tomorrow though."

"After all of this, I don't think I'll be able to sleep," she said.

"I don't think they'll attack again tonight, but Lancelot is getting more guards around the castle."

She shook her head. I couldn't blame her. My whole body was wired from killing a vampire and werewolf (not that I'm bragging or anything).

"We should try to get some sleep, considering it'll be our last chance before the battle," I said.

"Fine, but I'm not sleeping alone in a dark room," she declared.

"I'll sleep by the fire, take my bed," I offered.

She smiled her thanks and got into my bed. Will removed the cloth from his neck revealed three cuts from the vampire's claws. "How does it look?"

"You'll live. Besides, we heal faster than most people. I bet it'll be gone by morning."

"Alright. I'm going to try and go back to sleep."

"See you in the morning."

"Yeah, if I don't get woken up by ghosts or freaking vampires or other things trying to kill me …"

He rambled on for a while, but eventually it became gibberish as he drifted off to sleep. I sat by the fire, allowing its heat to comfort me. I don't remember falling asleep, but I knew I had when I saw Excalibur standing beside a flagpole. The flag was tattered, as if it had been through a difficult battle.

"You're lucky you have those powers. Most people would be dead after what you've been through," he said casually.

"Yeah, well most people don't spend most of their childhood as a test subject for an evil corporation either."

"Touché."

"Thanks for kicking in there," I paused. "I would've been too freaked out to react."

"Like I said, you must keep cool in those situations."

"I'm sorry your whole curse thing didn't get fixed when I killed the witch, but I'm glad you're helping me out."

"Don't mention it," he sighed. "Tomorrow will be the end of the prophecy, one way or another."

I nodded. "Do you think we'll be ok?"

"Nothing is certain in battle, but between my skills, your powers, and our allies, I think we'll be fine."

"Will it be like tonight was?"

"It'll be worse," he said honestly. "Battle is chaos. People die all around you, and there's nothing you can do about it. There is danger everywhere, and you must be aware of it. But don't worry, I'll help you."

My head began to hurt, so I started to rub my temples with my fingers.

"Are you alright?" he asked me.

I frowned. "My head hurts when I use my powers."

He nodded. "It wears your energy down when you use them too much; I can feel it. Like when you first got here, you passed out. The same thing happened with the witch when you stopped time. You should keep that in mind for tomorrow. You can't just stop time whenever you meet an enemy."

"I guess that explains it," I replied.

"You should get some rest. You'll need it."

"Big day tomorrow."

Excalibur agreed, "You have no idea."

I closed my eyes, and drifted off into a deep sleep. My last thought was that I hoped we would survive whatever tomorrow had in store for us.

17 EVIL UNLEASHED

My eyes fluttered open. Someone was knocking on our door. The room was lit by sunlight pouring through the window. The fireplace had gone out at some point during the night. It was Blaine.

"Our scouts have reported that the enemy is nearly here," he said cautiously. "It would be wise to prepare for battle."

That snapped me to attention. "How long until they get here?"

"Soon."

"Alright, I'll wake everyone up, and meet you in front of the castle."

I shut the door. Will was awake in his bed, staring at the ceiling. Jessica was still asleep. I walked over to her, and shook her shoulder gently. "Jess, they're going to be here soon. We have to get ready."

She mumbled some nonsense, but eventually sat up, rubbing the sleep from her eyes. "OK, I'll go get dressed."

Jessica left, closing the door quietly behind her. I gathered my armor that had been knocked off the table during the night. I piled it on the bed, and began to get ready for battle. Will had the opposite tactic, which was to continue lying in bed.

"So this thing's going down now?" he asked.

I latched the armor to my chest. "It will soon. You should probably get ready, dude."

"Alright, alright. But did the elves get me a shiny suit of armor? Nope! I get this old piece of junk," he said, pointing to a pile of armor that I hadn't noticed before.

I laughed. "I'm sure that armor's fine."

He began to put the heavy armor on, piece-by-piece. "Yeah, but it's not as shiny as yours."

"Suck it up."

Once I had all my armor on, I slung my bow and quiver of arrows over my shoulder, and slid Excalibur into its sheath around my waist. Will said he was taking his time putting on his armor, but I think he just didn't know how to put it on. Rather than argue with him, I decided to wait outside. Jessica was already waiting in the hallway. She was outfitted in modified leather armor, much like what I had on before, but hers had a metal section that covered her left shoulder and arm.

"Can you believe this?" she asked in an angered tone.

"Yeah, I know, right?" I paused for a moment. "So what exactly are we frustrated about?"

"They expect me to stay back in the castle during the battle! Can you believe that?" she fumed. "I mean, after all we've been through, I don't get to fight too?"

I thought hard. "Well, maybe it isn't such a bad idea—"

She opened her mouth to argue, but before she could say a word I quickly carried on my sentence, "Let me finish! I'm just saying that last night I was terrified, and that wasn't even the real battle. This is going to be much worse, and the only reason I'm still alive is because of my powers and Excalibur. I don't want you getting hurt because of something that I caused."

"Excuse me?" she sounded hurt. "Was I just in the background the whole time we were fighting killer snakes, witches, mice, and everything else? Francis, me and Will aren't just sticking by you because you're our only hope of getting back. We're here because we're your friends, and friends don't abandon each other … even in the face of an evil army. We've looked out for each other ever since we all arrived on The Island."

Several seconds of silence passed. "I guess I never looked at it like that. This whole time I've been too concerned about everything that I haven't given you guys enough credit," I conceded.

"I know, but we're all in this together, and we're going to make it through this together."

I nodded. "Alright. So you're sure you want to do this?"

"I can handle myself out there."

Before I could respond, Will barged through the door in his clunky armor. "Man, how cool do I look in this?"

I grinned. His sudden appearance completely killed the mood for our heart to heart conversation. Jessica frowned just to annoy him. "You look like a tool," she teased.

"Nah, I look like a champ," Will said to her, as she made her way down the hallway.

I shook my head at him. "C'mon."

The three of us walked to the front of the castle where Blaine was waiting. Camelot was full of people and guards rushing in every direction to get ready for battle. Silas had spent the night in the courtyard, and was still lounged out on the dirt, scaring people who walked by.

"Having fun?" I asked him.

"Yes, it's amusing how frightened people are of me," he said. "I find it quite entertaining."

"I'm sure you do," I chuckled. "So are you ready for today?"

He rolled his eyes. "Eating people in armor isn't appetizing. The metal just ruins the taste of blood and meat."

I stared at him. "You scare me sometimes."

"Good. But going back to your question, I am looking forward to causing some chaos."

I nodded, but our conversation was cut off by Blaine. "The enemy is in sight, and are making their way through the forest as we speak."

The four of us left Silas and quickly made our way to the walkway above the front gates. Our soldiers had taken their places on the path, standing side by side with bows and arrows at the ready. Once we reached the walkway, I could see the enemy approaching. They hadn't made it to the field yet, but they were moving along the path as far as my eyes could see.

"Are our men and the dwarves in the tunnels ready?" I asked Blaine.

Lancelot was walking along the path towards us, and answered my question, "Indeed. They are ready for battle, waiting for the signal to strike."

I nodded. "Good. How about the elves?"

Blaine pointed at the stables and marketplace behind us. I turned to see that a massive group of elves were occupying the area, ready with their bows and curved swords. There were so many of them, and they all looked intimidating. Marrek was leading many of them towards the towers and walkways to get them in place. He made his way up the stairs, and stopped when he reached us, his elves carrying on to their designated spots.

"My elves are ready for battle," he said as he passed.

I stared at the massive army heading for us. "Lancelot, you're in charge of our men here, OK?"

"I shall coordinate and lead them as best as I can. They will defend the castle to their last breath," he replied. "Usually the king leads the men, so might I ask where you'll be?"

He still had a grudge against me. "I'll be with Silas, taking out as many of them as we can before they reach the castle. Hopefully Silas will be able to use his fire to cut off or separate them."

"A wise strategy."

"What're these thingies for?" Will asked, reaching out to touch one of three large cauldrons that stood over the front gate.

"Mind your hand! They are filled with boiling hot oil that we can pour on them if they get close."

Will retracted his hand and grimaced, "Lovely."

"Then all we have to do is wait," I stated.

Lancelot and Blaine left to tend to last minute details. Marrek stayed with his soldiers. The three of us remained on the walkway, watching as the enemy got closer and closer. It was rather unnerving to see them approach the field. Clouds were rolling in, bringing a light drizzle of rain with them.

"Well this is just awesome," Will said as the rain fell.

"Hey, everyone knows it rains when there's a battle. You should've been expecting this," I told him.

The enemy had reached the field now, and were spreading out along the wide area. There were so many of them that I began to second guess my decision of staying here. They poured into the field in an endless wave. I hadn't been able to see any monsters so far, which made me glad. But then I saw the catapults. Three large catapults were being pulled by giant trolls who must've been at least four times bigger than me. Even though they were a fair distance from the castle, I could see how ugly they were. I'd rather not describe them, because even thinking about it grosses me out.

The front rows of their army initially appeared to be mostly armored men. Four or five rows back was completely comprised of minotaur and cyclops (who were really tall dudes with one eye). And then, as I looked harder, and as they came closer, I could see there actually were a ridiculous amount of hideous creatures scattered among the men. They were grouped together. I made out an entire section of goblins with a nasty shade of green skin.

This is going to be insane, I thought to myself.

The thundering roar of their footsteps made some of the men around us nervous. After what seemed forever, the last of their army stepped onto the field. There was a long moment in which each army sized up the other. This was not going to be an easy fight.

I stared forward with a dreadful anticipation of what was coming. I asked Lancelot, “So what happens now?”

Lancelot’s eyes narrowed as he studied the field. “Now, we prepare for battle. They will most likely begin with a charge; our archers will need to be ready.”

Adrenaline was rushing to my head as I psyched myself up for what was about to happen. The rain poured down now, beating against my armor. There was a sudden movement on their side, as several creatures began to fly off the ground, circling their army.

“What kind of evil are those things?” Jessica asked.

I squinted. “They’ve unleashed the harpies. I’ll take care of them. Lancelot, you’re in charge as soon as they attack.”

“What? No motivational speech?” Will asked.

“Shut up, Merlin,” I shouted, running to Silas.

As soon as I reached him, I jumped on the saddle, and strapped myself in. I could tell he was ready for battle.

“Has it begun?” he asked, taking off from the ground.

“Yeah, looks like they’re sending the harpies in first. We’re going to take them out so that Lancelot and our troops can focus on the ground.”

“Have you spoken to your troops yet?”

“Why is everyone so obsessed with a motivational speech?”

Silas hovered over the front gate. “It’s how it has always been.”

“Fine!” I raised my voice to address the army of Camelot. It carried much more loudly than I thought it would. As I spoke, I felt my stamina grow stronger and I hoped everyone else felt a surge of strength, too.

I bellowed, “I didn’t force any of you to be here today. You’re here because you are fighting for something you believe in. You’re here to protect your friends and your families. You’re here to make a stand against all that is evil in this world. We will win this battle. Not because it's foretold in some prophecy, not because we're stronger than they are, but because we're fighting for something we believe in. Some of us may die today, but we'll die for freedom, for honor, for all that is good. So fight with all your wisdom! Fight with all your strength! Do not back down, and we will take everything from them!"

A tremendous battle roar erupted from all the soldiers. Apparently I had done a good job.

"Are you happy?" I grumbled to Silas.

"It was quite inspiring," he encouraged.

"Good. Now let's end this."

Silas pumped his wings, and we began to soar towards the enemy army. The harpies were already on their way towards us. I grabbed my bow off of my back and hitched an arrow into it. I took careful aim, and pulled back on the string. I let out a small breath and released the arrow. A harpy plummeted to the ground, signalling the beginning of the battle. Silas shot a ball of fire at another harpy. It fell, engulfed in flames. I was quick to fire another shot, but the harpy dodged it. Silas began to chase one, gaining on it quickly.

Below us, the enemy army had begun their charge. I barely caught a glimpse of it because a harpy was chasing us, its talons posed for action. I turned my body, firing an arrow at it. The arrow pierced its heart, and it disappeared from my sight. The one Silas was chasing couldn't move fast enough, and was caught in his vicious bite. I lost track of a harpy that dove at me from above, clipping my shoulder. I cried out in pain as I felt the claws stabbing through my armor, digging into my skin. Silas flipped in the air, throwing the harpy off of me, and ripping it to shreds with his claws.

"Are you alright?" he shouted.

"Yeah, the armor caught most of it," I cringed, doing my best to ignore the pain.

Silas nodded and began to chase the two harpies that got past us. I took aim with another arrow, pegging one off, sending it into the moat. An arrow coming from the castle, most likely from Marrek or an elf, killed the other. Silas looped around, facing the army charging towards us. Many were armed with spears and pikes. Near the front were several long groups, protected by shields above them and at their sides. They were moving what appeared to be ladders towards the castle. I had little time to focus on them because the trolls were beginning to launch rocks on the catapults. Silas dodged one heading right for us, which smashed into one of the houses behind Camelot's wall.

"Silas, we need to take out those catapults!" I shouted.

He moved quickly, heading for the three catapults. Behind us, our men were launching giant stones from our own catapults. This crushed many of the men charging the castle. As we approached the catapults, several archers fired arrows at us, but none could hurt Silas so it was rather pointless. Silas launched a wave of fire at the first catapult, while I shot arrows rapidly at the trolls. The wooden catapult crumbled, and a troll hit the ground. We moved to the next catapult with the same strategy, but they were ready for us. One of the trolls fired a boulder at us. Silas dove left, and smashed the troll with his claws. I fired at another troll who operated the catapult. The arrow hit him right between the eyes. Silas sent a fireball at the catapult, burning it to a crisp. The final catapult was just as easy to take down. I fired arrows from a distance, killing the trolls, while Silas launched a stream of fire.

We had successfully taken out their long-range weapons, but that was a small victory. Heading back for the castle, I could see our troops firing thick clouds of arrows at the enemy, taking down most of them as they approached the castle. The constant barrage of arrows caused some chaos in the enemy ranks, but some got close enough to fire back, killing some of the soldiers on the walkway. The trap holes in the field had been triggered, and many of their soldiers fell into them on the charge. As we flew over, I could see dead bodies impaled by the sharp stakes at the bottom. The soldiers carrying the ladders had reached the moat, and were placing large planks of wood over the alligator-infested water. While taking volleys of arrows, they crossed the moat over the boards, and began to raise the ladders up against Camelot's wall.

A different situation was developing at the front gates. The soldiers and my friends were firing arrows down at goblins that were hacking at the chains on the drawbridge. I saw Will and Jessica doing their best to keep them off the gate, but there were too many of them. The goblins cut through the chains, and the drawbridge fell. They poured over the bridge, and began to hack at the gate. The cauldrons tipped over, pouring the oil on the goblins underneath. I could hear them screaming in agony before they died.

We couldn't help them out at that moment, because we had to separate the enemy so that our troops in the tunnels could attack.

"Silas, you need to use your fire to cut off their troops," I instructed.

He dove down and began to scorch everything in his path. His stream of fire killed many of their men, and forced them into different areas of the field. Soon we could give the signal to Blaine, and the dwarves would pop up for a surprise attack. I was starting to run out of arrows, as I shot as many of the minotaur as possible.

Rain continued to pour down on the battlefield. The sound of clashing swords rang out once the enemy soldiers had reached the top of the ladders. The elves and men had their hands full, battling the invaders on the walkway. Meanwhile, the goblins who hadn't been scalded were struggling trying to get through the main gate. I was about to say I hadn't seen any sign of the djinn yet, but an explosion suddenly rocked the gate, sending it in every direction.

That can't be good, I thought.

A hooded figure stood on the drawbridge, letting the goblins swarm through the broken gates.

The djinn, I realized. I reached to grab another arrow to kill it, but my hand came up empty. I was out. The enemy had breached the castle, attacking the elves at the gates, and the others on the walkway.

"Silas, we need to signal them to open the tunnels before the goblins overrun the castle. And I'm out of arrows; you'll need to drop me off somewhere. Keep attacking the enemies out on the field."

He swooped past the courtyard, where I jumped off, meeting up with Blaine. "You need to tell the dwarves to attack."

He nodded, and rushed into the castle to let them know. I ran down the path to the front gates where the elves were doing a good job at keeping the goblins at bay. I unleashed Excalibur and joined the fight. I pushed through the elves until I was on the front lines, fighting for my life against a horde of goblins. They snarled and growled as they came against us. I blocked one attack, only to quickly block another from the other side. It was madness. I stabbed and slashed at the goblins around me. Excalibur reacted to everything, moving to where I needed to be at the right time. The goblins were striking back just as fiercely, as numerous elves around me collapsed to the ground. With each goblin I killed, another replaced it.

Where are they all coming from? I wondered. It was a never-ending wave of ugliness. Swinging Excalibur, I began to slash my way towards the stairs, trying to reach my friends. Goblin blood splattered across my face after I pulled Excalibur out of the chest of yet another dead body. It was gross.

There were battles happening everywhere I looked. I dove on the ground, avoiding a sword meant for my neck. I grabbed a shield that belonged to a dead elf that lay beside me, and bashed the goblin's face with it. Armed with a shield now, I was able to be more aggressive, pushing and driving my way through the goblins until I reached the stairs. One of the elves was sticking with me, guarding my back as we made our way up the stone staircase. I lunged at a small goblin halfway up the stairs, and threw him to the ground, clearing a path to the top.

Battling along the walkways was much different from what I had just been through at the front gates. The walkway was wide, but not enough to be comfortable in battle. The attacking men climbing over the ladders were filling up space along the walkway, leaving little room to fight. I located Will and Jessica, who were fighting a group of men in front of one of the ladders. They must've run out of ammo in their guns, because they were defending themselves with swords. Lancelot was by the cauldrons with his hands full against three men. He did surprisingly well, but after defeating two of them, the third was moving in for a fatal strike.

"Lancelot!" I shouted over the commotion of battle.

He turned to see the blade heading right for him, and had just enough time to duck and kill the man. Lancelot gave me a nod of appreciation, realizing that I had just saved his life. The two of us worked together to clear the area above the gates. A ladder slammed against the wall by the cauldrons. We quickly moved for it, pushing together to send it outward. The ladder was heavy, but we managed to get it off the wall and it crashed to the ground. I turned to see my friends being driven back by the soldiers invading by the ladders. I rushed over to help them. Together, the three of us slashed our way through the troops, reaching the ladder. I attacked the men climbing up it, while Will and Jessica tried to push it over, but they were unsuccessful because of the added weight of enemy soldiers.

"It's too heavy!" Jessica called.

I was distracted with protecting the two of them. "Keep trying!"

"The stupid thing won't budge!" Will shouted in frustration and punched it. His powers kicked in, and Will's mind sent the ladder backwards with great force. "Never mind."

I would've laughed, but fighting for your life didn't really allow for an opportunity to do so. Behind us, a large goblin was charging at Jessica. It had its axe raised over its head and was about to swing when Jessica disappeared. The goblin stopped mid-swing, and scratched its head, confused. Jessica reappeared behind it, and stabbed it through the chest. It was a good thing we had our abilities, otherwise this battle may have ended up very differently. A large group of Camelot's soldiers were losing the fight on the walkway, which was driving us backwards along the wall. I was right back where I had started, above the gate.

"We need more troops up here!" Lancelot hissed to me. He was dealing with a similar situation on his side of the walkway. Another ladder was being raised up near the cauldrons. Lancelot was about to make a move towards it, but I stopped him.

"Let Merlin handle it."

He frowned as Will ran towards the ladder and took up a Jedi-like stance. The ladder trembled, and then flung backwards like the other had.

"You must be some sort of a wizard!" Lancelot exclaimed as we resumed the battle.

Will chuckled. "Yeah, I guess I am."

Taking a moment, I glanced out over the field. The tunnels had been opened, and our troops and the dwarves were pouring out of them, attacking their army from behind. Not only that, but I saw Aiden charging forward from the path, on a horse, leading a bunch of centaurs behind him. So that's where he went. Aiden had gotten the help of the centaurs! Although we had fresh help, the battle was far from over. Silas was doing his fire-breathing thing over the field. He also knocked the occasional ladder down as he soared past. The walkways were being filled with dark creatures now. Several minotaur were giving some of the men trouble. I pushed my way through until I came upon them. One grunted at me, holding its massive axe with both hands. I'll admit I was a little freaked out, but it wasn't as bad as the werewolf. It swung the axe at my head. I ducked and attacked with Excalibur. The minotaur was big and strong, but he was also slow. The rain made the walkway slippery, so I dove between its legs, sliding underneath it. I jumped onto its back with a clear shot at its head. Excalibur came down hard and unforgiving. The beast collapsed with a heavy thud. Another had seen what I had done and was charging at me. An arrow flew out of nowhere, colliding with the creature's chest. The minotaur slid off the walkway and fell to the ground. I looked to see where the arrow had come from. Marrek was holding a bow on the other side of where the minotaur had been.

I can't explain this, but I sensed that Camelot was holding well against the enemy. Squinting through the rain and darkness, I could see the dwarves and the others weren't having such luck. Though the attack from behind had taken a large chunk out of the enemy army, they still outnumbered our troops out there. They needed help, and fast!

"Silas!" I shouted to the dragon, who was lighting the dark battlefield with his destructive fire. He circled around, heading along the castle walls toward me. I stepped on the top of the wall and jumped off as he flew to me. Several arrows whizzed past me, but luckily none hit me. Silas caught me in the air with his massive claws, momentarily knocking the breath out of me. "We need to help our guys out there!" I called.

"I shall try to drop you gently," he said calmly, heading for the front lines on the field. He lowered his altitude and speed, releasing me at a clear spot.

I slid across the muddy field, stabilizing myself on one knee. I had no time to recover from the sudden drop, because the enemy troops were all around me. I pulled out Excalibur and charged forward, helping the dwarves near me. The rain and mud made the fight out here much harder than it was at the castle. My feet slipped, and I had to squint to see past the rain hitting me. One of the enemy soldiers managed to nick the side of my arm because I wasn't fast enough to react. There was so much going on that it was hard to focus. After killing one large man, I'd turn to see another charging at me, and then another and another.

A surreal side note: The whole time that this was happening, I kept hearing Queen's *Another One Bites The Dust* playing in my head.

Even though the battle was taking a toll on my body, we were slowly gaining ground, and getting closer to the castle.

I couldn't see Backura anywhere, but the dwarves fighting beside me were incredible warriors. Those guys were small, but man could they fight. Armed with axes, each dwarf packed a powerful attack that sent enemies flying backwards. Their size was also a weakness, as I saw several dwarves killed around me because they couldn't move fast enough. There were many casualties on both sides. I kicked a man in the chest, ducking another's sword right after. I slashed one man's back and then stabbed the one I had just kicked. Crazy.

Far ahead of me I could see the djinn. He was dressed in a black robe, with black armor underneath, and had a hood covering his head. He was tearing our soldiers apart one after another by stabbing them, or by firing blasts of dark magic. Either way, Camelot's men and dwarves were dying gruesome deaths. I did my best to fight my way towards the inevitable battle between me and the djinn, but there were so many people in the way. I looked again to see someone had beaten me there. Aiden was locked in combat with the leader of the enemy army. The two were a close match for each other. Aiden's swift and elegant movements countered the djinn's magic and attacks. I fought my way through the battlefield, trying to help my friend. The djinn proved to be quite powerful, gaining the upper hand in the fight after hitting Aiden with a bolt of black lightning. Aiden managed to get up to his feet, but he was no match for the wrath of the djinn. I stared, helpless, watching the djinn stab Aiden through the heart.

"AIDEN!" I shouted, unable to do anything.

I didn't make it there in time to save him. Aiden's body crumpled to the ground, lifeless. The djinn turned his gaze to me, over the many warriors that stood between us. He removed his hood, revealing his face. His head was bald, his skin pale. His eyes glowed a fiery red. An evil smile slid across his face, revealing pointed teeth. I glared at him. My body burned with rage over the death of my friend. I hacked my way towards the djinn, killing anything in my path, showing no mercy. This was going to end here and now.

After much bloodshed, I reached a clearing where the djinn was waiting for me. Everyone around us was fighting, but none dared to attack either of us. I don't know why they didn't, but it allowed me to focus my attention solely on the thing that had killed my friend. Aiden's body lay to the side of the clearing.

"Was he a friend of yours?" spat the djinn. His voice was cold and raspy.

I didn't respond.

"Oh, he was. Tsk tsk," the djinn taunted. "Elves should know better than to challenge a djinn."

I raised Excalibur, ready for him to make a move. He just smiled at me. "So you're the one who pulled it. I thought you'd be … taller."

"Sorry to disappoint," I countered with a dry voice.

"That's fine, you all look the same when you die."

The djinn fired a stream of lightning at me, but I was expecting it and dove to my right. The bolt hit the dirt behind me, sending it flying in all directions.

He smiled at me and crooned, “This is going to be fun.”

I lunged at him, swinging Excalibur at his side. He moved faster than I expected, blocking the attack, and countering with a fist to my face. I took several steps back from the hit.

Don't give in to frustration, Excalibur's voice spoke to me. *If you become angry, you will lose this fight.*

I had to cut off all emotions, especially those tied to Aiden.

“Why don't you just give me Excalibur, and I won't have to kill you and all your friends,” the djinn said, playing with my head. It was like this whole battle was a game to him.

“Or I could just kill you and call it a day.”

“Such spirit. Such … determination,” he said, circling me. “I could use someone like you.”

I ignored the comment and attacked him. This time I was quicker, moving with purpose with each swing. I gripped Excalibur over my head to attack. The djinn raised his sword, easily blocking it. He attacked me with a relentless push, moving me backwards. He was definitely stronger than me. (I haven't spent much time in a gym, you know?) I remained aware of my surroundings, careful not to slip in the mud, or trip on a dead body. I dodged his swing, which was meant for my head. I turned and retaliated, striking back. We were moving back and forth in the mud, neither of us letting up.

After blocking his sword only inches from my face, I kicked him in the chest, forcing him backwards. I moved quickly, trying to gain an advantage, but the djinn turned and sent another bolt at me. This one connected with its target. I flew a good fifteen feet backwards. My body crashed and slid through the mud. My chest-plate was singed from the dark magic, and my head was rattled. I slowly got to one knee, holding Excalibur in a feeble attempt to block the djinn. My eyes couldn't focus, I was so rattled from the hit, so I could only swing Excalibur blindly. I could hear the djinn laughing at me. Suddenly something hit me in the face. It was his foot. I landed on my back, eyes trying to focus on the black blur in front of me. My nose was bleeding from the kick, and my helmet was knocked off of my head. I could feel rain falling down on my face.

"I expected more from you," he spat in my face.

This was it. I used what energy I had, and focused on freezing time. As my eyes adjusted, I saw that I did it in the nick of time. The djinn had both hands gripped on his sword, which was headed right for me. My body was weak from the djinn's magic. The pain in my head told me that I couldn't hold time frozen for much longer. I began to crawl away from the djinn, not strong enough to do anything else. I inched my way along the mud as far as I could, before trying to get up. The headache was growing, and I could no longer hold time in place.

The djinn's sword plummeted into the ground. His sly grin turned into confusion. He turned around to see me trying to get to my feet. He began to laugh.

"Well, well, well," he cackled. "You were holding out on me. You know, we're not so different, you and I."

My vision had adjusted, and I was regaining energy as I stood to my feet. I tried to stall him by talking. "Yeah, except for the whole destroying the world thing," I said, wiping blood from my mouth. "Oh, and I have normal teeth … and hair."

He ignored my insult. "We're both powerful. That's what all of this is about anyway. Power. That sword will make me invincible, once I pry it from your cold, dead body."

My strength and senses returned to me, and I saw the djinn charging towards me, with his sword held high, swinging down for my head. I raised Excalibur up quickly to block the attack, pushing him back. I kept up the momentum I had by striking at him again and again. Each attack was blocked, but I wasn't giving him a chance to go on the offensive. Our swords locked, our faces inches apart.

"You don't have what it takes to beat me," he hissed. I pushed him back with all my strength. That was when everything hit me.

The death of Aiden.

The death of Galahad.

The Island.

Everything that I had been through.

I found the motivation and inner strength to fight back. I lunged at him, aiming Excalibur at his throat. He pushed my attack away with his sword, his face turning serious at my sudden aggression. Our swords clashed again and again, as I drove him back. Aiden had taught me to always be aware of my surroundings. The djinn should've taken the same lessons. He was too focused on my relentless attacks that he didn't see the trap hole behind him. Another swing forced his feet to the edge. He paused as he realized his situation. I used that second to my advantage, stabbing him through the heart with Excalibur, sliding it all the way through, until my face was right in front of his.

"That's for my friend," I growled through gritted teeth.

His eyes reflected the realization that he was about to die. I pulled Excalibur from his chest, and pushed him into the pit, his body falling on the sharp spikes below. I collapsed to my knees. I had killed him. I took a moment to recover from the duel. I looked around to see that the battle wasn't over. I was still too weak to stand, but I heard a familiar voice nearby.

"I don' believe it! 'E did it! 'E killed the djinn!" Chester, who was now at my side, announced. Seeing him helped me focus.

Malcom was defending our position from enemy soldiers. "Heavens! 'E looks pretty banged up, eh?"

"Course 'e does. Lost 'is 'elmet and everything," Chester replied, leaving me for a moment to kill a man who was charging at us. The otter returned moments later, trying to help me to my feet (which is pretty hard for an otter to do). "C'mon, let's get you up. We're not safe 'ere."

I managed to get to my feet. My body was in pain. The otters were able to protect me while I recovered from the battle-shock. My vision finally returned to normal, and I was able to focus on the combat around us. I snapped back to reality and rejoined the efforts. With the otters on either side of me, we fought our way back towards the castle. Although both sides had numerous casualties, we were definitely winning the battle.

Up in the sky, Silas was swooping down and picking off anyone that he could. I was too far away to see the walkways on the castle, but it looked like our side was beginning to repel the attacking army. A nearby knight of Camelot was battling with a goblin, and was having a hard time killing it. Lunging forward, I stabbed the goblin in the back, right as it was about to strike the knight down. The knight got to his feet, giving me a nod of appreciation, and then resumed battle. The madness and brutality was getting to me. I just wanted all the killing to be over. I didn't find any appeal in the violence of it all. I killed because I had no other choice. But on some of the faces around me, it was obvious they enjoyed the bloodshed of battle.

I kept fighting, trying to return to my friends. The space between me and the castle narrowed with each goblin and man I killed. The rain had stopped, but the clouds lingered. There would be no sun or moon to light the bloody scene after the battle was over. A large goblin—perhaps an orc—was charging at me. I blocked its initial attack, and countered by tripping it with my foot. The orc fell to the ground, and my blade stabbed into its defenseless body. A yelp of pain, followed by silence. The battle was ending. Small skirmishes still carried on, but our troops outnumbered them significantly, and then ...

It was over.

Our troops let out a mighty cheer, signaling victory. It didn't feel like victory to me as I looked at the carnage. In front of me lay a dead centaur. To my immediate left was an elf. The bodies of the goblins were grotesque, and I couldn't bear to see them among the bodies of those who fought on our side. I knew as I stared at those who gave their lives in this battle that the images would haunt me. The once green and open field was now puddled red and littered with bodies. I wiped Excalibur on the grass then sheathed it, for what I hoped was the last time.

People around me began to celebrate openly. I wasn't feeling celebratory. The sick feeling in my stomach proved to me again that I didn't belong there. The battlefield disgusted me. So much bloodshed and death … and I had caused it all. The worst part was some of the bodies weren't dead. I could hear the cries and groans of the injured and dying. I shut everything out of my mind, and headed for the castle. I had to make sure my friends were OK. The men around me were congratulating each other. The dwarves were looting the bodies, grabbing whatever gold or valuables they found. They were also taking armor from the dead, as well as swords or weaponry. Once the centaurs figured out that the battle was over they left as fast as they had come. I guess they weren't feeling very social. The trail of bodies continued all the way to the castle gates. The alligators were having a feast in the moat.

"You're OK!" Jessica shouted, running at me as I crossed the drawbridge.

I smiled. She wrapped her arms around me, which made me gasp in pain. She pulled back, eyeing the singed armor. "Are you hurt?"

"It's nothing I can't handle. Is Will …?"

She nodded. "He got hit in the shoulder with an arrow, but they said he'll be fine."

"That's good. And the others?"

"Blaine, Lancelot, and Marrek are fine. Did you see the centaurs Aiden brought?"

The sound of his name forced my eyes to the ground.

Jessica covered her mouth with a hand as she read my body language. "Oh no," she said, her eyes filling with tears.

"The djinn. I didn't get there fast enough …" I couldn't say more.

Will turned the corner. His armor and face were covered in blood spatter. He gripped his shoulder with his good arm. "On a scale of one to awesome, how awesome was that?"

The look on my face silenced him.

"Aiden's dead," Jessica informed him.

Will gave me a solemn look. "Sorry, I didn't know."

I shook my head. "Whatever. Let's just get out of here."

We walked up the path to the courtyard. As we made our way through Camelot, I saw some knights cheering and celebrating the victory, while others were dealing with the wounded or dead. Blaine was walking out of the castle when we had reached the courtyard, and Silas was lying down, trying to remove his armor.

"It's good to see that you are all alive," Blaine greeted us. "I've just informed the people in the tunnels that the battle is over and we stand victorious."

I nodded, but didn't smile. "Alright. I'll be in my room if there's any trouble or anything."

He bowed, and walked past us to attend to the remains of the battle. I walked over to Silas.

"Thanks for everything, Silas. I don't think we would've won without you. You're welcome to stay or leave, whatever you'd like."

"It has been an honor. I would gladly fight beside you again," he bowed his head and tilted it in thanks as he spoke. He took off, and I realized I would not see him again.

I sighed, and turned back to my friends. We walked down the hallway to our rooms. Jessica went inside her room, and Will and I stepped inside ours.

"Can you help me get this thing off of me?" I asked him, the pain too much to lift the armor alone. "And the shirt underneath."

Will lifted the armor off of me, as I growled in pain. He tossed the armor aside, and helped me pull off the shirt, revealing the extent of my wounds. My chest was burnt; black and bloody, similar to the wound from the witch. My face was also bloody and bruised. A large claw mark from the harpy covered my shoulder. I was in rough shape. I should have had Silas heal me before he left. But I hadn't thought of it.

Will gasped as he stared at my wounds. "Are you sure you're alright? I think you should sit down for a while."

He helped me over to the bed, and that was the last thing I remembered happening. Whether I blacked out, or just fell into the sleep of someone completely exhausted, I'm not sure. Images of the battle, the dead bodies, Aiden's death, and scenes from The Island flashed through my dreams. Excalibur did not visit them, nor did my family.

18 JUST THE BEGINNING

I blinked, not sure if I was awake, or still dreaming. I looked around the room and I could see that Will was lying in his bed, eating as usual. A white bandage was wrapped around his shoulder. Jessica was asleep on a chair beside my bed.

"What happened?" I croaked.

Will dropped his plate. "Hey buddy, you're awake!"

"Obviously. What happened?" I repeated. Bandages covered my chest and shoulder.

He walked over to me. Jessica woke up. She was pleased to see that I was awake. "You're awake!"

"Yes, we've established that. Now can someone please tell me what happened? The last thing I remember is coming here after the battle."

"You've gotta stop getting hit with that dark magic stuff, dude. It's not good for you," Will said.

Jessica took over, "You were banged up. The burns and cuts looked pretty bad. You passed out from exhaustion. You just needed to rest. You've been out for a day."

"Using my powers drained my energy. The djinn almost killed me."

"What happened out there?"

I told them my account of the battle, and then they told me theirs. Jessica shared my view on the battle and killing, but Will seemed to have enjoyed it. That worried me a little bit. The two of them had stuck to the walkways during the battle, clearing out anyone who came over the ladders. After their guns ran out of ammo, they had switched to swords.

"Where are the guns now?" I asked groggily.

Will pointed to the corner. "They're over there. We managed to find them in the aftermath of the battle while you were passed out."

"That's good. I don't want them getting in the wrong hands," I replied.

"Oh, are we leaving already?"

I gave him a firm look and said slowly, "I told you; we don't belong here. Besides, I have to help the others."

"*We* have to help the others," corrected Jessica.

"Right."

Will was still skeptical, "I still say we should stay here. You're king. It doesn't get any better than that."

I stared at him coldly.

He put his hands up in defense. "Alright, alright. We go back and help them."

"So what's the plan? Wait until you've recovered, and then try and get you to do your time-travel thing?" Jessica asked.

I shook my head, getting out of the bed, and on my feet. "No. We shouldn't stay here any longer than we have to. I've had enough of this place."

"Do you think that's a good idea? I mean, you're still recovering. Are you sure you can get us back? You said it yourself, using your powers takes away your energy," Jessica said.

"I'll be fine."

"What if you can't get us back? What if we wind up somewhere else again?" Jessica asked.

"I don't know," I sighed. "I'll try my best, but I have no idea how to control it."

"So what do we do with the guns?" Will asked. "They're kind

of useless now that they're out of ammo."

I thought for a moment. "Nimue. She'd be able to hide them in the lake without anyone finding them."

"What will happen to Camelot? They won't have a king anymore," Will persisted.

"Let's take one thing at a time, alright?" I snapped, my head hurting from all the talking. My friends backed off with their questions.

"We'll meet you in the courtyard when you're ready," Jess said, grabbing Will and the guns. They left the room, shutting the door behind them.

I let out a deep breath. I walked to the mirror, and began to pull the bandages off of my body. Underneath was a partially healed wound on my chest. The only thing I could thank The Island for was the ability to heal fast. I'd have been doomed without it. I took a different shirt from the table and pulled it over my head, then put the leather armor over it.

"What if I can't get us back?" I asked myself.

Excalibur's voice answered, *Don't think like that. One way or another, you'll get back.*

"How can you be sure?"

Because I know you, and you won't give up. You might not get there right away, but you'll get back eventually.

"What about you? Should I just stab you back in the rock?"

Dear God, no! It would just create another battle for power. You should leave me with Nimue. She'll be good company for me.

"Alright," I said, placing the sword in its sheath around my waist.

I left the room, and walked down the hallway towards the courtyard. When I reached the entrance, I could see that the sun was shining. It was a beautiful day, with a clear blue sky. I embraced the warmth of the sun. I spotted Will and Jessica sitting on the rock I had pulled Excalibur from. Blaine was with them.

"Merlin and Guinevere tell me that you are leaving," he said with a raised eyebrow.

I nodded. "There's somewhere else we need to be."

"Is it another quest?"

"Something like that."

Blaine sighed, "When will you return?"

I shrugged. "Who knows. I'm sure Camelot will be fine while I'm gone."

"But you'll be back?" he asked.

"Of course," I lied.

"Well then, I shall wait for your return. And let me say, it has been an honor serving you."

"It has been an honor to have met you. You have been a comforting friend to us," I replied.

He smiled. He didn't seem to want to linger. "Well, I have things to do, and history to record. Until we meet again."

I waved goodbye as he walked away.

"Good to go?" Will asked.

"Yup. Let's head to the lake."

The three of us made our way through Camelot. You wouldn't have known that there was a battle just over a day ago, except for a few collapsed buildings that were hit with boulders from the catapults, before Silas and I destroyed them. The bodies were gone. I wondered where they went? People scurried about, repairing any damage. Things were returning to normal. We had reached the gates when a voice called out to us.

"Where are you going?"

I turned to see Lancelot walking towards us. I rolled my eyes. Just who I wanted to see.

"We have to leave for a while," I told him. "Talk to Blaine if you need anything."

"I know we got off on the wrong foot, but I'd like to say, I'm proud to call you my king. You fought valiantly, and you saved my life. I am forever in your debt."

"Thanks, but it was nothing."

"You're too kind. Farewell," he said, his eyes lingering on Jessica for a moment. He bowed and walked away from us.

"Well whatdaya know," Will said. "He's a decent human being after all."

We laughed as we walked out of the gates of Camelot. The field was a mess. The battle had worn it down. The holes from the tunnels and traps dotted the ground. My mind flashed back to Aiden's death as we passed where he had died.

"You guys go on ahead, I'll catch up," I said, pausing at the spot.

Jess and Will moved on, leaving me alone. I walked away from the path towards the place Aiden was killed. I knelt on one knee.

"You were a good guy Aiden—or elf I should say," I whispered. "I will always remember the lessons you taught me. I'm sorry I couldn't save you."

I grabbed a handful of dirt, and scattered it on the ground for my fallen friend. I stood up, and ran to catch up with my friends. They didn't ask what that was about; I think they knew. Once we reached the forest, we took one last look back at the castle. It seemed to sparkle in the sunlight. It was hard to think that we were only here for such a short time after everything we'd been through. It felt like a lifetime.

"Do you think we'll ever come back here?" Jessica asked softly.

I stared at the castle. "Who knows, we might even bring the others here. Anything's possible."

"I think we should come back," Will stated. "They have good

food."

We laughed, and began the walk to the lake. I took one last glance at the castle and then it disappeared from view. Part of me was going to miss this place. And part of me wasn't. We walked in silence, taking in the fresh air and scenery. I knew we were getting close when we saw the mist. We stopped.

"You guys should wait here," I said. "Nimue only talked to me last time … and she's really creepy."

"I'm fine with avoiding creepy people," Will said, sitting down on a log.

Jess seemed like she wanted to come too, but she sat down as well. They handed me the guns, and I walked to the water's edge, careful not to step in. Playful laughter echoed across the lake. Nimue emerged from the water several feet from me.

"Well, well, well," she smiled, "you survived after all. I must admit I'm impressed."

"Thanks."

"What do you want?" she asked coldly. Her voice still sent shivers down my spine, which I found odd after all the monsters I'd encountered over the past few days. You'd think I'd have toughened up.

"I just want to ask you if you could hide these where no one will find them," I said, holding up the guns.

She stared at the guns for an unusually long time before answering, "Very well. Just throw them in and I shall keep them out of sight."

I tossed the guns into the lake. They splashed, causing ripples across the water.

"Is that it?" she asked me.

I shook my head, and pulled out Excalibur. "This too," I requested.

Before I could throw it, the sword glowed brightly. I let go of it, not knowing what was happening. Excalibur floated in the air, and grew brighter. I had to cover my eyes from the blinding light. My friends ran over in curiosity. The light suddenly disappeared. Where Excalibur had been moments ago was now … me. Not me, but a replica of me. He looked exactly like me, which freaked me right out (the real me).

"What's going on?" I asked, staring at my clone.

The clone stared at his body. He had Excalibur gripped in his right hand. A huge smile spread across his face.

"Francis, I'm free," he said.

I recognized the voice immediately. It was Excalibur.

"But how?" I asked, happy for him, but I'd be lying if I said I wasn't a little bit wigged out.

Nimue explained, "His curse wasn't lifted when you killed the witch, it lifted when you fulfilled the prophecy. After winning the battle, he was released from the curse."

His smile grew wider as the reality sunk in. "I'm free!"

"Does someone wanna explain what's going on?" Will asked. "Oh, and Francis you were right, she's pretty creepy."

Nimue turned her head sharply at Will. I'm pretty sure he flinched. I explained to my friends how the whole time Excalibur was a spirit trapped inside the sword. How we had been having conversations and how we assumed he would've been freed after I killed the witch. They took it all in, but couldn't hide the wonderment and surprise they felt inside.

"So what now?" I asked, staring at him.

He smiled. "Don't you see? This is perfect! I can return to Camelot as King Arthur, and no one would be the wiser. They'll think I'm you."

It took a moment for me to figure everything out. He would take my place, seeing as how he looked exactly like me.

"I guess everything turned out for you after all," I said.

He nodded, declaring, “I shall return to Camelot.”

“Maybe you should wait a day or two,” Jessica interrupted. “We just told everyone we were leaving.”

“Very well. I shall use that time to celebrate. I can tell them that Gwen and Merlin chose not to return,” he said. He grabbed my arm and patted me on the back, whispering in my ear, “I did not forget our arrangement. I have left my skills with you. Use them wisely.”

I nodded. “Thank you.”

He and I looked at one another for a full minute. I couldn’t believe I didn’t notice the resemblance when I saw him in my dreams. But then again, he usually had that hood over his head. In a weird way, I was going to miss his presence.

As if understanding what I was thinking, he smiled.

“Goodbye, Francis,” he said.

“See you later, Excalibur,” I replied. I wondered if that was true.

Excalibur left us to celebrate his freedom from the curse. I felt better knowing Camelot was left in good hands. He would be a great king, much better than I ever could have been.

“Am I the only one slightly weirded out at what just happened?” Will asked.

The question didn’t seem to warrant a response.

“Well, I guess that’s it,” I said. “It’s time we leave this place.”

“Not so fast,” Nimue said sharply. We turned to face her. “There’s something you should know before you go.”

“What’s that?” I asked, thinking nothing she could say would shock me.

I was wrong.

She rolled up her sleeve, revealing an all too familiar symbol. It was The Island’s logo. She was branded just like we were. That threw us completely for a loop.

"I don't understand," I said, trying to work it out in my head. "How is that possible?"

She sighed, and pulled her sleeve down again. "I used to be a scientist for Island Facilities. We were marked, just like you. Once you join them, there's no turning back."

I glared at her, suddenly no longer afraid. "You're one of them," I accused.

"Let me explain," she said. "I *used* to work for them. It was a different time. They didn't acquire orphans then. We used to run tests on animals or plants, but that all changed. They started bringing in these orphans, forcing us to experiment on them. Some of the scientists enjoyed using the human subjects, feeling it would save us countless months of work. Others, like myself, refused to. We tried to leave, but they wouldn't allow it, afraid we would leak information about what they were doing. My fellow scientists began to disappear. I'm assuming they were murdered. I knew they were coming for me. I injected myself with a hybrid compound that I created—one of a kind—and the next thing I knew, I wound up here. I managed to escape The Island, but at a price. I'm stuck here. No matter what I do, I can't leave this lake. Whatever that compound did, it gave me these abilities, and trapped me here. I've become a prisoner in a different time. The Island's influence runs deeper than you can imagine. If you think you're safe in the past, think again."

"You mean they killed their own scientists?" Jessica asked.

Nimue nodded. "Joining The Island meant signing your life away. They can do whatever they want with you, and no one cares. Some of the escaped scientists were captured and joined the orphans as test subjects."

"That's terrible."

"The Island is corrupt. They are hungry for power. And they will stop at nothing to get it. Even if it means changing the past."

"What do you mean?" I asked.

"For the years that I worked there, they had always wanted to achieve time manipulation. They've been trying every possibility, but nothing ever worked … until my compound."

"That's how we got here in the first place!" I told her. "They injected a compound in my head that gave me this ability. But why would they want to control time?"

"Isn't it obvious?"

I shook my head.

She rolled her black eyes in exasperation. "If they can manipulate the past, they can get anything they want. They can become the greatest power in the world. No one would be able to stand up against them. Control time, and you control the world. That's their goal."

I let out a deep breath. I was speechless.

"So everything they've done to us, to the others, was so that they ultimately can rule the world?" Jessica asked.

Nimue spoke urgently, "Yes. And that is why you must stop them."

"Stop them?" Will repeated.

"Yes, stop them," she barked at him. "Your goal is to free the other imprisoned children, but I'm saying you must do more than that. You must take the entire corporation down, Francis."

"And how am I supposed to do that?" I questioned her. "It's not exactly like I can prove anything."

"If you can get into their headquarters, you can relay all the research to the media. Once it's leaked, the world will see The Island's red hand."

"Whoa, whoa, whoa. Since when did they have a red hand?" Will butted in.

"It's a figure of speech, genius. It means their hands are bloody," Nimue snapped. "As I was saying, once the information is leaked, they will be shut down forever. If you free the kids, they will just get more. You have to shut the entire place down in order to truly free them. Besides, there are over 600 research centers in the world. This is the only way."

I took in everything she told us. We were only held in one of six hundred locations? There must be thousands of kids imprisoned. Nimue was right, the only way to beat The Island was to shut it down.

"Why didn't you tell me this when we first met?" I asked her.

She laughed. "Why would I waste my breath explaining this if you died on your quest, or in battle?"

"Point taken."

"Now, do you think you three can do that?"

I looked at my friends. "If there's anyone who could do it, it's us."

Jessica agreed.

Will raised his eyebrow. "So instead of doing a suicide mission to save the others, we're now doing a suicide mission to take down the entire corporation?"

I nodded.

"Yeah, I'm down for that."

Jessica and I laughed.

"I wish you the best of luck," Nimue said. "The fate of the world rests with you three."

"Thanks," I said, as she disappeared back into the water. I turned to my friends. "So?"

"So let's get out of this place, and save the world." Jessica said.

I looked to Will.

He nodded. "How do we get back?"

I was dreading that question long before it was asked. "I think we need to recreate the stress I was under at The Island. We were about to get shot, possibly die, or possibly get sent to different cells. I couldn't handle just another failed escape attempt. I definitely did not expect to wake up here, but we did."

"What are you getting at, Francis?" Jessica asked.

"Well, I thought we were going to die, and I somehow got us here. What if we put ourselves in danger again?"

"You mean you want us to stand in front of a bunch of archers so that you could try to get us home?"

I shrugged. "I don't know. But I don't think I'll just be able to stand here and get us there. I've gotten a lot better at controlling my ability, but I'm not there yet."

"I'm not real fond of becoming a pin cushion, Francis," Will groaned.

"Look, it was just a suggestion," I replied in frustration. "We're not getting back without taking a risk. What other choice do we have?"

We processed the options. Then Jessica spoke up, "Are you sure about this? From the sounds of it, if you can't trigger your abilities, we will all die."

"It's a big risk—believe me I know," I began, "but I can't think of another way."

"On a scale of one to Armageddon, how sure are you that this will work?" Will asked with a raised eyebrow.

I shrugged. The scale system we use never really gives us a positive answer. It's more of a joke, really. "Probably somewhere around the Titanic."

He sighed. "I'd rather not get shot again. Any other options for your suicide plan?"

"There's a cliff not too far from here. If we jump, the adrenaline and fear from the fall should help trigger my ability."

"It *should* trigger your ability?" Will said skeptically. "That's not at all reassuring."

Jessica remained calm. "And if it doesn't, we fall to our

deaths."

"One way or another I'm leaving this place," I began. "I will do everything I can to stop The Island and help the other kids like us. If you want to stay, that's fine, but I'm willing to take the risk. I'm like, ninety-five percent sure that this will work."

My friends considered the plan. Jessica was the first to speak, "Crazy risks have paid off for us so far, what's one more? If you think our best shot at getting back is jumping off a cliff, then I'll jump with you. But, I think we should at least wait one day. You try your best to send us back. If nothing happens, we'll go to Plan B and jump."

I smiled. Her confidence and faith in me never faltered. She was a good friend.

Our discussion continued for another ten minutes as we debated other possibilities. Nothing of significance came up. We made our way towards the cliff, and found a spot to spend the night. I did my best to try to send us back, but it only led to more frustration.

Morning came with no progress made. We had a final discussion about Plan B. No one (including myself) was really fond of the plan, but there was nothing left to try.

With our hearts set on the course of action, we walked to the cliff. Standing at the edge of it made me question my confidence. My legs began shaking. I took a few steps backward. Jess and Will were on either side of me. Jessica took my hand, and squeezed tightly.

"Are you sure about this?" she asked.

"No," I said grabbing Will's hand. "But there's no turning back now."

We stood there for a moment, looking at one another. Unspoken questions filled our eyes. The uncertainty of what was about to happen hung heavy in the air. My heart pounded so loud I could hear it in my ears. Then, it was as if we all were ready at the same time. I looked at Will. He nodded. I looked at Jess. She gave me the bravest smile she had. I gave their hands a squeeze, ensuring I had a tight grip on the two people who were not only my friends, they were my only family.

The three of us ran forward and jumped.

TIMELINE

JOURNEY TO SKELETON ISLAND

BY: STEVEN FOSTER

THE ADVENTURE CONTINUES IN THE
SECOND BOOK OF THE TIMELINE SERIES ...

ISBN: 978-0-9919839-8-8

CPSIA information can be obtained at www.ICGtesting.com
Printed in the USA
LVOW08s0044150414

381671LV00001B/27/P